This novel is entirely a work of fiction.

The names, characterisations of historical characters and locations portrayed in it are entirely a product of the author's imagination.

Any resemblance to actual persons, events ⌐ 'ities is coincidental.

First published on Amazon Books UK, 2021.

I would like to acknowledge the critiques and help by Gilly and Anne, and various other people who have commented on my novel.

For Meriel.

If, when you have read this novel, you enjoyed it, please consider posting an honest review to Amazon.

Best wishes

Lange

2022

Introduction

This is a work of fiction, though with a basis in fact, and the story is woven around some people of the time, though it is a work of imagination, not reality. The historical setting is historically accurate for the county of Northampton. It is primarily a narrative about what we nowadays call PTSD, which is quite common among soldiers. In the 17th Century, of course, it was not understood, and anyone suffering from it would not have been considered to be unfit for service.

In modern times, it has frequently been a fact that spies, informers, and counter-spies (which would be a better description of Robert) have been 'recruited' by blackmailing them, either through deliberate entrapment, or by surveillance revealing something which would compromise them if made public. Since people do not fundamentally change through history, that would be a likely way of recruiting such people 372 years ago too. This makes the threat of Robert being coerced into spying by his handlers a credible way of recruitment. From 1645 until 1653, Parliament's spymaster was Thomas Scot(t), who established a network of spies and informers, cryptographers, interceptors of letters, and so on, that would function almost as well today as it did then. The employment of double agents was also widespread, and disinformation was readily employed as a covert weapon. I have endeavoured to describe the awful consequences of the civil wars – known as the Great Rebellion at the time - on the English population, and on Robert Barker and his family in particular, as he struggles with his mental demons resulting from the war. The county of Northampton was especially badly affected, as it could be described as having been 'on the front line', with major Royalist and Parliamentary bases in close proximity across the county, as well as nearby in Oxfordshire, Buckinghamshire, Leicestershire, and Warwickshire.

LESLIE LANGE, 11 June 2021.

Table of Contents

Northampton 1649

Map derived by author from various historical sources and comparison with modern street plan

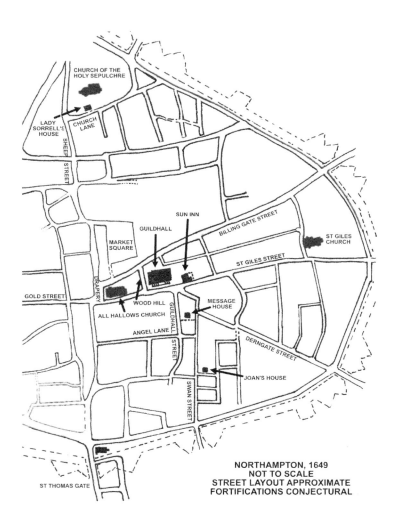

CHURCH OF THE HOLY SEPULCHRE

LADY SORRELL'S HOUSE

CHURCH LANE

SHEEP STREET

SUN INN

GUILDHALL

BILLING GATE STREET

MARKET SQUARE

ST GILES CHURCH

ST GILES STREET

DRAPERY

GOLD STREET

WOOD HILL

MESSAGE HOUSE

ALL HALLOWS CHURCH

GUILDHALL STREET

ANGEL LANE

DERNGATE STREET

JOAN'S HOUSE

SWAN STREET

ST THOMAS GATE

NORTHAMPTON, 1649
NOT TO SCALE
STREET LAYOUT APPROXIMATE
FORTIFICATIONS CONJECTURAL

List of Fictional Characters

Barker, John	Tanner, leather factor, and boot wholesale dealer of Rushden.
Barker, Elizabeth	John Barker's wife, and Robert's mother. Née Peck.
Barker, Robert	Son of the above. Volunteered for an execution, became a Parliamentary spy. Born 1622.
Barker, Amelia	Robert's wife, née Rately. Born 1625.
Barker, John (Johnny)	Robert and Amelia's son, born late 1643.
Rately, Jeanne	Amelia's sister, born 1629. "Joan the Whore"
Rately, Thomas	Amelia's uncle. Living in Wellingborough in poverty.
"Edwin": Marston, Edward	Keeps 'safe house'; owns Golden Lion tavern, in Wellingborough.
Adkin, Edward (Ned)	Casual farm labourer and ne'er-do-well.
Mawle, Edward (Ned)	John Barker's foreman and future partner.
Goodly, major Sam	Impostor. Of the Sorrell family.
Sorrell, Lady Margery	Widow of Sir James. Mother of Maud.

5

List of Historical Characters

Whalley, Colonel Edward — Colonel Edward Whalley's Regiment of Horse (New Model Army) under the Earl of Manchester. Later Administrative Major-General.

Whetham, Lieutenant Colonel Nathaniel — Military Governor of Northampton, 1645 - September 1649. Whetham's Regiment of Horse. (NMA). Married to Joanne Tressell.

Lydcott, Lieutenant Colonel Thomas — Took over from Whetham as Governor of Northampton. Lydcott's Regiment of Horse.

Grove, Captain John — Cromwell's quartermaster to 1643, then Whalley's second-in-command.

Ekins, John — Originally of Chester House, Irchester, bought Rushden Hall 1643. Died 1677. Wife Elizabeth Watson of Bletsoe, Bedfordshire. Married c.1649.

Bishop, Captain George — Marshal General of the Army. Involved with Thomas Scot, spymaster, as his right-hand man.

Scot(t), Thomas — Lawyer. Secretary of State from 1648. MP for Aylesbury. Regicide, prime mover with Cromwell, Vane, and Heselrige. Executed 1660. Spymaster 1648-53.

Waller, Sir William — Major-General of the Southern Association. Prime mover in the raising of the New Model Army. Known as "William the Conqueror". Emigrated to America. Died 1667.

Skippon, Sir Philip — Sergeant-major-general, in command of the foot soldiers of the New Model Army under Sir Thomas Fairfax. Executed 1660.

Prologue

I waited apprehensively on the scaffold, as the man was led out onto it, then kneeled to say a prayer with the priest, before he left this world for ever. Having finished the prayer, he stood, walked over to the block, where he was quickly blindfolded. Then he lay down, and calmly placed his head on it with the help of the waiting guards. The officer of the guard tapped me on the shoulder; I took up the axe, stepped forward, lifted it on high, and swung it downward in a well-aimed stroke, taking the man's head off in one clean cut. As a quiet murmur rose from the crowd, the officer of the guard held the severed head up, then threw it to the soldiers in front of the scaffold. I was quickly ushered away to change my clothes, after which I returned to my soldier's duties guarding the city of London.

I had agreed to perform this task due to the lure of the offer of gold. Gold that would be a great help to me and my family. I would be allowed to leave the army soon, and, I hoped, for good. But, never before had I killed a defenceless man in cold blood, in such a manner, and only for gold. I felt profoundly sick, then shocked at my rash decision. Maybe I would be damned in the sight of God; I knew not. That severed head would come to haunt me in my sleep many times thenceforth, as ever-present feelings of guilt and shame pervaded my soul.

For choosing to do this awful task, I received the personal thanks of General Cromwell himself. It was little comfort, considering the heavy price that I and my family would pay in the months to come, when my demons grew and made my life as if I had gone to Hell already. I near lost my wife and my mind. I will regret it to my dying day.

Chapter 1: Homecoming

I walked nervously to the door of the old house, my boots crunching in the fresh snow. After studying the heavy iron knocker for a few moments, I seized it, and rapped it twice. There was no reply. The house was silent. I reached out and rapped it twice again, harder this time, then called out, 'Father, Lia! Are y'in there?' There was still no answer. Nothing stirred. My officer, captain John Grove, called me. 'Robert! Come, we must seek shelter in the hall. Methinks they will be there.' I turned, nodded, said, 'Yes, sir,' and walked back to my horse, then turned again, and surveyed the old house and its neighbours. The holes made by musket balls were evident in the house walls; some of its neighbouring houses had suffered cannon fire, others had lost their thatch, some bore the scars of fire. Our village of Rushden had indeed suffered in the war.

I mounted my horse, and our small troop of twenty soldiers filed slowly along the High Street, towards the lane alongside the hall's park. There, a wicket gate gave access to the stableyard behind the house. It was getting dark now, on this gloomy winter's day, the sixth of February, 1649.

We had travelled with Colonel Whalley's column, a long, hard journey in the depth of winter, from the city of London to the County of Northampton; captain Grove's men had split from the column at Bedford, where we were quartered yesternight. It had taken us five gruelling days to make our way here. All of us were exhausted, cold, and damp through. The steep hills of the

Chilterns made driving the carts first uphill, then unhitching the horses, and using them to pull against ropes and blocks to ease the carts down the other side. When it was not freezing, we were mired in mud. How we longed for a warm fire and a comfortable bed!

For me, Trooper Robert Barker, it was harder than for my comrades. I had not seen my wife Amelia, and our young son Johnny, for nigh on six years. The army had ordered me to tasks that would keep us apart. After joining the troop bringing the king from Newmarket in Suffolk to Hampton Court Palace in '47, I was then ordered to guard London against mutiny and insurrection. Two miserable years under canvas within the city's walls. When the chance to do general Cromwell a great service was offered me, I accepted gladly, as it brought the chance to come home and mayhap leave the army. But it was not to be.

I was glad that I travelled with captain Grove's men; the roads were not safe for lone travellers, especially near Northampton. If deserters and refugees from the Royalists' armies were not enough, the local folk had suffered so much from both sides raiding them, and were hostile to soldiers. It was especially bad in '43 and '44, but since '48, Parliament's armies had mutinied too. When we left the thick earthen ramparts of London behind, as we travelled north, we saw more war damage, scarcer flocks and herds, fields left untended, and in some villages stones were thrown, even shots fired, at us. Typical was Soulbrook, the last village before Rushden. As we rode along the high street, a group of ragged men spread out before us, armed with pitchforks, old billhooks, scythes, and a rusty old sword or two. The captain lifted his arm, 'Column…. Halt!' Our sergeant-major yelled, 'Close up!' then Captain Grove moved closer to the group of villagers. 'We wish ye no harm! We do Parliament's business, let us pass!' The group of villagers waved their weapons, moved menacingly towards him. 'I ask ye again, let us by, do not give cause for force!' He turned in his saddle, and ordered, 'Firelocks at ready!' As one, we drew our carbines from our saddle holsters, and cocked them. The villagers' spokesman stepped forward, 'We 'ave nary a bite t'eat, captain. Soldiers took all we 'ave afore ye! All we 'ave!'

'Aye! Aye!' from behind him. The captain turned to the man.

'We would only pass through. We want nought of ye 'cept to pass freely 'pon the Commonwealth's highway. Pray let us pass peacefully.' Then added, 'Ye have my word.'

The villagers muttered and though one or two hotheads made threatening words, the group reluctantly moved over to let us pass. Our sergeant major shouted the order, 'Column, for'ard!' Four soldiers parted in pairs, keeping sight both of us and our would-be assailants, and the rest trotted past the downcast villagers. As the last of us departed, two or three villagers shouted insults, but nothing more. We all breathed a sigh of relief. Captain Grove shouted the order to uncock and holster firelocks. It was a sobering lesson for all, and left me worrying about what I would find in my home village of Rushden.

Rushden was damaged for sure, but not as badly as might have been. However, I knew that my mother had passed away while I was at the war, but did not know why or how. My father wrote that he had been given help by the new owner of the hall, Master John Ekins, whom I met briefly before I was ordered to the war. Father did not tell me that he had moved out of his house, with Amelia and our son, and Master Ekins gave them all quarters in the hall. We troopers were to garrison the hall, to replace the larger wartime garrison, which had moved elsewhere.

But I digress. At the stableyard, two grooms came out to help us with the horses, though mostly we had to unsaddle, unload, and settle our twenty-two horses ourselves, before we could go into the hall for food and some comfort. It was fully dark by the time we finished, and one of the grooms fetched Master Ekins to call us in to the back door, to a large room which, since the hall had been garrisoned, functioned as a dining room for the soldiers. One previously empty wing of the old house served as dormitory for the soldiers; I quickly learned that Amelia and Johnny, and my father, had adjoining rooms upstairs in the same wing. There was a roaring fire in the large hearth of the dining room, and we were soon able to remove our breastplates, helmets, and other soldierly equipment, and warm ourselves while the kitchen maids cooked food for us. The dining room was laid out with trestle tables and simple benches except for a large ornate table and chairs at the end nearest the kitchen - presumably for the Ekins family. Master Ekins came to me. 'Robert, is it not? Go into the scullery' – he pointed – 'and ye will have hot water to wash. You have clean clothes in your snapsack, I think? Change after ye've washed, and I or the good captain will take ye to your family.'

I thanked him, and did as he said. It was hot in the scullery, so I stripped off my clothes, and washed all over. It was so good to be free of the damned lice that had plagued us all on the road. Clean shirt, drawers, breeches and doublet back on, stockings, and shoes – heaven after the heavy cavalry boots – and I put on a coif, then came out, ready to meet my father and my wife and son. Johnny will not remember me. He was but a babe in arms when I was called to war. We will all be near strangers.

Master Ekins saw me and called me to him by the stairs in a corner of the room. 'Follow me', he said, and we went up the stairs to the next floor, then along a corridor. He knocked on the first door on the left. Amelia opened the door.

We were each shocked at the sight of the other. She spoke first, as Ekins quietly turned and went back to the stairs.

'Oh, Robbie, is it ye behind that beard? Is it really?'

'Aye, it is. And ye, Lia! How ye've changed! You were a mere girl when I left… You look so...different now.' We briefly embraced, and I kissed her, before she pulled away from me.

'Come, Robbie. Meet your son. He is much grown now.' She turned to the little boy, hiding behind the bed, clutching a toy as if it were a defence against strangers. 'It's your father, Johnny. Come back from the horrible war.' Johnny was having none of it, and ducked lower behind the bed. Amelia nipped around the bed, and caught him, then brought him to me. I picked him up and smiled at him.

'Let's look at ye, my son.' He had my ginger hair and grey eyes,

12

but his features were more Lia's.

I kissed him, as he tried to wriggle free. 'You're a fine, strong boy, Johnny. We'll have fun together, now I am home.' He wanted his mother, so I put him down, and he ran behind Lia's long kirtle. 'He does not know ye, Robbie. My, I wonder if I do now. You've changed so much.' I smiled at her, thinking of my inner demons that I dare not talk about, not even to her.

'There is a hardness about ye, Robbie. You look, well, careworn.'

'Aye, that sums me up,' I said. 'Careworn, tired of war, tired of the army, mayhap just tired.'

A knock at the door. Lia called, 'Come in.' It was my father, Master John Barker, leather and boot factor. I was learning his business when I was wrenched away from my family in '43. He walked towards me, then squinted at me in the subdued light of the room. I think he saw my shock at how he had aged since I last saw him.

'Aye Robert, how we have changed, my son. I am grown old with the cares of this world since your mother died. If it were not for Master Ekins…..' His voice trailed off. I saw tears forming in his eyes.

I stepped forward, shook his bony hand. He was not fifty, yet was thin, lined, grey of hair and face.

'We have all changed so much, father. War has brought us nought but pain and woe, but I am home now, for good, I hope. We must hope it will be better for the future now. And for Johnny.'

My father walked with a stick now; he moved slowly over to a chair and sat in it.

'Father, ye wrote that my mother passed away. If ye please, how, why?'

He looked up at me with rheumy eyes. 'Let us leave that till after we have eaten. I would know more of ye, son, what ye have done these last years.' I was surprised, but complied.

13

'I did, as ye know, go to Rockingham Castle in '43, but in '44, I was with the garrison at Northampton. We watched and raided Holdenby at first. I was assigned to major Lydcott, and went to battle at Towcester. Only local skirmishes, but then in '45 I was at Naseby.'

Hearing Amelia's sharp intake of breath, I paused and looked at her; she had paled, but I went on.

'We had to chase the Royalists after the battle, hunt them down. Then I was ordered to Kettering, and on to Newmarket. The king was taken to Newmarket in the June of '47, then to Hampton Court Palace. I was in the troop that took him there. After that, with unrest in London, I was ordered to help guard the city. I lived under canvas for the next two years. A chance came to do a great service for Cromwell, and with his thanks to me, I was sent back here. He shook my hand, ye know, thanked me personally."

'General Cromwell shook your hand, son?' My father was astonished. 'What great service led to that?'

'I may not say, father. All that matters is that I have come home. I hope they will pay me off now.'

Amelia looked a little doubtful, but said nothing. A knock on the door, and a voice said, 'Food ready!'

We all left the room, and went down to the dining hall. The other troopers were already seated, and the kitchen wenches were bringing out hot potage, bread, cheese, ale. It was not the greatest fare, but very welcome.

We could not converse at the table. The noise of twenty happy troopers was just too much. We all tucked in gratefully, except my father, who picked at his food, and ate little. He saw me looking at him, smiled weakly, and ate a little more. From time to time, he gave me a sidelong glance, to see if I was watching him still. Each time, he took another small bite. It was a worrying sight. Amelia noticed, and kicked my foot under the table, with a meaning look, and an almost imperceptible shake of her head.

After everyone had eaten, and the troopers returned to their quarters, Ekins came and sat with us. I asked my father again about my mother. Ekins said, 'It is hard for your father to speak of it, Robert. I'll tell ye, if he cannot.' My father demurred. 'Nay, Master John, it should be me that does.'

Amelia sat with downcast eyes as my father sighed heavily and started speaking.

'Your mother were attacked when fetching some milk. She did not return, so I went to seek her. I found her on the ground in Mill Lane, bleeding, and badly hurt. Afore she died, she said it was Ned Adkin. He had....' tears started to run down his cheeks. 'Had...his way with her.....she fought him bravely but he beat her.'

I was horrified, 'Ned Adkin? That drunken sot?'

'Aye. I heard he boasted of it. Had knocked at my door, asking for work a week afore. I refused him. It was his revenge, I....'

I stood up and paced the room, trying hard to control my anger. My first impulse was to go and kill the blackguard.

'Hold hard. Do nothing rash. Ned will have to answer to God, my son. As will we all for our sins in this life.'

My first blind fury turned into a grim, cold desire for revenge. 'H'mm. Mayhap God will not get his chance.' I turned to Amelia. 'I have not asked ye of your parents, Lia. What of them?'

She cast her eyes down again. 'Papa and Mama are gone near these last two year since. The king's troopers took all they had in '45. Father tried to stop them, so they fired the house. We moved to Uncle Tom's in Wellingborough for a time, but he had little himself. Papa had nought, no money, joined the Diggers on the common in '47. They were starving, then Cromwell's troopers came and took Papa...' Her voice trailed off, as tears ran down her cheeks. She wiped them away, 'My mother died soon after of an ague. Jeanne....I know not. I have not heard.'

I did not know what to say, so I stepped forward, and took her in my arms. After a few seconds, she pushed me away, and stood looking at me. 'I'm so sorry, Lia. I wish ye'd told me.'

'What good would it have done, husband? Could ye have come home? I think not.' I could only shake my head slowly. This was surely not the happy homecoming that I had expected.

Master Ekins spoke, after listening to all this. 'What is done is done, Robert. Ye can't undo it. Let us just drink to your safe homecoming. Be thankful for that at least.'

He called the kitchen maid, asked for strong ale. We all sat and drank somewhat glumly. Conversation was sparse now, as each of us was lost in our own thoughts.

Johnny was clearly tired now; it had been a long day, and much to cope with for a small boy. Amelia suggested we retire, so we all stood and retired to our rooms after wishing the others a good night. At least I could look forward to being in Amelia's arms once more, in a proper bed.

Chapter 2: Choice and Coercion

After so long away, 'twould have been good to make love with my wife again; but she said, 'Good night, husband,' turned away, and went to sleep. Mayhap I should have expected it. I could not be comfortable in a strange bed, and sleeping with my wife again, I did not sleep well.

My mind raced, flitting from topic to topic, worry to worry, doubt to doubt. Eventually, tiredness overtook me, and I slept a troubled sleep, during which dreams came and went. As deeper sleep came, so did my demons. A severed head bit me. I tried to push it away, but it turned and grinned at me. The more I tried, the more it came at me. In my dream, I yelled, 'Away with ye! Away wi' ye!' My tortured scream rent the cold air of the bedroom, waking Amelia with a start. She jumped out of the bed, and tried to shake me awake. 'Husband, husband, what ails ye? What is't?' I came awake then, panting, shaking. Amelia struck the flintlock kept by the bed, and blew the tinder alight, lit a length of slow-match, applied it to a candle. Meanwhile, Johnny sat up, and blearily asked us what was going on. Amelia shushed him, then held the candle near enough to look at me. I was still shaking, white, and sweating profusely. 'God's blood, Robert! What ails ye?' I looked at her with a feeling of terror. A knock came at the door, and it opened slowly. It was my father, from the room next door. Seeing the spectacle on and around our bed, he said, 'What is't, my son? Are ye sick?' Amelia turned to him, ''Twas just a bad nightmare father. Please leave us.'

He looked as if he would argue, but thought better of it, and left us alone again, saying as he was about to leave, 'I think ye're troubled, my son, to have such a nightmare.'

17

He quietly closed the heavy door.

Alone again, Amelia said to me, 'Ye must tell me what ails ye, Robert. I may help ye.'

'Nay, Wife, I.....cannot....dare not tell ye.'

She watched as I looked into the candle flame for a few moments, then I said, 'I...I have done.... dreadful things. I fear I am damned in the sight of God. I...may not say more.'

She wiped the sweat from my brow, a worried frown clouding her face.

'Get ye back to sleep Robbie. We needs must talk on the morrow.'

I lay down again, as she placed the candle on a nearby table, then got in beside me. This time, she moved close to me, and put an arm around me.

'I'm here. Your wife yet, Robbie.'

Sleep eluded me. I lay still, listening to her slowing breathing, as she drifted back into sleep. I could feel her warmth beside me. I thought to myself, 'So long, so long since we have been together. So, so much has happened.'

Yet again, my mind raced, and a little sleep came in fits and starts. All too soon a bell rang in the house somewhere, and people began to stir. The church clock struck seven. An unseen hand banged hard on each room door. 'Seven of the clock! Arise!' from the disembodied voice outside the room, then footsteps receded towards the staircase.

Wednesday 7th February 1649.

We arose, as I felt groggy still, and sat shivering in the icy room. Amelia put a new candle in the candlestick, and lit it. She inspected my face, and proclaimed me to look awful. My face, she said, was grey, haggard, eyes red and bleary. She fetched my clothes, then spoke to me again.

'Robbie, I will fetch hot water for us from the scullery.' Wrapping herself in a thick cloak, she pulled her shoes on, and went out of the door. I could hear her footsteps padding quietly along the corridor, and the stairs creaking as she descended. A few minutes later her footsteps returned, and she carried into the room a steaming pail of water. She placed it on the floor in front of me.

'Wash,' she said. "Twill make ye feel better.'

A glimmer of light began to seep into the room through the window as the first rays of the rising sun peeped into the room through the small window. I gladly washed my hands and face in the hot water, then stood, took off my shirt, washed my body some, and dried off. Then I dressed quickly, before the cold soaked into me again. 'I thank ye, wife,' I said; she smiled weakly, then washed her own hands and face, after which, her back to me, pulled her smock down to her waist and washed her upper body. She quickly replaced the smock, pulled a short petticoat over it, then a stiffened bodice, which she laced as swiftly as her cold hands allowed, and tied it. Next came a second thick petticoat, then a thick, but somewhat worn, woollen waistcoat, with two buttons missing, and her kirtle. She coiled her long dark hair into a bun, pinned it. She used to leave it free. She pinned a grey crosscloth and coif over it. She looked very much the Puritan woman of our time, dressed in brown coarse woollen kirtle, white apron, grey waistcoat and coif, plus the ubiquitous grey stockings and black Northampton shoes. I was truly taken aback to see her like this; when I had last seen her, she was a carefree young woman, dressed quite fashionably, with long hair, which she let down in the house. Not so now. Despite being only in her early twenties, she looked quite matronly.

She noticed my expression, and said, 'Tush, Robbie, think ye I would not grow up? Times have changed so much, and I with them. But 'tis yet me.'

'Aye,' I said, with a wan smile; she smiled back, then roused Johnny from his truckle bed, further along the room.

19

'I needs must get him ready. We may then break our fast.' A quick wash of his face and hands in the now only warm water, and pulling off his nightshirt, she dressed him rapidly in linen shirt, black breeches, coarse wool padded waistcoat. She pulled on his long woollen stockings and then his black shoes that were a smaller version of her own. I thought he looked like the miniature grown up that is the style of our children, though of course, he is but a small child. I wondered about his education. We must speak of it soon.

We trooped downstairs to the dining room, where several troopers were already eating their breakfast. I noticed John Grove sitting apart from them, and asked Amelia to sit opposite on one of the long benches with Johnny, as I took a place next to Grove. 'Good morrow, captain. I trust ye're well rested?'

'Aye, Robert. Good morrow Missus Barker, Johnny. Your father has already eaten and returned to his chamber. I must away presently. The eggs are good.'

He stood, bowed slightly to us, and left. A kitchen wench came in carrying a tray with a bowl of freshly boiled eggs, a jug of small ale, and one of milk, which she set out on the table between us. There were wooden plates on the table, each with a chunk of newly baked bread on it. It all smelled delicious, and I started to tuck in at once, then realised that I had forgotten my manners, and pushed the eggs and plates over towards Amelia and Johnny. I passed Amelia's pot with small ale, Johnny's pot with milk, then took my own.

'My best food since London!'Twas a hard journey in such weather, and army food is army food, no matter if in Bedford or a cheap inn.' I winked at Johnny, then smiled at Amelia. She returned my smile, passed Johnny a peeled egg.

'I see ye're not used to woman's company, husband. Ye must say Grace, Robert. We may not offend God, ye knows.'

A quick 'Thanks, Lord, for thy bounty, Amen,' and I grabbed another two eggs. Amelia looked at me with a raised eyebrow, but said nothing more, and tucked in herself.

We sat chatting after our breakfast, when captain Grove reappeared from the stairs. He walked over to us.

'If you would excuse me, Missus Barker. Robert, Master Ekins and I must speak with ye in private, if you please. Would ye come with me.' I looked at Amelia, who sat looking quizzically at me.

'I will come back as soon as I may.' I said, standing up as I spoke, and turned to follow captain Grove. He took me up two flights of stairs, to a small garret room. Master Ekins sat at a table by the window. The captain motioned me to a chair.

'Good morrow, sergeant-major! We must to business.'

Thought I, 'Sergeant-major. Hmm.'

I sat opposite Ekins as John Grove took the other chair and sat between us.

'There is much that must be done, Robert. Ye knows the stirrings of the Levellers and the Diggers. They must be watched. With Charles gone, there are new threats – from the Scots, the Irish, the French – and the army's unity must be preserved at all cost. At … all …. cost. Parliament itself is divided enough. Charles the son's advisors seek to exploit any division. Ye can help greatly. Ye knows the county of Northampton, ye're well educated, discreet. Ye have great value to us.'

He stopped and looked intently at me. Captain Grove spoke.

'The task has risk. If ye are discovered, your life could be forfeit. Master John and I think ye are well up to the task. If ye take it, ye will be promoted to sergeant major.'

I looked back at Ekins, as he continued.

'Take ye not the task lightly, Robert. Think on't carefully. The rewards are good, we can protect ye from discovery of your great service to general Cromwell; but this is your own choice, and for ye to consider if ye have the skill, the nerve for't. If ye do not take it, and leave the army, the pay that ye were offered….. may not be given to ye...in full. And ye will not have the protection of which we talk.'

I felt profoundly shocked at this. I did not know what to say. 'By whose order, pray?'

''Tis not for ye to know who ordered this. Only that ye would work for me and Captain Grove. 'Tis safer thus.'

'Safer? 'Tis so dangerous? Why so?'

Captain Grove answered. ''Tis not for ye to know. Nay – 'tis better that we do not answer it.'

Ekins offered, 'Ye would be well taught the necessary skills. After, 'tis your own ability that would be the key.' I was now feeling very unsettled.

'How would I be paid?' I said. 'What of my pay for serving general Cromwell? What of my regular army pay – I have had none these last two years.' Ekins answered that immediately.

'I would be your paymaster, Robert. Your paymaster and protector so much as I may, if ye take this task. Ye would needs trust me. I would not fail ye.'

The discussion dragged on, as my growing number of questions were answered, either by Master Ekins or the captain as the question demanded. We discussed secret messages, cryptography, dead letter boxes, indeed, all the aspects of intelligencing. Then, at once, I had a thought.

'Should I needs kill, what then? How should I do't? How should my soul be spared from damnation?'

Ekins and Grove looked at each other. Then Ekins replied, 'Think ye of this task, or the vengeance ye would take on Ned Adkin, Robert?'

My jaw dropped at this blunt question, then I recovered my composure. 'Sir, mayhap both. I have killed in battle, but...this… this is ….different, methinks.'

Grove replied, 'We hope ye need not kill for us. That invites discovery. Yet the other … matter … that is your own business, not Master Ekins's nor mine.'

I felt my face redden, as I realised that I had made a basic mistake. I must remember – discretion, discretion, discretion. If I wreak my vengeance on Ned, no-one, not a soul, must know that I have done it, nor how. And Ned must suffer, suffer greatly, before he dies at my hand, as he has made my father suffer.

The meeting continued for another half hour or so, then Ekins stood, and said, 'Robert, ye have much to think on. We will break now. Ye may have two days to think about this. Remember, ye are still a soldier, under army orders. Refuse, and ye may be sent elsewhere. Go to Amelia, enjoy time with her and your family. And ye are ordered to say nought of this conversation. Nought, till the time is right, and I will tell ye what to say to your family.'

As I descended the stairs, I considered the conversation. I realised that I had no choice other than to do what they wanted, and work for them, or again, I probably must leave Rushden and my family. Such a blow I could not inflict on Amelia, especially. She would be distraught. But how could I tell her that I must risk my life by becoming an intelligencer, if we are to remain together as a family? If I did not do it, I would not be paid, as so many soldiers of Parliament now. That has caused much unrest and mutinies. No, I could not refuse them. I would sleep on it, but do as they want was in truth my only option, God help me. What the war has brought us to! My mind was in turmoil once again. A turmoil that would grow until it came to near destroying me.

Chapter 3: Demons and Duty

I returned down the stairs in a very pensive mood. At the bottom of the stairs Amelia, little Johnny, and my father were standing in a small cluster, talking quietly. Amelia saw and called me, so I joined them. Amelia noticed my furrowed brow.

'Let us to our room, Robbie,' she said, and my father retorted, 'Nay lass. Let us away to my chamber.'

We followed him, and waited while he unlocked the door with a large key that he produced from deep within the folds of his gown. He went inside and motioned us in. As he moved to sit on his usual chair, near the small fireplace; I saw with some satisfaction that there was now a log burning merrily in it. Close to the nearer side of the fireplace was a settle, on which I and Amelia took our places, glad to be able to feel the warmth, while Johnny took his toy to the far end of the room, and sat on the floor, where he started to play with it. Amelia was the first to speak.

'I have told Robert of my parents, father. I think he will have questions of ye too.'

My father turned to me.

'My son, the war has sorely tried us all. We have much to tell ye.'

'Aye father. I did not know what happened here. I was ordered to remain in London, so could not come home. I am so sorry – nay, sickened – to hear of Lia's father and mother. Sore troubling indeed. But what of the Levellers and Diggers – they are hereabouts, I hear. Cromwell sees Levellers and Diggers as bad for England. Lord Cromwell is a hard Master, yet is honest and fair. He will do what he thinks best for England.'

My father was immediately angered.

'The man has no charity, I think. The Diggers in Wellingboro' are starving.'

'Aye, 'tis true. But he is in London, and does not see the truth of't.

'Tis hard, I know. But 'twas a hard fought war for us, and mayhap more is to come. England's enemies watch and wait.'

'Robert, Robert, time was when ye would not say such. What has become of ye, my son?'

I looked down, embarrassed, then up again into my father's eyes.

'I have seen much, father, done much. Much ill. Perchance am I damned in God's sight. 'Twas war. My eyes have seen too much to … to … go back to before. Many more are as am I become.'

I did not expect my father's reply. Shaking his head, he said, 'And ye may stay with the army, son? Leave your family yet more?'

I looked at Amelia, then back to him, wondering where this came from.

'I am still a soldier, father. The army may yet order me to war again. God help me."

I turned to Amelia, unsure of what to say to her.

'Wife, my love, I mayhap must serve England yet more. I cannot tell ye more than that. If I am ordered by the army, I must do my duty. I would have to do so or else be hanged as deserter. I am still under army orders.'

Amelia was now angry with me. She replied, 'Robert, if ye had been here, ye could have saved your mother from Ned's cruel hands. If he should….'

I put an arm round her, hoping to comfort her.

'Aye, wife, I know full well what Ned is. He will pay for what he did, I promise ye. But ye have Master Ekins and captain Grove to protect ye if I were sent away again.'

We fell silent, wistfully looking into the fire, at the fading flames. I suddenly recovered from my reverie, and said, 'Tush, it is midday, let us go and partake of Master Ekins's good food while we may.'

Taking Amelia's hand I led her, with Johnny in tow, out of the chamber, and down the stairs into the dining room. My father followed us at a short distance, with an even sadder look on his lined face.

On the trestles there was a simple lunch of bread and cheese, and jugs of ale. When we took a seat on a bench, a kitchen wench came, and offered a potage of mutton, pork, and beans. I and Amelia both accepted quickly; but my father gloomily waved the wench away, picked up a pot, poured himself some ale, and sipped it. I looked at him, but he would not return either my or Amelia's look. Johnny waved to him, but he did not notice – or maybe just pretended not to, I knew not.

While we awaited the potage, I turned to him.

'Father, I have time to myself this afternoon. I would see around the town, and would wish ye accompany me. It would please me much. I would see what has become of your merchanting business.'

I heard him grunt, still looking anywhere but at me. Amelia addressed him herself.

'Please father, 'twould please me too.'

He looked up at her.

'Aye, lass. I will to it.' Then, pointedly, 'For ye.'

I saw him smile weakly at her, still ignoring me. The wench returned carrying two bowls of steaming potage, putting them on the table before Amelia, then me. She returned to the kitchen, then came back with a small bowl for Johnny, which she placed before him. 'Master John, will ye not eat? The potage will warm ye.' Amelia and I stared at him intently.

'Oh, aye, wench. Just a little.' She had a bowl ready, which she put before him. John Barker thanked her, and asked for more ale – strong ale. Two or three minutes later, she returned with a jug of strong ale, to the concern of Amelia and myself, which we sought to hide from him. We all tucked into the hot, welcoming food, even my father, to my surprise, after his gloomy mood. It did little for the conversation, however.

Ekins and Grove had again disappeared, nowhere to be seen. I did not know it, but their horses had gone from the stable. They did not return until late afternoon, covered in snow from the near-blizzard that had blown up for a time outside. After the meal, Amelia took Johnny back to my father's chamber upstairs, where a new log was spitting fiercely in the fireplace, as it tried to get burning properly. Meanwhile, I and my father walked off out of the hall's yard into the lane beside the park, and thence along the High Street. Firstly, we went to our old family home, where my father produced another large key, unlocked the door, and we both went in. Much to my surprise, the furniture that I was once familiar with was no longer there. There was just a desk and chair, also small bench and stool, in what had been the parlour, and throughout the rest of the house the rooms were either stacked with sheets of thick boot leather, or else freshly made cavalry boots. I went upstairs to my and Amelia's old room, where, whilst my father remained downstairs, I found the floorboard that I could once prise up. I did so, and looked inside the cavity with some feeling of satisfaction. Then I went to one of the wall beams, again prised out a section of what is in reality a secret door, where I once had hidden my grandfather's poniard, checked the space, replaced the wood.

Back downstairs, my father gave me a door key identical to the one that he had opened the front door with.

'Ye may need this, son,' he said, 'Keep it safe.'

Outside, the light was beginning to dim in the short winter day, so we made a quick walk along the High Street, where my father pointed out damage to each building, and described how it happened. As we passed Ned Adkin's dilapidated hovel, my father went very quiet. Ned was nowhere to be seen. After we were past Ned's hovel, I looked quizzically at my father. 'In the tavern.' Neither of us spoke more about it. The sky had considerably darkened to the north east, and we both realised that snow was imminent, so returned as quickly as possible to the hall. The fire burning in the hall was a welcome sight.

I bade my father well, before going up the staircase, and knocked on his chamber door. On entering, I found Amelia sitting in my father's chair by the fire, and Johnny asleep on his bed.

'Your mare last night woke him, and he is now tired,' she explained, went over to the sleeping boy, and nudged him awake. She picked him up, and with Johnny protesting noisily, we went out into the corridor and into our own room. We both lay on the bed for a while, and I soon fell asleep too.

When we woke, footsteps going down the stairs told us that people were going down to supper. We got up, roused Johnny, and followed suit, with me having to carry my protesting son.

Supper being the main meal of the day, the dining room was full of people. All the troopers were there, but out of uniform except for breeches and doublets, and Grove and Ekins sat at the head table on their own. They both stood as we entered, doffed their caps, so I nodded, and slightly bowed my head, as much as I could do whilst carrying Johnny. Amelia smiled at them, which they both acknowledged with a smile and an inclination of their head.

There was a hearty meal, involving the ubiquitous potage again, though with beef, pork, and bacon this time, and a large mincemeat pie, after which the troopers became very noisy, especially as the ale loosened their tongues. My father came in just then, and sat near Amelia. The kitchen wench saw him, and brought him some left-overs, which he tucked into half-heartedly. My father saw me look him up and down. I realised that he had become very thin, hence his lack of colour and stooped stance. He saw me looking, but just looked down at his plate, and continued eating.

As the room resounded to more and more raucous singing and conversation – if yelling to each other over the din can be called that – I indicated to Amelia that I would like to go up to our room. Grove and Ekins, I noticed, had already departed. Back in our room, I suggested that we retire to bed; Amelia was clearly tired too, so she undressed and put Johnny to bed in his truckle, and then proceeded to disrobe herself. The room was not so cold this night, the wall adjacent to our room being quite hot from the fire that had been in my father's fireplace all day. We climbed gratefully into the bed in our smocks and pulled the heavy coverlet over us, then a fur over that. Cuddling together for warmth, both of us felt secure in each other's arms, and sleep soon overcame us.

But not for long. I had another terrible nightmare. It started with me demanding 'Away foul demon!' then I started to scream. As I tried to fend off the demon, I pushed Amelia away so hard that she fell out of the bed. She scrambled to her feet, and, as the previous night, got up and went through the motions of lighting a bedside candle, only to see me writhing in the bed, drenched in sweat and white as...well, driven snow, since the sheets were more grey.

'God be with us, husband, what ails ye? Why have ye this tortured soul so?'

She picked up her apron and wiped the sweat from my face, pulled back the covers, and fanned me with the apron. Johnny was now kneeling in his small bed, and crying as he tried to make some sense of what was happening. Amelia tried to comfort the child, and bade him lie down and go back to sleep. She may as well have asked him to fly. I now sat on the edge of the bed shaking. 'I...I....did a ....service for.... Lord Cromwell, that I ....I....cannot tell ye of. It haunts me greatly. I fear to sleep. I have no peace in sleep.'

She looked at me with a fearful look on her face.

'Robert, what sort of .... service? What is't that would haunt ye so?'

Before I could answer, a knock on our door heralded my father's

30

entry into our room. He looked at me with a look of mixed concern and inquisition. Taking hold of my upper arm, he spoke.

'Come ye with me, son. This must end.'

I was too shaken too resist, and stood up, allowing him to lead me into his chamber next door. As before, two or three inquisitive heads were looking along the corridor at us, but disappeared as we entered my father's doorway.

My father made me sit, then poured a goblet of wine. After a few gulps of the dark red wine, my face began slowly to feel more normal again.

'What have ye done that makes ye thus, Robert? Ye must tell me. Amelia fears greatly for ye.'

I sighed and looked up at him, 'Father, I may not say a word. Not to a soul. I did Lord Cromwell a great service, of which I must stay silent, or risk all our lives. It is a terrible...burden.' I could not help but look down at my hands, now wringing together, 'I would fain I had never done't, for I am damned forever.' I regretted the words as soon as I had spoken them.

My father looked at me with a worried look on his face.

'Ye volunteered … to kill, I think? Volunteered for money?'

I felt my face go pale, if that is possible. I looked into his eyes, but said nothing. I slowly gave a very weak nod, then could not stop myself bursting into tears.

'A father knows, son,' said my father, putting an arm around me, then gripping my shoulder. As my sobs subsided, he took me by both shoulders.

'Son, ye are not damned. Ye did what ye must. Use my chamber tonight. I will see to Johnny, and send your wife to ye.'

He left me, and went to Amelia. Two or three minutes later she entered my father's chamber, and looked at my tear-stained face, then sat beside me on the bed, which I had migrated to from the chair that I used moments before. Amelia put an arm around me, pulled me to her, and kissed me gently before we both took to the bed, wrapped in each other's arms. That night, we made love for the first time since I went to the army some six years or so before. Both of us sank into a deep sleep afterwards, and at seven o'clock, when my father knocked and entered his chamber we were still asleep in each other's arms. He turned quietly and left us there, as silently as he could, closing the door after him.

Thursday 8th February 1649.

My father dressed his grandson and took him down to breakfast, leaving Johnny to eat while he crossed the room to the top table. I heard what transpired afterwards, from Master Ekins himself.

'I beg your pardon, captain, Master Ekins. Master John, I must speak with ye privately.'

Ekins stood, and excusing himself, moved well away from the tables, 'What is't Master Barker?'

My father said, 'I know not what ye want of my son, or what he volunteered to do for Cromwell. but I must tell ye that he is in a sore distress. I beg ye to wait a while before ye press him to work for ye.' Master Ekins thought for a few moments, then, 'I did not know, Master John, but 'tis not unexpected. The war has exhausted many. I will give him as long as I am able.'

My father thanked Master Ekins, and returned to Johnny, who was still scoffing the gammon and fresh bread. He finished his own breakfast, asked Johnny to go with him, and the two returned to my and Amelia's room. Johnny, of course, wanted to know where his mother and father were. 'They are greatly tired, Johnny. We must let them sleep.'

Amelia and I woke to hear the hall clock strike nine, and we arose, washed and dressed. We were about to go out and down to the dining hall, when a knock came at our door, and my father entered. He looked surprised to see us up and dressed.

'Johnny and I have broken our fast, Robert. Ye need not worry on that account. If ye would break your own fast, there will be food, I think. I will see to Johnny.'

We were glad of that, so that we could have a little more time on our own.

We went down to the dining hall, while my father saw to my grandson's needs, taking him to the privy – a cold, unpleasant experience in such freezing weather. A new light had lit in both Amelia's eyes, and I hoped in mine, too. I felt much happier, and it was clear that we both felt like man and wife again. It had snowed quite hard overnight, and the snow lay some eight or nine inches deep. An icy wind blasted in from the north east, howling along the High Street like a demented wolf. It was not weather to be abroad, for sure. After Johnny and my father's return from the freezing outdoors, we were at table still, both eating a thick porridge and drinking small ale. Johnny ran to his mother, putting his arms around her waist, almost getting a face full of porridge as she struggled to keep the spoon straight. I had to smile, 'Tush, Johnny, ye would have a hat of porridge!' and grinned at our son. My father said, 'Robert, I have spoken with Master Ekins. Ye may rest for a few days. After your fast is broken, I would take ye to my house, and we will talk more.'

I thought that it was not weather to be walking the village, but agreed.

'Aye, father, 'twould be good.'

The breakfast over, Amelia and Johnny went off to the old hall's long gallery, where she could sit while Johnny ran about, and played, and while Amelia mulled over her concerns.

''Tis good of Master Ekins, to be so kind to us. But what does he yet want of Robert?'

Amelia asked the question, which would be for now unanswered.

Meanwhile, I and my father donned our heavy winter cloaks, took up stout staffs, and trudged through the deep snow out of the hall's

33

grounds, along the High Street, and towards the church, to my father's old house. I was surprised to find a log burning in the hearth of the parlour, and turned to my father questioningly.

'My foreman, Robert. Ned Mawle, he has been working. He is a faithful and hard-working man, and one day ye may see him as a partner, after I am with our Lord. Ye will need a partner then, I think.'

We took a seat each side of the hearth, and my father spent the next half hour explaining how he ran the business.

'I do not want to know what Master Ekins expects of ye, Robert, nor what ye have done that has distressed ye so. 'Tis not my concern. But I would have ye working with me as much as ye can.'

I explained that I hoped that I would be able to bring work as part of my tasks set by Master Ekins, since I would have to go to various towns around the area; and the New Model Army, as well as creating a demand for boots, also created additional demands from those who supply it with sundry other goods. I told my father with more hope than certainty that I and he should profit well from it all. The unrest too means that the demand for army boots is not going to subside for a few years yet. Maybe other leather goods also might be a possibility? Armies need much in the way of leather goods, and the county of Northampton knows about leather goods. All in all, it was a good discussion, and my mind was released from my woes for now.

Monday 12th February 1649.

As the next few days passed quickly, I felt more relaxed and absorbed by affairs of my father's business. Then, on the afternoon of the Monday next whilst I and my father were in the dining room, the front door bell sounded. A maid opened the door, and ushered in a man in military uniform, together with a small entourage of four troopers. They were brought into the dining room, but kept well away from my father and I, and there was no audible conversation between them, just a low murmur. The leader of the group was dressed as an officer, and I, carefully observing his clothes, sash, and side arms realised that his rank was a staff captain – one whom I had seen in London, but whose name I could not recall. Grove came into the room, the stranger and he exchanged salutes, and he requested the stranger follow him upstairs. I asked my father to come with me upstairs, but as we started to ascend the stairs, we found our way barred by two of the troopers. We had reluctantly to return to our table, where I called for a kitchen wench to bring more small ale. I racked my brain, but still could not recall the officer's name; the best that I could come up with was his first name, which I believed was George.

'He has come from the White Hall, I think. I saw him there,' I whispered to my father. 'Something is afoot.'

My father looked at me with a frown on his face, but said nothing.

'He is here about me, I'll warrant, Ekins has work for me,' I whispered.

After an hour, the staff captain and all four troopers reappeared, saluted Grove, who had led them to the dining room, thence through to the great hall, and they left by the front door. Ekins now appeared at the foot of the stairs, signalled to me to join him, and waited. I looked meaningfully at my father, who could only return my look with a worried stare. I walked over to Ekins.

'We must talk, Robert. It cannot wait, I fear.'

He led the way up to the small garret room, motioned to me to sit, then picking up a jug of wine and three goblets from the wall cupboard, joined me at the small table. Two minutes later, Grove joined us, and sat between us. He recounted what happened, as Master Ekins poured wine for us all.

'I had hoped that ye would have more time to rest, Robert; and I do not know how your father got wind of our asking to choose whether or not to work for us before we could talk further. But things move fast indeed, and we must ask ye to begin the work for us. 'Twill be an easy task, not too onerous. I would have ye go to Wellingborough and learn about the Diggers – or what is left of them.

We may not give ye a choice now. The army orders it.'

I could not suppress a sigh, picked up the goblet, and drank deeply.

'If 't must be, I must to't. When am I to leave for Wellingborough, Master?'

Captain Grove answered that.

'Ye must go under cover of dark, sergeant-major. No man must see ye leave.'

Ekins added, 'I will have your orders and warrant for the agent at Wellingborough. Ye will have a billet at the address in your orders. Your orders will be readied for you to depart at six of the clock this night.'

''Tis a dangerful road by dark, sir. The river will be in flood.'

Grove agreed, 'Aye, 'tis that. But mayhap more dangerful in light of day, Robert. Ye knows the locality well, I think. Ye must not be discovered.'

Master Ekins cut in. 'If needs be, ye may stay at an inn overnight, if 'tis too dark, or snow too deep. But better not, if 't may be avoided.'

Grove spoke again.

'If ye must stay at an inn, ye must not disclose where ye go. Learn to lie. Have a story ready. And God be with ye.'

As I drained the goblet, Master Ekins informed me that my orders were to be delivered to me in my and Amelia's room, then dismissed me. I now had the unenviable task of telling Amelia. She would be very angry. And distraught, if I were any judge.

I walked slowly down the stairs, with my mind unquiet again, and fearing the prospect of telling Amelia.

In the dining room, I saw my father still sitting there alone, and walked across to sit by him. I came out with the unwelcome news at once.

'I must away this night, father. No man may know of my purpose, nor where I go.'

He was lost for words, and did not answer, as I went on. 'I must go to Amelia, and tell her.'

I stood, smiled weakly at him, turned, and walked back to the stairs, my mind in a whirl.

Amelia was devastated by my news. I heard my father come to our door and enter without ado. Amelia was sat in a chair, her shoulders hunched, her face streaked with tears. I sat opposite her on the bed, my head in my hands. I looked up at my father, with pleading eyes.

'Father, I must go. I cannot break my oath. I know Lia is upset, but 'twill only be for a few days.' The three of us conversed a little more, and Amelia eventually agreed to wish me a safe journey, and a quick return to her. A knock came at the door, and Master Ekins entered, carrying a sealed letter. He looked at the tearful face of Amelia, and my worried look and said to her, 'Fear not, Robert will return safely. It is but a small task.'

Then he handed the packet to me, 'Here are your orders Robert. Open them before ye leave Rushden, memorise, then burn them. God be with ye.' I could only groan inwardly as I saluted him.

The hall clock had struck five. It was almost dark already, and a light snow was falling. There was much to do to prepare for the journey. I took my orders up to the garret room, taking a lanthorn with me, both to light the narrow stairs, and to read the orders by. I sat reading the orders for a while, tore off the address in Wellingborough that I was to use, then returned downstairs to our room, where I immediately put the paper on the burning log in the hearth, and watched thoughtfully as it charred, burst into flame, and finally became ash. I poked it well with a poker, until it could not possibly be read. I quickly put some clothes in my snapsack, where my poniard was still secreted. Then I put my heavy winter cloak around my shoulders, pulled my hat well down, and went out to the stables to ready my horse. I took my tuck and horse pistol, and a bandolier of shot and powder from the gun room and placed them on a table near the horse, then proceeded to saddle up, strap on the pistol in its leather case, and then the bandolier. Making sure I could not be seen, I removed the poniard from my snapsack, which I strapped on the horse the other side to the bandolier, and fitted the poniard into my breeches, where it was not openly visible. I asked one of the two grooms to come and watch over my horse for a few minutes while I went up to say my goodbyes, came down again, and took charge of my horse. After the groom had scuttled back into the warmth of the stableroom, I checked that no-one was about, walked the horse out to the wicket gate in Hall Lane. The half moon was already high up in a clear sky – it was a bitterly cold night – and with the deep snow muffling the sound of hooves and boots, I mounted, and rode away.

Chapter 4: Testing Time

At the first junction of the narrow lane outside Rushden, I took the Irchester road, and rode slowly away from the warmth, comfort, and safety of the hall. I was now alone in a hostile world.

Wellingborough is but six miles from Rushden Hall, and the only real difficulty I expected was the river Nene crossing at Little Irchester. The river has a large flood plain for much of its passage through the county of Northampton, and the narrow medieval bridge at the hamlet of Chester-on-the-Water is one of few places where it can impede crossing in winter due to water rising well above the road either side of the old bridge. If flooding were deep, it could be risky to attempt a crossing in the darkness. The journey through Irchester took less than an hour, and with the snow and moonlight, the road proved easy to follow. Having made good time, I soon approached the bridge, where it was clear that the water level was considerably higher than normal. The Nene is not a fast-flowing river, so I decided to aim my horse carefully for the bridge, and if the water level became too deep, I could turn around and seek an overnight stay at Chester House, close by the river half a mile back. As I steered my horse through the dark water, the level crept up almost to her belly, so I reined her in and inched forward until we started up the steep ramp to the bridge, and the going eased. Down through shallower floodwater again on the far side, and to my relief, I had crossed without any drama. A mile further on I reached the centre of the small town. I quickly found the agent's house – the sign of the fleece – in Angel Lane. I heard a church clock strike nine; not too late an hour to arrive. A few minutes later, I walked my horse along the alley to the side of the house, found its small stable, and tethered the animal while I went around to the front door and knocked. A voice from within called, 'Who is't?'

'Ekins's man.'

As the door opened, the scruffy-looking man inside asked for my password. I hastily gave it then slipped quickly inside. 'What be your business 'ere?'

I answered, 'I am come from Rushden to collect despatches for Master John Ekins at the hall. He would have word of the Diggers.'

The occupant gave his name as Edwin, which I guessed swiftly was not his real name.

'Bed your 'oss, maister, then we talk.'

He ushered me through the house to a back door, handed me a lanthorn, opened the door, and pointed to the rear stable. I trudged wearily through the snow to the stable, tied up my horse securely, then removed her saddle and other accoutrements, especially my pistol and snapsack. I made sure my horse had fodder and water for the night, spread a blanket over her, and returned to the house carrying my pistol, bandolier, and snapsack.

Inside, Edwin was heating some left-over potage, mostly an assortment of vegetables and barley, and indicated to me that I should sit on the settle in the stuffy kitchen.

'Maid ain't t'ere, maister. Ye'll 'ave to do wi' me makin' some eats.'

He brought me a jug of good ale and then spooned out the steaming potage from a large pot on the kitchen fireplace crane into a wooden bowl. Next came some hot bread, and, unusually in these sparse times, butter. I was only too pleased to get a hot meal inside me after the freezing journey.

'What be your name, maister?'

I had to think for a second, then said, 'Hob.'

With a sidelong look,'Y'ain't from these parts?'

'Oh, aye,' I said. 'I were born and bred Rushden. Been away at the war these six year.'

Edwin looked me up and down with raised eyebrows. I decided to continue.

'Can't get away from the army. Seems they are worried 'bout the

Diggers. D'ye know much 'bout them, Master Edwin?'

'Arr, they be roun' 'ere f'sure. Skippon's men left many wi' nought in Wellin'borough. Burned their 'ouses 'bout their 'eads. What'd ye do, if 'ee'd lorst all, maister? Sit'n starve, mebbe? Oi think not.'

I was surprised at this, but nodded in agreement.

'D'ye know Tom Rately, Edwin?' This brought a quick look of astonishment, then narrowed eyes. 'What's 'e t'ye, maister?'

My first test. I had to think on my feet.

'He is of possible interest. Don't know him, meself. He is in Wellingborough yet?'

He looked warily at me. Then spoke slowly, as if weighing every word.

'Oh, aye. Gort in wi'em Diggers on't common,'e did.'

'Did he, indeed? I would speak with him, mayhap?' Then hastily, 'I am not a threat, good sir.' Edwin thought, spat in the fire, thought some more.

'We does maister Ekins' business fust. Then we sees.'

I tried to look nonchalant, and shrugged.

'As ye wish, Master Edwin. I be here two days, more, mayhap. Soonest done, soonest gone, methinks.'

After finishing eating, Edwin showed me to an empty bedroom behind the kitchen and scullery. 'Maid usual sleeps 'ere when 'er stays. It'll do fer 'ee.'

I thanked him, dumped my snapsack on the floor by the bed, then took my pistol out of its holster, checked it, set it to half cock, and placed it on a small table by the bed, next to the candle and tinderbox. I had left my damp cloak near the kitchen cooking fire to dry, along with my hat. I quickly undressed to my shirt and breeches, removed my boots, and lay on the bed under its thick, coarse blanket. Sleep did not come easily, with unfamiliar noises from the town waking me

41

from time to time, as well as creaks from the house.

Tuesday 13th February, 1649

When the town's church clocks struck six, I was already awake again, and listening to the various sounds of my strange surroundings. Musing about Edwin, I didn't feel that I could trust this man; there was something about him that made me feel very suspicious. Perhaps this is what I would have to get used to during my intelligencing missions, I thought, but then, he should be on my side – or was he? Doubt and suspicion are strange, unsettling bedfellows. I heard footsteps coming closer to the door of the room, picked up the pistol, and cocked it, then covered it with the blanket. A knock came at the door, and a middle aged woman entered.

'Toime to rise, maister. Ye can break your fast soon, Ed be 'bout a'ready. 'e would speak wi' 'ee soon as may be.'

She put down a small pail of obviously hot water, replaced the candle in the holder with a lit one, and went out to the kitchen. I uncocked my pistol, and returned it to its holster, before taking off my shirt, after which I made welcome use of the hot water to wash my face and upper body, found fresh stockings and changed into them, and then dressed fully again.

In the kitchen, Edwin was sitting with a plate of fresh bread, some butter and cheese, which he was eating quickly, whilst scrutinising a piece of paper that he put down and picked up again at intervals. His clay pipe lay on the table alongside the paper. He looked up as I entered, and grunted, motioning me to sit opposite him. The maid asked if I would have eggs – she had bought them fresh in the early market – and I smiled at her, nodding appreciatively. There was already a wooden plate of fresh bread, no doubt from the early market too, I presumed, and a lump of fresh butter. It made a welcome change from the usual potage at the hall, especially in this freezing weather. Five minutes later, two fresh-boiled eggs were deposited on my plate.

After finishing the breakfast, Edwin had lit his pipe and sat there puffing at it, whilst looking dispassionately but minutely at me.

'Good eats?'

I nodded, saying, 'We must to business, I think.'

We removed ourselves to the parlour, and Edwin began the conversation.

'There be two concerns 'bout the Diggers, maister 'Ob. One, they disturb the peace; two, they be 'cited to 't by mischief-makers.'

I had to respond with a noncommittal 'Aye, 'tis about the size of 't, I guess.'

Edwin continued.

'That there be mischief-makers, I know not. Folks be 'ungry, must feed theyselves. Diggin' 'n' plantin', 'tis all they c'n do. There be little work.'

'What of boot making?' I said. 'Army needs boots.'

'Aye, but army ain't pop'lar 'ere, since '43 they burned many 'ouses. Two year since, they took some Diggers away. Ain't bin seen yet. Crom'll be 'nother tyrant, men say, like Charlie.'

'Have ye a report for Master John? I am to bring one.' I said, wanting to get the business over as soon as possible. Edwin showed me the paper.

'Ye mays read 't. Full'n be ciphered 'n sealed. I'll gie 't'ee anon.'

I immediately raised an eyebrow.

'So secret, Master Edwin? What be so secret 'bout the Diggers, pray?'

'Not fer thine eyes, maister. Oi 'ave me orders.'

The conversation had taken an odd turn, methought. I decided to try a different tack.

'Master Edwin, who leads the Diggers? Does ye know? And what of the Levellers – be they not a greater threat?'

Edwin looked at me with a suspicious expression on his thin face.

'Diggers ha'n't no leaders, maister. Theys ain't Levellers, fer all that folks says they be.'

No leaders, indeed? Someone must lead them, I thought to myself. This man was less than truthful. Ekins wouldn't be pleased.

'I think Master John wants names, man. Do ye watch the Diggers?'

Now it was Edwin's turn to look rather less than pleased.

'Watch 'em? Be diggin' so int'rest'n? Nay. Theys ain't no trouble.'

We sparred with words for a while, then I changed the subject.

'Well, Master Edwin, I would be pleased to speak with Tom Rately. Will ye help? Know ye the man?'

Edwin looked at his hands, then again spoke slowly.

'Aye, Oi knows 'im. Ye wun't get ought from 'im.'

'Mayhap that be my problem, Master Edwin.' An uneasy silence followed, then Edwin spoke again.

'Ye can try 'is 'ouse. Poor place, Wilby Rud. Fourth 'ouse from th' 'igh Street. On left.'

I thanked him, and indicated that I would go there now.

I donned my heavy cloak and broad-brimmed hat, and left the house by the front door. It was a very short walk to the marketplace, which had a few meagre-looking stalls selling bread, a chicken or two, some rabbits, pheasants, ducks, eggs. One stall sold rather unappetising-looking pies. Another was selling some threadbare clothes. I studiously avoided the stallholders trying to drag me to see their wares, and within five minutes found Tom's house on the Wilby Road. It looked very run-down, like so much of the town – indeed, most towns – now. I rapped on the front door. A muffled voice answered, and then the door opened with much creaking of its rusty hinges. Amelia's uncle peered out at me. His face was haggard, his clothes would have looked at home with the rubbish. I was disconcerted; this man was a few years ago quite prosperous, dressed well, had a decent house.

'Who be 'ee?'

''Tis Robert, Amelia's Robert.' Tom peered at me with rheumy eyes. I guessed his eyesight was poor.

'Robert? Robert? Amelia?'

'Your niece Amelia. I be her husband. I come to enquire about ye for her.'

Tom stepped back then, and waved me in. The house was in a terrible state, stank of God-knows-what. With difficulty I kept a straight face, pushed past the door, then waited as Tom struggled to close it. I realised from the state of the house that Tom was now a pauper, and lived alone.

''Tis years since I saw ye, Robert. Ye've changed so much. How be Amelia?'

I assured him that I and my family were well.

'Ye have had a hard time, methinks, Uncle. What of your wife? What of Jeanne? She lived with ye, I think?'

Tom proceeded to tell me that Amelia's aunt had died in '48, when the troopers from Northampton came to arrest the Diggers' leaders. Tom evaded them, but was in dire straits since, and lived almost like a beggar. As I had surmised, his eyes were not good enough to stitch shoes now, and anyway, there were few jobs. I asked again about Jeanne.

'She left. I would say to Northampton. Be work there, may be married, I know not. She were looking for a man to marry in Wellin'borough, but didn't find to her likin'. Mostly poor 'ereabouts.' That was new!

'Ye were with the Diggers, ye say? What of them?'

Tom spoke with bitterness in his voice.

'All we wanted was food, work. We live on the parish now, alms. Rich won't give us time o' day, let alone money. We talked o' justice for all. Justice. And Justice' – he spat the word – 'Pentlow, that FINE man, he asked for soldiers to be sent. Nine of us taken to Northam'ton! No word since. They'd be 'anged. Justice! What justice?'

He spat in the small fire in the hearth. Looking up at me, he said, 'Crom'll's justice, that be! Now ye'll be for Crom'll!'

I put my hand in my purse, and took a sovereign out.

'Please, Uncle, take it. I would do more. I will-' Tom cut me off.

'I want no such charity!'

'Uncle, I was in London. I knew not about your ..... state. I would see what can be done. Ye are family. My father mayhap would also help.'

Tom shook his head, pointed at the door.

'Be ye gone now.'

'I bid ye well, uncle. Please – I was not here.'

I opened the door, and left. It was a pensive Robert that ventured into the Golden Lion tavern a few minutes later, asked for a jug of best ale, and found a quiet corner. The landlord brought the jug and a pot over, and looking at me said, 'Welcome, stranger. Ye looks troubled.'

'Aye, I be sore troubled. I ... visited my ... kinsman and found him in a bad state. The town is much distressed, I think.' The landlord pulled up a stool sat on it opposite me.

''Tis that. Townsfolk supported Parliament, yet they do us ill. Many have lost all. Your kinsman be..?'

'Tom Rately. He lost all. His wife, besides. My wife's kinsman, her uncle.'

'Tom Rately, is 't? He were a good man. A leader o' the Diggers. He were lucky to hide from Skippon's men.' I could not suppress my look of surprise.

46

'A leader of the Diggers, ye say? I knew it not.'

'Oh, aye. Strong supporter o' Winstanley too. Durst not say it now, mind. Parliament yet 'ounds us wi' its spies an' informers. We thought to do better, now Charles Steward be gorn. Crom'll, he be as bad. Cares nought for likes 'n us.'

I thought that I might try a probe.

'Know ye of Jeanne Rately, landlord?' The man looked even more shocked than I myself.

"Jeanne, ye say? Aye, indeed. A bitch if e'er there be one. She marrit an officer – a major – from the garrison at Northam'ton. His name.....Berry, I think. Posted to Belvoir, last I 'eard. She were lookin' for a man wi' money. An' found un. She be your kinswoman?' I nodded cautiously.

'Wife's sister. My wife would have news of Jeanne.'

'Well rid, methinks.'

I thanked the landlord, and asked for some food, the least I could do was to buy some, with such information forthcoming. This news was hardly welcome! I would have to tell Amelia carefully. She would be near distraught to hear about it, I thought.

It proved to be a tasty, but somewhat meagre meal, mostly a bean potage with other vegetables that were available in the market. It was hot and filling, so I was well satisfied. I had much to think about, not least my dislike and suspicion of Edwin. I resolved to be back in Rushden the same night – if the weather held. I finished the meal and three pots of the good ale, paid my tally, and thanked the landlord for his hospitality. Leaving the tavern, now filling with customers, I walked briskly back to Angel Lane, little more than an alley off the High Street, with its ramshackle houses and back courts. The front door was unlocked when I arrived, so I entered. There was no sign of 'Edwin', but the maid was still about, and she ushered me into the parlour, where a feeble log fire gave a semblance of warmth. After removing my cloak and thick felt hat, both of which she took to the

47

kitchen to warm again, I settled myself in a chair by the fireplace. The maid came back in, and proffered a folded, unsealed document.

''e says Oi've ter gie yer this'n letter, maister. Says ye's ter read an' 'e'll seal 't afore ye takes 't away. Would 'ee care fer a small ale?' I took the letter, shaking my head.

'Have ye any hot broth, mistress? 'Twould be most welcome wi' this cold.' She scowled at me, but nodded, and left me to read the letter.

The letter was a report for Grove and Ekins. The handwriting was barely legible, and the spelling, being kind to it, was erratic. I made what sense I could of it, which was essentially that the Diggers were still a threat to the peace of the town, and they should be watched carefully. No leaders had appeared to replace the ones taken away to Northampton. Examining it very carefully and closely, I thought that I could detect hidden writing between the rough lines of scrawl, but couldn't be sure; I thought better of trying to expose what was written in secret ink before getting back to Rushden Hall. Maybe Edwin would say something. If he did not, I mused, there was something underhand about it. The maid came back in carrying a bowl of broth, which she placed on a small and rickety table near the chairs, and held her hand out for the letter. I gave it to her, just thanked her for her solicitude, and decided that I would go and ready my horse for the road after drinking the broth. I wanted no delay leaving. I heard the town's church clock strike two, and realised that I would need to saddle up within the next hour and a half.

The mutton broth was quite hot, and warmed me considerably. I took the bowl to the kitchen, recovered my cloak and hat, and repaired to the stable. My horse had fed enough, and had drunk plenty of water, so I need not worry about that. I removed the blanket, replaced it with a saddle cloth, and the saddle, tightened the girth, and checked that the reins and other straps were secure and ready. I made sure that my pistol's outer case was ready to receive it, and that the bandolier was secured on the other side of the saddle. I replenished the fodder and returned to the house. Edwin was sitting in the kitchen now, with both the letter that I had read, now sealed, and another letter already sealed, secured to it with a ribbon. I quickly removed my cloak and high-crown hat, and sat on a stool opposite Edwin. I thought that maybe I should offer Edwin some money for my bed and board, but the latter declined, saying that he was well rewarded for his work. I told him that I would leave as soon as it was dark, and Edwin didn't demur. He handed me the two letters, and asked me to accompany him to the parlour. We sat in the two chairs, one each side of the small hearth. Edwin started by saying that his letter to the Master Ekins is important, and needed be delivered into his hands as soon as may be. The one that I had read was secondary. He was pleased to have me as a guest, and I would be welcome to return. I replied with my own pleasantry – insincere though I felt it to be - and also thanked him for Tom Rately's address.

'I was pleased to meet him, but he had nought of value about the Diggers. I will scribe my own report at the hall.'

Edwin again eyed me a bit suspiciously.

''Twill soon be dark. Best go when ye be ready.'

'Aye, I fear crossing of the Nene at Chester. River were well up when I came. May have risen more. 'Twill do so if snow thaws.'

Edwin bade me go, and fare well, so I put the letters in the hidden pocket in my doublet, whereupon I realised that I had a bill of exchange, supposed to be part payment for the service to Cromwell, still in the pocket. I must have a care not to lose it, or get it wet, I realised. I and Edwin returned to the kitchen, where I donned my cloak and high-crown hat again, picked up my snapsack and pistol from the bedroom, said my goodbyes, and left for the stable.

It was near enough dark now, so I strapped the snapsack across my back, put the pistol into the leather casing and fastened it in. I led my horse out into the alleyway, thence out onto Angel Lane. There was almost no-one about, and those that were had wrapped themselves well into thick cloaks and pulled their hats down against the bitter wind. No-one, I guessed, would even notice me. I mounted my horse, and headed south down the High Street, and then London Road to the river. The moon was now well above the horizon, and I could see that the river had fortunately risen only slightly, so I walked my horse slowly into the icy water that flooded over the road either side of the bridge. At its deepest, it was only two or three inches higher than when I came, but the crossing is risky here, and I had to go even more cautiously until I was across the narrow bridge. The road was now very slippery, and my horse was reluctant, so I dismounted, and walked her slowly along for the half mile until the Irchester turn. There, the road is more level, and less used, so it was both easier to follow, and less treacherous underfoot. I remounted the horse, and walked her slowly forward. Her hooves sank into the snow, both quietening our passage, and inspiring both my horse and myself to have more confidence. I soon passed through Irchester's main street, and settled into an easy walking pace for the three miles to Rushden.

It took about an hour to enter Rushden, by a back lane, which runs almost parallel to the High Street, until I found the turning into the narrow lane that should lead alongside the grounds of the hall, and the wicket gate to the stables. Except this time, in the dark, I took the wrong turning. I found myself in Mill Lane, where, I remembered, the ne'er-do-well Ned Adkin had raped and beaten my poor mother. As chance would have it, the lane comes out close by my father's house, and lying in the lane, drunk insensible, was the same Ned Adkin, snoring as only drunks can. It was obvious why he had walked up this narrow lane: he needed to shit. He was too drunk even to find a privy, and his breeches were lowered, leaving his buttocks exposed to the world and the biting cold. 'Perchance he will be well bitten by the frost,' I thought, then looked back at him, as an idea formed in my mind. I would consider it more back at the hall. At the High Street, there were no people about, no lights in any houses but the hall. I turned my horse along the street to the lane alongside the hall grounds, found the wicket gate, dismounted, and walked my horse slowly, as quietly as I could, to the stable. I found a candle and tinderbox, and after tethering my horse in a vacant stall, I lit the candle. Off with my pistol, bandolier, saddle and saddlecloth, covered the horse with a thick blanket after I had given her a perfunctory brush down, made sure there was fodder and water for her, and then crept into the scullery passage of the hall. Once inside, I pulled off my wet boots, took off my cloak and hat, and apart from the odd creak of the stairs, made my way almost silently to my and Amelia's room. She was asleep in the bed, but woke as I entered, and sleepily asked who was there.

''Tis Robert, Lia, I be back from my task. I will join ye quickly.'

I had become aware of my clothes itching since Wellingborough; they had some lice in them – damn Edwin's house, I thought. I tore off my clothes – all of them – found a nightshirt from my snapsack, put it on quickly, and joined Amelia in bed. I was glad when she cuddled up to me, and whispered, 'Are ye all right, Robbie? Did the task go well?'

'Aye, thankfully it did, my love. Let us to sleep, I will tell ye on the morrow.'

We entwined ourselves around each other, and quickly fell asleep.

Wednesday 14th February, 1649

The knocker-up woke us at six o'clock as usual. I immediately disentangled myself from Amelia, got out of bed, and lit the candles. Whilst I was doing this, Amelia put a cloak over her smock, shoes on, and went out to bring a small pail of hot water from the scullery. She was back within a few minutes. It would be a while before our room was warmed a little by the heat from the hearth in my father's adjoining chamber. We both had a quick wash in the hot water, and dressed as quickly as our complicated clothing permitted. As soon as we were dressed, before Amelia could rouse Johnny, I said, 'Hold hard,

I have something to tell ye, Lia.'

She looked round at me with a worried frown.

'I have news of your uncle, and also of Jeanne.'

I spoke quietly, telling her about my encounter with Tom Rately, and what I thought of her uncle's state; then about my conversation with the landlord of the Golden Lion tavern. She was not surprised, but was saddened at her uncle's bad state; but of Jeanne, she was, as I had feared, profoundly shocked. Her younger sister had always been such a friend and confidant to her, the description of her as a 'bitch' came as a barely believable bolt from the blue.

'How could it be so with Jeanne? She be married? And not tell me?'

''Twould seem so, my love. I think not why she could not write to ye all this time. There may be more to this than I learned. Ye must be patient, mayhap I shall hear more of her. Let us not mither just now, my love. We must ready Johnny to break his fast.' I kissed her gently, then moved to wake and pick up Johnny from his truckle bed.

When Johnny was up, washed and dressed, we descended to the dining hall, where John Ekins was already at his place at the top table, eating from a large bowl of porridge, steaming in the cool air of the hall. The log in the hall fireplace was yet to burn up properly. He inclined his head as I and Amelia entered, which I acknowledged with a cheery 'Good morrow, Master Ekins,' and we seated ourselves at one of the four trestle tables. There was no sign of captain Grove as yet.

The kitchen wench brought three bowls of steaming porridge, asked if we wanted small ale or best ale, and if cheese would suit with the hot fresh bread already on the table. I asked for best ale, whilst Amelia opted for small ale for her and milk for Johnny, and they both asked for some cheese. There was no butter today. I quickly said an approximation of Grace, and we started eating before the porridge cooled too much. We had almost finished eating when captain Grove appeared, and strode straight over to me.

'Good morrow, Master Robert, Missus Barker. May I take the despatches, if ye please, Robert?' I duly handed over the sealed letters, as Amelia looked at me and then captain Grove questioningly. With a quick nod, he turned and strode back whence he had come. I looked at Amelia with a raised eyebrow, but said nothing about the interruption. After eating, we arose and headed for the stairs. As I came by Master Ekins, I asked Amelia to take Johnny to the long gallery. I asked if I might obtain writing materials. Ekins gave a perfunctory 'Certainly. I will send them to your room,' and resumed eating his breakfast. I inclined my head, then went upstairs to my room and waited. I did not have to wait long before a knock at the door ensued. I opened the door to find Grove standing there, looking a little red-faced. He handed over paper, quill, ink, and sand shaker, then said, 'When your report is writ, please come to the room atop the stairs.'

I nodded in acknowledgement, took the materials, and sat at the room's only small table to compose my report. It did not take long before I felt it sufficiently done, dried the ink, then went up the stairs to the garret room. Ekins was already sitting there, with Grove to his side. Ekins motioned me to the remaining seat. 'What think ye of the task, sergeant-major? And of the agent, Master Edwin?' I handed over my report, then gave a verbal assessment.

'The task was easily done, Master. Edwin – if that be his name – I do not like. I think he be....untrustworthy, mayhap has other masters than yourself and the captain. He wanted me to speak not with Lia's uncle, Tom Rately, that I discovered was once a leader of the Diggers. I learned more from the landlord at the Golden Lion tavern. He, I would broach, is honest.'

Grove and Ekins looked at each other. Ekins spoke.

'Ye have done well, Robert, very well. We too, have our suspicions of Master Edwin. Can ye say more of him?'

'He looks, behaves ….. sly, suspiciously. I think that he says what he would guess that I want to hear. He tried to avoid giving Tom Rately's whereabouts. Tom said nought to me that I feel less than

53

honest. Edwin showed me his letter to the captain; but I saw it had more hidden in it. He would have me learn that the Diggers are a great mischief, a danger to the peace. I think not. They be poor people who would merely eat. Gerrard Winstanley, he be far from Wellingborough. His writ incites people, as those who be hungry cleave to those who would help them. And Parliament, Lord Cromwell, help them not. No more do the rich of the county of Northampton.'

Grove and Ekins looked at each other again, before Grove turned to me.

'A forthright assessing of the state at Wellingborough, Master Robert. Ye are perceptive.'

Ekins added, 'Master Robert, ye have done well indeed. What has passed in here must not – NOT – be repeated. We needs must maintain the deception that we trust Master Edwin. Now, we would acquaint ye with what we want of ye.'

I nodded, wondered what that would mean, 'I understand, sir.' In truth, I did not.

Ekins next passed on the briefing that would stun but excite me, and that, should she learn of it, dismay Amelia.

'Do ye know of those who plot to bring back Charles the son?'

I had certainly heard of this issue, but knew nought of it.

'They be few, we have learnt, but they would grow stronger. They be, we have learnt, among us, even in Rushden yet. And, mark this well, they would stop at nought. They be most dangerous. Ye must take utmost care, Robert.'

I felt myself pale somewhat, and nodded solemnly – though I felt anything but solemn.

'Their leader be well known to those whom we serve. The earl of Northampton. He is powerful, he has ambitions, he is most dangerous. If ye take not cares enough, a knife will soon be in your ribs.'

54

As he saw me blanch, "Tis good that ye are afeared, Robert. A man that has no fear makes not a good intelligencer.'

'I see that, Master John.'

'Presently, we would have ye in Wellingborough more times. 'Tis good that ye can use Edwin's house. Let him learn that ye're watching the Diggers. Your man at the Golden Lion may know more, Robert. Make good friendship with him. There may be others yet. The market, the church. But do not make yourself stand out. Be a good townsman. Ye would have more on Jeanne; make much use of that.'

Now I wanted answers.

'What of the plotters, Master John? Why for they be so dangerous?' Grove answered this.

'Aye, Robert, I will answer. They would kill Cromwell, bring back Charles the son, and place him on the throne. Ye may see that such as my lord Northampton would profit greatly, should he hand young Charles the throne. He would be sorely in debt to the earl and others of his group. That prospect makes them most dangerous indeed.'

Ekins added more.

'Captain, Robert needs must be taught some necessary craft. How to write secret messages, secret writing. And more.'

He turned to me, and handed over Edwin's letter, which now had lines of small brown writing between the lines of inked script.

'Ye may read this, Robert, and see the secret ink writ within it. Ye must learn to do't.'

My mind spun as I read the secret message. It described myself, Robert, as gullible, and unlikely to find the good intelligence like that which he, Edwin, is providing. The good Master Ekins should be most grateful to Edwin, it said. I looked up at Grove, realising that it was, in fact, Edwin that was the fool, and he was taking Grove and Ekins for fools too. I would truly relish this job!

'Be here, in this chamber, at nine of the clock on the morrow, sergeant-major.'

'Aye, captain. If I may, Master John,' I addressed myself to Ekins, 'I have yet my bill of exchange, the part payment for my service to Cromwell, with me. Could ye provide safe keeping for't, if it please ye?'

Ekins agreed, suggesting that my father already had the means to safely store it, but he would handle the matter, and tell me afterwards what he had done.

Chapter 5: Wiles and Wellingborough

My training unsurprisingly took rather longer than a week; I had so much to learn. Ciphering and deciphering alone was a big subject, with my having to learn about coding by substitution codes, Alberti's substitution, and finally, steganography, by far the most secure, but hard to decipher, much used by governments. Grove impressed upon me that since Parliament had outlawed ciphered letters in '44, it would be dangerous indeed to be caught with any without very good reason.

Grove cautioned me, 'Ye must hide your real secrets from Edwin, yet let him think ye a fool. Code something of no importance with a single substitution, leave it so Edwin may find, decipher, and make copy of't. Edwin will think ye poor intelligencer. But ye will know better. Other times we may give ye a writ that we want Edwin to read.'

Following my indoctrination into the mysteries of ciphers, I was then taught about finding and managing sources, vital for any intelligencer. And finally – somewhat to my surprise – how to kill silently, and so as not to be detected as the murder it would be. I demurred at first, then realised that this could aid my vengeance on Master Adkin. I became a good and attentive pupil to that subject!

After the meeting, I went downstairs in again a pensive mood. How would I tell Amelia that I will be spending much time upstairs, and then when that is over, I will have to return to Wellingborough? This time, I may be there longer. She will not be happy at the prospect of my going away again, and I may not even tell her why, or what I am to do – much less of my plan regarding Ned Adkin, now forming in my mind. I dare not tell her that I may now be at serious risk of my life in the process. My, oh my, what had I got myself into? At least, after the training, 27th February or thereabouts, the snow will have much receded, except it would be replaced by a glutinous quagmire on the roads, and a very swollen River Nene, potentially meaning that this time I would have quite a detour through Irthlingborough and Finedon if the narrow stone bridge at Chester-on-the-Water were badly flooded.   And the days were getting rather longer, making moving around unseen harder. I thought much about how to broach the subject of my leaving again, and decided to start by speaking to my father, after the midday meal, when Amelia would have taken Johnny upstairs to the long gallery to play for a while.

'Father, I must talk with ye in private. If it please ye, in your chamber.'

My father looked at me enquiringly, but agreed, and haltingly led the way up to his room-cum-office. There was a log in the hearth burning idly, so we both pulled a chair close to it.

'We must speak quietly, I wish not to be overheard,' I said.

My father could only nod, though looked rather worried, as I continued.

'I must away again, father, for a few days. I will visit Tom Rately while away. Could ye help him, perchance? His eyes be dim, but mayhap there be work for him? Even a little silver would help him, he lives on alms.'

My father was taken aback, though his daughter-in-law had told him that I had found Tom in a poor way.

'I could help with silver, but work…. Tom was ne'er a cordwainer. He were a bocher, a keeper of sheep, no more'n that. If his eyes be dim, 'twould be harder yet to give'un work.'

'Father, I would like to help him. Lia would be well pleased. But Tom is a proud man. He would take not my sovereign, and I see why. Silver is less …. obvious. He needs good clothes, shoes. We must surely help.'

My father put his head to it, then, 'Aye, let us help him. I have a sovereign in silver. Take it, do, give it to him. Or ye can buy stuff for 'im.'

He counted out some silver shillings, groats, and pennies, and gave them to me. I put them in my purse for now.

'Son, Master Ekins has given me your bill of exchange to keep safe. It be in my strongbox – over there,' pointing to a large iron box, with heavy locks, behind his bed.

'My thanks to ye, father, I had been carrying it with me.'

"Tis for a large sum. A large sum, indeed. 'T must have been great service for Cromwell, indeed.'

'Aye, father. 'twas, but I still may not speak of it.'

He said no more on the subject, though looked at me with a worried frown.

I broached my other point.

'Father, Lia knows not that I go away again. In a fortnight. I fear she will not be pleased. Nor will ye. But I have my orders.'

'Son, Master Ekins has told me. Ye must tell your wife this day. Pray do not let it fester. She must have time to be ready for't.'

I breathed a sigh of relief. Smiling, 'My thanks again, father. I will to't.'

I left my father's chamber forthwith, and went to the long gallery, where Amelia was sitting sewing, and Johnny was playing with his toy.

'Lia, my love, I must tell ye news. I am ordered to go away again, in a fortnight. But 'twill not be bad; I will have silver for your uncle Tom. I would buy clothes and shoes for him, 'twould help him much.'

Amelia adopted a resigned look, 'Aye, Robbie, I expected such. So, to Wellingborough again?' 'Aye, not far. Though I may be away longer, I think. I have much work to do.'

An unexpected question came from her, 'This will be not the last time, methinks. There is much unquiet in the land, I guess your task be about that?'

I thought for a moment, then decided that the truth would be the best option.

'Aye wife, 'tis why I must go. Parliament ... lord Cromwell is a ... demanding master.'

Another unexpected question followed.

'My husband, be it danger to yourself?' Again, I thought the truth the best course of action.

'Mayhap 't will .... could be so. I would take a care, my love. A great care.'

Then came the most awkward question.

'Can ye tell me more of it?'

'Nay, wife. I may not tell a soul. 'Tis enough that danger mayhap stalks me; I would not that it stalks ye too.'

Then thinking it might be politic, ''Tis of great import. Now there be no king, there be much mischief afoot. Needs must that I do my duty, my love.'

Amelia deduced that it would be wise to ask no more awkward questions – for now.

'God will be with ye, my husband, He will keep ye safe. For me. We must pray each Sunday, Robert. 'Twill help greatly to ease my fears.'

'H'mm,' thought I, 'a small price to pay, if it will make my task easier to bear.'

'We shall, my dear, we shall indeed.' I meant it – when I said it.

I kept my word, as a good husband should. That Sunday, morning and afternoon, I, Amelia and Johnny attended the austere Puritan service in the church of Rushden, Saint Mary's, which had been stripped of all its stained glass, its organ, pews, and altars. The service was conducted around a stark wooden table, with its small congregation sitting on rough wooden benches. Despite that, the preacher was not one of the more fire-and-brimstone variety that had been so prevalent since the Great Rebellion, and I was thankful for that, at least. Amelia seemed very pleased with the gloomy sermon. I decided not to disabuse her of my real feelings about it. 'So long as she be happy,' I thought, 'but I would not that she becomes a grim faced Puritan harridan.' My first insincerity to her, God forgive me.

As we rose to file out that first Sunday afternoon, I was taken aback to notice Ned Adkin skulking about supposedly listening to the sermon. I smiled grimly to myself, as I thought about the retribution I had planned to come for that blackguard. The preacher bowed slightly as I and my family left the church, and I inclined my head in return, as did Amelia. Back at the hall, Amelia remarked how the sermon had made her feel much better. Whilst I wondered how that might be after such a gloomy diatribe, I smiled weakly at her, and said nought. My second insincerity to her. I just hoped that she wouldn't expect me to bow and scrape to a god that could allow the awful things that I had seen and done during the war.

The days passed quickly by as my training progressed. Then came the day when I had to return to Wellingborough.

Tuesday, 27th February.

I readied myself to leave for Wellingborough again. The moon had waned to around a quarter, so, though it was a fairly clear sky, the night was dark and forbidding as I again reached the river Nene at Chester-on-the-Water. It was obvious that the river was much too much in flood to attempt a crossing on such a dark night, so I turned my horse around, and headed to Chester House nearby, which was still owned by a member of the Ekins family. Maybe I could make use of that and gain the use of a room in the house and a good breakfast next morning. By the time I was walking my horse through the grounds, I was beginning to think better of the idea – it would cause too many awkward questions - and looked for the estate manager's cottage, which I found easily with its well-lit windows. I walked the horse up to the cottage and dismounted, then knocked on the front door. A voice demanded to know who was there; I answered, 'Robert Barker, come from Rushden Hall.' The door opened and flooded me with light. I stepped forward, and said to the man, 'I would ask ye for a bed for the night, if it please you. The Nene is too flooded to risk the bridge this dark night.'

The man looked me up and down, and then grunted. 'Stable your 'oss, then be back quick smart.'

He pointed at the nearby stable block. I thanked him, and did as he bade me, soon returning carrying my snapsack, pistol, and bandolier. When the man opened the door again to my knock, he was less than pleased to see the weapons I was carrying. I saw his fearful expression, and said, 'I be on business for Master Ekins at Rushden Hall. 'Tis business for the Ruling Council. The roads be not safe in these troubled times.'

The man carefully looked me up and down, before letting me in, and introduced himself as Dennis Plowman, Tom Ekins' man.

'I be most thankful, Master Plowman. There be no inn this side of th'river. I would pay ye for your hospitality. 'Tis no night to be sleeping in a field.'

Dennis still looked somewhat askance at me, and wanted to know where I was going, why out so late.

'Orders. Master Ekins had a visitor, left this day, then Master Ekins ordered me away this night. My wife was not pleased I can tell ye!'

I grinned at Dennis, whose wife appeared from, I assumed, the kitchen. She smiled at me.

'Come through, Master Robert, warm yourself in the kitchen. Fire be low, but ye look chilled through.'

I did as she bade, and took my cloak and hat off in the warm kitchen. Dennis' wife – I learned that she was Mary – clucked around me like a mother hen, getting me some strong ale, and heating some broth. Dennis himself joined me with a pot of strong ale, and soon the conversation became quite convivial. I had an idea.

'I heard say the Diggers be up to mischief around these parts, Master Dennis.'

'Diggers, maister Robert? Nay, nay. What mischief could they do? Attack ye wi' 'oe?'

He laughed fit to bust. 'Ye lookin' for Diggers, maister? Where do ye go?'

'North, Master Dennis. Leicester town, first. Then we see. I would see my wife's uncle, Tom Rately in Wellin'borough on th'way. 'E were in wi' Diggers, I think.'

Dennis looked surprised.

'Tom … Rately, 'ee say? Ye must know 'e were a leader o' Diggers. 'Idin' 'way, he be, since Skippon's men took th'others. Ye ain't come t'arrest 'un, Oi 'opes?'

I assured him that I had not, just my wife wanted news of her uncle.

'Ye ain't one o' Skippon's men, be ye?'

'Nay, man, I were under Edward Whalley. Report to Master John Ekins at Rushden Hall now.'

Then, thinking quickly. 'And captain John Grove.'

That seemed to satisfy Dennis, and he lit his clay pipe, puffing away for the next five minutes, while no-one spoke. Then Mary bustled in.

'Maister Robert must be tired, husband. 'E can sleep in our kitchen, methinks. 'Twill be warm for 'im.'

So I ended up spending an incredibly uncomfortable night partly on the settle and from time to time on the stone floor, when I slipped and fell off it. 'At least it be warm,' I thought, miserably, rubbing my bruised elbows and head, 'E'en Edwin's lice-ridden place be better'n this! If only Lia could see me…'

Wednesday 28 February 1649.

Dennis and Mary were up soon after first light, Mary coming into the kitchen to find me in something of a heap on the floor.

'Tush Robert, have ye hurt yourself?' I roused myself wearily.

'Nay, Missus Mary, 'part from a few bruises. 'Twas a bad night, though, I fear.'

She helped me to get up and sit on the settle, then started to set a new fire and do the necessary to make a breakfast. I sat for a couple of minutes, then said, 'I will away, Missus Mary. I will break my fast in Wellingborough.'

I stood up groggily, found some cold water, and splashed it on my face, with a deal of shivering. After making sure that my belongings were in my snapsack, I thanked her, then headed to the stables to ready my horse. Half an hour later, I was riding slowly towards the exit of the grounds onto the Irchester Road, where I turned left to the Wellingborough road, and the river. The river was still well up, and the bridge in a lake of floodwater, which I eased my horse very gingerly through. I knew the road to be straight – more or less – but it was quite badly rutted after the winter, so I allowed the horse to find her own footing as she inched closer to the bridge parapet, visible above the water. This would have been very dangerous indeed, I thought, as the bridge came steadily nearer, and the horse felt for a sound footing from time to time. Once at the bridge's steep ramp, the going became easier, and the horse gradually sped up, until she was walking over the level middle section, then slowed at the ramp down on the Wellingborough side. Here, the water was shallower, and I was soon riding along the London Road into the town, as before. I heard a town church clock strike eight o'clock as I turned into Angel Lane. A few minutes later, my horse was tied up in Edwin's stable, and I was knocking on the front door. Edwin's gruff voice boomed out, 'who be that?' from inside, which I answered with my password. The door creaked open, and I was able to enter, past a grumpy looking Edwin.

'My apologies, Master Edwin. The floodwater was too bad. I stayed overnight at Chester House. Edwin grunted. ''Ave ye brook yer fast?'

'Nay, Master Edwin. I came early as I might.'

Edwin yelled. 'Jen! Mistress! Some eats fer maister 'Ob, if ye please!'

The middle aged maid appeared, saw me, and frowned. ''Im agin.'

'Bed your 'oss, maister, 'n Oi'll see what Oi 'ave.' I voiced my thanks, went outside, walked round to the stable, and attended to my horse. At least Edwin keeps a good stable, I thought, as I removed my saddle, and made my horse comfortable for her stay. I picked up my snapsack, bandolier, and pistol, and headed for the back door of the house. Inside, the hot kitchen was as stuffy as before; I removed my cloak and hat, which Jen draped over a chair near the fire. This time Edwin took me upstairs to a small bedroom that looked as if it hadn't been slept in for a decade. It would have to do for now. I put my snapsack on the floor, which I noticed was thick in dust, then made use of a small, rough table to place my pistol and bandolier somewhere. The bed had just a hair mattress, no blankets. It looked as though the next night would be little better than the previous one! I came down the creaky stairs to the parlour, and into the kitchen, where mistress Jen had placed a plate with a piece of bread, butter and gammon for me on the table. Edwin sat the other side, puffing at his clay pipe and humming to himself.

''Ow went it wi' the cap'n and maister Ekins, maister 'Ob?'

I spoke through a mouthful of bread and butter. ''T went well, Master Edwin.'

I continued to down my breakfast. Jen brought a pot of small ale, which I swigged appreciatively; it helped the still warm, soggy bread down.

'Aye? Ye're back soon, maister 'Ob.'

I took another swig, and swallowed the half chewed bread.

'Aye indeed. There be much mischief afoot, I fear. Master Ekins is much afeared of what guz on in our county.'

Edwin smiled slyly. ''N' ye're 'ere ter watch they Diggers, I think?'

I smiled as slyly as I could muster.

'Oh, aye. I would learn more 'bout Jeanne Rately, too. My wife were sore upset when I tell 'er 'bout Jeanne. Wants me to talk to 'er uncle agin, too.'

Edwin cocked an eyebrow.

'Used t'be close to Uncle Tom, d'ye see. And Jeanne. The war changed all.'

Edwin nodded sagely. 'Aye, 't did indeed. Oi used ter be boot stitcher. Not a bit o' such work in Wellin'borough now. Maister Ekins, 'e pays well, so Oi do what he arsk.'

I thought to myself, now why say that? Had he discovered my real name? Rushden made boots, maybe he wanted work? H'mm. It paid to be suspicious.

'Aye, Master Edwin, times be 'ard for county o' Northam'ton.' I was about to ask Edwin how he came to work for Ekins, then thought better of it, and changed the subject.

'There be much roguery 'bout since the war ended. The roads be not safe for travellers.'

Edwin looked up as if he had been prodded.

'Ye've soldiers' weapons, maister 'Ob. Ye could look after yourself, I think.'

'Aye, yet there be many rogue bands 'bout. One man against, maybe six, eight......' Then I added, 'Army can only do so much. While there be fears of ..... those who would....are...for the young Steward, I think.' Edwin waved a bony hand.

67

"'E be in 'Olland, they say. 'N' on'y a boy. 'As no trups.' I thought that I would end that conversation. 'I'll go to Tom's this morn. Make my wife happy.' Edwin had different ideas.

"Ob, what did 'ee do in the war?' Now that was a surprise!

'Many things, Master Edwin. I was at Naseby. Cromwell's second cavalry. 'Twas a hard fight. And Marston Trussell. Gives me mares some nights. I was to leave the army, but Master Ekins had other designs for me.'

Edwin looked quizzically at me but said no more, and relit his pipe, puffing at it with gusto. He sat there examining me with half closed eyes, until I said, 'I must to my billet, Master Edwin, and leave for Tom's.'

I got up, and headed back up the rickety stairs.

In the bedroom, I removed my poniard from the snapsack, and fitted it into my breeches, then put my pistol in the snapsack instead, and tied the top of the snapsack with a double knot. Whoever tried to rummage around in it would have to cut the knot. I left a simply ciphered message in the snapsack near the top as Grove instructed, where it could be easily found. I came down the stairs again, retrieved and donned my cloak and hat, and set off for Wilby Road. It had started to drizzle now, making it an unpleasant walk to Tom Rately's. Tom was surprised to see me again, but let me come inside the unkempt house. It was obvious that he had made some attempt to clean and tidy it a bit, and at least it smelt less noxious than last time. He and I talked for some time about the events of the last two or three years, and I learned more of how he had come to be in such a parlous situation. I told Tom that Amelia was pleased but shocked to hear about him and the news of her sister, then proffered the silver that my father had handed to me to help Tom. This time, Tom took it gladly. Well, maybe not gladly, but with good grace.

'The silver should help ye some, uncle. My father would help ye more, when I return next. We must not neglect families, they be all we have.'

Tom nodded, then came out with another shock for me.

'The tale of Jeanne, 'tis not true, Robert. She is not marrit, not to James Berry, anyways. She was his whore.'

'His whore, uncle? God's blood! How came ye to know such?'

''Twould have been too much for my wife to bear, Robert. I have my ... sources of news. The Diggers be far 'n' wide now, wi' so many poor. They does no 'arm, but Crom'll is afeared o' them. If ye would learn of the truth, the Diggers know much. But ye must tread wi' great care.'

I asked, "Do ye know more of Jeanne? Where she be?' The answer pointed me to a decision.

'She be in Northam'ton. Whoring for staff officers in Army 'eadquarters.'

My stunned expression brought more.

'If ye would know more, ye must away to Northam'ton. Could start wi' marshal general of 'orse, a Cap'n Lawrence, last I 'eard. An' Jeanne, she be known as Joan the Whore.'

I recovered some of my composure. 'Joan the Whore? 'Tis an awful thing to call her! Ye have given me much to think 'bout, uncle. Much indeed.'

'Ye can not walk in to army buildings, Robert. Ye would need a letter from such as Master Ekins. Or your captain Grove, methinks. Else ye would be arrested now.'

'Would I?' thought I. 'I have my password. Or maybe find the officer by other means.'

I resolved to travel to Northampton on the morrow, and endeavour to discover more. Now, as the conversation moved on, a new revelation stunned me more still – if that were possible.

Tom asked, 'Where do ye stay, Robert?'

'At the house of Edwin, sign o' the fleece in Angel Lane.'

'Edwin, 'e calls hisself? Nay, 'e's Edward. Edward Marston. Looks like a beggar, but 'e be well orff – 'e owns the Golden Lion tavern, 'e do.'

My jaw dropped open.

'Din't ye know? 'Ow do ye know 'im?'

I recovered my composure enough to answer, 'He works for John Ekins. Sends him news of such as Diggers. I be 'ere to take despatches for Master Ekins.'

Tom laughed a cynical laugh. ''E'll be takin' Ekins fer a fool, Robert. 'E's no friend o' Crom'll or Parli'ment.'

'What of the landlord at Golden Lion, Uncle Tom? He seems a good man.'

Another cynical laugh. 'Oh, aye. 'Seems' roight 'nough. Ed'll hear ye were at th' tavern, I'll be bound. Ye must not place your trust in Master Wally at th' tavern. He be in Ed's pocket, aright.'

'God's blood, man! Be none in Wellingborough to be trusted?' I added quickly, ''Cept ye, 'o course. Well, if ye can't trust family, who can ye trust?'

Tom laughed his cynical laugh again.

'What of Joan, er, Jeanne, Master Robert? She be family!'

'Aye. Aye indeed, uncle.' Tom now cautioned me.

'Edward must not be trusted. 'E says 'e 'as sympathy wi' th' Diggers. But, mark ye well. Edward would do anything fer silver. 'E'd give up Diggers soon as look at 'em, if 'e were offered enough. And ye.'

I was very thoughtful when I left Tom a while later, and decided to look around for another tavern. I walked slowly around the town centre, until I noticed The Star of Bethlehem tavern in Sheep Street, and went inside. A matronly, buxom woman greeted me.

'Good morrow, maister. Ye be a stranger, I think?'

'Good morrow, Missus. I would have food and good ale, if you please. Strong ale.'

She made a small curtsey, and swept an ample arm around, 'Make yourself at 'ome, maister.'

I spotted a corner table with a vacant chair, and sat down in it after removing my cloak, draping it over the chair back. I rubbed my eyes, then my chin, then sat with my head in my hands, thinking about the conversation, Edwin/Edward, Jeanne/Joan, Tom, and all that had passed between me and Tom. I will tell Edwin that I will leave for home next morning – but will instead head for Northampton. When the buxom woman brought my ale, I asked her if she knew of a good inn in Northampton.

'Drapers' Arms, by Guildhall. Just off Marketplace. Best I know of, mayhap full o' troopers now.' I thanked her and poured myself a pot of the ale, which I absentmindedly started to sup. She returned after two or three minutes with a large bowl of stewed lamb and vegetables, steaming well, and a plate of warm bread. I smiled my thanks to her, and started to tuck in. The food was surprisingly good for these straitened times, and my appetite grew as I tucked into it. I found the meal more than I could eat, and as soon as I put down my knife and spoon, the bar woman came over with penny pipe and slow match. The room was getting busier now, so I decided not to try to get her to talk other than about pleasantries. Word could spread all too quickly in a small town, and get back to Edwin or any other dangerous character. I could well do without any drama. I puffed away at the penny-pipe, trying to look as if I hadn't a care in the world, but my mind was far from relaxed. When I had finished the jug of ale and the pipe, I paid my tally, donned my cloak, and left the tavern with a cheery 'Thank ye much, Missus,' to the bar woman. I walked slowly back to Angel Lane, and Edwin's – nay, Edward's – miserable dwelling. As in the visit before, Edwin was nowhere to be seen, only his maid was about. She was sitting in the kitchen asleep at the table with a pot of ale in front of her, her head lolling on her chest, and snoring like a rusty door hinge. As I entered the kitchen, she

71

spluttered, and woke quickly. Seeing me, 'Oh, maister 'tis ye. Yer business done?'

'Aye, enough for this day. Mayhap I could have quill, ink, and paper, mistress Jen? If ye please?'

A disgruntled Jen replied, 'Arr, I s'pose, maister. Oi'll get 'em fer ye sharp.'

She disappeared into the parlour and up the stairs. Her footsteps creaked their way down the stairs two or three minutes later, and she shuffled into the kitchen with the items in a grubby hand. I took charge of them with, 'I thank ye kindly, mistress,' and a smile, then I too went up the same stairs to the small bedroom. I was surprised to see that the floor had been swept, and blankets put on the old bed. When I inspected my snapsack, I was not surprised to see that the twine had been cut, and a new, badly made knot replacing the one I had left that morning.

'So someone looked well at my clothes,' I thought with a grim smile, 'I hope 'twas a goodly lot of information they found!'

Having removed my cloak and hat, I sat on the bed, with the small table pulled up close, and spread the paper, then pulled out a cipher sheet from my secret pocket, and laid out a message at the top. I quickly ciphered the message, folded the sheet, and put the cipher sheet back in my secret pocket. Then I wrote out a second message, that read, 'Talked to TR again. Little of value. E helpful. No new words of Diggers. H', coded it with the simple substitution cipher, and stuffed the coded message in the top of my snapsack. As before, I tied the top of it with a length of twine, and a neat, unusual knot. Then I donned cloak and hat, took the quill and ink back down to Jen, and left the house again. I decided to return to the Star of Bethlehem. I could while away an hour or two, have a good repast in the early evening, then return to Angel Lane. If the tavern were empty, I maybe could see what I could learn from the barmaid.

The market stalls had partly dispersed when I headed out for The Star of Bethlehem tavern, and there were few people left shopping in the marketplace. I walked steadily to Sheep Street, and then back to The Star of Bethlehem. There were only two other people in the tavern's taproom, so I picked the corner furthest from both, and sat there, at an empty table, which had scraps of food and puddles of ale left on it. The buxom barmaid appeared, and seeing me sitting there, came straight over.

'A jug o' best ale, maister?'

I smiled my approval, and added that I would like to eat later, too. She went away, and minutes later returned with a jug of best ale, a pot, and a clout to wipe the table top down. I asked her if she would sit with me for a while, I would like to ask her for some information.

'Aye, maister, though I mayhap will needs serve others.'

She sat in the next chair. I asked her if she knew Jeanne Rately for starters, and might know more of her whereabouts. She thought, then, 'That would be Joan the Whore, I think?'

I thought to myself, 'God's blood, she be well known indeed.'

'Aye, so I be told. She be my wife's sister. Wife has heard nought of her since '47, she would seek to have news of Jeanne..er, Joan.'

'Yer wife's sister? Oh, Oi be sorry for ye. And her. That be why ye would go to Northam'ton, I think?'

I nodded.

'Ye may have news of her at Drapers' Arms, or mayhap The Sun inn. That be near th'marketplace, maister. Army officers billeted there.'

'Aye, Missus. I heard she were with a Major Berry. But mayhap is no longer. I hear tell she likes staff officers.'

73

The barmaid looked a little taken aback.

'Maister, I knows not tha' much. Ye would do be'er ter talk wi' me 'usband. Jim. Oi'll send 'un out.'

She got up, and returned to the back room. A few minutes later a rather fat, typical landlord with dirty apron and arms like hams, came out, and sat next to me.

'Me Mary say ye arsk 'bout Jeanne Rately, maister. Maister...er?'

'Hob, landlord. Ye be Jim, I think? I seek news of Jeanne, for my wife. Jeanne be her sister.'

Jim replied in a voice a bit too loud for my comfort.

'Maister 'Ob, ye do well t'leave that Joan be. She be poison. Aye, I 'ear tell she loikes they army toipes. Officers, 'specially. Been whorin' fer 'em these past two year I thinks.'

Having looked me up and down a few times, Jim gave voice to his curiosity.

'Be 'ee army toipe, maister 'Ob? Ye looks army.'

I thought a half truth advisable.

'Militia. Sergeant-major. I would leave the army, but it won't let me go. Times be too … worrisome, what wi' Diggers, Levellers, an' king not long dead.'

I smiled at Jim, but he didn't return my smile.

''Er'll loike 'ee, then, maister! 'Er be easy ter foind at Northam'ton. Arsk any army officer. All officers knows 'er – theys all 've ridden 'er, Oi'll be bound!'

I had ceased to show any surprise at what I was told. But what would Amelia say if she heard this conversation? What, indeed! I changed the conversation.

'Master landlord, your wife says The Sun inn or Drapers' Arms be good to look for a room at Northampton. What say ye?'

'Ye would go, then? Aye, Sun be where 'igh-ups stay. Lot of 'igh-ups at Northam'ton. Mayhap 'ave to share. Drapers, m'mm, few there, more rooms. Fer what ye wants, Sun be be'er.'

I thanked him most kindly, then asked if I might have some food.

'Aye, maister. Me Mary'll bring it uvver.' He stood up. 'Take a care, maister. 'er be poison, loike Oi says,' and returned to the back room.

I had much to ponder – and I hadn't noticed one of the other two drinkers watching me closely, listening to the conversation. After some while, Mary appeared, and headed over to me with a bowl of mutton and bean potage and a plate of bread and cheese.

'Ye would 'ave 'nother jug of ale, maister?'

I replied that I would, but small ale, which she brought, along with a pipe of tobacco and slow match. I needed to keep a clear head.

Chapter 6: Northampton Beckons

It was late afternoon when I walked back to Angel Lane, and Edwin's threadbare house. Edwin was there now, and looked questioningly at me as I entered through the back door.

'Good morrow, Master Edwin,'

'Good morrow, maister 'Ob. Did ye 'ave a useful day?'

'I did indeed, a trifle cold, but 'twas most interesting. I would go back to Rushden on the morrow, Master Edwin, and will take your letters for ye to Master Ekins.' Edwin raised an eyebrow.

'Oh, aye, I will 'ave a despatch for ye. Perchance ye will 'ave a thimble o' tobacco and an ale wi' me?'

I was going to say no, but changed my mind, 'I thank ye, Master. I will indeed,' and made to sit on the settle, but Edwin waved a bony hand.

'We will to th' parlour, methinks.'

Each of us took a chair in the parlour, and Jen appeared carrying a jug of small ale, an extra pipe with tobacco, and two pots. I pulled up the rickety table, and she put the jug and other things on it. Edwin thanked her, and poured a pot each, then proceeded to make small talk to go with the small ale. I felt somewhat lulled into a sense of relaxation as the conversation progressed, and both of us puffed at our pipes and supped our ale. A sudden question brought me up short: 'Did ye find out more 'bout Joan, maister 'Ob?'

'Nought I did not know aready. I were the more interested in the Diggers, and going to Tom's house, to bring him a bit o' help, too.'

'Oh, aye? I 'eard ye were arskin' 'round 'bout Joan.'

I had learned to lie whilst keeping a straight face.

'Aye, but like I say, nought I did not know. Master Ekins's work comes first.'

Edwin smiled his sly smile, and changed the subject to the scarce food and high prices. I hadn't shopped for food since London, only eaten in taverns or Ekins' hall. So I asked for more about the issue, and Edwin was happy to comply. We talked for well over an hour, and I felt it time that I should make my excuses, and go up to the room for an earlier than usual night.

Thursday 1st March 1649.

The next morning, I woke at around seven o'clock, after a night of poor sleep and some bad dreams. I had noticed that the second piece of twine that I had tied through the top of my snapsack had not been tampered with, so gave it no further thought. I was soon dressed and down to break my fast. There was, as before, a good breakfast of eggs, bread, butter, and this time some cheese, washed down with small ale. I picked up the letters that Edwin wanted taken to John Ekins, and went upstairs to ready myself for travel. By the time I left the house to prepare my horse, I heard a town clock strike eight. I soon bade farewell to Edwin and his maid Jen, and set off for Northampton. I had told Edwin that I would head for Finedon, because, with it now having rained for most of the night, the river would be even more swollen at Chester-on-the-Water. Edwin agreed with me. However, when I left Angel Lane, instead of going north up the High Street, and turning right for Finedon, I turned left into Wilby Road, and past Amelia's uncle's house. It was but a little over twelve miles to Northampton, and it is a good, flat road, so about two hours ride in this weather. I would have plenty of time. I found Wilby a somewhat damaged village, much as I had expected, given its location. As I approached downwind of Northampton, I was appalled at the stench of excrement; I was not used to it as badly as this, not even in London. All towns stank, but this was exceptional; the army had near quadrupled the population of men, plus as many horses, and they all produced far more ordure than the nightmen could cope with. The city of Northampton was strongly walled, though rough repairs to the old walls were evident, as well as extensive earthwork outer walls and bastions. At the St Giles gate, I was stopped by two soldiers who wanted to know why I was wanting to enter the city. I stated that I had come on personal business, but was a serving soldier, and so gave them my rank and password, and named captain Grove as my superior. They briefly conferred, and then let me through, providing they knew where I would stay. I said that I intended to seek a room at the Sun inn, or if not there, the Drapers' Arms. That seemed to satisfy them, and I was allowed to enter. Having asked directions of the soldiers, I rode straight to the marketplace, turned left down Wood Hill, then left again past the Guildhall; I soon found the Sun inn, where after tying my horse, I went inside to ask for a room.

The landlord too asked if I was army, so I gave my rank, and that I worked for captain Grove in Rushden. The landlord had a small room available. It was not the best, but he could offer good food, and the room was paid for by the army. I gladly accepted it, and a maid was called to show me where it was. I said, 'Mistress, I thank ye, but would bed my horse first, if ye please.' She told me to do so, and indicated where the stable was, so I took my horse to the stable behind the inn, tethered her in a stall, removed her saddle and other accoutrements, threw a blanket over her, and made sure that she had fodder and water. I returned to the back door of the inn, carrying my snapsack, pistol, and bandolier. The landlord saw me, and called the maid again. She looked a little wary at the sight of my pistol and tuck, but said nothing, and led me up two flights of stairs to a garret room. The bed, at least, looked as good as anything that I had made use of whilst in the army, and there was a well made table, piss-pot, pail, and some basic things such as a stoneware jug. My only concern was a lack of any way to lock the door. Well, I thought, it should be safe with all these soldiers staying here! The maid told me that the previous occupant had been an army officer of middling rank. They normally only take officers at the Sun. She told me that I would be roused at seven, and a maid would bring hot water for my ablutions. I had seen the privy outside the back door, so apart from eating, I was ready to settle in.

Northampton was something of a surprise for me. I had expected a large city, whereas in fact it was fairly compact, with most houses being thatched, many with the thatch in a poor condition, and in this area of abundant limestone, only the bigger houses and public buildings were stone-built. Most artisans' houses were timber framed, and a lot of them looked decrepit. Northampton was not a very prosperous city before the Great Rebellion; and though the army setting up its headquarters in the city at the end of 1642, from which leather workers and boot-makers profited, with seven long years of war, there had been little opportunity for many residents to repair their houses. The main body of the soldiery quartered in the city were in the old castle on its mound, in makeshift timber lean-to buildings built within its medieval walls. The quarters there were damp and cold, and though junior officers and such as sergeants and sergeant majors had usually to accept quarters within the castle, more senior officers were quartered comfortably in the two biggest inns in the city, the Sun and the Drapers' Arms. The military governor, lieutenant colonel Nathaniel Whetham was even more comfortably quartered in Haselrigge House, not far from the city centre, and convenient for the castle if the need should arise. The castle would be a last-ditch strongpoint if the walls were breached in the event of a determined siege, which was unlikely now.

Having changed into a clean shirt, along with washing hands, face, and upper body, brushing mud off my boots, and generally tidying myself up, I went down to order an evening meal. The fare was excellent, being prepared to the standard expected by senior officers in the commandery. I found myself sharing my table with a staff captain and two majors. After a meal of broth, beef potage, and a mincemeat pie, followed by jugs of wine and strong ale all round, I decided to drop a comment about Jeanne, specifically that she was my wife's sister, and my wife had charged me to get news of Jeanne. One of the majors, an officer of foot, knew her, and replied that she was around the city.

'Ye would well avoid that hussy, sergeant-major. She is well-known as a whore, but not a pox-ridden purveyor of a ha'penny dalliance against an alleyway wall. She is a whore of quality, friends in high echelons, that 'un.'

I thought it best to drop the subject, but the captain said more.

'She be in the Sun on the morrow, I think.'

I thanked him, and changed the subject, asking if the Diggers were troubling the peace of Northampton. The other major, a cavalryman, answered.

'Nay. Not troubling the peace, but they be around. Many wi' nought now. They needs must feed they families.'

The noise in the room had by now gone up by two orders of decibels, and raucous singing started, as well as even more raucous joke telling. The higher the officers' rank, the more bawdy the jokes, a popular one being about a lady of quality having hoisted up her voluminous skirts, and sitting on the privy, when a rat ran up inside her skirts, and bit her in her privy place; this raised particularly raucous laughing, though I did not think it overmuch droll. Conversation had become almost impossible, unless shouting oneself hoarse, so I decided to sit and sup some more ale, then excuse myself, and away to bed. Nine of the clock had struck by the Guildhall clock some time since, when I rose unsteadily, bade my three companions a good night's sleep, and wobbled up the two flights of stairs to my room. The strong ale having taken over, it was not long before I had swapped my day clothes for a smock, retired to the comfortable bed, and drifted into a relatively dreamless sleep. A visit to the piss-pot a while later did little to suppress the effects of the alcohol, and I was rapidly back in a deep sleep.

I did not hear footsteps come up the stairs, and my room door open. It was the feel of cold steel hard against my throat that woke me, in the pitch dark room. A voice hissed by my ear, 'What do 'ee want wi' Joan, Robert?' The words brought me wide awake abruptly, and I stammered, 'Nought save for news for my wife.' The voice hissed again. 'That best be all, stranger, or yer life be forfeit.' Then the blade and its owner were gone. I got out of bed, shaking like an autumn leaf, and with difficulty lit a candle. I was all the more shocked that my assailant knew my real name. That was deeply worrying in itself; but why the concern about Jeanne? Why was she so important that my life was now threatened, just because of wanting to talk to her? What had I stumbled on? I resolved to depart next morning, return to Rushden, and report to Grove and Ekins.

Friday 2nd March 1649.

As I was doing my ablutions and dressing the next morning, a knock came on my room door.

I called, 'Enter.' A staff captain came in, and announced that my presence was required in the office of Governor Whetham in the Guildhall at ten of the clock. I thanked the officer, who saluted and left, and I continued my dressing, whilst wondering what I was wanted for. A good breakfast, I thought, would stand me in good stead for what could be a difficult meeting. Did it have to do with my enquiries about Jeanne in Wellingborough, I wondered?

It was indeed a good breakfast: eggs, bread, butter, ham. I tucked in with gusto, and washed it all down with a generous quantity of small ale. My mind was racing, my apprehension growing. I resolved still to depart this day, mayhap after I had met with Nat Whetham, or yet after a midday meal. But depart I would. I would go south of the river Nene, through back roads, a journey of some eighteen miles, about three and a half hours' riding on a good day, but if I left by late afternoon, I could do it even if it meant arriving in the dark. Then a thought struck me. If I arrived in the dark, I might find Ned Adkin again….and...and….settle the score. The thought of that cheered me somewhat. It was almost a new moon, so the night would be dark indeed, though on the first of March, the days were much longer now; only three weeks from the equinox, it would not be truly dark until perhaps near eight o'clock in the evening.

After finishing my breakfast, and making use of the privy, for which I had to wait a while, I returned to my room. I donned my cloak and high-crown hat, then tuck and pistol, descended to the ground floor, and set off for the Guildhall. It was close by, out of the door, and turn right. I walked briskly, and after a two minute walk I was outside the old Guildhall, at the top of its double flight of outdoor stairs. It had guards on each door. I went to the first door, and told one of the guards that I had been summoned by Governor Whetham.

The guard accompanied me inside, taking charge of my tuck and pistol, which he lodged in a room just inside the door, then showed me along the building to a range of offices. The Governor resided in the grandest of the offices, once the lair of the Guild Master. The soldier knocked on the door, and it was opened by a very ordinary looking man, but clad in the finest quality clothes. He spoke with a soft Dorset burr.

'Ye're sergeant-major Barker, I think? Come in, come in and take a seat. Trooper, leave us, if ye please.'

The door closed behind me, as I inclined my head, saying, 'Good morrow, Master Governor. Ye would speak with me?'

'Aye, aye. But first, will ye take a sack with me, Robert?'

I indicated that I would, and the Governor poured out two goblets from a jug.

'Now, my good sergeant-major, what is't that ye would do here in Northam'ton? What is your regiment?'

I wasn't sure how to answer this, so said, 'My regiment was Edward Whalley's regiment of horse, sir. Whalley is no longer its colonel, so I know not what has become of it. I report to captain John Grove, lately colonel Whalley's adjutant, and Master John Ekins of Rushden Hall.'

'And your purpose here in Northam'ton?'

'I be here on my own account, sir. I would speak to my wife's sister, Jeanne Rately, that my wife has not had news of for near two year.'

The Governor looked at me intently for a few moments.

'Nay, sergeant-major, that be your excuse for to be here. I ask your purpose from Master Ekins.' 'My orders are …. not for anyone to know but Master Ekins and the good captain, sir.'

Whetham sighed loudly. 'Master Ekins be not on the army payroll, man. He is of the Ruling Council, I'll warrant?' I nodded.

'Aye, I would so expect. His service be to Tom Scot, I think. As then be your'n. His man here would be marshal general Bishop.'

I immediately realised this was the man whom I had seen in the hall at Rushden. Staff captain George Bishop. Before I could say more, the Governor went on, 'My good sergeant-major, I would help ye, if ye would let me. There be much mischief afoot in these parts, many intelligencers, many working against Parliament. They needs must be contained.'

I acknowledged this with a polite, 'Thank you, sir.'

Next, the Governor added, "What of Jeanne Rately, Joan the Whore, sergeant-major? Ye were … visited?...by a man who threatened ye in your bed, this last night, am I not correct?'

I was visibly taken aback. 'Aye sir, that I were. He – if it were he – held a blade to my throat, and would know of my purpose in seeking Jeanne...er, Joan. He threatened … death to me, if I do not leave Northam'ton.'

'God's blood, man! What be of such import that ye are threatened so for seeking a whore?'

I ventured, 'Joan mayhap be a way to garner influence among officers here?'

'Robert, sergeant-major, ye will accept my help. Ye brings arms into Northam'ton. That needs written permission from me, since ye are not in uniform. I will write one this morn. Ye will needs have a password, which I will also give ye. Then shall ye have access to army premises, to the city, as ye wish. And I would wish ye God's blessings for your task.'

After writing out the permit for arms, and giving me both the permit and the password, the Governor said to me, 'Ye are welcome to seek my help as ye needs it. If ye please, get your midday food, then return to me. I would give ye a letter for Master Ekins. 'Tis of the greatest import. Ye're to be sure that he gets it. Understood, sergeant-major?'

I walked back to the Sun inn, where I bought a hearty midday meal and very good ale. I mused that I had not had such good fare for all of my time in the army, indeed seldom anything so good even before the war came, when my mother cooked for our family, and good food was locally plentiful. It was far from plentiful now for most people, yet the officers of the New Model Army fared very well indeed at the Sun! I realised that I should be back at the Governor's office, so settled my bill, and returned to the Guildhall, where I was allowed straight in by the guards on the door. I was even allowed to find my own way to Nat Whetham's office, to my surprise. The latter was sitting at the ornate desk writing, and rose to greet me as he called 'Enter!' in response to my cautious knock at the door. 'Take ye a chair, my boy.'

I took a chair opposite him, and waited for him to speak.

'Ye shall have my letter to Master Ekins presently. But there is more that I would tell ye. I desire that ye have a higher rank, so ye can serve me better, and remain at the Sun, where the most intelligence is to be had. I wish Master Scot to lift ye to staff captain. Now, your side arms. I note that ye have an army horse-pistol, tuck, and a long dagger. They will not serve ye well, if ye would be an intelligencer, sergeant-major. A tuck, mayhap. Ye needs must have a pocket pistol and a small dagger, not a cannon and that overlong bodkin ye secretes in your breeches.'

Seeing my look of astonishment, 'Aye, I have seen it, and others will too, I'll warrant. 'Tis too long if ye be assailed close, or if ye must deal with an enemy secretly. Short, sharp, keep it well hidden, with ye always, if ye would save your life.'

'Sir, the horse-pistol is army issue. A pocket pistol would be greatly beyond my pocket. The bodkin, 'tis my grandfather's poniard. It has saved my life in battle many times.'

'Aye, sergeant-major, I am sure it has, but ye're not in high battle now. 'Twill be a war of shadows. I will request Master Ekins equip ye as I do tell ye.'

I inclined my head and thanked him.

'Now, sergeant-major, what know ye of Joan the Whore?'

'More than I have told, nought of much import. Jeanne Ratley be my wife's younger sister. Her parents and she left Irthlingborough when Royalist troopers burned her father's house. They lived with her uncle, Tom Rately, but he suffered greatly when Parliament's troopers came and took the leaders of the Diggers and with them Jeanne's own father in '47. Her mother died of an ague soon after. She left Tom's but I know not when, nor of Tom's wife, her aunt. Jeanne is bitter for sure, I think. Sore bitter. Against Cromwell and Parliament. Diggers now say Cromwell be no better'n king Charles. Tom says that Jeanne be here in Northam'ton, so I came to seek her.'

Whetham looked thoughtful, and steepled his fingers in front of his mouth.

'H'mm, a sorry tale. Diggers be little threat. But Joan the Whore....she whores for my officers. I would know which ones. And why would your seeking her bring your assailant in the night?' Clearing his throat, he went on, 'That question vexes me much. When your rank be confirmed, mayhap ye can learn more of my officers. I would learn more, much more, of Joan. So use your new rank well, sergeant-major Barker.'

My 'Yes, sir,' brought more.

'Sergeant-major, I would have ye return to Rushden this night. My letter informs Master Ekins and captain Grove of my intent for ye. Their orders are clear, and to be confirmed by Secretary Scot quickly. I would that ye are here, in this office, one week hence. Those be your orders, serge-...er, captain Barker.'

My eyebrows ascended, then I recovered myself, and asked Whetham how he knew of the assailant. 'Do ye think ye are th'only intelligencer in Northam'ton? To your orders, man.'

I began to think of protesting – as my wife surely will – but thought better of it. Now, I have my orders for sure.

'Aye, sir. I will to't.'

Whetham meanwhile sealed the letter in front of me, and as soon as the seal cooled, handed it over.

'Keep this safe, captain. With your life. Now, go, and God be with ye.'

I secreted it in the hidden pocket inside my doublet, stood, saluted, and left the office. My mind was now in an even bigger whirl, as I tried to comprehend the events of the past twelve, twenty-four, hours. What can I tell Amelia, I thought, and what will she say?

"Twill not go well, I think,' I said out loud, as I left the Guildhall's sumptuous interior, and headed back up the street, in a fine drizzle, back to the Sun inn. I resolved to have a small meal and two or three pots of ale, so that I could sit and turn it all over in my mind, before venturing out onto the road back home to Rushden.

On my return to the inn, I ordered a jug of small ale and a pot, and asked if I could have a small meal, before leaving. I made sure to ask in a loud voice, in case ears were flapping – as they undoubtedly were. I found a table in a corner, and presently a wench brought me the jug of ale and a pot, then offered bread, butter, and roast gammon or cheese. I asked for cheese. I was joined by another officer, a cornet, just as the wench returned to my table with the snack. We exchanged a few pleasantries, until the cornet commented, 'I heard ye say that ye leaves this afternoon?'

I confirmed the truth of that, and added that I had new orders, and would have to return. The cornet looked at me with a curious expression, but changed the subject to the weather and the bad roads. We chatted for a while until I heard the Guildhall clock strike four.

'I must ready my horse, and depart, I think.'

We said our goodbyes, I paid my tally, went up to my room, shoved my clothes into my snapsack, then out to the stable for readying my horse. A voice whispered in the dark stable, 'Be ye gone, 'n dun't 'ee come lookin' fer Joan n' more, maister. Mind 'ee well my warnin'.'

I looked around, feeling shocked, but the owner of the voice had disappeared already into the shadows and vanished. I proceeded to saddle my horse, and attached my accoutrements to the saddle. Finally, I fitted my snapsack across my back, walked the horse out of the stableyard, and set off towards the centre of the city, past All Hallows' Church, then left towards St. Thomas' gate.

Chapter 7: Retribution and Religiosity

I headed for the bridge over the river Nene, here somewhat silted up, caused by the many weirs that are along its course to service watermills. The bridge was wide and would be an easy passage over the river, then I took the road for Cogenhoe and Grendon. I kept to an easy pace, despite it being a rather winding road. I expected to get into Rushden around nine of the clock, maybe a little later. As I expected, it was a dark night, with little of the waning moon left, and I had to rely on my horse's sense to keep to the narrow country roads. In case it grew too dark, I had brought an old lanthorn to light the way, as much as its horn windows would allow – but I did not want to be too easily seen. The road to Grendon curved around the park of Castle Ashby, so it was relatively easy to keep the castle on my right, and let my horse find her way, though I was careful to avoid any possibility of alerting the guards stationed at the castle's park perimeter. I did not want challenging questions. Once I found the turn to Wollaston, however, the going was less easy, and I lit the lanthorn to light the way. It was still early when Wollaston came into view across the Wellingborough road, and I was surprised to see troopers riding south at this time of night on the road towards Olney; troopers that appeared to be in something of a hurry. The column soon passed, and I was able to cross and continue towards Irchester on what was a wider and better kept road. From Irchester, I knew my way back to Rushden like the back of my hand, even though the night was almost pitch dark. The drizzle had petered out, giving me and my horse some much welcome relief from the chill wetness of it. I entered Rushden by the narrow back lanes, using the lanthorn until I reached Mill Lane, where I extinguished it, and dismounted, preferring to continue on foot. There, sure enough, in the dark and out of sight of the High Street, was the prone form of Ned Adkin, snoring in his usual drunken stupor at this time of the evening. I tied my horse loosely, and approached Ned with some care to be quiet. Then leaning over him, I decided to try a prod.

The man snuffled, spluttered a little but did not wake. I stood up just enough to look carefully around. Not a light was in sight, and on this dark night, in my dark clothing, I would not be seen without a lantern or candle. I felt the man's clothing, undid his breeches and pulled them down to expose his buttocks. Next, I slipped out the poniard, with the other hand parted Ned's buttocks, slipped the weapon's tip into his arse, then pushed hard until almost all of its length was in the sleeping man's guts. Ned barely stirred, just spluttered a bit, snored loudly a couple of times, then returned a little hesitantly to his rhythmic loud snoring. I twisted the narrow blade around a little, before pulling it out, wiped the blade on the inside of Ned's filthy breeches and returned the weapon to its scabbard and its usual hiding place. Afterwards, keeping low, I returned to my waiting horse. I looked back at the prone form, and could not resist a grim smile. Then I mounted my horse again and rode slowly away from Ned's loudly snoring form to the back lane, turned left, then left again at the next lane leading to the High Street further along. The street was dark apart from a dim light in the hall itself, so I rode along to the far side of the park, dismounted and walked my horse into Hall Lane leading to the hall's wicket gate, through the wicket gate, and into the stable. I settled my horse, and bedded her down for the night, before going into the hall by the scullery passage door, as before. Once inside the door, I removed the poniard from its hiding place, and returned it to my snapsack, which I had taken off before I entered. Thence up the stairs to my and Amelia's room. I felt my way to the small table by the bed, blew up the faintly smouldering slow match, and lit the candle. Amelia twitched and woke up, then sleepily whispered, 'Is't ye Robert?'

'Aye, wife, 'tis me. I would join ye.'

Quickly I took off my cloak, hat, doublet, shoes and breeches, slipped into the bed beside my wife, and blew out the candle. I moved across to Amelia, and put an arm around her, but she did not respond. I was too tired anyway to bother her more, and whispered 'Sleep well,' before making myself comfortable and slipping into a troubled sleep. I was too wound up to sleep properly, but it mattered not. We could talk in the morning, after I had reported to captain Grove and Master Ekins.

Saturday 3rd March 1649.

Next morning, we were both woken as usual by the knocker-upper, lit two candles, and Amelia went down to the scullery for a pail of hot water as she habitually did. After about half an hour we and young Johnny were dressed, and ready to break our fast. Amelia said to me, 'Husband, 'tis glad I am that ye're back. We must go to church firstly, and pray to God our thanks at your safe homecoming.'

After the events of the last day, I felt angered at this, 'Tush, woman, 'tis not Sunday! I would break my fast, and then must report to captain Grove and Master Ekins post-haste.'

Amelia would have none of it. I did not feel like giving in to this; she had never been so religiously inclined before, and I was still in a state of high tension.

'Ye will be damned if ye deny God, Robert.'

My temper took over rapidly.

'God did not bring me back safe, my horse did! There be plenty of time to pray Sundays. What has brought this on?'

She looked at me with pity in her eyes; that wound me up further.

'I have seen God's light, and it is good, Robert. Ye must seek it too, and ye will be saved.'

With my being still tired after the events of the last two days, my temper snapped.

'Enough, woman! I will not be denied by ye! Hold your tongue,'

I turned, stomped off and down the stairs to the dining hall, making sure that I had the letter for Grove and Ekins safe in my hidden pocket. As I entered the hall, the two gentlemen were sitting together at the top table, and signalled to me to join them, which I did promptly.

'Good morrow, Master, captain. Master, I have an urgent letter for ye from Governor Whetham in Northampton.'

I handed John Ekins the sealed letter. Ekins looked at captain Grove, who looked back in some astonishment.

'Your orders were for Wellingborough, sergeant-major. What had ye to do with Northampton and the Governor?'

'The letter will explain much, if not all, Master Ekins. I am to return to the Governor's office one week hence.'

Ekins broke the seal, and opened the letter, then quickly read the two pages of it. He looked back up at me with a puzzled frown.

'This is most …. most ….. improper, sergeant-major. Why were ye in Northampton?'

'We must talk in private, Master. I think this too, er, easily heard by flapping ears in this hall.'

Master Ekins looked at me in some disbelief.

'Very well. Break your fast, then we repair to the room above.'

We continued to eat and drink in near silence. Whilst we ate, Amelia had brought Johnny down to the hall, and sat with Johnny somewhat disconsolately as far away as she could be from the top table, but nonetheless, watched me intently as we ate. When I had finished my food, I, Master Ekins, and captain Grove stood and headed for the stairs without my acknowledging that Amelia was there. In truth, I felt too angry with her.

In the garret room, I proceeded to recount the events and what I had discovered in Wellingborough. The revelation that Jeanne was not married after all, and was in fact whoring for high-ranking officers in

Northampton amazed both captain Grove and Master Ekins, as indeed did the next revelation that Edwin was not Edwin, but actually Edward Marston, owner of the Golden Lion tavern. I commented, 'Your intelligence was not good, Master Ekins, captain. It came from Edwin, mayhap?' The captain and Master Ekins both acknowledged that it was so.

'So your doubts about Master Edwin were well-founded, sergeant-major…. er, it would seem now, captain. Ye must have much impressed Nat Whetham.'

I recounted my unpleasant experience in the Sun inn.

''Twould seem that Jeanne, or Joan, is more than a whore, Master John. But what? Intelligencer? Or something else? That is what Governor Whetham would have me discover. I think, he is a worried man.'

Master Ekins replied first.

'So 'twould seem, indeed. Your life be much in danger now, Robert. What of your wife and son? What think she of 't all?'

'I have said nought yet. She is only concerned that she drags me to church to thank God for my safe return yet again to Rushden.'

Master Ekins sat and thought for a few moments.

' H'mm. She will not be pleased with your news. I can arrange weapons. From the store here in the hall. Ye will hand back your horse-pistol forthwith. But what of your tuck? And the bodkin ye hides about your person?'

The second time someone had shown me that I had not hidden it well.

'The horse-pistol is a cannon indeed. It is in the gun room of the stable. The tuck, I would keep. The bodkin, my grandfather's poniard, I will put back whence it came, in my father's house. 'Tis too long to defend against such as at the Sun inn, though it saved my life many times during the war.'

93

Now captain John Grove added to the conversation.

'Weapons are easy to find for ye, Robert, but ye will needs use them well. I will advise ye before ye return to Northampton. Ye must talk with your father as well as your wife. He would have your help with his business, and ye will be unable to do so.'

Master Ekins added more still.

'Now ye knows whom we work for, ye needs must hold your tongue on 't. Else ye would be in great calamity. Even your wife, your father, may not know the details of your tasks and who they are for. Pay great heed, Robert. Your life may be in danger from not only your enemies. Think on 't, and take good care.'

I decided to raise the issue of Amelia and how she would react to all this.

'What of Amelia, Master Ekins, captain? I have not told her of Jeanne's whoring, nor of my new orders. What thinks ye I should do?'

Master Ekins was again first to answer.

''Tis a marvellous thorny problem for ye, Robert. 'Tis your decision, but Amelia should not be told too much. Aye, Jeanne or Joan be a whore. Aye, she be in Northam'ton yet. Ye would find her if ye can. Ye may not tell her what ye does. Or for whom higher than the Governor.'

As I acknowledged Master Ekins' words, and sat looking thoughtful, captain Grove added a caution.

'Ye must use your discretion in all things now. Fail, and 'twill be calamitous for ye and your wife. 'Tis a big responsibility.'

I felt like a heavy load had descended on my shoulders as I stepped out of the garret room, and down the stairs, to find my wife and son. I found her sitting in the hall still, talking to my father.

'Good morrow, father. I would speak with ye, but first must speak alone with Amelia. If ye please, would ye leave us alone.'

He looked at me with a hurt expression, but rose and left us alone.

When my father had left the hall, I began.

'Wife, I have news of Jeanne. News that I did not wish to hear, or to have to tell ye. Jeanne did not leave Northampton with Major Berry. She is a whore, and is yet in Northampton town.'

I let the news sink in, as Amelia's face registered first the shock, then disbelief.

'How came ye to this news, husband? Jeanne would not, I think.'

I assured her that it was unquestionably the truth.

'I know not who she whores for now. She lives by friending officers of Governor Whetham's staff...and so much as to be known as Joan the Whore. It is a, er, great concern to the good colonel.'

At that moment, captain Grove appeared at the foot of the staircase, and strode over to me. 'Captain, Master Ekins would speak more with ye, when ye have done with your family, if ye please.'

Amelia looked at me with widening eyes, as Grove retreated back up the stairs, 'Ca..cap..tain? Captain, husband? What passes to make ye captain?'

'Aye, wife. On the Governor's order. I needs must tell ye, I am ordered to return to Northampton in one week, to the Governor. He would have me do work of greatest import. More, I cannot say.' Amelia blinked, sitting speechless for a few moments.

'Husband, will ye be in harm's way?'

I had now to improvise.

'More, I cannot tell ye. Must not. I must seek my father now.'

I left a confounded Amelia sitting at the table, and climbed the stairs to my father's chamber, knocked, and entered. My father was sitting at his desk writing, but looked up, and put his quill down as I walked towards him.

'Father, I have news. Item, one. Jeanne. I have discovered that she whores for officers of Northampton's garrison, so much that she is known as Joan the Whore. Item, two. I am ordered to return to Northampton, to a task of greatest import for Governor Whetham. I am now made captain. I may not tell ye more. I will not be able to help your business. For now. Could ye raise Ned Mawle to partner? Grant him a quarter of the business, mayhap?'

It was my father's turn to sit open mouthed, looking at me as if I had sprouted a second head.

I said to him, ''Tis so sudden, father, I know. So much to take in, I think. But,'tis a fair notion about Ned Mawle, I have thought much on't. I know not when colonel Whetham will release me.'

My father, like Amelia, blinked in surprise, then, 'Son, what have ye got yourself into?' Then recovering his composure some, 'In these times of danger, what of your…. This work, be it risk to your body and soul?'

I answered as best I could.

'Body, aye, mayhap. I must take great care. My soul be damned a'ready from the war.'

His curiosity was much roused, and he could not help himself.

'Who do ye work for – Gener'l Cromwell? He be much hated in these parts. Much as king were before 'un.'

I had to fend off the question. I did not want to lie to my father any more than to my wife.

'Father, I may not tell ye. I know that Cromwell be much hated, aye, but he is not the king. He is but a tool of Parliament, the Ruling Council. We must obey Parliament.'

'Robert, son, what does Amelia say? She will be sore hurt by this.'

I tried to sound more apologetic now, 'Aye, 'tis true. I have no choice, I am ordered to work for the Governor.' Seeing my father's hurt expression, I went on, 'She is more sore hurt by the news of Jeanne. I can tell ye little more, except, Jeanne has a house in Northampton town. She gives cause for great concern to the Governor, because of her whoring with his officers. She is there and not there. I could not find her.'

My father clearly did not know what to say, so did not say anything. Then I carried on.

'Amelia seems much taken with God, methinks. 'Twill be harder to bear Jeanne's whoredom, for her, I think. And I will not be with Lia all the days.'

'Aye, son, that I have noticed. She went to hear a preacher – a presbyter, and has been much smitten by his words. 'Tis not good for her, but 'tis not for me to tell her.'

I decided to bring the conversation to a swift end, and returned to the garret room, as ordered.

I found John Grove sitting at the table, with a small array of weapons in front of him.

'Captain, I recovered your horse-cannon from the gun room. Ye may take either this pocket pistolet, or this two barrel pistolet. The two-barrel is less reliable. If 'twere me, I would take the pocket pistolet.'

I picked it up and examined it. The horse-pistol was unquestionably big and heavy, seriously unwieldy if it were not used on horseback; but the pocket pistol was no lightweight, either, as it was some ten inches from butt to muzzle. It might not be easily concealed, certainly not in a pocket, but it was less than half the size of the horse-pistol, and half the weight. I decided to opt for it.

'Now, Robert, a small knife. Have ye still your old bodkin?' I indicated a 'yes'.

'I have a secret place for 't. In my father's house. 'Twill go back there.'

Captain Grove pointed to a robust looking knife, with a blade about six inches long, and two very sharp edges. 'This would do ye well. But unless ye would have a smaller knife?'

I looked analytically at each knife in turn, and picked a thinner one with a five inch blade that was wickedly sharp, with an equally wicked point. 'This, captain.'

"Twill suit well, methinks.' Grove passed it to me, and asked for my signature against an inventory list for each item. I had to grin.

'Must keep books in order, Robert. Lord Cromwell be a stickler for such things. When the fast post-rider brings your papers from London, we must talk again. Go now to your family.'

I thanked him, and left the room, but not yet back to Amelia. I needed to get rid of the poniard, which was still in my snapsack. I went to my and Amelia's room, took out the poniard from my snapsack, and fitted it into my breeches as I had been doing through the war. Then I donned cloak and hat, quickly went down the stairs, and out of the front door of the hall. About ten minutes later I entered my father's house. I found Ned Mawle working in the old parlour. We exchanged greetings.

'Ned, I must go upstairs to my old room, I have not used it these five years, I would spend a little time there. If ye please, I would not be disturbed.'

Ned looked a little put out, but nodded, and I ascended the creaky stairs to my old room. I could not lock the door, but there was a stool in the room, which I placed against the door, effectively preventing it from being opened more than a few inches. Then I removed the secret panel, took out the poniard, and replaced it in the hidden compartment, afterwards replacing the panel. I sighed quietly as I reminisced, went over to the stool, and took it away from the door as quietly as I could. I carried it over by the window, then sat on it, looking out at the dismal day outside. It was a cold day, and the drizzle that often falls near the river had turned to a light snowfall – unusual for early March – but it did not settle. I got up, reached for the window, and opened it, then looked out on the grey-green fields behind the old house. So much had changed, I could scarce believe it. A month ago, I was a lowly common soldier expecting to return to a comfortable...well, if not comfortable, more normal, home life and helping my father run the business that he had built up during my long years in the army of Parliament. I felt a deep nostalgia for a time when my life was looking good, and my future reasonably secure. Now I had no idea what my future would be, and I was worried that I and Amelia and our son might drift apart. My father looked like an old man. Much could depend on Ned Mawle. Then there was that other Ned. Would he die? Did anyone see me, that dark night? I did not think so, but could not be absolutely certain. My life now was a series of what-ifs. I sighed again, closed the window, left the room, and descended the stairs. Ned was still there, working away at the accounts ledger. 'Are ye happy, Ned?' The other man looked up in some astonishment.

'Me? Oh, aye, 'tis better 'ere in Rushden now. Yer father be a fair man to work fer. I 'ave little to be worrit about.'

I came to a decision. 'My father and myself, we would seek to better your lot. I cannot help my father as I would wish. My father will talk with me about 't soon. God willing.'

Ned looked surprised, 'Thank 'ee, maister Robert. God keep 'ee well,' and returned to his work.

As I was about to go out of the front door, Ned spoke again.

'Folk do say that Ned Adkin be sore poorly, Robert. 'E as… defiled yer ma. 'E be sufferin' much. Shittin' blood, this morrow, folk say.'

I looked at him with feigned shock. 'He be so? God's blood! Yet I would shed nary a tear for that blackguard, Ned. Too much ale. His guts be marvellous pickled, I think. 'Tis not unwelcome news, methinks. God's punishment, perchance.'

As Ned nodded in agreement, I turned, then walked out of the front door and back to the hall.

I returned to the dining hall to find my father comforting Amelia, who clearly had been crying. As I entered, my father called me to come to the table. 'Your Amelia be sore upset, captain.' He emphasised 'captain'. ''T should be ye comfort her, not myself.' I sighed.

'Aye. I have much on my mind father. I can not take this mithering 'bout godliness too.'

I turned to Amelia, 'I am sorry, Lia. So much to think on. I need your… understanding. Not your harsh tongue. I would 'twas as we once were, but that cannot be. So much has changed.'

She nodded a tearful face in my direction, but said nothing. Then, I turned to my father.

'Father, I spent a little time in our old room at your house this morn. I wanted quiet for a while. Ned was working. He told me that blackguard Adkin is sore ill. Shitting blood, he say. Perchance God works in a wondrous way, and Ned Adkin pays the price for soaking so much ale. The news pleases me much, as 'twill ye, I think.' My father nodded slowly, with a look on his face that I could not fathom.

'I take no joy in his distress, Robert. As ye says, God perchance has wrought punishment on Ned.' I looked quizzically at my father sitting there with downcast eyes, not meeting my gaze. Did he know, I thought? Or just suspect?

'We must decide on Ned Mawle's future, father. He be a good man.'

My father did not demur, so I continued.

'Governor Whetham requires much of my time, father, so I would be away much. I may not help ye, so this time could be right to make Ned Mawle a partner. I would suggest a quarter of your business.'

My father thought for a few moments, 'Son, ye has't right. I will do't afore ye leave for Northam'ton. Ye will inherit when the Lord takes me, and Ned would be a good partner for ye too.'

Amelia chipped in, ''Twill be a goodly while afore the Lord calls ye, father in law.'

I, looking at my father's thin, lined face, was not so sure, but said nothing. She carried on, 'Methought Robert may be called afore ye, father, as he would put his soul in danger so, lately.' I felt a pang of anger again, flashed an angry look towards her, but thought better of voicing my anger, and merely said, 'I will take great care.'

A sigh from Amelia brought a response from me, 'Tush, wife, we cannot all put your God before our earthly Master's demands.'

She looked down at her hands, and the conversation returned to the present.

'Father, I would that my duties are soon over. But 'tis out of my hands.'

'I knows, son, ye must do as ye be ordered. These be trying times for us all.'

My and Amelia's relationship remained tense as over the next few days I received some further weapons training from captain Grove, and the time of my departure grew ever nearer. My father drew up a simple deed of partnership for Ned, and with it, promised Ned a pay increase as business might permit. Both I and my father voiced our gratitude to Ned for his hard work, and wished him well for the future. News came every day about that other Ned, who, it was said, was raving with dreadful pain more and more, so that he could be heard fifty yards away across the High Street, and a prayer was said for him by the local preacher in church on that Sunday. Two days later, on Tuesday the 6th of March, 1649, his ordeal came to a permanent end. No tears were shed in the little town of Rushden, however the tavern keeper moaned at how his profits were down, now that Ned Adkin could no longer drink himself insensible several times a week, every week. He found himself the butt of numerous ribbings from other townspeople, and rather than Ned's demise being a source of mourning, it had instead become a cause of some welcome raised spirits. No one knew of any Adkin family members nearby, and since Ned had poured what little money he had down his throat, he was to be given a pauper's funeral the following week, when I was to be back in Northampton.

The letter from Thomas Scot came with a fast Parliament post-rider on the same day that Ned breathed his last. My captaincy – a staff captain's rank – was confirmed by marshal general Bishop, countersigned by Secretary Scot, and my terms of service were laid down in it. I was to be paid largely by results, and reasonable expenses would be reimbursed. My pay was to be at the discretion of Governor of Northampton lieutenant colonel Nathaniel Whetham, as was the duration of my service. In public, as opposed to covert, I will be allowed to wear the blue sash with single gold stitch line of a captain of the regiment of horse of colonel Whetham, and likewise a matching blue ribbon in my hat band. Now that the commission had arrived, I would have to return to Northampton early on the morning of Thursday, 8th March. Though it had passed new moon, the night would again be dark, so rather than risk the bad roads, especially as rain was making the roads into quagmires in that early Spring, I decided to set off as soon as it was light enough in the morning. I would be there, God willing, by the early afternoon, the time of my previous meeting with Whetham.

Meanwhile, as the week wore on, Amelia became more and more tense and determined to get me into church to say prayers for my safe return, and the friction between us grew relentlessly. After my commission arrived, she became very vocal about her demands.

'Husband, ye must join me at church, to pray for your soul, and for your safe passage.'

I inched towards losing my temper again, as I tried to balance the competing demands on my shortening time.

'Wife, ye are free to go on your own account, I will not stop ye. But I must do my work.'

'Husband, ye are damned if ye sees not God's light, and bask in the glory of His sun.'

'Wife, hold your tongue! Ye shrieks like a demented Anabaptist at Paul's Cross. I will not have it. Enough, I say.'

Red in the face now, she cried, 'Care ye not for your wife, your son? God's love is for us all, and ye denies it! If damned ye would be, I would ye not return to us, your family.'

I had become exasperated, 'Enough, wife! I churched with ye last Sunday. I have much to ponder. Godliness is not my first care at this time. On the morrow, if – if – I am prepared, we may to church and pray. Else, go on your own account.'

My father, hearing the exchange, came to us.

'Be still, if you please, both of ye. Amelia, Robert has much of import to do. Pray do not excite him so. And Robert, son, I know ye are angered, but have a care for your marriage. I would fain not see ye all in such a turmoil.'

Amelia pursed her lips and stalked off with a face like thunder, whilst I said, 'Aye father, this mithering makes me sore angry. I dare not make mistakes; 'twould be a danger to my life.'

103

My father squeezed my arm, gave me a half smile, and, sadly, 'Aye, I know 't. I know it, son.'

Releasing my arm, he walked away in the direction Amelia had gone a few moments before.

Captain Grove overheard our raised voices, and came down to the foot of the staircase. He walked over to me, now sitting trying to dampen my roused temper.

'Captain, your wife is much upset. If ye please, come to the garret.'

We ascended the stairs to the garret room, where Grove went to the wall cupboard, and brought out a jug, a bottle of wine, and two goblets. He poured a goblet and passed it to me. Little did he or I realise that alcohol would worsen my unsettled state of mind and my nightmares.

'Drink this, captain, 'twill help settle ye.'

I did as I was told, whilst he poured another glass, and sipped the wine.

'I would advise ye, Robert, make peace with your wife. If 'twould please her, go to church for a while and pray with her. Do not leave with this hanging over ye.'

I sat and stared into the goblet, lost in my thoughts.

'Do ye hear me, Robert? I would fain ye do not leave with this festering in ye. The danger to your life, man. 'Twould be made greater thus.'

I raised my eyes until Grove looked into my face, and I sighed deeply.

'Aye, captain, 'tis so. Amelia tries my patience marvellously. She has changed since my return to Rushden. I know her not now.'

'Self pity helps ye not at all. Ye will be on your own resource in Northampton. A knife in your ribs for your distracted mind? Is that your wish?'

I slowly shook my head. 'Nay, ye are right. I will offer her a

104

bargain. If she do leave me be, we can to church tomorrow after the noon. For mayhap an hour.'

He filled my goblet again.

'Drink this, then go to her, and make your peace.' I felt truly downcast as I left captain Grove and descended the dark staircase to the dining hall again. I knew it would only be a temporary truce with Amelia, and the thought was deeply concerning. If only I could turn back the clock five years!

I entered the dining hall, but it was empty of people, so I climbed the stairs again to try my and Amelia's room. That, too, was empty. Next, I tried my father's chamber, where I discovered my father at his desk writing again. 'Father, I do not know what to say to Lia. Nor where she is. I would make my peace with her before I must leave on the morrow.'

My father looked up, put his quill down, and came over to me, motioning me to one of the two chairs placed by the hearth.

''Tis a vexing question, son, but ye needs must find an answer.'

'Aye father, do ye know of her whereabouts?'

'She is to the church with Johnny. I could not dissuade her.'

I sighed, and threw up my hands in despair.

'She cleaves to that damned preacher. And his God. Mayhap I should stay in Northampton. God's blood, Joan the Whore would be more a wife than Amelia now!'

My father adopted a look of horror at the last words.

''Tis a harsh thing to say, son. I understand your anger, but I beg ye, not such a final act.'

My answer filled him with dread.

'Father, a man needs… comfort, not such a tongue as Lia's is now. And a man has needs. She has become no wife now. I know not what to do.'

My father suggested we both go down to the hall, find a kitchen

105

wench to bring ale, then wait for Amelia. We did not have to wait long, before she came in from the front door, entered the dining hall, and headed for the stairs. Father called her, and she turned reluctantly and walked across the room. Her face looked stern.

As my father started to speak, I put a hand on his arm, and butted in.

'Amelia, I should not say this. In Northampton I were twice threatened with death if I did not desist from seeking Joan the Whore. 'Tis yet more pressing to seek her, discover why she is of so much import that someone would kill to keep me from her. I am ordered to seek her. Methought ye would be my pillar, not drag on me like a… a… leaden weight.'

I let this sink in, as my father looked astonished, then worried, whilst Amelia looked…… impassive. 'I came home to my wife. Now, I know not what ye are. My judge? My scourge? Ye are not my wife now, forsooth. I would hear why, what has made ye so.'

My father looked at Amelia intently, as she spoke very quietly.

'If ye has abandoned God, ye are indeed not my husband.'

I thought for a few moments.

"I have not abandoned God. But ye know I have killed in the war. And since. 'Twas my work, Lia. I did not seek such work. Mayhap I must kill again, I know not. There be much mischief in England now, it would have us all in jeopardy if 'twere to succeed. 'Tis my task to seek and destroy such mischief as I am ordered.' Then a moment later I added, 'Even if Joan be part of that mischief.'

Amelia did not answer, but fiddled with one of the ribbons tying her petticoats.

I thought, in for a penny, nought to lose, and carried on.

'Amelia, should I stay in Northampton, perchance? Do ye truly wish my safe return? Would ye be wife, or scourge?'

At this, she rose and fled sobbing from the dining hall. My father

106

took my arm.

'Son, ye did not say your life were so much in danger. I, your father, would support ye as I may. But that was cruel of ye.'

'Aye, I do know, father. But Amelia, I truly know not what I should do or say to her.'

I stood, and turned again to my father.

'I may not return to Northampton in this worrisome condition. Ye learned enough of my service for Lord Cromwell to see that I would not be safe, nor Amelia, if I turn away from this task. Amelia, she, she turns her mind from me, will not hear me. Could ye help, perchance? If it would please ye?'

My father nodded sadly.

'I will try again, my son.'

I had not noticed Master Ekins standing back in the shadows, and he stepped forward.

'Captain, with me, if ye please.'

He took me to his private office, where he pointed to a chair, poured and proffered a goblet of sack. So much wine this day! But I took the goblet, and sat down, facing him.

'Robert, ye are not the first to return from the war, and find your wife thus. Ye and Amelia both be changed by the war. 'Tis hard, but 'twill take time. I will help ye both, if ye'll let me. Your task be of too great import to fail due to this, this difficulty, with your wife. If ye please, may I bring her here?'

'Aye, mayhap ye can help, Master John.'

Ekins rang a small bell on his desk, and moments later a woman appeared from a concealed door to ask his requirement.

'Mistress Jane, would ye to Missus Amelia's room, and bring her here, if ye please?'

Jane gave a small curtsey, and left by the main office door. A few minutes later, she returned, and showed a tearful, downcast Amelia

107

into the office, and left again, by the concealed door. Ekins rose, motioned Amelia to a chair, then offered her a goblet. She accepted the goblet, all the while not looking at me.

'Robert, Amelia, I have known ye both since ye were little more than children. It pains me greatly to see ye so, at each other's throat. First, Amelia, I heard Robert tell of his new task in Northampton. 'Tis a heavy burden, indeed, that he carries. And ye may not know much of 't. I would tell ye that Robert has no choice. He must carry out his orders or be charged with desertion. Ye both would be in grave danger were he to refuse. Ye, Amelia, must understand Robert's position. Concern for ye and your child, your marriage. Second, Robert, ye have been deeply troubled by the war, and your other tasks since '45. But ye are not alone. Many a wife has been sore affected by her husband's absence at the war. Robert, ye have seen so much killing, dreadful acts of war. Ye cannot see God as your Amelia does, now. Ye love each other, do ye not? I would ye both make your peace with each other. Ye must each see the other's view.'

Amelia spoke first.

'I cannot bring Robert into God's light, Master John.'

'My dear young woman, there be none of God's light on a battlefield. There be none of God's light shining on Robert's new tasks. He must – MUST - do his work under the shadows, the dark shadows that fall on England at this moment.'

She sat there looking at Ekins impassively, so he continued.

'Amelia, Robert loves ye very much. I beg ye not to reject his love. God would not thank ye for that. I would leave ye both to talk awhile.'

He rose and left his office, with Amelia sitting looking down at her clasped hands. I came to a decision.

'Lia, I was at Marston Trussell. My regiment chased king Charles's troops from Naseby, trapped them 'tween church and river. We killed every last one. No quarter. Their women and children sought refuge in the church. 'Twas no refuge. My captain ordered me to kill a woman your age with babe in arms. She looked into my eyes as I raised my pistol and shot her. Ne'er will I ever forget that look. When I see ye, I see her face, bloodied and black from my pistol shot. I see her fall, drop her babe. I see my captain step forward, kill the babe with his boot. Where be God that day? Where the preacher? Fled, I think…' My voice trailed off. I recovered my composure. 'Lia, I love ye dearly, but your faith I cannot share. I see that woman's face all my days. I would 'twere not so, but 't cannot be undone. War makes wild animals of good men. I have done … other... awful things, I may not tell ye of. Truly, your faith I cannot share.'

As the blood drained from Amelia's face, she sat looking into my eyes with a hand over her mouth, before rising from the chair, taking my hand for a moment, then running from the office. I sat still, staring into the goblet, and intermittently sipping absent-mindedly from it.

It was a sorrowful, red-eyed Amelia that returned ten minutes later. She walked cautiously to the same chair, and sat looking tearfully at me.

'Robbie, my husband, I.. had.. not known. I hoped that ye would see God's light healing ye. Ye are so, so, changed. I think, I know ye not. What would I do?'

'Lia, I am so sorry to have told ye. I needs have your comfort, your love, not your harsh words, not your, your preaching. I wear my shame and guilt each day; I bear great fear all my days. I dare not tell ye more, lest ye bear the same fear as I.' She reached out, and took my hand.

'I would that we be as once we were.'

'My love, so do I. So do I indeed. It cannot yet be. There be forces in England that would bring Charles the son to the throne. That would mean more war. If my tasks thwart that a trifle, 'tis worth it. I would not that we live in fear of more war.' She looked at me sadly, as John Ekins came back into the office. He saw Amelia holding my hand.

'On the morrow, take ye both time together. I would that ye enjoy your time tomorrow, afore Robert must return to Governor Whetham.' He smiled at us, as we rose, thanked him kindly, and left his office, after which we went down to the dining hall, where my worried father sat nervously twirling the corner of his gown.

'I hope ye have made your peace. 'Twas so sad to see ye at each other's throat.'

We both nervously smiled our affirmation. When we were sat down, I called the wench and ordered a jug of small beer and three pots. I started the conversation.

'I would seek more about Jeanne, or Joan. What makes her of such import? Not whoring, I'll be bound.'

'Aye, 'tis queer. Mayhap she carries letters? Money? Yet, who for? And who from?'

'That could make her traitor.' I said.

My wife's hand shot to her mouth, as before in Ekins' office.

'She could be traitor? My sister Jeanne? Nay, surely.'

The wench approached, so we fell silent until she had put the drinks down, and returned slowly to the kitchen, methought with her ears flapping.

'Not so difficult to be a traitor, Lia.' from my father.

I added, 'If not traitor, why whore only for officers ranked captain, or major? Or higher, perchance? She whores for more than the money, I'll be bound.'

We looked at each other, and sat thinking about the implications of that, until I spoke again. 'That is what I must discover.'

At that point, we changed the topic of conversation to the next day, and I and Amelia's day off before I would leave for Northampton. We did not think anything of the wench hovering just behind the kitchen door. Shortly the troopers would return to the hall for their evening repast, so we decided to stay put, especially as Johnny had been playing contentedly all this time close by. I called for the kitchen wench, and she arrived almost instantly, leaving me wondering if she had been listening. I ordered our meal and best ale. She brought the best ale, and about a quarter hour later, the meal itself which we all tucked into with, for once, some gusto. My father suggested, as the nights were now so much lighter, we leave Johnny with him after we had eaten, and take a walk in the evening sun. We were glad to accept his offer, and wandered off around the hall's expansive park, holding hands, and talking quietly.

On our return, the sun was very low in the sky, and Johnny was becoming tired and cantankerous, so we took him up to bed. It had been a long and arduous day for us both too; we resolved on an early night, and for the first time for a while after we had readied ourselves for bed, lay in each other's arms, each comforting the other as the light gradually left our room in total darkness. I, especially, slept better than for a long time, and by morning, both of us woke refreshed and obviously less tense, much less unhappy. We would have a welcome day of freedom from our life's cares, and even if it proved rainy, we would do our utmost to enjoy it, while it lasted.

Chapter 8: Deceit and Death

Thursday 8th March 1649.

After we had all broken our fast, we found a maid who would look after Johnny for a couple of pennies for the day, and we dressed for the still cold weather – there was some frost on the ground even though it was March – and set off to wander around the park and the village. My father had perked up somewhat too. John Ekins found him at a trestle, and called him over to join him at his usual place at the top table. They had an earnest conversation about myself and Amelia, as they both realised how much we all had achieved the day before, and thanked God that it had ended so well. The only elephant in the room was tomorrow, when I had to depart once more for Northampton, and an uncertain future. Both John Ekins and my father realised that I could not have undertaken such a dangerous task with myself and Amelia at war in Rushden; and neither of them relished the possibility of having to tell Amelia that I would never return. If my mission were to go badly wrong, I could easily stop a pistol ball or an assassin's blade.

My father left to make his almost daily contact with Ned Mawle at the old house, and bring Ned up to date with my impending departure. My father could clearly no longer cope easily with the day to day running of his business, and I would have been a very welcome assistant, but it clearly could not be, yet. My father and Ned went through the books, decided the work priorities for the next few days, then proceeded to discuss further Ned having a quarter of the business himself, as soon as the arrangements could be put into writing. The events of Tuesday had slammed the brakes on putting that into effect. Ned did not demur, yet my father sensed that he was not happy. 'What gives ye unquiet, Ned?' Father asked him. Ned's answer worried him not a little.

'Maister John, I think't not fair that I does most work, yet gets but a quarter.'

My father felt and looked a bit offended; he tried to persuade Ned otherwise.

'Ned, ye has been my foreman for longtime now. I seek to reward ye, not sell ye short.' Ned did not answer immediately, so my father continued.

''Tis still my business, Ned. Ye have done well from't.'

Looking down, Ned replied, 'Aye, 'tis true. But 'twill ne'er be my business, maister John, an' wi' maister Robert away, much load lands on me.'

'Aye, that I knows. Master Robert will come back. The war has asked much of us all; I ask no more of ye, Ned, only to reward ye for your hard work. Let us do this, and your lot should grow better.'

My father sought a way to get his way without putting his foot down hard, or making Ned feel disgruntled. He did not want to lose Ned, but who had put this into his head, this most contented man?

'But is't reward enough, maister John?'

My father thought for a moment, and decided to seek the cause of his discontent.

'What has changed, Master Ned? Ye were content with my offer a few days past.' Ned looked away, his face betraying guilt.

'My wife has pressed me hard, maister.' Both my father and I knew Ned's wife, Liza, and did not believe his reply. She was a quiet woman who would not be so bold.

'Are ye sure 'twas your wife, Ned? Not someone other?' Ned just sat looking guilty, and did not volunteer a reply.

'Very well. We shall let it rest till Robert be back. I had thought ye more faithful, Ned.'

With that, my father sent Ned home, then decided to check stock inventory against the ledger. He was most surprised to see that it did not match. Some stock of finished boots was not there.

After his stock check, my father walked slowly back to the hall, deep in thought. He decided not to tell myself or Amelia, but thought perhaps he could discuss it with Master Ekins after I had left for Northampton. I had enough on my plate with my mission in Northampton, and did not need more worry – or so my father thought. Events on the morrow would change that dramatically.

Friday 9th March 1649.

The morning seemed normal, as I, Amelia, and Johnny went down to the dining hall early to break our fast. My father joined us five minutes later, and he and I set to discussing the offer to Ned Mawle.

'I know not why he now objects to my offer,' said my father. He wondered if Ned had been influenced by another, and I replied that Liza, Ned's mousey wife, was likely not the source. We were sitting nearer than usual to the doorway leading to the kitchen and scullery, and I suddenly noticed the kitchen wench hiding in the shadows, just within the doorway, watching us intently. I called her over. She came to the table, looking apprehensive.

'Ye spy on us, mistress. Why, pray?'

'Nay, I ne'er, maister.' I looked at her face, saw that her guilt was obvious.

'She lies,' said my father.

'Why do ye spy on us? Who for?' I stood up to confront her.

She stood silently scowling at me. I demanded an answer, deftly pulled my dagger out, fingered its sharp edge so that she could see. The hussy spat at me, and made to turn away, but I caught her arm, pulled her back, and made her face me, back against the wall. She tried to claw my face, so my next move was to tear apart her rough bodice and smock, revealing her breasts, and pressed the point of my knife into her left breast until it started to bleed. Amelia looked on in fixated horror.

'Answer me!' The young hussy remained defiant.

114

'Would that I slice your paps, wench? Why do ye spy on us?' I pressed the knife harder.

'Nay, stop, maister, I tell ye, I tell ye!'

'Speak the-' as a shot rang out, and with a small fountain of blood and bone fragments, she keeled over sideways in front of me. She was dead as she hit the floor. I turned and sprinted towards where the shot had come from, through the cloud of gunpowder smoke into the scullery, my knife still drawn, but there was no sign of the assailant.

'Where went he?' I snapped to the terrified scullery maid; she pointed to the outer door. I went out and saw the figure galloping away on a horse from the stable – without a saddle. The figure was wearing militia uniform. I wiped my blade on a kitchen cloth, returned it to its scabbard, then came back into the hall to find my father struggling to support Amelia, who had fainted. I helped him to lift her, and bring her round. Captain Grove appeared from the stairs, followed by Master Ekins a few seconds later. 'What is't, Robert?' from Grove.

'Captain, if you please, a roll call of your troopers. One killed the wench. She were spying on us. I had her about to tell why, and…. this. One of your troopers, I think, killed her.'

Grove paled, then turned and went back up the stairs to check the troopers, some of whom were coming now, alerted by the shot.

I turned round to my father, 'Can ye see to Amelia for now?'

He replied with a 'yes, surely', then I addressed myself to Master Ekins, who stood, looking in shock at his kitchen wench.

'Captain, I suspected someone here of passing secrets, but Emily? Nay, she be… were… a mere fifteen year old. Poor lass.' he said, his voice shaking as he spoke.

'Master Ekins, she were the tool of another. He has fled. Captain Grove may tell who is missing from roll call. 'Tis not just secrets, 'tis making mischief. Ye knows now the problem with Ned Mawle. He is put up to't, I am certain.'

Amelia was fully conscious now, and shakily stood up. She looked in horrified fascination at the blood spattered up the wall, on my doublet and hose, then down at Emily's shattered face, and immediately retched, then vomited onto the floor. The ball had hit Emily at the angle of her jaw, instantly shattering the bone into fragments, helping it to cut major blood vessels. Whoever it was that killed her was a very good shot. I addressed Master Ekins.

'I must help Amelia, Master John. Excuse me, if ye please.'

I turned to Amelia. She looked up at me with her face as white as a sheet; she had never seen anyone shot dead before close to, not even when Royalist troopers had rampaged through Rushden in '45. I took her hand, but she pulled it back.

'Robbie, I feel that I know ye not. How could ye be so cruel with that poor wench?'

'Better I got the truth from her than she be taken to Whetham's gaol. Would ye rather she went to the governor's brutes or the press? If she be found a spy, and charged with treason, know ye the punishment? Do ye? Come.'

I took her hand again, pulled her towards me, and helped her upstairs to our room with my arm around her waist to steady her. Meanwhile my father kept an eye on Johnny, who seemed completely unfazed by events.

Back in our room, I talked quietly to Amelia.

'Lia, my love, this is war. We do not play games. I had not expected a spy here in the hall… but they be everywhere, 't seems. See ye why I must go back to Northampton now, and find Jeanne?' She nodded, but it was clear that she was still shaking, still reluctant, and I embraced her, stroked her face. When we moved apart, she realised that the blood on my doublet was now on her clothing too. She took off her waistcoat and apron, shuddered, and threw them down, then found others and put them on.

'Robbie, ye must change your doublet too. Let us get Emily's blood off both our clothes. We may not do't, if we let it dry.'

I smiled weakly at her, and did as she bade, changing into fresh doublet and breeches, as she dabbed the blood away with a cloth dampened in cold water.

'Lia,' I said, 'I am so sorry ye should see war so close, yourself. But war comes to visit us when we least want it. Aye, I am changed, ye knows. Yet I love ye as ever.' I kissed her, as she smiled a very wan smile.

We embraced again, as I said, 'I must back down to the hall, will ye come with me?'

She nodded, and we returned to the dining hall together. Captain Grove had now returned with the muster roll. As I approached him, he turned, and said, 'Captain, the man missing be trooper Watterson. I would not have thought it of him.'

Ekins chipped in. 'Will Watterson, indeed? A friend of Ned Mawle.'

My father and I looked at each other as the implication sank in. My father spoke first.

'We must speak with Ned, methinks, Robert.'

'Aye, indeed, and mayhap not be so easy on Ned.'

Amelia, who had walked a little apart from me as we entered the hall, looked at me with worried quizzicality.

'Worry not, Lia. I'll not stick him with my blade,' and gave a little laugh. But I did not say that Ned would not get to see the point of my blade…

I turned my attention now to Master Ekins.

'Sir, I must speak with Ned. I must write my report of this day for Governor Whetham, lest I should be late at Northampton. Mayhap ye could make a report also to back up mine?'

'Aye, captain, 'tis a fair notion. Captain Grove will take some

117

troopers to look for Will Watterson post-haste. We both know his house, his friends. If we take him, ye would need troopers to escort him to Northampton with ye.'

I saluted, and asked my father to stay in the hall while I went to speak to Ned Mawle. Alone. I returned to my and Amelia's room, swapped my coif for my high-crown hat with its ribbon of regimental rank, donned my sash of rank, my thick cloak, then left the hall via the scullery passage door and the side alley. A few minutes later, I was in the front room of the old house, and standing in front of Ned Mawle.

'Master Ned, I would know who has urged your discontent with my and my father's offer?'

Ned squirmed in his seat, and weakly replied, 'None, maister Robert.' It was an obvious lie.

'Ned, I have known ye for ten year, have I not? Do ye not think I would know when ye lies?'

Ned sat there, silent, looking down guiltily.

''Twas Will Watterson, I think?' Ned nodded.

'He gave me money, maister. Five shillin'.'

'Five shillings, Ned? Is that all your trust, your loyalty, be worth? Methought better of ye. And I be captain Robert to ye.' Ned said nothing. 'What more did Will say to ye, Ned? He would have ye spy on us, methinks.' Ned still said nothing.

I pulled my dagger out from the sheath behind my back, fingered its sharp edge.

'What will't take to get the truth from ye, Ned?' I stroked Ned's ear with the blade, felt him flinch.

'I knows he spies, Ned. His young agent.. he shot her dead this morn. To stop her telling who she spied for. That could be your fate too, Ned. If ye do not tell.' This time, I drew the sharp edge of the blade across Ned's ear, drawing blood. Ned yelped.

'I know not who he spies for, captain Robert. He wants word of

118

what ye does for maister Ekins, why ye go ter Northam'ton, why ye seek Joan Rately.' I was alarmed, but not surprised.

'Indeed? Methought as much. I need more. Have ye heard of Royalist dissidents hereabouts?' Ned looked up at me now, with a scared expression.

'Aye, ye needs be scared, Ned. Ye have put your life in danger from Will's masters, from me and my masters. Have ye heard of the Swordsmen?' Ned looked surprised at this.

'Aye, captain, I hear tell of them. I know not who they be.'

'Ye knows Jeanne – not Joan - Rately, Ned? How come?' Ned was a little more forthcoming.

'Will, 'e arsk why ye would speak wi' 'er. Bain't yer wife a Rately, captain?'

''Tis for me to ask the questions, Ned.' Realising that I probably would not get any more from Ned, I carried on. 'Ned, ye must needs prove yourself to me now, if ye would be a partner. If Will Watterson be taken by captain Grove's militia, be assured, he will be questioned by such as I, but far harsher than I. If ye have more to say, now is your time. Else, if the militia does not find Will, and ye sees him, ye tells Master Ekins, or captain Grove, or I. Do I make myself clear?'

In a very chastened voice Ned answered, 'Aye, captain. Ye're most clear.'

I bade him good morrow and returned to the hall, where I joined Ekins and Grove for a meeting in the garret room.

I described my interrogation of Ned Mawle, the result of which rather surprised captain Grove and Master Ekins. They had not expected him to be so easily turned spy.

I said, 'There be more to Jeanne Rately than we may guess. But what is't? Is she a spy? I would not have thought her capable. I would also know how Ned Mawle has heard of the Swordsmen.' Master

Ekins and Grove looked at each other, then at me in surprise; they did not know of Prince Rupert's gang of friends, either. 'Captain, perchance ye can tell us of the Swordsmen yourself?'

'I may not, Master Ekins. They're not widely known of. If ye please, it may not be spoken of outside this room.' Grove realised that I knew much more than I could tell them. I said, 'I would know if your troopers find Will, captain. I fear he will be dangerous if left at large. I will go now, and scribe my report.'

We broke up the meeting, and I went to my and Amelia's room. She was not there, so I got out ink, quill, and paper, and started writing.

My report was in three parts. First part, an account of events in Rushden. Second part, problems remaining to be resolved. Third part, my approach to resolving them. It was succinct, and clearly written, though I say it myself. I folded it, sealed it, and committed it to the same secret pocket in my doublet as my other papers. It would not leave me until I was in Whetham's office. Then I went downstairs to find Amelia. I met my father coming up the stairs, and asked if he knew where to find my wife and son.

They had gone to the long gallery, so I asked my father to accompany me to our room.

Once shut in my and Amelia's room, I sat my father down, and opened on the subject of Ned Mawle. 'I have made Ned talk some, father. He was for sure stirred by trooper Watterson. Watterson seems to be the main spy, though I may have that wrong. Watterson paid him five shillings to make mischief with ye.' My father was stung by this revelation.

'Five shillin'? On'y five shillin', Robert? That all it took to buy him?'

'Aye, a mere five shillings. I have told him that he must earn my trust, if he would be our partner.'

''Tis a good notion, son. God's blood, what a marvellous pickle we have here. Dead wench, dead partnership, all in one day.'

I decided to speak about Lia. 'I am much unquieted by Lia, father. She knows not how to... how to... understand me, now, I think. She is shocked by war, by my work, I cannot help that, though I am so sorry it be so.' My father looked thoughtful.

'I am... likewise, my son. I have not seen ye so, so, brutal, Robert. I have not seen war. I know 'tis bad for men's souls. But I had not thought it so... cruel.'

'I was at Marston Trussell, father. Know ye of 't?'

''Twas bad, I hear.'

'Aye, father. I have told Lia. I was ordered to kill a woman of Lia's age. In the church. 'T haunts me as much as, as all my service in the war. I see her face yet.' My father looked at me, but said naught. 'Ye knows not what more I have done and seen. I would ye do not know. Nor Lia, yet. I hope she do not see my work. Nor ye.' My father sighed. I went on.

'I am damned in God's sight, I think. 'Twill not be fixed with more prayer. What is done, cannot be undone.'

'Nay, ye must do your orders. More war may yet come. What of ye then?' I shrugged.

'Mayhap I must be an active soldier again, I know not. If ye please, will ye keep Lia and Johnny safe to my return?'

'Ye knows I will.' He stood. 'Let us finish. I must work, too, my son.' With that, he turned and returned to his own chamber, and closed the door. I decided to find Lia, and headed for the long gallery. Before I had gone far, I met Master Ekins, with marshal general Bishop. Ekins asked me to join them. He introduced George Bishop to me, and we exchanged pleasantries, before repairing to Ekins' office.

In the office, Bishop came quickly to the point. 'Master Ekins, now spring is here, we must relieve ye of half your militia. People need food. Farms must plough and sow. And ye have kept your, let us say, present garrison, for two months. More troopers will be brought to array, and your present militia must then go home. Captain Grove will train a fresh garrison.' Ekins was about to speak, but I cut in.

'My apologies, Master Ekins, ye can not keep militia so long. Thirty days, on the old terms. It could be a cause of dissent if ye keep militia longer, methinks. Better they do not desert. Or do as trooper Watterson.' Captain Bishop looked at each of us in turn, his eyebrows raised.

'What of this trooper, Master Ekins?'

'This morn he shot my kitchen wench; she were working for him. He be now a fugitive.'

I added, 'Captain, 'tis why he shot her that be of more import. He were making mischief, a-spying. She were his intelligencer. A poor one, I think.'

Ekins added. 'And now she be dead.'

A "h'mm" from Bishop preceded a few moments thought. 'Do ye know of his masters, captain, Master Ekins?' We didn't, and I, though I had my suspicions, preferred to keep quiet, then decided to invoke my own work.

'Captain Bishop, my master be Governor Nat Whetham, of Northampton's garrison. I go to him on the morrow. I would discuss 't with him.' Bishop nodded sagely.

'Aye, captain Barker, I do know of your own tasks. Tom Scot will have my report on my return to London. I would speak with ye again, ten days from now.' I stood up, and asked to be excused.

'Master Ekins, I would find Lia. She be badly shaken by the wench's killing. Captain Bishop, I bid ye good day.' And with that, I bowed slightly, saluted, and left the office, to head for the long gallery.

I found Lia sitting stitching an apron whilst Johnny played with his toy a few feet away. She looked up unsmiling as I approached her.

122

'Oh, Robert, 'tis ye.' I smiled at her. Kissed her cheek.

'Will Watterson has stirred a wasp's nest. I would be with ye sooner, but marshal general Bishop is here. I had needs speak with him and Master Ekins. Let us to the hall, we will sup and talk.'

She dutifully nodded, stood, called Johnny to her, and we trio proceeded along the long corridor and downstairs to the hall. We found a trestle in the now empty room well away from the door whence came Emily on this fateful morning. Her blood had been washed off the wall and floor, but still the old panelling showed where it had been. Lia looked at it and shuddered.

'Poor girl, Robert. Shot down so young.' I agreed, and suggested she sit with her back to the scene, steering Johnny to sit close to her. I walked over to the doorway, and looked in, then went further in, and looked into the kitchen, where the maids were now cooking the midday food.

'Jug of small ale, with two pots, if ye please, mistress, and milk for the boy.' One of the maids turned to me, and nodded, so I returned to the trestle, and sat opposite Amelia. She still looked pale and her eyes still betrayed that she had been crying, but she looked up into my face as I spoke.

'My wife, we must talk now. Ye must not tell of this.' I spotted the maid walking towards us, and stopped. After she had deposited the drinks on the trestle, and had returned to the kitchen, I started again.

'This is 'tween ye and me only. The garrison goes home soon. 'Twill be necessary we find new men to train. But half as many.' She looked at me as if totally uninterested. I continued.

'I would not that ye be afeared. There may be more mischief makers among them. Captain Grove would be a-lookout for them. On my return, so will I. Methought that ye may feel safer should we take a house in Northampton town, but ye would be, er, closer to my work as well as I. 'T may not be pretty. I would spare ye such.' A weak smile.

'Your father, husband. What of him?'

123

''Tis ye I think of. My father be here, and 'tis but a few hours ride from Northampton.' I paused, and looked at her questioningly. 'What thinks ye, Lia? Stay here in the hall, so we be apart, or take house in Northampton?' She looked vacantly at me.

'Do as ye think fit, husband.' Now I was feeling both hurt and anxious for her.

'Lia, I love ye and Johnny so much, I would ye be safe as may be. I wish ye to be happy. Tell me what ye wish I do.' She smiled weakly again, but said naught.

''Tis a sunny day. Let us take a turn of the park.' I stood, and held my hand out to her. She dutifully stood up, but ignored my hand. I looked at her despairingly.

'What is't, Lia? Be ye unwell?' She spoke hesitatingly.

'Ye are not the Robbie that I married. The Robbie I married, he were a gentle soul. Ye are so cruel. But I am your wife, I must obey ye yet.' A tear ran down her cheek. Johnny sensed that something was wrong, and started snivelling. I looked down at him, and realised that this is no conversation for a six-year old to hear.

'Let us back up to our chamber. I will ask Master Ekins for the borrow of his maid to see to Johnny, then we can talk freely.' Whilst I took Johnny's hand and steered him towards the stairs, Lia walked gloomily in front, and proceeded up the stairs, leaving me looking at her back with a growing sense of despair as we mounted the stairs. What had seemed such a good day dawning had become a nightmare, a day when all my hopes were dashed again, and fear had taken over. And all because I had spotted a lowly kitchen maid keeping us under close surveillance. 'Why has this world become one of fear so?' I thought, as we opened our room door and entered.

I was in for another shock. My snapsack had been rifled, and my clothes were strewn about, also my writing materials had clearly been visited by whoever rifled my snapsack. Amelia looked at the scene, and burst into tears. I took her gently and sat her down, made sure she was able to wait for me, then hurried to my father's room, and knocked on the door. My father came to the door, unlocked and opened it, and peered at me.

'Father, if you please, come. And lock your door.' My father did as he was asked, and followed me back to my and Amelia's room. When he saw the scene, and Amelia still crying, he looked at me in shock.

'What goes here? Who…?' He quickly recovered his wits.

'Robert, Amelia needs your love and care, she be greatly shocked. While ye take care of her, I would fetch maister John.' I indicated that captain Grove should come too. I sat alongside Amelia, took her in my arm, and was still holding her when Master Ekins and captain Grove knocked and entered. They surveyed the scene, and looked at each other in disbelief. Master Ekins was first to speak.

'So we have another traitor in our midst.' I nodded, and said, 'Master Ekins, I worry 'bout Lia. Thinks ye she be safe, whilst I be working away?'

Ekins thought a moment, then, 'I think she should move to a chamber in my wing of the house.'

'I did wonder if a house in Northampton would be safer for us, but Lia mayhap would be too close to my work.' Captain Grove answered that.

'Northampton be unsafe at this time, captain. 'Tis said there be much mischief afoot in the city.'

Ekins added, 'Aye, and Will Watterson be free yet. He perhance has another in my house. But another – what? Maid, trooper, servant?'

Grove suggested, 'Captain, when your wife be a little better, we all needs must talk again. Did the, the, intruder take anything? Did ye keep any letters in your chamber?'

'Nay, captain John, none but on my person. Could be to affright me – and 'specially Lia – that I do not go to Northampton?'

The conversation concluded that we should talk after the midday meal, when perhaps Amelia was feeling less shaken, and could be left in my father's care for a while. I tried to calm Johnny. 'My child, your mother be a little poorly. Can ye be grown up, and look after her?' The child nodded vigorously, as children do, but looked somewhat doubtful; as I arose, I ruffled his hair, and suggested to Amelia that we go for some food now, before the troopers came in for theirs. She stood up mechanically, and walked down the stairs behind her family into the hall. I pointed to a trestle, and said to Johnny, 'Would ye take your mother to that table for me?'

The child again nodded, and grabbed his mother's hand, pulling her in the required direction. They took a seat on the bench, and waited. I did as before, asked a kitchen maid if the food was ready, and requested some for each of us, as well as a jug of best ale, two pots, plus some milk for Johnny. Doing my best to be attentive to her, I sat holding Amelia's hand across the trestle table. I tried to assure her that whoever had invaded our room was unlikely to be a danger to her.

'Mayhap a chance thief, my love. 'Tis not always the worst.' An almost imperceptible nod. ''Twill feel safer when Will be caught. Mayhap he be far away, mayhap close by. But hiding, I think. He must come out for food. Then perchance he would be caught.'

She smiled weakly again, but said nothing. The kitchen maid brought the jug of ale, two pots, and Johnny's milk, and set it all in front of us. I thanked the maid, then poured some of the ale for Amelia, and filled my own pot. She sipped a little, then set the pot down again. ''Twill make ye feel better, Lia, if ye drink some more.' She took another sip.

A few minutes later, the maid appeared with three wooden plates, spoons, and a bowl of steaming potage with a ladle, as usual.

'Would ye have some gammon, maister? Fresh baked.' I signified a 'yes', and she left to fetch the food. When she returned with the bread, butter, and gammon, I bade her wait, cut a piece off the gammon, and asked her to eat it. She did so without demur. Then I asked her to sup some of the potage, which she also did without demur. After I dismissed the maid, I sniffed the butter and bread. All seemed good. Amelia, meanwhile, sat impassively looking on. I smiled at her.

'Lest someone would make me or thee ill. Methought the food be good, but a message to the maids goes not go amiss.' I smiled again, she smiled weakly back. "Tis good, my love, 'twill help ye feel better.' I spooned some out onto her plate, passed it to her, then the same for Johnny, finally for myself. Taking a hunk of bread and a slice of the gammon, I started to tuck in, then thought better of it. Putting my hands together, 'We thank ye, Lord, for thy bounty. Amen.' Then I commenced eating. It took a lot of persuading to get Amelia to eat, but after a while she did, and some colour returned to her cheeks; she perked up a little, even smiling at me and Johnny from time to time. When we had finished eating, I summoned the maid again. Did the kitchen have some sugared almonds, or fruit? The maid signified 'yes', so I asked for some to be brought to the table. She brought a bowl of the sugared almonds, and three small apples. Even Amelia's eyes lit up at the sight of the almonds, and she took several, whilst Johnny grabbed a handful. I wagged a finger at him. 'Greedy, Johnny! Greed be a sin. Ye must leave some for your mother and I.' Johnny pouted, put two back, and started to chew one. Amelia had clearly got some of her calm back.

'Tush, Robbie, ye does not like almonds!'

I laughed, for the first time in days, and she laughed too. It was such a welcome feeling. I took an apple, and split it in two with my knife. It was worm-eaten so I tried another. That looked better, so I divided it into segments, and ate it with feigned pleasure, pretending to push a segment into Johnny's mouth from time to time. From time to time, Amelia also took a segment and ate it.

Chapter 9: Anxieties and Approaches

My father appeared in the dining hall, saw Amelia, myself, and Johnny, sitting together, looking like a normal happy family, though I could still detect some tension, and I myself a feeling of some anxiety lest our happiness should be blown away again. He walked over to us, and took a seat.

'Ye goes to Northampton, on the morrow, Robert. 'Tis a sunny day now, if ye both would walk a little, I would find help to see to Johnny.' We were immediately grateful for his kind offer, and thanked him, saying that we would be delighted to walk in the sunshine, which we had wanted to do before Will Watterson wrecked our plan, and better now than never.

I elected to collect our cloaks from our room, and my high-crown hat of course, and within five minutes we were out walking in the fresh air. Both of us knew that we would have to confront the security situation on our return, but it was good to escape our worldly cares for a little while. A matter that had not escaped our notice was that we could not expect to live courtesy of John Ekins' generosity for much longer. Though we could not make other arrangements until my return from Northampton, it was a subject that had to be addressed. And addressed soon, for the government money that had kept the garrison at the hall would soon be cut.

I and Amelia walked around the hall grounds and then the village itself for two hours. Both of us had relaxed some more by the time we returned to the hall, and to the cares of the world that affected us directly. While Amelia collected Johnny from a helpful maid, and gave her a silver penny or two for her trouble, I had to proceed to a meeting in Master Ekins' office. I went upstairs, and knocked on his door.

Ekins' voice said, 'Enter,' and in I went, to find captain John Grove sitting opposite Master Ekins. They were already discussing something of import. 'Take a seat, if ye please, captain.'

128

I sat in the vacant chair.

'We be giving thought to the garrison, captain,' from John Grove, 'Since 'twill affect ye, your opinion be of import.'

'Aye, 'tis what I wished to raise with ye both. Two matters vex us, methinks. Amelia, whilst I be in Northampton, and our housing on my return.'

Master Ekins answered first, 'Amelia and Johnny need not vex ye, Robert. There be room enough here to find them safe lodging. 'Tis what happens after Parliament shrink the garrison that concerns me.'

We spent the next quarter hour discussing the possibilities; since no actual word had come from either Thomas Scot, George Bishop, or the Treasurers-at-War, the actual implications for the financial consequences remained unknown.

'Perchance the bigger question be security, Robert,' said Master Ekins.

'Aye, and security apart, 'twould be possible to move Amelia, Johnny, and I to the old house, but we needs must have a maid-of-all-work at least. We could make room for us, but a maid, too? And a kitchen? 'Twould be good to build on the house, but in these times? And 'twould take two seasons, likely. Business would not be good, and if the army leaves, money could become short,' I said.

We chewed it over some more, and the decision that we arrived at became for I and my family to stay in the hall, with the proviso that we might have to pay some rent, and for a servant, if the financial constrictions from the Treasurer-at-War became too much. I also pointed out that my contract from Tom Scot did not guarantee any sort of salary, just 'payment on result', so was at Whetham's whim. It was far from an ideal situation; but the Treasury was strapped for cash and bullion to make more coin, so it was not likely to change soon. The war had been an expensive business, with loans from the London merchants to Parliament being set at an interest rate of eight percent – and it probably wasn't over yet. With these thoughts in mind, as well as my impending departure in the morning, I felt it best to leave the meeting to find Amelia, and let her know the results of our deliberations. I resolved to raise the problem that it posed with both my father and Governor Whetham. Ideally, I would need a speedy result in respect of Jeanne Rately aka "Joan the Whore" and her so far unknown controllers – if they exist. That would allow me a chance to return to helping my father in the leather business, and some sort of regular income. Serving the Rump Parliament needed more than faith and beliefs.

When I found Amelia in our room, I apprised her of the situation. Much to my surprise, she did not raise any great objections, and expressed a hope that my tasks in Northampton would soon be over.

'Possibly we could live in your father's house, and rent a barn for storing the leather?' she said.

'Aye, 'twould make room enough, but could ye return to housework again, Lia, if we could not house a maid?' She shrugged.

'If needs must, husband, 'tis boring in the hall with nought to keep me busy, no-one to talk with like myself, and Johnny is hardly good company.'

I must be honest and admit that I hadn't considered such a possibility. Boredom for a still young Amelia was not wise. She could dwell on our problems too easily, too much.

'Let us think on't on my return, my love. We will find a solution, I think.' But I was a little less confident than I let on. I still had my bill of exchange, perhaps that would solve much if I exchanged it for gold, but I had not told her how much it was for, nor even, so far, of its existence. Only my father knew of it – and Master Ekins, of course.

It was time to seek our evening meal, so I suggested we go downstairs to the hall, and then did my best to remain cheerful so as to keep up Lia's spirits, especially now that she seemed to have put the early morning's events behind her. I would not want to leave for Northampton wondering what I would be returning to later here in

130

Rushden. When we reached the hall, already the first troop was there, and bawdy jokes were being swapped by the troopers. 'Tha's a good'un,' I heard one say, and guffaws echoed round the hall. I smiled at Lia, and pointed to a trestle nearby.

Having been across to the kitchen and requested food and drink, I returned to my family, and started to make small talk about the nice weather that day.

"Twas pleasant out this day, Lia,' smiling at her.

'Aye, husband, 'twas so. Birds be a-singing, and signs of Spring a'ready. I would we could walk together more,' she said, winking at Johnny, and smiling at him. I, however, sensing her air of tenseness, thought that I should reassure her.

'On the morrow, mayhap I would learn more from Governor Whetham. 'Tis said that the Scots may start war again, and perchance Cromwell be away in Ireland, fighting the Papist forces there afore long. 'Tis quieter in England now, so mayhap the army will go home.'

'There be troops yet at Northampton.' I was a little taken aback; I did not really want to discuss this touchy matter.

'Aye, but Colonel Whalley's regiment was ordered to London, 'tis much troubled there now. Captain Grove be of Whalley's command. Why be he at Rushden, not in London? Methinks he'll be recalled soon.'

At this, one of the troopers, who had heard me, came over and asked that he sit with us.

'Captain, if ye please, quiet your voice. My men fear they be called to Lunnon, may rebel.'

I could not hide my surprise. 'Sergeant, my wife worries about our position here. We but muse about it.' The Sergeant nodded.

'Rumours abound, captain, sir. Some say th' Scots may come south again, loike '48. We ain't not bin paid fer months. They'd go 'um, if'n they could.' It was my turn to nod.

131

'Aye, sergeant. Parliament has no moneys. These be difficult times. Would ye have Charles return?' The sergeant looked at me cautiously.

'We ain't n' be'er orf, be we, cap'n? No pay. Woives, childer starves. Yet Crum'll, if'n he take army t'Irelan', dorn't 'elp any on us, do 'e?'

'Ruling Council governs us folks, man. Not Oliver Cromwell. I met him in London, he's a good man, but he do as Council orders.' The sergeant stood up.

'Arr, s'pose so,' and excused himself before returning to his troopers. I spoke very quietly to Amelia. 'We should take great care with what we say when others are near us, Lia.'

'What passes when ye are in Northampton, husband?'

'I would speak with Master Ekins on't afore I depart.'

A kitchen wench appeared with our jug of small ale and pots, and a pot of milk for Johnny. I smiled my thanks, then I said to Amelia, 'Methinks Johnny could drink small ale now, my dear. If he would have 't.'

She nodded, as the kitchen wench appeared on her way back to us carrying our bowl of potage, bread, and cheese. Wooden plates and spoons were already on the trestle table as usual, so as soon as the wench had put our food down and turned away, I spooned some out onto our plates, and quickly said an approximation of Grace. 'It pleases Amelia some,' I thought to myself. We immediately afterwards tucked in.

After our meal, we went our separate ways again, Amelia and Johnny to the long gallery, I to Ekins' office once more. I knocked, and was summoned.

'Ah, 'tis ye, captain. Methought 'twould be captain Grove.'

I thought it a good lead-in to talking about my departure, and told Ekins of my and Amelia's concerns again, after hearing the sergeant's comments.

132

'H'mmm, as ye say, times be a-changing. The army perchance goes to Scotland, the Council has no money, and dissent grows. Do ye have a suggestion, captain?'

'Dissent be a strong motive, Master John. We have not power to stop 't, lest the Council step in. Men needs must be paid, parish relief be not good for proud men. Or their families. Perchance when I return, ye could pay against the bill of exchange, Master? Mayhap Governor Whetham would arrange regular pay for me, but we needs would move to the city, methinks, work reg'lar for th'army there. Also, what of captain Grove, Master? His regiment may want him back." Ekins looked very thoughtfully at me, and tugged at his beard before he answered me.

'Aye, methought that. What comes after, I know not. Could ye take his place here?' This was a surprise notion coming from Ekins, though one that I had wondered about myself.

'Aye, but I would need pay, too, Master John. I could not work for my father and the army too. There be Amelia - and Johnny - to consider in all this. Did ye know that she be bored here? She needs work or a companion. A companion to talk well with her, not child's talk.' Ekins was himself surprised at this, too. Not having his own wife, he had not thought about it.

'There be much to think on, Robert. I would move Amelia and your Johnny to my wing of the house. I will look after them. More, I cannot promise. Would I had a wife myself, to keep Amelia company. 'Twould be good for both, I think.' I thanked him, and excused myself, then went to my and Amelia's room, to prepare for the journey.

Saturday 10th March 1649.

The next morning, after a night when my nightmares had not been too disruptive to our sleep, we broke our fast together as a family, before I set out again for Northampton. I planned to dine at the Sun inn, then visit Whetham, if I made good time on the journey. My journey did not go quite as planned, however.

133

I had decided to take a quicker route, and so crossed the Nene over the old bridge between Wollaston and Wilby village, which went smoothly; but after the crossroads for Earl's Barton, I was confronted by three rough-looking, ragged characters who had appeared from the scrub land at the side of the highway. They were only armed with staves, one of them ordered me to stop and hand over my money. I pulled out my pistol, took it off half cock, then aimed it in the direction of the one who looked like their leader.

'Well, my fine fellows, which of you would depart this world first?'

I put my spare hand on the grip of my tuck, and slightly pulled the short sword out of its scabbard, before pushing it back with a sharp 'clack'. The would-be highwaymen looked at each other, then thought better of their assault, and ran off the side of the road into the scrubland near to the Nene. I didn't look back, but set my pistol back to half cock, pocketed it again, and spurred my horse until I had left them well behind. It was a somewhat unnerving incident though, which should not have happened on what was an important military road. Before I arrived at Northampton's St Giles gate, I donned my officer's sash, and when I encountered the two sentries was only asked for my password, then was quickly waved through. I was at the Sun inn by midday, was allocated a better room than on my last visit, and was soon in the tap room waiting for my lunch. As before, it was an excellent repast of good lamb and pork potage, with peas and beans, bread and fresh butter, a goodly slice of gammon ham, plus a jug of best ale to wash it all down. It set me up wonderfully for my meeting with the governor. I paid my tally, collected my cloak, and set off on foot for the nearby Guildhall.

At the Guildhall, I had to wait for Whetham to finish his own lunch, before being asked into his office. I used the time well, chatting amiably with two troopers who were waiting to go on guard duty. It was a good opportunity to gently pump them for information. I learnt that this evening, Saturday, is definitely the evening when "Joan the

Whore" would come a-visiting one of the senior officers at the Sun. They didn't know which officer, but she had to enter through the tap room where most officers, including myself, took their meals. It seemed that she had found a new paramour, and was anxious to make good the liaison as quickly as she could. I also learnt that there were troop movements in the offing, as some officers had been given advance notice of moving to the city of Nottingham, prior to mustering for marching North. But my informant didn't know when that would be. I asked about dissenters, but then my informants clammed up. That subject was obviously a very sensitive one, so I asked if they had been paid. No, they hadn't seen any pay for over a year. I commiserated with them, and just said that the Treasurers-at-War had no ready money yet. At this point, I was called into Whetham's office. This time, I was not required to leave my tuck or pistol behind. The staff captain's sash had its advantages, I thought, as much as did getting to know Whetham personally.

I handed my reports to Whetham, who opened and read them quickly but carefully.

'There is yet more,' said I, 'And I have learned more from your troopers in the hall.'

Whetham was clearly interested, and the conversation began in earnest. I recounted the events of the previous morning, as well as my interrogation of Ned Mawle, and followed that with an account of my chat with the Guildhall guards. Whetham was impressed with me.

'Ye has a way with the common troopers, captain. 'Tis good.'

Now was the time to broach the subject of pay and the immediate future. I ran through what I had discussed with John Ekins, and added that if I were to be a successful intelligencer, I did not need financial worry to add to my concerns. Whetham considered this carefully, twirling his moustache as he did so.

'Aye, I do see your predicament, captain. I will tell ye what I may. Troops will go to the North, aye, but that be months away. Of greater import is manning currently in Rushden and Northampton, since there is now little risk of the war starting up again here. Captain Grove will indeed return to his regiment in due time. I know not when, but I knows that George Bishop would replace the garrison troopers. He and I are much concerned at their loyalty, we do not need garrisons that would turn their coat at the first sight of an enemy, the Treaasurers-at-War have not the funds to pay them all that is due, so the troopers' loyalty is questionable. Rushden is to be reduced to six troopers and a sergeant. They could well be under your command. But only if, as ye says, ye be paid as a regular soldier. I will, if ye wish it, recommend it to Secretary Scot. The new garrison would need be at Rushden hall, as now. So ye and your family might remain at the hall. I could not guarantee that the garrison or your position would remain at the hall for more than one season. Ye must see that. Much would depend on what ye discover about "Joan the Whore". I hear say that she may be with the dissenters. If ye can prove it, your future would be altered.' He thought for a few seconds, twirled his wide moustache again before continuing.

'Would it not be better for your son to be here in Northampton? There be a good free grammar school here. No such school in Rushden, I think, or would ye that he might stay with your wife's - uncle? - Tom Rately, in Wellingborough?'

The conversation meandered through other options, leaving me much to ponder when I left his office almost two hours later. I walked Northampton's streets slowly for a time, then decided that I should return to the Sun, freshen up, then eat, and wait for Jeanne Rately. After my return, doing my ablutions and donning fresh clothes, it did not take long after my meal, when, quietly supping my ale, I spotted a woman walking in, dressed impeccably, and with beautifully cut clothes, whom I realised was Jeanne. I approached her at once, and extended a hand.

'Jeanne, is't ye? Robert, your sister Amelia's husband.'

She turned to look at me, looked me up and down, then said, 'I have no sister. Away.'

I took another step forward, blocking her way.

'Mistress, ye are Jeanne Rately, are ye not? Amelia would only know that ye fares well.'

She stopped, looked at me with a disdainful expression on her face,which, close up, was very....lovely.

'Aye, captain, I be she. I know ye not, nor your wife. If ye please, I would pass.'

She brushed past me, and walked over to a staff major who was sitting at the far end of the room, wearing the sash of a regiment that I did not recognise, only the gold stitching as on my own sash and hat ribbon. They clearly knew each other, and ascended the stairs together almost at once. I returned to my ale, then commenced watching for her return. I would remember the face of her military companion, also the colour of his staff major's sash and uniform. Whetham could enlighten me with the regiment and a name; there were few staff majors around. With some care, perhaps she could be tailed, and her home be discovered, I thought. So long as I did not betray myself in the process. Perchance bribe a link boy? There must be link boys aplenty in Northampton. While I was musing over all this, Jeanne reappeared, though the major did not. She looked around, then headed outside. I decided to follow her, but did not want to be seen to do so, so I went into the adjoining room, and left by its side door. I could see Jeanne walking rather shakily away from the inn, so, hanging back while she put more space between herself and the inn, I noted that she walked along the street opposite the inn, then turned left. I walked a bit faster until I reached the corner, and she had disappeared, so I decided to walk further along the street. As I passed what I assumed was Derngate Street, I spotted her walking along it, so turned right and followed her again. She followed the street around a right hand bend, then turned left after about 150 yards into a narrow lane. About twenty yards on she made to enter a set-back house, which I assumed was her home. By the time I reached the dark spot where I last saw her, she was nowhere to be seen. I stood and looked at the house, unsure how to proceed, when suddenly a female voice whispered in my ear.

'Tush, Robbie, are ye so desperate to fuck me that ye follows me home like a lapdog?'

Astonished, I spun round, to find her standing unsteadily in front of me. I could smell her scent, a surprise, since few women – other than whores – wore scent now. She grinned at me.

'Well, Robbie? Are ye desperate?'

I felt her hand on my crotch, squeezing and rubbing, she was almost in my face now, and I could smell her breath, a strange smell. I gripped her arms and pushed her away.

'Jeanne, ye knows I be married. Desist. I would just talk to ye.'

She indicated that I should go with her, and I followed her into her house, which, whilst plain and looking rather shabby outside, with rotting thatch, looked if not luxurious, rather well-appointed inside. Several fragrant candles were lit already, and she turned round and looked up into my face again.

'Come, Robbie, ye knows that ye wants me. Why else follow a whore?'

I pushed her away again, at which she deftly pulled the lacing of her bodice and smock, both of which fell undone, exposing her woman's charms, and slurring her words, then spoke again.

'Am I not lovely, Robbie? Lovelier than your cow Amelia! Come fuck me, Robbie. I'll not charge ye this once,' and giggled.

Shocked, I slapped her across her face, at which she flopped backwards onto a chair set with cushions, and promptly passed out. I looked askance at her, then saw an opportunity. I checked that she was breathing, and shook her, thinking she was but drunk, and might waken. She did not. Again, I noticed the strange smell on her breath, and flushed complexion.

138

I looked around the room, and spotted a large writing box, which I tried to open. It was locked. I looked for the key, but could not see it anywhere, so searched for something to open the lock. I found a large needle, and with that, managed to unlock it. Inside, there were writing materials, 'Odd,' I thought, 'I knew not that she could write.'

I found two, no, three seals, wax, and enciphered letters hidden under the writing materials. One of the seals carried the sign of a sealed knot. 'Evidence enough,' I thought, but then she moaned a little, and passed out again. I thought better of looking further at the box, closed it, and used the needle to lock it, with a little more awkward manipulation of the lever. She was starting to come round a little, so I pulled her up.

'Have ye taken overmuch wine, Jeanne?' She grunted, then a slight shake of her head.

I let her be, then I went into the rear kitchen, found a glass goblet – glass! Expensive, I thought – put some cold water in it from a stoneware jug, then went back and splashed it into her face. She groaned, then groggily sat forward, realised that her bodice was open and pulled it together a little, then held her head in her hands.

'What have ye taken, Jeanne?' She rubbed at her eyes, which were now very bloodshot, and managed to get out, '...my 'pothecary...give me....potion...' before passing out yet again. Some more cold water poured over her head and face. She came round again.

'Over.....m-m-much, R-Robbie. Potion. 'Tis good, dulls the senses... God's blood, my head…...'

I returned to the kitchen, and found what appeared to be a jug of small ale, then poured some into the emptied goblet. I held it for her to drink from. As she came round more, she talked a little.

'Robbie, how thinks ye I may do this…. whoring…. without a potion? 'T gives me…. desire….' Her voice still slurred, but she looked a little better.

'Ye makes much money, Jeanne,' I posited, sweeping my arm

around, indicating her surroundings.

'Aye, aye. 'Tis true. But my looks. When they fade, what would I have then?'

I thought that I would do a little fishing.

'Is't all ye does, Jeanne? Whore for army officers?' She looked at me guiltily now.

"Tis all I may do, Robbie. I be damned anyway.'

'Who were the major this night, Jeanne?' She was instantly alert enough to realise what I was asking.

'I'll not tell ye that.'

'I can find out, woman.' She looked daggers at me. I thought she might spit at me.

'Aye, no doubt. But I'll not tell ye.'

I judged that she would survive now, so bade her farewell, and left her house, carefully scanning the street as I went, in case of an ambush. No-one accosted me, and as I turned right into Swan Street – it was not, as I thought, Derngate Street - it was less dark, a few houses with light showing, so I cautiously walked back to Angel Lane, then Guildhall Street, and came out opposite the Sun inn. I was very relieved to enter its warm tap room again.

Chapter 10: Encounters

Back inside the Sun's comfortable tap room, I ordered a jug of best ale and a penny-pipe of tobacco, and sat in the corner to ponder this evening's events. It was quite a Pandora's box that I was peeping into. My first thought was that Jeanne clearly must hate what she is doing, else why take a potion that maybe could kill her? She was a gorgeous young woman, beautifully dressed, so she should have been able to find a decent husband quite easily, even in these straitened, volatile times. It didn't make sense. Then there were the writing materials in her box, the seals, the enciphered letters – evidence of treason. Firstly, so far as I knew, as most women, she couldn't read or write. Had she learned to? Who had taught her, if so? What was her association with such dangerous bedfellows? I inwardly smiled at my pun, then thought no more of it, as the major whom she had gone upstairs with appeared at the other end of the room. I allowed him to settle, like myself, with a pipe and a jug of ale, and then sidled over to his table, asked if I might join him. The major was happy to share my company. We introduced ourselves. The major gave me his name as Sam Goodly. I chatted amiably with him, then posed the question I was itching to ask.

'Major, I know not your colours. Pray, what regiment do you serve?'

I was surprised at his answer.

'Fairfax's Life Guards. We were to march to London, but I was seconded to Northampton to serve Governor Whetham, much as yourself. These times are trying, methinks.'

He spoke with a very refined accent, which I now understood: what remained of Fairfax's regiment of foot was but twenty gentlemen. Gentlemen. This might be significant! I did not wish to betray any more curiosity, but casually as I could muster, I asked another burning question.

'Ye knows my wife's sister Jeanne, I think. My wife would have

141

news of her.'

The major's eyebrows rose.

'Aye, she is lovely lass. She is called Joan, I may say. Why does your wife need news of Joan, if I may be so bold?' I had my answer ready.

'While I were serving and away, her parents' house were burned. That were in '45, after Naseby, retreating troopers of the king. Her mother died soon after. Then in '47, her father was taken, and my wife heard no more of her. Amelia, my wife, thought her sister be dead." The major looked genuinely sorry.

'Aye, a sorry tale. Many more could say similar, I think.'

"T pleased me much to see her here. I would speak with her soon, my wife would be pleased greatly to hear she be well.'

I changed the topic of conversation, and the impending move of troops to the North.

'I do hope I would not be for service in the North. There be many rumours. My Amelia would be sore upset, if the army take me away from her again. We were parted for more than five year.'

My new-found friend nodded a commiserative nod.

'Aye, my wife too. My wife is in Essex, near the village of Grays. If I were not ordered to stay in Northampton, I would be close to her. 'Tis not far from the Tower to Grays. My regiment was at Naseby, many other battles. I have fought across England these seven years.'

'Ye were at Naseby? My regiment, too. I were in Cromwell's second line of horse troops.'

We spent the next hour or so chatting about our war experiences, getting more inebriated as the evening wore on, and eventually departed for our beds, apparently firm friends. I was well pleased with my progress. I decided to approach Governor Whetham in the morning, after writing up what would be now a rather long report.

The door of my room had a bolt, which I decided to make use of.

I struggled to get undressed, and ready to retire, when there was a knock at the door. I picked up my knife, then cautiously pulled back the bolt and opened the door a little. There was a young boy standing there, who passed me a sealed letter, then turned and left without a word. I closed and bolted the door again. I slipped my knife under the seal – which I did not recognise – and opened the letter. It was nonsense, and made not the slightest sense to me.

'My dear James, the crow has flown. Ye must await its return. The cow is back in the field. She must be milked soon. God keep ye. 23.'

I read and reread it, but it made little more sense. '23', I deduced, must be code for an intelligencer – but for which side? Who was James? Who are the 'crow' and the 'cow'? Then as I remembered that someone else had this room before I did, I must find out who that was. But the 'crow' and the 'cow' made no sense – unless the 'cow' could be Jeanne/Joan. Maybe. I thought that I might have received the letter by mistake; as a precaution, I pulled a chair across so that if anyone entered via the door, not impossible, despite its bolt, in the dark they would walk into the chair, make a noise and wake me. I looked around for another obstacle, and decided to move the small table to a position where anyone avoiding the chair would probably walk into that, too. God's blood, I was getting paranoid! No, better safe than sorry. At that I retired to my bed, but not before checking my pistol was at half cock, and putting it and my knife in the bed beside me. I was soon asleep, though did not sleep very well. I was too tense and anxious, as well as perhaps too inebriated to sleep properly.

I woke only around two hours later, needing my piss-pot, and then was wide awake, and my mind set to work, thinking about Jeanne/Joan. She was so different to Amelia. Younger, yes, but full of life, and….no, maybe not that. Maybe her attempt to get me to have sex with her was just the potion...but would Amelia be so….forward, so bold and unafraid, even with a potion? Women simply did not do such bold things. Was Jeanne or Joan trying to entrap me into her world of espionage? Or was she…..? What? Being used? God's blood, she was so lovely! She could entrap Oliver Cromwell himself, I thought, grinning to myself. How much to tell Whetham? I thought for a while, and then decided that I should watch for her at the Sun, then slip out, making sure I wasn't followed, go to her house, break in, and search more thoroughly. If I told Whetham about the seal with the sealed knot motif, she would be arrested, and…...what, beaten? Put to the hot irons? I shuddered. No, I could not let her suffer that. I needed to know more, much more. Could I persuade her to talk to me? Would she talk more readily if I fu...no, mustn't think like that. I couldn't break faith with Amelia – and her sister might yet give me the pox. It was not far from dawn when I finally slept again.

Sunday 11th March 1649.

I was woken by the Guildhall clock striking seven, and my head was pounding. There was a pail of cold water in my room, so I stripped off my night clothing, and thoroughly washed myself. The cold water brought me round to something near full wakefulness, and a good towelling with the coarse linen towel hanging by the door completed the exercise. My beard had grown, and I really must find a barber, I thought. Donning clean clothing, dressing as far as my coif, I put the pistol in my pocket, folded the letter and secreted it in my doublet, then donned my sash and trusty knife, and I was ready to break my fast. My stomach lurched somewhat at the thought of food, but I gingerly descended the stairs, and called to a tap room wench for small ale and food, then sat near where I made friends with staff major Goodly the night before. Goodly, however, was nowhere to be seen, even though the room was close to full with army officers of two or three different regiments.

The wench brought me a jug of small ale in a pewter jug, with a pewter pot. I was astonished to see pewter in an inn. Next she brought a plate of boiled eggs, bread, butter, and fish. I realised that it was Sunday. The light breakfast suited me in my present state, and whilst I ate it more slowly than usual, I watched the goings-on at the other tables scattered along the lengthy room. There was nothing out of the ordinary to take my attention. I sat still for a while after eating my fill, gradually feeling better as I drank more, and the solid food quieted my very unsettled stomach. Eventually my head cleared, and I began to think clearly and objectively again. I realised that I must go back to my room, and would need quill, ink, and several sheets of paper. When the taproom wench appeared, I requested the writing materials and implements, and headed with them back to the room.

Someone had rifled through my belongings while I was eating breakfast. It mattered little, since I had no papers or anything else of use to an intelligencer except what I had in my doublet's secret pocket – and, of course, I was wearing the doublet. Before commencing to write, I was careful to bolt the door again. I set up the table so that I more or less faced the door, with the light from the small window falling on the table. I spent the next hour composing and writing my reports. I had decided to leave out anything about finding the seals, particularly the sealed knot one, though mentioning writing materials in Jeanne's house – but not the box – could be risking her arrest. I folded each report carefully and put it in my doublet's inner pocket with the letter from the night before. I checked my pistol, made sure my knife was secure in its sheath and easily reached, and donned my belt and tuck. Then I put on my cloak and hat, and went downstairs to set out for Governor Whetham's office. Five minutes walk later, I was sitting in the Guildhall, waiting Whetham's pleasure and admittance to his office. A senior officer came out of Whetham's office, and after a few more minutes' wait, Whetham came to his door, and signalled to me to come in. He was surprised to see me so soon after the meeting the day before.

He was even more surprised to read my account of the evening.

The most surprising aspect of my report to colonel Whetham was discovering that he had a staff major of whom he had never heard, and of whose presence at the Sun inn he was totally unaware. Banging his desk in a fit of temper, his Dorset accent suddenly came to the fore.

'Am Oi nart Gov'nor o' this city? Why be this...this...stranger 'ere in our midst, 'n' Oi nart be told? What says ye, captain?' I was more than a little taken aback by his ferocious anger, and stammered.

'I could not say, c-c-colonel. Just w-what he told me.' Whetham looked at me, red-faced. 'M-m-mayhap I could discover more, colonel.'

Whetham's flash of temper subsided into simmering anger.

'If ye please, captain, join me in a sack.' He poured a goblet of the fortified wine each, and handed one to me. We sipped the wine for a minute or two.

'Robert, ye did well to bring 't to me. I must wroite to Tom Scart this day, by fast post roider. Oi'll 'ave arnswers, by 'eaven, Oi will!' He banged his fist on the desk again, making me jump. I thought that I might make a point, and change the subject a little at the same time.

'Colonel, if I may. I would learn more of our Jeanne or Joan, however she be known; the major too. But, what of her previous paramour, major Berry? How came he here?'

The governor looked at me with an eyebrow raised.

'I can vouch for Jim Berry, captain.'

'So do Joan seek to discover secrets of these majors, or do Sam Goodly be here to....to....help her? Or do we see it wrong, perchance?'

Whetham stroked and pulled at his beard, studying me pensively before answering.

'Captain, this whore, your sister in law, would she have ye fuck her, ye says? Think ye she did the same with our major?'

'She were with him an hour or more. Upstairs, colonel. Do looks deceive, perchance? I should search our major's chamber, I think. And I will seek to search Joan's house while she be with the major next.' I thought for a second or two. 'Colonel, what say ye order the major to

146

come to ye here. Talk with him yourself, while I search his chamber.'

Whetham thought, then nodded slowly.

'Aye, captain, I will to't this day. For two of the clock – nay, three a-clock. Ye needs must watch for his leaving the Sun.'

'Aye, sir. 'Tis a good plan.'

I took my leave of Whetham, after agreeing to visit him in his quarters in Haselrigge House that evening. It would be a good walk across the city, but I would find a link boy to show me the way, since I did not yet know Northampton well enough myself.

Back at the Sun, I asked for a jug of small ale and a penny-pipe of tobacco, and sat in a corner of the tap room, watching the comings and goings, whilst ruminating at length about the recent events. So much in one short day! I had not exposed Jeanne to Whetham's gaolers – yet. But the clock was ticking for that ever more loudly. I must get to the bottom of her involvement as quickly as I could. Major Goodly appeared from upstairs at the other end of the room, saw me, and sidled over, a little unsteadily. Doffing his hat, he greeted me, and asked to sit with me. I was pleased to let him. In a few minutes, Goodly too was puffing at a penny-pipe of tobacco, and supping at his ale. He looked somewhat the worse for wear.

'God's blood, Robert, the ale here! My head throbs as if 'twere beaten with Thor's hammer. I drank wine too. Too much, too much.'

He sat and rubbed his forehead, then closed his eyes and rubbed them too. They looked so red that he struggled to keep them open. I felt some sympathy for him, but then thought better of it. Wine and best ale? The man's a fool! Or is he? Is it an act? We had been intermittently exchanging some innocuous chat, when a cornet came in the door, looked around, spotted major Goodly, and passed him a letter, saying that he was summoned to Governor Whetham's office in the Guildhall at three o'clock. Goodly looked surprised, then put out. He thanked the cornet, then groaned and rubbed his head some more.

'What does he want, Robert? Ye talks with him, I think?' I

shrugged.

'Mayhap expects ye do him the courtesy of meeting him and introducing yourself.'

Goodly squinted at me through his bloodshot eyes.

'Aye, 'twill be that. If I can discover his office.'

'Out of the door there, turn right. Along the street. The Guildhall cannot be missed. Up the stairs and announce yourself to the guards, one will lead you.' He thanked me, then leaned back in the chair, closed his eyes. I thought that I would probe a little.

'Do ye lie with Joan, Sam? 'Twould be a good coupling, I'll warrant,' with a broad smile and a wink.

"Tis not your business, Robert.' came his curt reply.

'Oh, come, come, major, Joan be a comely lass that any man would wish to lie with,' with a grin. Goodly, however, was not amused. 'I would not betray my wife so, Robert. 'Twould break her heart.' I thought it best to apologise and say no more. 'I thought ye went with her,' I said, lamely, and let the subject drop.

Our conversation stuttered on, then all at once, Sam said, 'What do ye do here, Robert?'

I was at once on my guard.

'My place be in Rushden. I bring reports to Governor Whetham, discuss them, take reports back. Keep an eye out for them Diggers, too.'

'Diggers, indeed? Here?' I thought 'that's interesting – he's unaware of them?'

'Aye, hereabouts. Wellin'borough mostly. They don't cause mischief, but 't seems the Council frets about them.' The major showed sudden interest.

'Why would that be, Robert?' I thought that I would stir things up a little.

'I know not, major. Cromwell had their leaders arrested a while back. Joan's father be a Digger.' From Sam Goodly's raised eyebrows and paling face, I had obviously struck a nerve. 'Oh, aye. Joan's father be Tom Rately. I know him well. He be no mischief maker, I think.'

Sam's surprise was evident, as he said, 'Well, well. Joan will not be a chip off the block, methinks. Whores are always mischief makers.'

I thought to myself, 'how knows he that she be a whore, if he knows her not, and lies with her not?' but decided to play dumb. 'Joan keeps some officers happy, I think. She be bold, but not....bright.' The major looked at me pensively. Maybe he was musing about me as much as I was musing about Goodly himself. We had been talking about two hours now. I heard the Guildhall clock strike twelve, and thought it would soon be time to eat. I had already had a busy and long morning, one that raised many more questions than it provided answers. I spotted a taproom wench and called her over. 'Mistress, when will food be ready, if ye please?'

'Not long. What would ye have, maister?'

I asked for small ale and whatever food would be ready, as it came. My companion shook his head. 'I would wait a while, wench.'

Half an hour later, the taproom wench returned with jug and pot in hand, pewter ones, as before, placed them before me.

'Good inn, this, Sam.' The major nodded.

'Aye. Pewter pots and plates are hard to come by in inns these days.'

I poured myself a pot of small ale, and took a swig.

"Tis a goodly ale they serve, indeed. All this chat makes a man dry.' I smiled at my companion, who smiled back, but with more than a touch of insincerity, I reckoned.

'Is your chamber good, Sam?'

"Tis comfortable.'

'Where be your chamber, Sam? I have a chamber at the back. 'Tis comfortable. Quiet, too.'

'Mine is at the front. Not so quiet. I would prefer 'twere up another floor.'

'So ye're down here, Sam?'

'Nay, first floor. Too close to the street. Market starts early.'

I nodded. It would help me find the major's room after he had gone to see Whetham. Our conversation tailed off somewhat, when the wench appeared carrying a tray with a bowl of steaming potage, bread, butter, some sliced meats, and some form of brown pickle. It smelled delicious as she placed it on the table in front of me, and turned to go. I addressed Sam.

'My wife would that I say Grace now. A man loses the habit in the army. The food smells too good for such ... religious nonsense.' I grinned at Sam, and started to tuck in.

The major looked a little pained, but said nothing, just watched me tucking noisily into the potage. I was of course really enjoying it. The Guildhall clock struck one just after I finished eating, and patted my stomach, then belched loudly.

'That was good indeed, Sam. I would that the food at Rushden hall were half as good.'

My companion adopted an air of disgust.

"Tis clear to all the taproom that ye enjoys your food, Robert. I would get mine own shortly. If ye please, excuse me for now.' He stood, gave a slight bow, and walked out to the privy, which was outside in the inn's rear yard. I was happy to be on my own for a while, so that I had time to think about our conversation. I realised that staff major Sam Goodly had something to hide. The question was, what. Also, what was his relationship with Joan – if indeed, there was one? He went upstairs apparently with her the evening before, but did they go to his room? Did they do so for the purpose of a session with a whore, or for another reason?

I had sat thinking for long enough; it was time to get to work. It would be more than an hour and a half before Sam Goodly set off to see Whetham. I decided to return to my room for a while, and come back down soon after three o'clock. I could use the time to write another report; it would be useful for when I myself went to see Whetham at Haselrigge House. I had kept the paper, ink, quill and sand shaker. Now I got them out, and tentatively started writing. It was hard to describe both what transpired and my thoughts on how they fitted together. I had been writing for some time, when I heard the Guildhall clock strike three. I put the writing materials away, and was careful to fold the paper and commit it to my doublet's secret pocket, away from prying eyes. I went downstairs, and found the landlord.

'Pray remind me, sir, if ye please, which chamber is major Goodly's?'

The landlord thought for a second. 'Chamber three on the first floor. But he has left some minutes ago.'

I feigned a casual reply. 'Aye, 't matters not. I would leave him a note.'

Having thanked the landlord, I went back upstairs, and found Goodly's room – it had a Roman three, III, on its door, easy for maids who could not read to identify it. The door was locked, as I expected. I tried my own key. Of course, it did not fit properly, but with some wiggling around, I managed to get the bolt back, and entered the room. The room was unexpectedly tidy, and the major had a writing box similar to Jeanne's. I had a large needle – I had thought to bring one – and rapidly unlocked it. Looking carefully through the sheets of paper, and two seals, there was nothing incriminating, even the seals were mere family crests. Then I noticed something: there was a second small bottle of ink, except that it was not normal ink. It had a pale yellowish colour. Invisible ink? I carefully examined the sheets of paper again, but slanting them against the light elicited no hint of secret writing. I decided to lock the box, then have a look at what else was in the room. There was nothing obvious to rouse suspicions. Goodly had a leather case which bore his initials carved into the leather, S.H.G. Then something struck me. A staff major in Fairfax's employ would surely have something with the army cipher on it; there was nothing of the sort. The man was simply too careful too; that alone roused suspicion. I made sure that there were no tell-tale signs of my intrusion, then looking very carefully out of the door along the corridor each way, I left quickly, and with some difficulty managed to trip the latch again. I slipped quietly back to my own room, then sat and thought carefully about what I knew. I was no further forward. Maybe Whetham's letter to Tom Scot would elicit some information. But that would be two or three days away yet, if not more. I needed a different plan of attack. Could I perhaps recruit a maid to keep her eyes open for me? Then another thought struck me. Did Jeanne or Joan the Whore have a maid? Surely, she must do. Bribery, maybe? But then, whores' maids were usually loyal, so not easy to recruit. Mayhap bribery could get a street urchin to keep watch and report back to me for a few pennies.

I thought it worth asking downstairs if there were a reliable link boy used by the inn. A link boy sees much, hears much. Now there's a thought! It would not be dark when I set out for Haselrigge House, so I could perhaps borrow a stable lad or a lad employed for menial tasks in the inn or its kitchen as a guide, ask for him to be fed at the house, then have him light the way back. That would give ample opportunity to sound him out. Have to be careful what you say to such lads, though, or they'll tell you what they think you want to hear; pay too much, and it has the same effect.

Another possibility could be to visit Jeanne unexpectedly during the day. What would her reaction be, I wondered. Maybe as a last resort use some ….. persuasion, like the sharp knife. That didn't look like a good option for the moment, though.

I realised that I had been thinking about Sam Goodly and Jeanne, and mulling over my options for quite a while when Sam Goodly walked in. He looked a little flustered, so I waved and called to him, and signalled to him to come and join me.

152

'Ye looks a little put out, Sam. Would ye care to join me in a good ale?'

Sam smiled weakly at me, and indicated that he would indeed welcome some good ale and company, so I called to the taproom wench. 'Another pot and a jug of good ale, if you please, wench.'

It took her very little time to fill a jug from one of the barrels, bring another pot and deposit them on the table.

I winked at her. 'I thank ye kindly.' This wench seemed particularly friendly, and I thought it worthwhile making the most of that; she might just be useful. After she returned to her post, I turned to Goodly.

'How did ye find the Governor, Sam?' The other looked at me with a tired expression.

'He is a hard man, Robert. I felt that I was being …. interrogated.' I feigned sympathy.

'Be that so, Sam? He be very direct, I think. But, surely ye have not given him cause to interrogate ye, perchance?' Goodly looked a little guilty.

"Twould seem so, my man. I have done nought to give him cause, surely.' He squirmed in his chair. 'He says that he knows Tom Fairfax, believes he should know all Fairfax's majors, but not myself. He does not trust me, I think.' I answered, with as much sincerity as I could feign.

'He were same with me. He places much on knowing a man.' After this, I thought it best to change the subject to my forthcoming visit to Whetham.

'He has summoned me to sup with him at his quarters this night, Sam. Mayhap he has't in mind to interrogate me too,' and laughed.

Sam smiled weakly at me, but did not laugh. I thought that perhaps he sensed the insincerity in my joke.

We chatted until the Guildhall clock struck five, then Goodly said,

153

'Robert, captain, I must take my leave of ye. I wish ye well with the Governor this night.'

He stood, doffed his hat, saluted, and left to return to his chamber. I signalled to the taproom wench to come over. She came to my table, and I asked her to sit with me for a short while. First, I asked her name. She told me it was Emma.

'Well, mistress Emma, may I ask ye, what do ye know of major Goodly? He ….. interests me.'

She looked a little puzzled. 'Why, cap'n, what do 'ee ask o' me?'

I tried to put it diplomatically.

'Mayhap ye cleans his chamber? See his comings and goings? I would know him a little better, that be all.'

"Ee would I be yer spy, sir?'

I thought that was rather bluntly put, and looked around for flapping ears.

'I would pay ye, if that be your concern.'

"Ow much, sir?'

I looked intently at her.

'What is your pay at the inn, lass?'

She looked back just as intently.

'Two silver pennies a week, sir. I may get more for, er, extra services.'

I kept a straight face.

'Very well, Emma. For good, honest information, a silver penny a day. I do not ask ye to put yourself in danger, I stress.'

Her eyes lit up.

"Tis a goodly offer sir. My 'and on't.'

We briefly shook hands, as I scanned the room for prying eyes and ears again, and found none. I thought that I would do a little fishing.

'Methought that the major, er, entertained Joan the Whore in his chamber. Yet he swears not. Do ye know of't?'

She looked at me sharply.

"Twould be val'ble information, sir. I shouldn't tell such tales. Fer three pennies, I would tell 'ee.'

She cautiously held out her hand, palm uppermost.

'Three? Mayhap two be enough?'

'Joan be bad news, sir. 'Ee says no danger. I would not have a bodkin in my ribs.'

Well, I thought, that's interesting!

'Three it be.'

She looked around nervously.

"E do, b't they dun't lie together. I hear't 'em talkin'. 'E give 'er le'ers, methinks. She take 'em som'ere. Oi dun't knows where. Oi knows where 'e gets 'em though. But that'll be more, sir.'

'Would ye come outside, Emma? Too near flappin' ears here.'

We walked outside, with me slapping her bottom and laughing, as if I were after a tad of whoring. We moved away from the inn, to where we couldn't be overheard.

'Two pennies, Emma?'

'Three, 'n' Oi shows 'ee.'

'Done.'

She took my hand, and led me along Guildhall Street, near the fifth house, where she turned up a narrow alley.

'Winder, four along. See thet missin' pane? 'E stops there, t' piss agin the wall. If'n ye watch 'im careful loike, 'ee'll see him pass le'er through the pane. Sometoime, 'e puts 'un in, other toime, takes 'un out.'

I can only say that I was most grateful.

'Four penn'orth, lass. Seven pence for ye.'

She took it quickly, and hid it in her bodice.

155

'Thank'ee koindly, sir.'

I led her back to the inn, where we walked in holding hands, and giggling, as if we had come from an assignment against a wall rather than what we actually did. She played her part remarkably well, I thought. Maybe she spied for anyone, for a price? She played a dangerous game, after all! What I would have to tell Whetham… or should I?

Chapter 11: Emma, 'Arry and Espionage

I had much to mull over, but I realised that it was time to borrow a lad from the inn, and make my way to Haselrigge House for my supper and meeting with Whetham. I found the landlord, and asked if I might borrow a lad to guide me. The landlord found me a slightly ragged looking youth of about fourteen who could be spared. His name, I discovered, was Jem. He knew the city well, and was easily able to take me to Haselrigge House, proving to be a surprisingly open and interesting companion for one so young and uneducated. I cautiously pumped him for information about my fellow officers at the inn, then raised the thorny subject of "Joan the Whore". Jem was clearly not happy to hear her name mentioned. I sought to calm his fears by telling the lad that she was my sister-in-law, and I wanted to learn more about her for my wife. Jem would have none of it.

'Why so fearful, Jem?' He kept his mouth tightly closed.

We passed All Hallows church, then Drapery, and entered a narrow road opposite, which I learned from Jem was Gold Street. Gold Street was quiet, barely a soul about, but as we passed a dark alley two assailants burst out of the alleyway, and the leader ran at me from behind, waving a long dagger.

'Oi tol' 'ee ter fergit Joan, an' not come back! Now 'ee pays th' proice!'

I instinctively pulled my short dagger out of its sheath with my left hand, spinning round to my right as the man tried to bring his dagger up to my throat. My assailant was not fast enough, as I deployed an old soldier's trick, put my shoulder into the man's chest, sweeping my assailant's arm upwards with my own right arm, and slammed the sharp dagger into his ribs with my left hand, straight into his liver, pulling the sharp knife to the right before I withdrew it. The man staggered, sank to his knees, then keeled over dead in a second or two as a major artery dumped his blood pressure. The second man wasn't so bold, and turned to run, though I tried in vain to catch him. Jem looked on, meanwhile, wide-eyed in astonishment and admiration. I returned to him, and beckoned him forward, after wiping my knife on the man's ragged jerkin. Jem helped me turn the man onto his back.

'Know ye him?'

Jem shook his head.

'Oi've see' 'un afore, sir, but dunno who 'e be.'

I did a quick search of the man's clothing, but it revealed nothing.

'Oi 'eard what 'e said, sir. That be why Oi wun't talk 'bout Joan. 'Er be piys'n.'

'He can't hurt ye now, lad. I would pay well for anything ye could tell.'

The lad shook his head. I thought it better not to press him any further, as we continued along Gold Street, then Marefair, to Haselrigge House. I rapped the large iron knocker, then was asked in by an usher, and brought Jem with me.

'Would ye feed the lad well, take him to the kitchen, if ye please?'

The usher nodded, and told Jem to wait where he was, took my cloak and tuck, then showed me into the great hall, where Whetham was sitting smoking a pipe. I heard the usher telling the lad to go with him, and their footsteps faded away somewhere in the house.

I went through the formalities with Whetham, following which the latter introduced me to his wife Joanne, who had just come in to join us. I thought them most gracious hosts, as we all sipped wine and exchanged small talk. Whetham saw that I was a little dishevelled, then noticed some blood on my doublet.

'Have ye been in a fight, captain?'

I recounted the story of my attackers, leaving out any reference to "Joan the Whore" for now, and asked for Whetham to arrange for the man's body to be removed and the affair smoothed over with the city's constable and watch. Whetham rang a small bell, and the usher appeared again. They had a brief whispered conversation, then the usher departed.

'Consider it done,' said Whetham. A few moments later, a butler appeared, and bade us go to the dining room, where supper was served.

I was led into the dining room on the arm of Joanne Whetham. I was astonished at the lovely fare set out on the long carved oak table. Courses of game, chicken, lamb, and a variety of pies and sweetmeats. Unlike the fare set out for nobility or royalty, it was not highly decorated, but it was beautifully presented in a plain, unpretentious way. The three of us took our chairs, with Nat Whetham at the head of the table, his wife on his left, and me on his right. The butler proceeded to serve us the delights spread out on the table, along with a superb red wine and good ale. I had not seen or eaten such fare since '47, when my troop brought King Charles to Hampton Court Palace – and this was better than even Hampton Court's kitchen provided. The Governor and his wife certainly did not stint themselves. After we had eaten our fill, Whetham asked me to accompany him to his private closet, whilst Joanne sought the company of her maids in the saloon of this capacious old house. The meeting was now ready to start.

Whetham was the first to speak, after we had settled into his comfortable closet, with a good sack and a pipe of tobacco each.

'Your attackers, captain, were they those who attacked ye before in your room at the Sun?'

'Aye, Governor, I would judge them so. The one that tried to stick me said I did not heed his warning to leave Joan alone. But what may we learn from that? He were a poor assassin, forsooth, and I be not so sure that Joan knows about it.'

Whetham's eyebrows shot up.

'So what think ye, Robert?'

I thought a moment before answering.

'I do think that more be at play here.'

Whetham looked pensive, as we looked at each other waiting for the conversation to continue.

'What do ye think of major Goodly, sir?'

'I think he be not what he seems. I have asked Tom Scot about him. What do ye think, Robert?'

'He be very educated, refined, not like army officers I know. He seems, well, too sensitive, too quick to turn his nose up at me.'

'H'mmm. So methought, too. He could be a king's man, I think. I know not his real name. He be evasive. But who be his commander? I cannot say.'

We sat there puffing at our pipes, both looking and feeling pensive now. I spoke first.

'I hear that he do not lie with Joan, though they tarry in his chamber for an hour or more. I also hear that he passes letters through the window of a house near the Sun.'

At this, Whetham's eyebrows shot up again.

'Do he now? God's blood! He works for someone, I think, but the army? I think not. Ye must watch him more, Robert. And Joan. She mayhap would respond to my gaol keeper's persuasion.'

I inwardly groaned at the thought.

'There may be a better way, sir. As ye knows, she wants to lay with me.'

Whetham laughed.

'Oh, ye're a good catch, Robert! But she be your sister-in-law, is that not so? Quite a hussy, methinks. 'Twould be illegal.'

I nodded.

'Aye, she be poison. She be so pretty, sir, hard to resist her charms. But 'twould give me a way into her house.'

'Or mayhap she into your chamber, captain!'

He grinned widely, and slapped me on the leg.

'Ye would not disappoint her, I think.'

He winked at me, but I blushed at the thought. I had been faithful to Amelia all these years of separation, and now….. this.

'Oh, tush, captain. I jest. But I take your point. Go to it, man. Do your duty. 'Twould not be a hard task.'

"Twould break Amelia's heart, Governor.'

'Then tell her not, man!'

'Aye, but should I get the clap off her, what would I say to Amelia then? What of my marriage?'

Silence descended on the room as both of us realised the implication of this conversation. Whetham was playing a dangerous game with my life now. And Joan was the spark that could ignite the gunpowder store. I wondered what Oliver Cromwell would think of this exchange between me and Whetham.

Whetham was the first to resume speaking.

'Ye must use your discretion, captain. Your task is to get the information that I and Tom Scot need, by whatever means ye deem necessary, even if ye must lay with Joan.'

I nodded cautiously, and thoughts of Joan flashed through my mind.

'Aye, sir. I will to't. Joan may yield much, if I play it well. But torture in your gaol? Nay, I could not. My wife would know. My family has suffered enough, methinks.'

The Governor did not demur, but reminded me that torture was always there as a last resort.

'I be not a barbarian, Robert. I be a family man, too, ye knows.'

'H'mm,' I thought to myself. 'And what would your family think of this conversation, I wonder?'

Our conversation gradually petered out as the effects of alcohol, good food, and the latening hour took their toll on the two of us. I realised that I had a possibly perilous walk back to the Sun, and sought to take my leave. Whetham bade me wait until his wife had joined us, and had a chance to get to know me better; no doubt he wanted her opinion of me. He called the usher and asked him to fetch Joanne.

Joanne walked in a minute or so later, and joined us. She was a most gracious lady, of about forty years, expensively and elegantly dressed, but not ostentatiously or showily bedecked in jewellery or other baubles, just small pearl earrings, and a fine gold necklace with a · locket. I thought her most charming and indeed handsome. We all exchanged small talk for about twenty minutes, at which point I again begged to be permitted to leave. My host called the usher, and my blood-spattered cloak and tuck were brought – the sight of which roused a small shudder from Joanne. He also brought a now ruddy-cheeked Jem, who looked very pleased with himself, and carrying a link ready for the walk back. I offered my host and his wife my most grateful thanks for a lovely evening and the excellent repast, also offering the couple my carefully crafted compliments about the meal so as not to sound overly flattering. They were graciously received, and both Whetham and Joanne conferred God's good luck on me, before I collected Jem, and we departed from the house. We walked back briskly, with me anxiously scanning every alleyway we passed.

Jem joked, 'Sir, 'ee'll know every jetty in Northam'ton by toime we're back!'

'Better safe than sorry, son,' and winked at him.

We got back to the inn with no further incident, much to my relief, and Jem turned to me beaming.

'Oi'll see if'n Oi c'n get 'ee more on Joan, sir. 'Twould be moi thankin' 'ee fer a foine ev'nin'!'

He was clearly impressed at my close relationship with Whetham and his wife. I smiled at him.

162

'My pleasure, lad.'

I was in for another worrying shock when I entered the taproom: Emma had been found in the back yard with her throat cut. "Joan the Whore" indeed, if it were to protect her, or whoever she worked for, was poison indeed, a very dangerous woman to know. But why kill this poor, innocent young woman? A sharp warning, surely, would have sufficed. As I realised, the threat was aimed at I myself, not truly because of Emma's help a few hours ago. Jem would need to be carefully warned not to risk his own life. I was rapidly learning the risks of intelligencing in these febrile times. Who, however, was the key to it all? I must find out, and quickly.

Back in my room, I could not get my mind off the thought that I had caused Emma's death, perhaps I had been too careless; perhaps she had talked; perhaps we had been seen opposite the house with the broken window. The thoughts went on and on, round and round. With each new spin of thought, my sense of guilt grew greater and greater, my anxiety ever deeper. I was tired and the effects of alcohol were taking their toll, so after a while of tossing and turning, I fell into a troubled sleep.

That night, my nightmares returned with a vengeance. This time, however, it was Jeanne's lovely face taunting me, and the sight of Emma's bloodied body languishing in the back yard. I awoke, not screaming, but with a sense of terror, and sweating profusely. Sleep would not sit comfortably with me for more nights to come. I began to feel that I was becoming a wreck, a shadow of my once youthful, healthy self. It was not a good feeling.

Monday 12th March 1649.

The following morning, it was a morose, bleary-eyed, pale Robert Barker that came down to break my fast. I barely responded to my fellow officers' cheery 'good morrows', and when Sam Goodly came and sat with me, I barely spoke. Sam asked me what was wrong.

'I am much troubled, Sam. I may not talk about 't. I must to

Governor Whetham's chamber this morning.'

'Come, Robert, the Governor is not so bad, surely? He would not roast ye upon an open fire!'

I smiled but weakly, as my head spun again.

"Tis not the Governor, Sam. My troubles be elsewhere.'

After eating, indeed leaving much of my breakfast of eggs, ham, bread and butter, I went back to my room, and lay down for a while. It did not help, so I dressed to go out, and headed for the Guildhall. When I reached the Guildhall, Whetham had not yet arrived, and I had to sit in the guardroom and sup small ale with one of the guards while I waited. I took the opportunity to ask the guard what he knew of Jeanne/Joan. The guard was aware of her, but, put simply, knew no more than rumour.

'What is rumoured, trooper?'

'Joan would kill to protect her position. 'Tis said she killed a maid at the Sun yesternight. Cut her throat from ear to ear, 'tis said, sir.'

I felt both my temper rising and a growing sense of despair.

'Trooper, that be hardly rumour. Who but Joan would do't to a simple kitchen maid?'

The trooper reddened.

'Aye, 'tis so. Joan be said as vicious. Poison. Jealous, ye sees. Maid had a.... a…...an … assig..nation with an officer, 'tis said. Joan did't out of jealousy.'

'H'mm. 'Tis not oft that a woman of such beauty and wealth as Joan be envious of a kitchen maid.' The trooper looked at me quizzically, but said no more, and we sat in silence until Whetham came in a little after eight of the clock. He went straight to his office. The trooper waited a few minutes, then went out with me in tow, and knocked on Whetham's door.

'What is't? I would not be disturbed, man.'

164

I pushed past the trooper.

'Development, sir. I fear we needs must speak.'

Whetham scowled, then told me to enter and close the door.

I recounted what had happened to Emma, and the rumours about it, as well as my own disquiet about it all. Whetham was not in a good temper.

'Welcome to intelligencing, captain. Ye must condition yourself to't. There be much more at stake than a mere maid.'

I felt chastened, but Whetham continued.

'I have a letter from Tom Scot this morrow. We thought right about major Goodly. Scot knows of a Major Sam Goodhay, but he be in London yet. With his regiment. Your Sam Goodly be an impostor.'

I was too tired to even register surprise. Whetham continued.

'He may yet be of use to me, to ye. Ye needs find urchins to watch the house with the broken window. Prove Emma's claim – or not. Ragamuffins that would not turn a head. Do't, and do't quickly.'

I nodded.

'Aye sir. 'Twill be done. But Joan. I would watch her closely. Mayhap visit her house. She be a vixen! I never knew a woman with such cunning.'

It was Whetham's turn to nod.

'If ye please, leave me in peace, man. Get to your tasks.' He flapped a dismissive hand at me.

I stood, saluted, and left. On my way back to the Sun, I thought much about my next steps. First, I would go back to the taproom, get a jug of best ale, then to my room to try to get some sleep. I was too tired and anxious to think clearly. Then a good lunch, after which I would walk to Joan's house, on the way seek to pick up a street ragamuffin who looked like a possible leader, and get him to assemble a group to watch the message drop. Then I would eat supper early, and try to relax more, before retiring early too. It sounded like a fair plan.

Back at the Sun, I called for a jug of best ale and a penny-pipe of tobacco, and sat in the near empty room, puffing at the pipe, whilst I drank the ale, and thought about Amelia and home. That made me feel even more unsettled and guilty, so I transferred my thoughts back to Northampton, and the prosperity, yet run-down atmosphere, of this bustling fortified city. Despite the years of war – its fortifications were much strengthened by late '43 after the army moved in – it had clearly done well from the money spent by the troopers and the army quartermaster's department. The latter supplied all kinds of equipment, luxuries, food and so on. So different to Rushden and Wellingborough, which had suffered greatly, and were now impoverished, as indeed were many towns in the area. My father had sold hundreds of pairs of army boots to the quartermaster's department, and he too had prospered; so I could not be too critical of Northampton's merchants and tradespeople. Even in wartime, some need to prosper so that the rest may pick up some of the crumbs from their table. Having finished the ale and the pipe, I paid, and retired to my room, which appeared not to have been rifled or disturbed, even by a chamber maid. I took off my cloak and hat, then doublet and boots, sidearms, even shirt, bolted the door, and took to the bed. A troubled sleep soon overtook me, and that gave way to a deep sleep for a while.

I woke up suddenly, to hear loud banging on my room door. It was a chambermaid who couldn't get in to clean and tidy it. Much relieved, I got up, put my drawers on quickly, walked over to the door, and pulled back the bolt. It opened, and a somewhat dishevelled forty-ish woman carrying a mop, bucket and other room cleaning materials entered. I was relieved, almost glad, to see her, a little normality in this mad world I had become ensnared in. I realised that I had slept for a long time, replaced my clothes and coif, put my pistol in my pocket, and left her as I went down to find some lunch. The taproom was already quite busy, but luckily I found my usual seat in the corner, and called the serving wench over to order my food and some small ale. I spotted Goodly further up the room, and when the latter looked my way, waved to him. Goodly waved back, but resumed his conversation with two officers from another regiment whom he was talking to. I was happy to be left alone this time, and when a delicious smelling meal was brought to my table, I tucked into it with relish. It had a simple potage based on root vegetables and some pieces of pork, supplemented with an excellent piece of almond stuffed chicken, and the usual bread and butter. The serving wench asked if I would be wanting a dessert – honey glazed baked pears – and I eagerly accepted.

I did not eat all of the food by any means, but I was feeling well stuffed by the end of the meal. I looked forward to a decent walk in the direction of Swan Street, and Jeanne's house. I would need to be stealthy and keep alert, if she was not to spot me, so I decided on a brisk walk around the market square first. The fresh air, and the smells of the Monday market enlivened me greatly. On my round of the market square, I surveyed the ragamuffins that congregate around the market cross. One lad, taller than the others, took my eye. I signalled to the lad to come to me.

The lad's name, he told me, was 'Arry.

'Harry, I could use a good lad like yourself. Be ye trustworthy? A worker?'

The lad nodded vigourously.

'Well, Harry, could ye pick a group of your friends, just as honest as ye, to keep watch for a few days on a house for me? Ye, and they, must not be seen to be watching the house.'

The lad beamed and again nodded vigourously.

'What 'ouse, maister?'

"Tis off Guildhall Street. I would know who comes and goes to the house. Day and night.'

Harry was keen.

"Tis easy, maister! Four on us c'd do that. 'Ow much?'

I offered a silver penny a day.

'Penny an' 'alf, maister?'

'A penny if ye watches, plus a half penny if ye does well.'

'Done!' came the reply.

'I show ye the house, ye must not mistake it. And ye must NOT be seen! Follow me, not too close.'

The lad followed me as I walked across the market square, along St Giles Street, down Wood Hill, then Billing Street before turning right into Derngate, thence Swan Street. After we were out of sight of the Sun inn or other prying eyes, I slipped into a side alleyway near enough opposite the alley in which the house stood and called to the lad to join me.

'The house is in the jetty over the road, fourth along, broken window. Now we take great care. Understand?'

The lad nodded seriously.

I walked further along the jetty towards Swan Street, in the shadow of the house walls either side. Close to the end, I indicated to the lad where to look. Harry was not fazed by the exposed position to be watched.

'We c'n 'ang around, maister, play games. Best place c'd be 'long tha' jatty uvver there.'

'I leave it to ye, lad. Do your job well, and I shall reward ye and your pals well. Now return to the marketplace and pick your pals. I will find ye in the marketplace on the morrow, eleven of the clock.'

The lad nodded, and left, whilst I headed back along the jetty, then left towards Jeanne's, aka "Joan the Whore's", house off Swan Street.

Exercising great caution, I picked a spot where I could watch

Jeanne's house from the corner of the lane and Angel Street; I felt exposed there. I decided to go further along Angel Street, turned up the next lane, from which I hoped to double back and approach Jeanne's house from the other side. Luckily, it proved a good decision; I found a jetty between two houses a few doors up the street across from Jeanne's house, slipped across the narrow lane where I emerged, then found another narrow jetty from which I could observe Jeanne's house from good cover. It looked almost empty, abandoned.

I stood back, taking care not to show myself, for some two hours, when Jeanne's maid appeared. She walked along the lane, turned in and opened Jeanne's front door using a key. It looked as if Jeanne was not at home, but I noticed that she called to her mistress, whom I heard shout an answer, from upstairs. So, I thought, she must sleep during the day. Important to know, if I were to break in and search the house thoroughly. About half an hour later still, I was surprised to see Sam Goodly walk up the lane from the same direction, go to the front door and knock. The door opened, and I just made out Jeanne in the darkness of the interior. She called him inside, closed and locked the door. H'mm, this was becoming interesting! She did not look to be dressed in her finery, indeed, I thought that she was still in her sleeping attire.

About twenty minutes later, the door opened again, and Goodly came out. He turned around, and said something to Jeanne that I could not hear; then Goodly turned back and headed back whence he came. I noticed that his expression was, well, not a happy one. What were the implications of this pantomime? Could it be that Jeanne was working for Goodly, and had not performed her task well enough? It certainly looked as though Goodly was a main cog in the machine. Whetham, I thought, would be very interested in this development.

I waited and watched for another twenty minutes or so, then turned away, walked back along the narrow jetty, turned right, and followed the longer jetty until it emerged onto Swan Street close to Guildhall Street. It would be a useful short cut, giving good cover for

169

my next surveillance foray to Jeanne's house.

The rest of the afternoon and evening passed without incident. There was no appearance of Jeanne at the Sun, nor did Goodly appear until mid-evening. Seeing Goodly, I beckoned to him, and signalled to join me for a chat. Goodly just about acknowledged me, but did not join me. He still looked an unhappy man. I saw him order best ale, after which he found a chair in a quiet corner, and sat alone. An officer of major Lydcott's troop joined me and made small talk for a while, which I responded to distractedly, as my attention was still discreetly focused on Goodly. I decided on an early night, walked towards the stairs, and on the way, diverted to Goodly's lone corner.

'Ye are quiet this eve, Sam, be something wrong?'

Goodly looked up at me, with a seemingly chastened smile.

'Oh, aye, I am much troubled, Robert. Much on my mind. I am poor company this eve, I think.'

'Nought I may help ye with?'

The other man shook his head.

'Nay, 'tis not a matter I would share.'

'Then I wish ye a good night.'

I smiled, bowed my head a little, and proceeded to go back to my room. I had much to consider now. An early night, mayhap, but not to sleep, I thought.

I mulled over various scenarios, firmed up my plans for the next few days, and before I could undress, fell asleep in the chair. I woke when the banging of doors nearby roused me from my slumber, and I realised that the candle had burned almost out; I undressed quickly, took everything off, and fell into bed after putting a new candle in the candlestick, using the piss-pot, and making sure that my door was properly bolted. I was too tired to sort through my clothes for a clean smock, and again fell asleep almost at once.

Chapter 12: Incest and Intelligence

My guilt was weighing me down more than ever, as I sought to overcome my nightmares with the aid of ale and wine. Far from helping, it fed my unquietness of mind, but I did not realise it at the time.

Tuesday 13th March 1649.

Apart from a repeat of the previous night's nightmare around three o'clock in the morning, and a call of nature about an hour later, I slept more or less undisturbed. It was a welcome change from some of my previous nights. I woke next morning when the Guildhall clock struck seven o'clock, and a few market traders in the square started to arrive, with their horses, mules, and carts carrying a variety of produce and goods.

I took myself to the taproom to break my fast just after the Guildhall clock struck eight. It was almost empty, so I decided to visit the privy first, for once. After that mission, I returned to a now moderately busy taproom, ordered food and small ale, and made a bee-line for my usual seat. There was as yet no sign of Sam Goodly, but I surmised that the latter would soon make his presence felt. A new wench appeared carrying my food, jug, and pot, and deposited them on my table. Apart from thanking her, I said nothing. I ate slowly for once, savouring the food, then sat there sipping at my small ale. When the wench returned, I requested a penny-pipe, and soon sat quietly surveying the scene through growing clouds of tobacco smoke. There was no sign of Goodly still, and though I remained there until the Guildhall clock struck nine, Goodly had still not appeared. I decided that I would sit there for a while longer, then go to the market square to find 'Arry. Almost three quarters of an hour later there was still no sign of Sam Goodly, so I paid for the food, returned to my room, donned my outdoor clothes, and headed out for the square. I found 'Arry by the market cross after a few minutes wait, sat on the base of the cross, and invited the lad to sit by me.

'What news, Harry?' The lad smiled up at me.

'Two men went to th'winder, maister. Both army. First 'un, 'e walked slow loike, lookin' about 'im, loike 'e were frit o' summat. Took a piss in front o' th'winder, give a packet to summun insoide, through brukken pane.'

He went on to describe Goodly perfectly – it could only have been Goodly from the description. 'Second 'un, 'e were less frit. Did same. Took a piss agin th' wall, an' this'un took packet from summun insoide.'

He went on to describe an army officer, but wearing colours that I had seen on several officers in the Sun.

'Well done, lad. Penny for now. If ye can give more description of the second one, there'll be more silver. If others come, I would know, too. And give ye more yet.'

I handed the lad the silver penny, for which 'Arry beamed his thanks.

'Second one, what colour were his hair? Beard? Sash? I need to find the man.'

'Arry was as before keen to please me.

'Oi'll see it be done, sir. Din't see 'im meself, Oi'll try to get what 'ee needs.'

Off he scuttled, leaving me pleased with what I had already achieved. I decided to wait before reporting to Whetham. I wanted to make the right impression on the Governor, even if I held back for a day or two.

I sat in the early Spring sunshine, watching the people coming and going to the market stalls, seeing what they bought, marvelling at the variety of business going on in this bustling city, comparing it with the miserable places that I saw on the journey up from London, and, indeed, in the poverty-stricken town of Wellingborough. Such a

173

contrast! My, Amelia would love it here, I thought. I began to feel more relaxed, less anxious, for the first time in days. So much so that I almost nodded off. Pulling myself up sharp, as I heard the Guildhall clock strike twelve – God's blood, I had been here nigh on two hours – I decided to return to the Sun, get some lunch, then use the time after to keep watch on Jeanne's house again. I needed to understand her daily routine.

As usual, lunch at the Sun was a relaxed affair, even more so on this Tuesday, with good food and ale, and I was somewhat reluctant to get back to work, and head out for the back alley to keep watch on Joan the Whore's house. I waited, waited, waited, then, suddenly, Goodly appeared again, this time in civilian clothes, not his uniform. He was wearing a look like thunder, as he reached Jeanne's house, and turned left towards her front door. She was obviously expecting him, as the front door opened before he reached it, and after a brief greeting, he stepped smartly inside. He reappeared about a quarter hour later, amid a heated exchange between himself and Jeanne. I heard him snap, 'Ye have been warned!' I could hardly believe my eyes.

He briefly turned towards Jeanne, said something more, then marched down her front path to the street, and turned back towards the Sun. This time, however, he walked a few yards, stopped, turned around, and walked briskly in the opposite direction. I had no option but to follow him. I walked quickly back to the back alley, then sprinted along it for a few houses, back up another jetty to the roadway, and watched as Goodly stalked past. He was clearly in some sort of huff. I repeated the manoeuvre, and reappeared again in shade near the roadway; this time, Goodly did not reappear. I risked getting closer to the road, but there was no sign of Goodly in either direction. He could not have gone far before either going into a house or else turning off. There were several narrow lanes off Swan Street, the first of which was just yards from the alley; I decided to keep watch from my hidden spot, and see if he reappeared. I did not have to wait long,

174

perhaps half an hour, when Goodly appeared at the junction of the lane with Swan Street, looked about him, then turned back towards the Sun and the city centre. I let him get to the bend near the Sun, slipped out of my hiding place, and carefully entered the narrow lane. It was mostly small artisans' houses, not much better than hovels, but one took my attention, one that looked more salubrious than the others. On the door was a small sealed knot sign. It had to be the house. I made a mental note of it, then retraced my steps.

I returned via the back alley to watch Jeanne's house, but no-one else went to her door, nor did she appear. After the Guildhall clock struck five, I thought it time to return to the Sun for my evening meal. I could look out for Goodly from my usual chair, and now that I knew there was another officer involved, I could carefully observe the other officers in the room to see if any were watching me myself.

Rather than my usual high-crown hat, I donned my coif, leaving my cloak in my room, before going down to the taproom and ordering my meal. This night, the room was unusually quiet for this hour. It was a Tuesday, so no accounting for the quietness, and I sat in silence eating my supper, after which I ordered a penny-pipe, and sat ruminating within my cloud of blue fug. It was after six before the officers started to appear, and almost all together. From what little of their conversation that I picked up, seemingly there had been some sort of military conference or service in the Guildhall, so that would account for the quiet followed by the mass of officers. One man was not among them, though – Sam Goodly. I sat and watched carefully, scrutinised each officer whose face I could see. None appeared to pay me any particular attention. After an hour and a half of this, I decided to see if I could get some company. I managed to get a couple of captains to come and join me, and engaged myself in small talk with them. It was almost nine o'clock before Goodly appeared, in his uniform as usual, rather than the civvies of earlier; he waved to me, and came across to join me. He seemed to be in better spirits than when I had watched him go to Jeanne's house earlier.

175

He and I chatted for an hour or so, when Goodly announced that he would be off to bed, so I concurred that I had had enough of the evening. We walked up the stairs together, then went our separate ways. I removed my clothes, had a wash – my long hair was dusty from the afternoon of secret surveillance – and having to remove the smock too, retired to my bed after dousing the candles. I fell asleep remarkably quickly into a dreamless sleep. It was, however, to prove a memorable night.

I had been asleep for about two and a half hours, when I slowly awoke to the pleasurable sensation of a hand massaging my erect penis, and the unmistakable feel of a naked woman's body against my own naked back. Jeanne's voice whispered in my ear.

'Would your God-bitten wife do this for ye, Robbie? I think not!'

Her voice whispered a variety of erotic comments into my ear, as her hand moved more vigorously, rousing me more and more. I could not resist its effect on me, as my passion burgeoned rapidly.

'Can ye feel my wet c-'

'No-o-o-o -!'

I couldn't stop myself coming.

'Oh, your dried up wife has starved ye of love, Robbie. Did I please ye well?'

Yet the hand was still gently massaging my cock, rubbing slowly up, down, up, down. We lay there for a few minutes in silence, as I could not help enjoying the sensation. I felt her tongue on my nipple, and started to get strongly aroused again, when, in one deft movement, she pushed my shoulder down onto the bed, swung her knee over, and straddled me, lowering herself onto my rapidly hardening manhood. She took over with her body, until I came again, and then slipped easily off me, and lay beside me panting. I lay back exhausted from her attentions.

'Did ye enjoy that, Robbie? Am I not a good lover? Ye would make love to me again, I think!'

176

I had never expected such of a woman! Coupling, according to the church, was a wifely duty, not a pleasure. I grunted an answer and slipped into a deep, satisfied, sleep.

I was woken three hours later by another terrifying nightmare, to find that I was alone. My God, she was indeed good. She satisfied me, yet left me craving for more of her. Then the thought hit me like a cannonball: I had betrayed my wife. And our son. Yet, Jeanne was such a different lover to my staid wife; no religious clap-trap, no guilt, just unalloyed enjoyment. Women simply did not do such things! I had never even seen Amelia naked, yet I had seen her beautiful sister with not a stitch on. I wanted Jeanne more than ever. Why should I feel guilty? After all, my wife would not have done what Jeanne did, I told myself. Then again, it was all in my line of duty, as Whetham told me; and it was hardly an onerous task. I fumbled to light a candle, got up, found the piss-pot, and emptied my bladder before returning to bed. I blew out the candle, and fell asleep again. I awoke after about half an hour with a sudden uneasiness, an overwhelming sense of guilt and anxiety. So this was how Jeanne hooked her targets. Maybe this was what Goodly and Jeanne's argument was about – hooking me. How did she get into my room? I was sure I had locked the door – though had not bolted it, nor set any obstacles for the unwary intruder. I got up, lit the candle again, walked over to the door and checked it. It was definitely locked. I put the bolt on, set a chair by it, then returned to bed and very troubled sleep until it was time to get up.

Wednesday 14th March 1649.

I rose at seven o'clock as usual, had a good wash. I could smell Jeanne's scent on me, and was particularly keen to eradicate it – it was the smell of my guilt, my eternal shame. Clean shirt, clean drawers, brushed hair, trimmed my moustache and beard, then outer clothes, and I was more than ready for breaking my fast; I needed it much more than usual after the events in the night. I hoped that it would assuage the nagging guilt at my having betrayed Amelia, and the anxious thought that in the eyes of the church and the law what I had

177

done was illegal. It was incest. God's blood, what had I done? Was I not damned enough already? Then Jeanne's tinkling laugh rang out in my head, and the feeling of craving for her rose up again. What should I do, what should I do? I descended the stairs to break my fast, hoping that the food would reduce my guilty feelings, my craving for Jeanne's favour.

Breakfast was normal, except as the day before, Sam Goodly was conspicuous by his absence; what differed, however, was that I noticed one of the officers paying me rather a lot of attention. I made a particular effort to memorise the man's uniform and physical characteristics. Whilst I was eating, I noticed the man frequently glanced over at me, and unless I had sprouted two heads, there was only one logical explanation, because I had never spoken to him, or even seen him, previously.

After my breakfast, I noticed that the strange officer had disappeared. I decided to collect my outerwear from my room, head for the market square to make contact again with 'Arry, and see if the lad had any more information for me. The work, I hoped, would take my troubled mind off all my woes. Having readied myself, I ventured out towards the market, and had not even entered the open area, when an excited, bright-eyed 'Arry whistled to me softly from a jetty near All Hallows church. I looked quickly around me, then slipped into the jetty. 'Arry was anxious to tell me about his information, so I asked him to come into the church, where we could sit and talk quietly without being overheard. I entered at the side door, saw that the church's cavernous interior was still virtually empty, picked a pew where anyone approaching would be easily detected, and sat down. Within two minutes, 'Arry slipped into the seat behind me, leant forward, and told me his tale. I was all ears – and was surprised at the amount of information forthcoming. First off was the description of the other officer who had visited the house with the missing window pane. I was pleased to hear that the description fitted my own description of the officer who was watching me at breakfast time. The second piece of information was even better: yet another officer had been spotted at the window, and 'Arry also gave me a detailed description of the man. Very pleased with the lad's excellent efforts, I handed him three silver pennies. The lad was most grateful, and keen to continue watching. I decided on a bolder plan: could the street urchins follow any of these officers, to find out if there were any other houses they used to pass letters, and, indeed, if they used any other local taverns? The lad was only too pleased to earn more money for himself and his pals, so, yes, they would be glad do it. He beamed at me with the widest of wide smiles. This could be valuable information indeed, and the chances of the lads being seen as spying on their targets was small, I thought, since street urchins would follow anyone who looked a possible hit for begging a silver coin or two. If they were seen following a target, and the target spotted them, all they had to do was beg for money. The worst likely to happen to any of them was a clip around the ear or maybe a boot up the rear end.

The next task for me was to present my intelligence report to Whetham. I thought that my best option was a succinct written report, which, if I could not gain audience with Whetham, could be handed to a guard for personal delivery. It would need couching in careful language, so that if someone other than Whetham opened it, it would not arouse undue suspicion, since I did not know who was trustworthy in the febrile atmosphere in the city, even soldiers. I headed back to the Sun, after thanking 'Arry again for his efforts, then up to my room, where I bolted the door, got out my writing materials, and proceeded to write my report.

By the time I had finished my report, sealed it, and secreted it, I heard the Guildhall clock strike midday. My first port of call must be to eat. I did not fancy confronting Whetham on an empty stomach, in case his ire descended on me again. I guessed that Whetham would probably be best approached at Haselrigge House, just after lunch, so proceeded to the taproom, and ordered some food and small ale. I did not want to befuddle my head with the strong stuff. After the food

179

arrived, I ate slowly, and glanced around the room, taking a peek at who was there every so often. As on Tuesday, there was no sign of Sam Goodly, nor did the officer who was so interested in me appear, though others drifted in, in ones and twos. Some waved to me, but none joined me at my table. After my meal was finished, I decided on a penny-pipe, and sat looking contented in my corner, blowing clouds of pungent blue smoke. I must have been a picture of geniality, despite my anxious feelings. I heard the Guildhall clock strike one o'clock, waited about a quarter hour longer, then settled my bill. After collecting my outerwear and sidearms, I ventured out towards the Guildhall, where I found 'Arry and his pals congregating. I knew the way to Haselrigge House now, but thought it would be wise to ask 'Arry and his pals to accompany me, so they could look out for possible assailants. The lad was only too happy to oblige, and two of his younger companions tagged along too.

I had a merry chat with 'Arry and his pals as I made my way along Gold Street and Marefair, reaching the front door of Haselrigge House without incident, for which I was mightily relieved. 'Arry looked wide-eyed as we approached the towering three storey house, and I asked 'Arry if he and his pals could amuse themselves while I was inside. 'Arry could hardly believe his eyes when I knocked the ornate knocker, Whetham's usher appeared, and called me inside.

I have to admit that Whetham was not best pleased to see me. His meal was barely over, and he was looking forward to a quiet snooze over a glass of sack and a pipe of tobacco before he had to make his way back to the Guildhall by two o'clock. Nonetheless, he asked me to accompany him to his closet, and we sat facing each other as I gave him my report, then proceeded to enlarge on it as soon as he had read it. When Whetham heard what I had to say, he had to agree that this was important enough to disturb his post-lunch reverie. He was particularly surprised about the strange officer whom I described, and whom 'Arry and his pals had observed at the window with the missing pane, handing a packet to whoever was inside. My description of the colours that the man wore truly hit the spot; he was wearing the colours of Colonel Harley's regiment of foot which was quartered in St James's Palace, in London. So what was an officer of this regiment doing in Northampton? I pointed out that Sam Goodly, too, was wearing the colours of Fairfax's Life Guards, another regiment quartered in London – or at least, what was left of it was. Whetham still awaited the messenger with more information from Tom Scot that could provide more information about who Sam Goodly could be; now he needed do the same again for the newcomer. However, given that both were somehow involved in espionage, both were likely to be impostors, and maybe not known in London.

Whetham's next step was to interrogate me about my encounter with "Joan the Whore" during the previous night. I could do no more than say that I awaited the next development – if indeed there was one. I surely expected that there would be. Whetham had made it clear that if I did not get information about what she was up to soon, his men would "persuade" her that she should tell all, a deeply disturbing notion for me. She was my kin, after all, and whatever she had done, whatever I thought of her, I could not let her go to those cruel brutes. I inwardly shuddered at the thought of what they would do to Jeanne. Not only that, I was convinced that Jeanne was but a lowly actor in a far bigger game, and knew little if anything more than the real name of her controller, Sam Goodly.

Whetham was undoubtedly pleased with my progress, and was happy to spend a little time chatting to me over a goblet of sack. I, on the other hand, was nervous that alcohol, especially strong wine, could dull my senses, and that could be dangerous for me. I accepted a small drink of the sweet fortified wine, but sipped sparingly of it as we talked.

Almost an hour had passed when I emerged from the front door of the house. I was relieved to see 'Arry and his pals still there. They scuttled behind me for the most part as I headed back to the marketplace. Gold Street was the danger zone, and I was especially vigilant walking along that narrow and dark street, also getting my comrades to keep a good lookout too. Nothing happened, but at times I had an uneasy feeling that I was being watched – a vague, prickly feeling at the back of my neck that I could not explain other than I sensed the proximity of someone too interested in my activities. That someone kept out of sight; there were several even darker jetties leading off the street, and it was too easy for an observer to keep well hidden in one.

When I and my young comrades emerged into the marketplace from Drapery, I gave 'Arry two pennies for their trouble, and thanked them all for their company. 'Arry was well pleased, he would be very happy to do my bidding again if needed. Then, on the opposite side of the marketplace, I spotted the strange officer walking diagonally across the square.

'Be that the man ye saw at the broken window, Harry?'

'Arry nodded vigorously.

'Aye sir. 'Twas definitely 'im.'

'Good. Could ye and your pals follow him, if ye please, and tell me where he goes to?'

Yes, indeed they could, and scuttled off after the man's retreating figure. He appeared to be heading towards Sheep Street, beyond which was Horsefair and a maze of old winding streets. Many of those streets contained tumbledown old houses with poorer citizens, and indeed, two streets were occupied by the main body of local "ladies of the night". It was not only a far from salubrious area, but it could be extremely dangerous for the unwary, who could fall prey to cutpurses and other petty criminals of all stripes. The army had failed to clean up the area, and in fact, many troopers were known to seek the company and dubious "charms" of the ladies of the night there – with some ending up with their throat cut in the process. It was a part of the city that I had no wish to enter. Yet my young comrades had no fear of going into there; many of the occupants of the houses were just as poor and ragged as they themselves, so they were unlikely to be attacked. Later in the day, the officer reappeared at the Sun, so I slipped out, and looked for 'Arry. There he was, close to the Guildhall side of the marketplace, and he had surprising news for me. The man did not go into the maze of streets, instead visiting a house near the church of the Holy Sepulchre. It was set well back off Church Lane, and he entered it down a narrow jetty, through a tradesman's entrance. The lad gave me a good description for the house and where it was situated, and earned himself another penny for doing so. My God, thought I, this lad is getting expensive! But he was gaining intelligence that I could not have easily obtained myself – certainly not without considerable risk to my safety, and I really appreciated his enthusiastic help.

I returned to the Sun, where I enjoyed an uneventful supper, a light meal, this Wednesday evening, and found a couple of other officers to whom I could chat over a good ale and a penny-pipe. I found myself in gregarious company, and also was able to engage in conversation about rumours and goings-on in the garrison, which all added to my insight into the state of things in both Northampton and the Midlands generally. It was a worthwhile evening, and I repaired to my bed a contented man for once, but with one exception: my craving for another visitation from Jeanne. It was stronger still, now. I started thinking.

'God's blood, if only Amelia were as good in bed as her younger sister. 'Tis a shame that Jeanne commits treason, she is a lovely girl.'

After a good wash to remove the dust and street grime of the day, I succumbed to the power of the good ale and good company, and was soon snoring like an old porker. Apart from a rather unpleasant nightmare waking me several times in the early hours, and a need to make use of my piss-pot, I had an uneventful night, and woke at my usual seven o'clock feeling refreshed and rather more relaxed and less anxious than of late. On this Thursday morning, the marketplace was already a-buzz with the noise and shouts of the stallholders, as the city woke to a beautiful early spring day.

Chapter 13: Goodly and Badly

Thursday 15th March 1649.

I washed and dressed before going down for breakfast, relishing the welcoming smell of boiled eggs and bacon. Sitting in my usual corner, I was surprised to see Sam Goodly walking towards me. Goodly waved a cheery 'good morrow', and asked to join me. I wasted no time in expressing my surprise at seeing Sam after his absence for the last two mornings. Goodly explained that he had not been well, and also had an altercation with a more senior officer – he did not say whom – so I, realising that it was a fabrication, did not pursue the topic.

"Tis a beautiful day, Sam. I feel glad to be alive this morn.'

Goodly smiled at me benignly.

'Aye, Robert, 'tis for sure a lovely day. Spring is with us, and welcome after all that damned snow and frost. Methought 'twould never end.'

We chatted away easily for a while, when Goodly changed the subject.

'What have ye been up to, Robert? Ye seem busy of late.'

I, fortunately had a ready answer.

'Oh, aye, Whetham works me hard. He be a hard taskmaster, and hard to please with it.'

'What does he have ye do, Robert? If I may ask.'

I had to improvise quickly; it was as well that I had become adept at lying.

'There be much I may not tell ye. But mostly administrative tasks for Whetham's masters in London, and reports on goings-on in Northampton. Very boring, I may say. 'Tis better to be busy than footloose, I think.'

Goodly nodded sagely.

'Aye, I have time on my hands. 'Tis hard to fill the hours some days.'

I thought to myself, 'aye, ye lying devil', but kept a straight face.

'What do ye do, Sam? There seem not much for soldiers to do in the city, especially of your exalted rank.'

Goodly was also ready for the question.

'This and that. Reports mostly, as ye says. I must report to Whetham, and also Fairfax himself. 'Tis hardly onerous, methinks!'

Now I thought that I would probe a little.

'I see ye some days in the city. Walking about.'

Goodly's eyebrows lifted, but he stayed calm.

'Forsooth? I have not seen ye. I go for walks to kill time. Like ye, I have no men here, they be all in London.'

I knew that to be a lie; none of Fairfax's Life Guards had any troopers reporting to them.

'My regiment has gone to make up numbers in other garrisons. Lincoln, Rutland, Leicester, Nottingham. I know not what our generals would achieve with breaking up a regiment such as Rossiter's cavalry. We are a body of men, we work best together.'

Goodly was surprised.

'Ye are in Rossiter's cavalry? I did not know ye're a cavalryman.'

'Did ye not? Methought ye would know my colours.'

Goodly reddened, and was obviously making up a fabrication.

'I have been with Fairfax for three years. I have ….. forgotten other regimental colours.'

I had had enough of the mild sparring.

'Methinks I must take my leave of ye, Sam. I would bid ye a good day.'

I stood, doffed my hat to Goodly, saluted, and started to return to my room.

'And I wish ye a good day, too, Robert.'

He did not return my salute – bad manners when both of us were in uniform – but I took little notice. What I did know however, was that Goodly was well aware that I was a cavalryman, since he had, in an earlier conversation, claimed to be at Naseby. We had talked about my regimental role in that decisive battle, as well as Goodly's probably fictional role. It was a bad mistake for an intelligencer to make, I thought.

After donning my outerwear and sidearms, I ventured out of the inn, turning right up Drapery then Sheep Street towards All Hallows church, then right again towards the church of the Holy Sepulchre. This avoided the marketplace, where I would be mobbed by 'Arry and his pals. It was a back street route that passed the end of Church Lane, where I again turned right, and walked slowly along the lane looking for the house that the strange officer visited on Monday. I soon found it, and examined it carefully as I passed, though trying to look as if I were merely looking around me. It was a good house, large, well maintained. This was no ordinary artisan's house; nor did it look like a churchman's dwelling. Past it, I noticed a narrow jetty on my side of the lane, which was well shaded, so turned into it. Standing in the shade, virtually invisible from the lane itself, I had a good view of the house. I could also see along the jetty opposite, where 'Arry had described the officer going, before using a side gate. I mulled over having a closer look, but realised that the jetty opposite was too well lit by the morning sun, and decided not to attempt any further reconnaissance. After a few minutes, I turned left out of the jetty, and retraced my steps back to Sheep Street, then the marketplace. 'Arry of course spotted me, and came galloping across.

'Harry, if ye please, I would like ye be more discrete. Or mayhap make a show of begging,'

The lad immediately looked a bit crestfallen.

'I know ye means well, but 'tis risky for us both.'

187

I told the lad to follow at a distance, and entered the side door of All Hallows church, which was again almost empty. As before, I sat close to the middle, where anyone approaching would be obvious. 'Arry came in, spotted me at once, and sat behind me.

'Have ye any news, Harry?'

The lad said that he had nothing new.

'Mayhap ye could find out more about the house in Church Lane for me?'

'Arry indicated that he and his pals could certainly do such an easy task.

'Name of the house, who lives in it, anything else ye can discover, Harry.'

The lad left me sitting there to find his pals and I assumed that they had wandered off in the direction of the house. Although I was correct in my assumption, I was shocked and angry that about two o'clock in the afternoon, 'Arry and one of his pals were found with their throats cut on the side of Sheep Street, near Church Lane. Two more senseless deaths, I thought, as a large wave of guilt enveloped me. I was getting too close for someone's comfort.

'Damn their eyes!' I said out loud, as I sat in my corner seat in the Sun inn, making another officer at my table jump, and he asked me what was wrong. I apologised.

'I were lost in my thoughts.'

The other officer looked at me quizzically, but said no more about it, and then started to talk about the latest rumours.

After lunch, I took a bold decision; I walked to All Hallows church, going in by my usual side door. I looked around for the preacher, and eventually found him in his vestry. I asked if the preacher could spare me time to ask a private question. The preacher was happy to do so, and I ventured, 'Do ye know Church Lane, father, near the church of the Holy Sepulchre?' The preacher certainly did.

'I wonder if ye knows a large house on the side of the lane nearest the church?'

The preacher again averred that he knew the house well. So I asked the question for which I was itching to get an answer.

'Know ye who lives there, mayhap?'

The preacher thought for a few moments.

'I knows not his name, captain, but I know that he be very well off. Keeps himself to himself, and I believe that he rarely goes out.'

'Do he live alone in that large house?'

The preacher did not know, but considered it unlikely; such a large house would need a staff to run it, maybe three or four people at least. I wondered if he could find out the name of the owner. Now the preacher became wary.

'Why do ye need to know, captain?'

I thought it best to answer truthfully.

"Tis army business, preacher. I may not tell ye – or anyone else but Governor Whetham.'

'Ah, Governor Whetham, indeed. I would that the Governor ask me himself, if ye please. There be too many strange happenings in the city, I fear, too many killings. These be perilous times.'

'Aye, 'tis so,' I said. 'Indeed, my own life has been threatened. I will ask the Governor when next I see him. I thank ye for your help.'

I would have left, but the preacher continued.

'My son, I would ask that ye stay awhile, and say a prayer for the poor souls who have lost their lives in Northampton, and the other victims of the cruel wars hereabouts. 'Twould be good for your soul, mayhap.'

I nodded my compliance, went into the body of the church, where I sat, apparently in silent prayer. In fact my mind was in much turmoil, and I was contemplating my immediate future, what I might do next. I no longer had 'Arry to turn to. Nonetheless, my stay in the quiet of the great church salved my troubled mind a little, and I was grateful for it. After about an hour, I stood, said a loud 'Amen', bowed to the altar, walked out of the church into the afternoon sunshine, and on to the marketplace.

The marketplace was still busy, despite being well into the afternoon, and the stallholders appeared to be doing well. I effected to amble round the stalls and see what was for sale, since it would give me further time for reflection. I might also bump into one of 'Arry's former pals, though that might be a forlorn hope now.

There was no sign of 'Arry's erstwhile pals, though probably they will have spotted me and kept well away from me. After about an hour of wandering around the stalls, many of which were now putting their wares away ready to go home, I decided that I had seen enough, though I had noticed a nice silver locket on a secondhand goods stall, and bought it as a present to give Amelia on my next trip home. It was two groats, quite a lot of money, but she would no doubt appreciate it, especially if I could find a good silver chain for it next market day. I felt the need to try to get back into her good books, because, God knows, I had betrayed her with Jeanne, and that was likely to be repeated. My guilt loomed larger than ever. I ambled back to the Sun, repaired to my room for a quick wash and brush-up, and then came down for an early supper. With the taproom almost empty, when the wench brought my food, I tried to open conversation with her. She was very wary, clearly only too conscious of Emma's fate four days ago. I assured her that I wasn't going to ask her to go outside with me, just a little chat. I asked her about Emma's family.

"Er mother died givin' 'er birth, maister. 'Er looked arfter 'er faither, 'e be on un's own now. Lorst wi'out 'er.'

'No brother or sisters?'

'Nay, 'er were fust chil'.'

My guilt welled up even more at that.

'I be so sorry, mistress. Would that I could help her father.'

'Aye sir. But 'ee can't. 'E'd 'ate 'ee fer causin' 'er death.'

I tried in vain to assuage my conscience a little.

"Twas only an innocent romp, mistress. Would that I could find her killer.'

She turned up her nose, and flounced back to the kitchen. I felt so helpless – as indeed I did about 'Arry and his pal, too. I realised that I did not even know the pal's name. I wondered if I could pay for the two lads to be buried properly in hallowed ground.

I looked at the food balefully, and after a few sips of good ale, started to eat slowly. It was of course potage, mutton and some root vegetables flavoured with a herb or two. I soldiered on with little enthusiasm for the food, and looked up glumly as Sam Goodly arrived and asked to join me. A wave of my hand, and Goodly took that as a 'please do'. He looked at me enquiringly.

'What ails ye, Robert? Ye looks troubled.'

I replied reasonably honestly.

'Emma's murder, Sam. The other wenches blame me for having a romp with her. Why should that be grounds to kill her so? Envy? Would that I could find her killer.'

Goodly looked at me searchingly.

'Were it just a romp, Robert? Or mayhap ye gave cause. She had admirers, did ye not know? As ye said, envy, perchance. 'Tis a strong urge for some.'

I nodded, still gloomily, distractedly.

'I be not good company this night, Sam. Mayhap ye could find a more genial topic?'

Sam changed the subject, and talked about the latest rumour, that the regiments in Northampton are to go to Scotland, and be replaced by others. He wondered if I had heard this one. It led to a long discussion about events in the North and Scotland, as the long war still raged on far away, and the stories of atrocities in Ireland and sieges, and bandit bands roaming the countryside abounded. It was hardly an uplifting conversation, but at least I was distracted from my guilty feelings, and both of us agreed to retire to bed after our conversation fizzled out.

I took to my bed feeling tired and sleepy, and rapidly fell asleep, having forgotten to extinguish the candle. After some time I was woken, as two nights ago, to the sensation of firstly a hand gently stroking my penis, followed by the unmistakeable feel of a woman's naked body against my back. Jeanne's voice whispered in my ear.

'Do ye enjoy this, Robbie? Of course ye does!'

She kept it going for a little while, then just as I was almost ready to come, she took her hand away, and got up out of the bed. I turned on my back scrutinising her lovely body as she slipped on her clothes and fastened them. I had not realised that she had an outfit that incorporated her undergarments with the outer ones, made so that she could pull the ribbon fastening, to cause them to fall apart, and slip off. She looked at me smiling.

'Robbie, my services come at a price. Ye must pay the price.'

'And the price is...?' I said.

'Information, my dear. There be a rumour that Richmond castle has fallen to Parliament, and that Northampton garrison will be changed for other troops soon, and sent to the North. My masters would like to know the truth of that rumour.'

She turned and walked to the door.

'Ye has two days.'

She opened the door, left, and closed it silently. Dazed, I got up, locked and bolted the door. Now I was bursting with sexual tension, and sought in vain to relieve it. I spent the rest of the night tossing and turning, and when I heard the Guildhall clock strike seven, I blearily arose from my bed, and washed myself, before sitting on the edge of

192

the bed and thinking about what I should do next.

'So that is how she hooks her catches,' I thought, bitterly. 'I have betrayed my wife for ..... this!' I burst into tears of frustration and remorse, which slowly subsided, and I realised that I must ready myself for work. I grabbed the pail of water left in my room last night by the maid, and splashed more on my face and head. After drying it off, I dressed in a clean shirt and drawers, then sat in the chair nearby, thought a little more. I wrote another sheet of my report to Whetham. The latter would be overjoyed, I thought bitterly, now he will expect me to betray Amelia again and again with Jeanne. Whetham would want to do… What? I realised that Whetham would see it as a chance to plant false information. God's blood, how will this end? More needless deaths? My own, mayhap? Then "Joan the Whore". If they take her, Whetham's men would wreck her beautiful body with red hot irons, burning oil, trying to get more information from her, that she almost certainly does not have. Then take her naked into the square and press her to death in front of a baying crowd. I shuddered involuntarily. I must not allow that to happen. Amelia would never forgive me if I did, even if she forgave me for betraying her with Jeanne. I would not forgive myself – how could I? Whatever Jeanne had been forced to do – I was certain, forced – she does not deserve such a horrible end, poor woman. My guilt and remorse burgeoned the more I considered it all. Nathaniel Whetham was ruthless, I knew; and I wondered how the man would react to his own or Joanne's sister going to such a fate? He must have feelings, surely. I, Robert Barker, would do my best to save Jeanne from the atrocious fate that awaited her if Whetham's men should take her – even at the risk of her life and, indeed, my own. I was damned enough already, I reasoned. I did not need even more damnation in the church's or Amelia's eyes.

Friday 16th March 1649.

A knock on my door jolted me out of my gloomy reverie. It was only the chambermaid come to change the pail, take my piss-pot away, and so on, but it provoked me to don my coif and go downstairs to

193

break my fast. I was certainly hungry, inevitable after the bad night, and Jeanne/Joan's machination. No eggs this morning, instead some lovely thick slices of gammon roasted with honey and herbs, with good fresh bread and butter, fruit if I wanted it, and whatever ale I wished. I opted for small ale, on the grounds that I needed a clear head to present the news to colonel Whetham.

I decided to find another corner, mainly because I wanted to be alone, but it was not to be. I found myself in the company of several other officers – and one of them was the one who was so interested in me previously. I discovered the man's name was Jim Roding, an unusual name, and certainly not from Northampton area, yet he spoke with a local accent. I assumed that the name was not genuine. I felt that I recognised the man close to, but could not place him. That, I concluded, was worrying. I was too distracted with thoughts of what I would say to Whetham to devote any more thought to the man. Whetham might know him anyway.

The breakfast improved my mood a little, and when it was over, and I had done the other necessaries of life, I donned my cloak and hat and walked to the Guildhall. It was not far off nine o'clock when I entered the hall, and asked to see Whetham. The latter initially declined to see me, so I gave my written report to his aide, and asked that it be given to Whetham at once for his urgent attention. The aide took it, and disappeared into Whetham's office. Ten minutes later firstly the aide, then Whetham himself came out, and called to me to come in. I apologised for the intrusion, but Whetham brushed it aside.

'Nay, 'tis excellent news, captain! I must hear more of this news. Ye have made good progress indeed, we must make good use of your efforts, and gain more from it. 'Tis a pity that so many deaths have occurred, but it cannot be helped. That is the world of the intelligencer.'

'Aye, sir,' I said. 'I would seek to have the two lads buried in consecrated ground. They were ragamuffins, yet good lads, did not deserve to die so.'

194

'Your scruples will get ye killed, man. They were only street ragamuffins.'

'I caused their deaths, sir, and I would make what repair I can. It weighs heavily on my conscience.'

Whetham was anxious to get on with the matters in hand.

'As ye wish captain. We have two matters to deal with. The preacher; if he do know who owns the large house in Church Lane, and "Joan the Whore". I will summon the preacher here, and ask him myself. 'Twill be done this day. As for Joan, your Jeanne, we must make use of her. Ye will wait while I pen a letter to Secretary Scot, complaining about the changes to my garrison. That will do 't. Ye can say that your task were to take it to the Parliament post-riders. Make sure that ye gets it back. It must not go to Scot.'

'Nay, of course, sir.'

'This Joan the Whore, she knows much, I fear. I would question her myself ere long.'

'I think not, sir. She be but a small cog in a much larger machine. This officer, Jim Roding – do ye know him? He be very interested in myself, and he uses the house with the broken window. He also goes to the large house in Church Lane. Major Goodly seems to know it not. Joan, I be sure, knows little. She be just the bait to hook the catches they want.'

Whetham looked at me with anger on his face.

'Would ye countermand me, captain? 'Tis my decision, not thine.'

It was inviting trouble, but I stood my ground.

'Aye sir, but she be my sister-in-law. I cannot, in all conscience, give her up to your brutes. My wife would not forgive me, and I would not forgive myself.'

Whetham was clearly riled.

'Captain, then I will wait for the results of your efforts. But 'twill still be my decision. If ye please, wait outside while I pen the letter.'

Whilst I waited, I applied my mind to the matter of Jim Roding, who wore the uniform of a captain in Harley's regiment of foot. I suddenly realised where I had seen that face before. I was near certain that it was Will Watterson's face, the man who shot and killed Emily, Ekins' young kitchen maid. When Whetham came out to me, I would pass on the information. This man indeed should be interrogated by Whetham's torturers. Yet even then, he is not the man in charge of this nest of spies. He probably would not know who that was. They were too careful to ensure that no-one had contact with more than one above, one below, their station. I mused that Tom Scot's organisation appeared less professional, if my own experience was anything to judge by.

A quarter of an hour later, Whetham emerged and called me in. He gave me the letter that I was to pass to Jeanne/"Joan the Whore". I took the opportunity to mention Jim/Will.

'Sir, I have recalled where I saw Jim Roding before. I believe that he were Will Watterson, that killed Master Ekins' kitchen maid. I saw trooper Watterson but briefly, but I would swear 'tis he.' Whetham was pleased with that, and his face softened.

'I will not order him arrested yet. Ye must find out more.'

'Aye, sir, each one of them contacts but one above and one below in their net. They be careful that one being taken cannot bring down the others.'

'H'mm,' came the answer from Whetham. 'If ye please, see your preacher and order him to come here at two of the clock.'

I bowed and saluted, stowed the letter in my secret pocket, and walked out of the Guildhall into the spring sunshine. My next stop would be All Hallows church again.

Inside the church there was no sign of the preacher, so I decided to sit and wait, and quietly review the events of the last days. I realised who had almost certainly killed poor Emma at the inn, and 'Arry and his pal. It had to be Master Roding/Watterson, or whatever his real name was. I was intrigued that whilst Roding had a local accent, like myself, Sam Goodly did not. His accent was that of a gentleman, and probably a London gentleman at that. Could he be a bigger cog in the machinations of this scheming group? So far as I knew, Goodly had not lain with Jeanne, nor killed anyone; but he would have been capable of ordering a killing, surely? Just then, a door that I had not noticed swung noisily open, and the preacher emerged blinking in the bright interior of the nave.

'Oh, ye again. What do ye want this time?'

I ignored the discourteous greeting, and spoke sweetly.

'Master preacher, I have talked with Governor Whetham this morrow, and I must tell ye that he orders that ye go to him in his office in the Guildhall at two of the clock.'

The preacher snorted.

'Huh! Do he, indeed? Captain, my ORDERS come from God alone. Whetham may request that I go to him, and I may choose not to.'

I was much angered, but tried my best to hide it.

'I am the messenger, preacher. Mayhap he would arrest ye, if ye think yourself a higher authority in Northampton than he. With respect, I suggest that ye do as he asks.'

The preacher looked daggers at me, but said nothing, merely turned away and walked to the altar table, where he carefully – too carefully, methought – rearranged some flowers in a small vase. I took my leave and walked out of the church. Once outside, I said to myself, 'Humph! The man be a fool, methinks!'

I walked into the market square, and sat on the base of the cross in the sunshine, spending the next hour or so weighing up my next move. That large house was clearly the key – but who owned it? And how could I find out? I could ride to De La Pré Abbey, home of the Zouche

Tate family; if I could gain entry to the house, they might know. But it was a fair ride from the city centre. Comparing my options, I decided to opt for a more logical, if a more risky approach, to solve the problem. I would walk back to the church of the Holy Sepulchre, and ask the vicar there, even though it might get back to either the owner of the house or the leader of the group of plotters. I set out to walk up Sheep Street, past Church Lane, and entered the round nave of the old church on the far side. The vicar was in his office within the church, writing in the parish record book. I approached him cautiously.

'Good morrow, preacher. I am here on behalf of Governor Whetham. May I ask ye a question, if ye please? The large house, on Church Lane. Do ye know whose house it be?'

The preacher looked at me owlishly, but seemed happy to answer the question.

'Aye captain. Ye are captain, I think?'

Yes, I am captain Robert Barker, I told him.

'Captain, it is owned by Lady Margery Sorrell. Very fine lady, good patron of our venerable church here. Her husband, Sir James Sorrell, was killed at Naseby. He was a good patron of this church. I know of no children, unfortunately. What do Colonel Whetham want with her, if ye please?'

I had to think quickly.

'He wishes to know of influential people in Northampton, preacher. I know not why.'

The vicar seemed happy with the answer, so I bade him a good day, and took my leave. I had not expected such an answer, but it made sense, if she were a Royalist – likely, since she is an aristocrat - she might be in league with the dissident Royalist groups secretly scheming away against Parliament. There were many unhappy Royalists in the county of Northampton, and they would undoubtedly want Charles the son on the throne, with a notable very few exceptions. But would she be involved in gathering intelligence, I

198

wondered? Also, I noted wryly, were such women playing a key role in this Northampton cat and mouse game? Another thought struck me. If her husband was at Naseby, he would likely not be elderly, so Lady Margery would probably be fairly young. That could make her a dangerous adversary. What age would she be, thirty five, forty at most? Educated, intelligent, angry perhaps. She would be a very dangerous woman. This I must communicate to Whetham. More importantly, I and Whetham would need to plant someone inside the house, if we could find a young woman – or young man, even – who could approach her and ask for employment. I noticed a young woman walking from Sheep Fair carrying a basket, heading for the market. An idea took root in my mind. I decided to approach her.

Chapter 14: Maud and Mawle

Today, Friday, 16th March, I made a decision that would make my guilt a hundredfold worse. I should have discovered the real name of the young woman walking towards me before taking her to Governor Whetham and certain arrest for treason, with all that that implied. I recount here the story with profound sorrow and remorse, both for myself and even more so for the young woman herself.

'What cheer, mistress?' I said, 'Ye would shop in the market, I think?' She smiled at me.

'Aye, my mistress would have fresh produce for her supper. She is fussy about her food.'

I noticed her refined voice. It should have warned me, but sadly, did not.

'Do ye work for Lady Sorrell, perchance?' She nodded and smiled again.

'Aye. She is a good woman to work for, but demanding, I fear.'

'What be your name, mistress? Mayhap I will see ye again here,' I smiled back at her.

'I am Maud, Master….er, captain? Who be ye, pray?' I saluted her.

'Captain Robert Barker, mistress Maud. I report to Governor Whetham. I must repair to the Guildhall, and make my report to him. He be a demanding Master, too!'

I doffed my hat, smiled again, and took my leave of her. A plan formed in my mind: possibly she could be induced to go with me to see Whetham, and handed over to the Governor. If she were arrested, Lady Sorrell would then be in need of a maid. I thought Whetham would be pleased with such a plan, and felt pleased with myself for thinking of it. At very least, Maud could be interrogated about Lady Margery Sorrell; that alone could elicit some useful intelligence. I turned and walked off towards the Guildhall, thinking as I went. Maud was a pleasant, innocent young woman, not especially pretty, but what one would call a 'comely lass'. I was young enough, if need be, to cultivate her friendship.....or maybe seduce her, even, if Whetham required it. I would seem a good catch to such a lass; few officers would take a second glance at a mere maid. I felt a pang of guilt, but put it out of my mind. After all, I told myself, I had a job to do, and do it I must. It would be less reprehensible than being seduced by my wife's sister, after all.

I walked to the Guildhall in a few minutes, and asked if Whetham was still there. The guard thought he was, and volunteered to go and ask if I might have a quick word. The guard came back a couple of minutes later and told me to go in. Whetham was not particularly pleased to see me again, but invited me to take a seat. 'What is't this time?' he said, with a note of impatience in his voice.

'I would not have troubled ye, sir, but I have discovered more of value. The owner of the large house be one Lady Margery Sorrell. I have identified her maid, and made her acquaintance in the marketplace. We have opportunity, sir, to place our intelligencer in the house, or I could, er, bed the maid, methinks, if need be. The vicar of the church of the Holy Sepulchre told me more. He said that Sir James Sorrell were killed at Naseby, so Lady Margery be on her own.'

'Did he indeed? Lost your scruples, too, now, I think.' I reddened, but did not rise to the bait.

Then I said, 'I could easily bring the maid to ye, Governor, for interrogation and arrest. Lady Margery would then need another.'

Whetham sat there looking at me, and twirling his moustache.

'H'mm, 'tis a good plan. Progress, indeed.'

We sat looking at each other for a couple of minutes whilst Whetham considered the matter.

'Bring me the maid, captain. I would speak with her myself.'

'I will do 't Governor, but I must wait until she comes to market again. 'Twill not be long, I think. Lady Margery likes her food fresh, it seems, so her maid will return on the morrow.'

201

"Tis quite a nest of vipers, methinks. We needs must catch them all, pull their fangs.'

I agreed wholeheartedly.

'Aye sir, vipers indeed. Joan the Whore be but a small cog in their wheel. 'Tis the ones who control her that we must catch.'

'H'mm. They all commit treason, captain. Ye must discover yet more about them.'

I was somewhat discomfited by this comment, but thought better than to answer back this time. 'Lady Margery mayhap be a dangerous enemy, sir. If Sir James were at Naseby, he could not be old. So Lady Margery be probably young, educated, angry at her husband's death. She will not be easy to catch, methinks.'

'Aye, 'tis true. Ye must do what ye think required. Get to 't, captain. I bid ye good day.'

He flapped a dismissive hand at me and returned to his paperwork. I stood, doffed my hat, saluted Whetham, then left his office and the Guildhall, and returned to the Sun for some lunch, since it was now well past midday.

Lunch was not especially appetising, just a rather minimal potage consisting of some bits of mutton in a mashed up mix of swede, turnip, carrot, and onions, in a thick broth, and flavoured with parsley and..... some other herb that I did not recognise. It was filling, that much I accepted, but not to the usual standard of the Sun's good home cooking. After the potage, the maid brought some apple pie flavoured with cinnamon, and including honey and rosehips. Now that was more like it, I thought, and I wolfed it down, then washed it all down with a generous pot of best beer. It was not long after I finished the meal that I felt drowsy, had to shake myself up, and go out for a brisk walk to clear my head. I noticed Maud again, not heading into the market, but out of the marketplace and in the direction of Bridge Street. I thought it worthwhile to follow her. She walked quite a way down Bridge Street, then turned left into Angel Lane, then left again

202

up Guildhall Street. She then turned right into the alley on which stood the house with the missing window pane. She walked to the very door, knocked, and when it opened, went inside, much to my surprise. I was watching from my hiding place across the road, out of view of the street. A few minutes later, along came none other than staff major Sam Goodly, who also turned into the alley, knocked on the door, and when it opened, immediately entered too. It was a good hour before they emerged, though not together; Goodly came out first, and walked back up the street towards the Sun inn. Ten minutes later, Maud emerged, and as I saw her turn the other way – retracing her steps - I decided to head back to the marketplace by the quickest route, past the Guildhall. I did not have long to wait, before she emerged from Bridge Street, and strode purposefully along Drapery towards the marketplace. I walked just as briskly across her path, and deliberately almost collided with her.

'Oh, mistress Maud, 'tis ye! I beg your pardon. Mistress, may I ask ye, if ye please, to come with me to the Guildhall? The Governor wishes to speak with ye.' She looked rather put out.

'Why, pray, captain? Why does the Governor wish to speak with a mere lady's maid such as I?'

I played all innocent.

'Mistress, I know not. He would speak with ye about your Lady Margery, I expect. I know that he would make her acquaintance.'

Tut-tutting, 'Could it not wait, captain?'

'Nay, mistress, he be an impatient man. If ye please, it would not take long.'

I offered her my arm, whilst thinking that I might have to take her at pistol point, if she refused. Fortunately, she did not, just took my arm, and walked with me. I led her into the Guildhall, and asked a guard inside to announce me and mistress…? 'Smith,' she said.

'Captain Barker and mistress Smith to speak with the

Governor, as he instructed earlier.'

Whetham was clearly in a foul mood at yet another interruption, but quickly realised that I had Lady Margery's maid for him to speak with..... or rather, interrogate. He tried to look welcoming.

'Come in, come in, both of ye. I be pleased to see ye here.'

He chatted cheerily with both of us, and offered us each a goblet of sack. He gently questioned Maud about Lady Margery, but she was largely non-committal about her employer. I, after a few minutes of this, asked Whetham if I might have a quick word outside the office. He and I both exited the office, and Whetham closed the door behind us. I spoke very quietly.

'Sir, I followed her this afternoon to the house with the broken window. She went in, then Sam Goodly came along and went in, too. They were in there an hour or so. I know not why. I took a shorter route, caught her on Drapery, and asked her to come here with me.'

Whetham realised what I was saying, and in a voice loud enough for her to hear, said, 'Very good, captain. We must return to the young lady, she will feel neglected.'

He opened the door, waved me in, then followed me, and closed the door. The questioning started in earnest now. He opened by speaking plainly.

'Mistress, I think that ye and your employer have links to a Royalist agitator group. That be an illegal, treasonous matter.' Maud looked thunderstruck. She tried to protest, but he held his hand up to quiet her, and continued.

'Ye have been observed, mistress, in the company of a known person and at a house known to be involved with the group. I would know more of ye, and your friends, if ye value your life.'

Maud stayed tight-lipped, despite both I and Whetham urging her to talk. I told her that not talking was a great mistake, but she would not budge. Whetham looked at me and sighed.

'Captain, if she will not tell us, I must arrest her, and as ye well know, my men will make her talk.'

I felt an awful pang of guilt at this. I knew only too well what it would mean. I felt great regret at having brought her to Whetham, but it was too late now. I turned to her one last time, 'Maud, ye are a fine young woman. I must urge ye to answer our questions, and truthfully. Do ye not know what awaits ye in the Governor's prison? The terrible pain of the gaolers' "persuasion" methods? Ye are so foolish to stay silent.'

Maud looked at me with a sour expression, then spat in my face. I wiped my face, then turned back to Whetham.

'I fear that ye must have your men do their worst, Governor.'

A tear escaped from one of Maud's eyes, but she would say nothing more. Whetham called for his guard, who came in, and asked what was wanted of him.

'If ye please, tell my gaolers to come and arrest and shackle this foolish young lady, and house her in the cells.'

The man looked at her with sorrow showing on his face.

'Very good, sir.'

He returned with two heavy, rough looking men a few minutes later, who bolted shackles on her wrists, and led her away. I watched her retreating form with a growing sense of disgust at what I guessed they would do, as my guilt threatened to overwhelm me. I turned back to Whetham.

'I wish there were a less…. brutal way to make her talk, Governor. 'T fair makes my flesh crawl.' Whetham frowned at me.

"Tis not your fault, captain. Ye have a job to do, and did it well. If she has sense, which I much doubt, she will soon talk. I have seen her type before, man. Would rather die in agony than talk and save her skin.'

I, with deepest regret, knew that to be right. All for the sake of a

205

would-be tyrant like Charles the son, I thought. I took my leave of Whetham feeling saddened and guilty, and walked slowly to the Sun, where I went in to the taproom, found my favourite corner, and called for a pot and a large jug of their best ale and a penny-pipe of tobacco.

As I sat and puffed at my pipe, in between sips of the ale, I thought again of Jeanne, and what would happen to her, if Whetham were to get her in his clutches. I must get more evidence, discover more of the real identity of Sam Goodly, who seemed to be controlling them all – or so I believed - and whether there were any more that we knew nothing of. The more I thought, the more depressed and guilty I felt. I wondered how to find out more about Lady Margery Sorrell, and, indeed, her allegedly dead husband. I wanted to know Sir James' regiment, so I needed to find a man who could tell me more. Could that man be John Grove, I wondered? I needed to leave this cauldron of traitors and killers for a while, and be back with my wife, son, and my father, and the ordinary world back home in Rushden. Mayhap I could write to George Bishop, the marshal general; he surely would know, but it would take about five or six days to get an answer – and that prompted a thought, too: Whetham had said nothing of his reply from Tom Scot. At that moment, who should enter but Sam Goodly; he spotted me instantly, and came over to me. I had no choice but to invite Goodly to sit with me, though I felt uncomfortable at the thought. Goodly was quite cheerful, in the event.

'Have ye heard any more good rumours, Robert?' I answered truthfully.

'Nay, Sam. All seems quiet. I would 'twere less quiet. When there be no rumours, there usually be something afoot.'

Goodly gave a sardonic laugh, and agreed with me.

'A good rumour does a man a power of good,' he said, grinning broadly. "Tis a grand way to relieve the boredom, I think! Mayhap we should start one or two.' and laughed raucously. I had to laugh with him, but was screaming inside. Indeed, I felt my stomach churning with apprehension and remorse for what I had done in taking Maud to Whetham. The feeling was eating away at me. Nonetheless, I had to make small talk, if nothing else. I could not allow my feelings to let me down.

'Sam, I would so much like to go home to my family. A man can only be separated for so long. I miss them so much.'

Goodly was surprised at my change of tone.

'Aye, I know that feeling well, Robert. I have not seen my wife for so long, it hurts. I do not do well to be here, yet may not return home. 'Tis a pretty quandary for me.'

'Aye, 'tis so. Amelia and I, we be like strangers. I would ask Whetham to let me home for a day or two, methinks. 'Twould do me good, and my family too.'

'Mayhap I should do the same, Robert. Unhappy wives do not help us.' Then added ominously, 'When the fox be away, the chickens come out to play.'

I called the serving wench over.

'I would have food, if ye please, mistress. And more good ale. Mayhap my friend here too."

Goodly nodded vigorously.

'Aye, my stomach has a great void, wench. It needs well filling. What have ye to fill the void, if ye please?'

'We 'ave a good beef potage, sir, wi' plums an' ground vegetables. Barley, too. In thick broth made wi' beef fat. Sweetmeats too.'

Goodly's eyes lit up.

"Twill do most well, mistress. Two, if ye please, with more best ale and tobacco.'

She gave a small curtsey, then returned to the kitchen. No matter what his mood, I thought, Goodly surely likes his food! She returned almost at once.

'Sirs, we 'ave a goodly capon pie, if ye both would prefer. Fresh made this day. Good wine, too, if 'twould be preferred.'

Goodly's eyes lit up even more.

'Aye, that would be most welcome, mistress. And for ye, Robert?'

I concurred; the potage, however good, was daily fare, and I needed change. I hoped it would lift my mood.

'Have ye any sack, wench?'

She nodded, so I went on.

'Sack, too, if ye please.'

Looking at Goodly.

'And for ye, Sam?'

Sam nodded too. It would be a fine meal this night! I had developed a taste for sack, after being introduced to it at Whetham's house, and now had a thirst for it.

The meal lifted both of our spirits, and I was grateful for that. After two goblets of sack, I was feeling almost merry. By mid evening, we were singing bawdy songs and telling jokes along with the other soldiers who had now filled the room. I had temporarily forgotten about my guilt at handing Maud over to Whetham and his brutes, not to put too fine a point on it. Both of us retired to our respective rooms not long after the Guildhall clock struck nine, well lubricated with good wine and ale, and sated with a fine meal of capon pie. I, with difficulty, managed to extract myself from my outer clothes, and flopped onto my bed without undressing further, after which I immediately fell into a deep inebriated sleep, without even extinguishing the candles. I was not to know that three hours later I would have one of my worst nightmares ever, as Maud came back to haunt my sleep as only a demon in a nightmare can. I woke screaming and thrashing in my bed, so that the inhabitant of the next room came out and banged on my door. An ashen-faced me made my way to my room door, opened it, and apologised profusely to my irate neighbour, explained that I sometimes suffered terrifying nightmares due to what I saw in the war. My neighbour was not amused, but grumpily returned to his own room, and left me to try to regain my equilibrium and return to some sort of sleep.

Sleep, however, evaded me for much of the rest of the night. Every time I closed my eyes and started to drift into sleep, I was woken by apparitions of Maud, 'Arry and his pal, and Emma, tearing at my subconscious with red hot irons and pincers.

Saturday 17th March 1649.

By morning, I was a wreck. Even pouring lashings of cold water over my head did little to reignite life in my stiff limbs and body. I found a clean shirt and drawers, thanks to the maid who 'does' my room each day, and dressed as best I could in order to go down to break my fast. When I appeared in the taproom, and shakily meandered to my usual table, several officers looked at me, and joked that I must have truly had a good time with some bawdy wench last night, followed by asking what she had done to me to make me look so awful. I smiled as best I could, just stayed silent and wobbled to my chair and flopped into it. Even the serving wench looked at me askance, when she came to take my order.

'Are ye unwell, captain? Your eyes look like overripe strawberries! And your face… God's blood, ye must've 'ad a good toime indeed larst noight..'

I offhandedly ordered my food and small ale, and sat staring into space until she put the food on my table and departed with a 'Do ye want ought else, sir?' I just groaned and shook my aching head.

Sam Goodly appeared, equally wobblingly came over to my table and sat down opposite me.

'God in heaven, Robert, ye looks poorly, man. What ails ye?'

I could not think of a better answer than, 'My demons came to haunt me, Sam. I fear that sack and I agree not well.'

Sam did not look so well himself, I thought. Another man who suffered last night, his eyes looked red, too. But neither of us spoke until the serving wench came to ask Sam what he would have for breakfast. I slowly, very slowly and gingerly, managed to force down a boiled egg and some bread and butter, but then felt sick, and sat still, somehow managing to keep it down with difficulty. After sipping some small ale, I felt a little better, so sipped more at intervals until I began to feel a little better still, and a smattering of colour returned to my cheeks. There was cold meat with the eggs, and eating some of that with bread and butter also revived me a little. As I revived, Sam looked at me, and said, 'What demons were they that troubled ye so, Robert?'

'Private ones, I cannot tell of them.'

Sam cocked an eyebrow, so I said, 'I fear the war stays with me, though I would ward it off. I want to have time at home with my Amelia. That would help me greatly.'

'Aye, the war affects us sorely, Robert. But ye must put it behind ye, or ye will be sick for sure.' I nodded wordlessly, but said nothing, just took some more sips of the small ale. I resolved to go to Whetham and ask for a short leave of absence.

I reached Whetham's office as the latter arrived soon after nine o'clock struck, and was going to admonish me for troubling him again, but he noticed my haggard face and red eyes, and asked what I wanted, was something wrong with me?

'I would return to my home for two or three days, Governor. I am in sore need of some rest.' Whetham considered for a few seconds.

'Very well, captain, be back here three days hence.'

I thanked him, saluted and left. I returned to the Sun, asked that my room be held for three days till my return – the army paid for it, so I would not need to – and then saddled my horse, took my snapsack and weapons, and set off for home. I decided to take the fastest route, via St Giles Gate, then to Wellingborough, across the Nene, and into Rushden via Chester-on-the-Water, Irchester, and the back road into the little town. I arrived at the hall without incident at shortly after eleven o'clock, asking a groom to see to my horse, and passing him a silver penny for his trouble.

I expected Amelia to be pleased at my return; it was disappointing to get a somewhat cool, though surprised, reception, when I walked into the hall, and she spotted me coming. She gave me a perfunctory kiss on the cheek.

'Husband, ye do not look well, I think.'

Then she just stood and waited for my reply. My father, however, had heard the noise downstairs, and came down; he walked across to me, and was genuinely pleased to see me, shaking my hand, and clapping me on the back.

'What cheer, son? How long with us this time?'

'I be so tired, father. I asked Governor Whetham for a few days off. I must be back three days hence, but 'tis better than nothing. I miss Amelia and Johnny greatly, and yourself, of course. Whetham be a hard taskmaster, I think.'

My father turned to Amelia.

'Come daughter, are ye not pleased to see your husband? He misses ye and Johnny. Do ye not miss him too?'

She looked a little gloomily, saying, 'Aye father, but I would 'twere for good.'

I understood her feelings only too well.

'Wife, if ye knew Whetham, ye would know that he be uncommon

211

difficult to please. He were not happy to allow me even this small time away. I have much work of great import.'

I turned back to my father, 'Father, I would talk alone, if ye please.'

I and he went upstairs to the garret room and sat down. I began.

'Father, I am very sorely troubled. Three people are dead in Northampton because of me, and a fourth soon too, perchance. 'Tis likely Whetham will put Jeanne, too, to his torturers unless I somehow may deter him. He is a ruthless, cruel man, and I feel so much guilt.'

My father was rarely lost for words, but this left him speechless. He stroked his grey beard.

'I know not what ye do for Whetham, so may not give ye much counsel. Mayhap ye must one day confide in your wife? I fear I am too old to take your troubles on my shoulders as well as my own.' Peering into my eyes, he carried on.

'I see truly that your troubles be great, son. Could ye ask that master Ekins help ye? Or captain Grove, whilst he still be here?'

I replied that I would talk to Grove soon anyway, but was concerned about my wife, and her coolness to me. I was surprised to hear from my father that my wife had cooled on the church too; the preacher had been caught by another villager in bed with his wife, and therefore had been hounded out of the locality, whilst the villager publicly beat his wife in retribution.

I responded. 'So the preacher were a true Christian believer! Mayhap he would have tried his luck with Amelia too, if she were as stupid as that wife.'

My father's eyebrows rose, but he did not respond to that.

'Amelia will come round to ye, son. She would have ye back, not away in Northam'ton. 'Tis not far, yet ye could be on th'moon, for all she know.'

'Father, I would that I were on the moon. 'Twould be a happier place than Whetham's employ.'

He asked what I was doing for Whetham.

''Tis hard for me to say. But….. Northampton be...plagued with traitors. 'Tis my task to uncover them, give them to Colonel Whetham. Royalist traitors, father.'

'I see,' said he.

'Nay, ye do not, father. Truly, ye do not indeed.'

After which conversation, I rose, and returned to the hall below.

On our return to the hall, we were met by Master John Ekins, who was evidently pleased to see me, and shook hands with me vigorously.

'Ye looks careworn, Robert,' he said, 'Whetham works ye too hard, I think.'

'Aye, Master Ekins, he do that indeed. He be not pleased for me to have a rest, but allowed me home for three days. I would talk with captain Grove. He be here still?'

'Aye, but not for long, Robert. He is to be sent to the North, methinks.'

'Indeed? Methought that the last northern pinprick had fallen? Richmond?'

Ekins assured me that, so far as he knew, it was not yet so. The army had ordered many pairs of boots from my father and they were to be sent to Nottingham.

'Nottingham? Why Nottingham?'

Grove had appeared behind us.

'Cromwell's army has many without boots, Robert. Men march barefoot. The boots will newly equip them for taking Richmond,' said Grove.

Ekins added, 'And stockings from Coventry, too. Yet, the Council has little money, so will they pay? I know not.'

So this was what Jeanne wanted to know, I realised. They would attack Cromwell before he could make Richmond, and mayhap Scottish troopers would come to their aid again. Yet another sally into the North. My father was shaking me out of my reverie.

'Robert, are ye with us? What be this to ye?'

'Father, I may not say.'

I looked up at Ekins, who looked back knowingly, and asked if he might speak with me alone.

After my father had left us, I told him what had happened, with Jeanne seducing me, and asking me to get information on troop movements if I wanted her more. Ekins was not overly surprised. I said, 'She is but a pawn in the game of that nest of vipers, Master John, but Whetham would take her and let his men have her to try to get more information. But she knows nought, I am certain. The intelligencers are too well organised. None in the nest has contact with more than one above, one below. I cannot let Whetham have her. Amelia would never forgive me.'

The other man looked very thoughtful. 'Aye, Robert, I understand that. What may I do to help ye?'

'John Grove may help me for sure. I would ask him for a morsel of information.'

'He will soon be called away, so now is the time, Robert. My little garrison is to be halved.'

I knew of this, but still asked if I might talk with John Grove. Ekins went out and fetched him. I greeted captain Grove eagerly.

'Good morrow, captain, what cheer? I would like to ask ye a question. Do ye know a Royalist soldier, and officer mayhap, Sir James Sorrell?' Grove searched his memory.

'I have heard of him, I think. He were at Naseby, methinks. Killed there, I hear.'

Neither he nor I spoke for a few moments, then Grove asked, 'Captain, why do ye ask of him?'

'First, may I ask ye if ye have met a major Sam Goodly? He wears the colours of Fairfax's Life Guards.'

Now Grove was on rather more familiar territory.

'That name is wrong, Robert. I know a major Sam Goodhow. But he would be in London. Fairfax's Life Guards are at St James's Palace, or by now, mayhap, the Tower.'

'Aye, that meets with my knowledge. He says that he were at Naseby. I think not?'

'The earl of Essex's Life Guards were at Naseby, Robert, but they were disbanded last year, and some officers given to Fairfax. Fairfax retains a few as his personal bodyguard. None would be in Northampton. No reason, unless Fairfax himself were there.'

Now I ventured to explain. 'Lady Sorrell has a large house in Northampton, but 'tis said that her husband died at Naseby. Methinks this gentlewoman would not be the head of the group. This major Sam Goodly resides with the officers of Whetham's headquarters, but is unknown to Whetham and Secretary Scot, and has no work to do. Yet he goes to a house to pass messages and take messages, we believe for a Royalist agitator group. Another officer has appeared, too. He calls himself Jim Roding, but I swear he be Will Watterson. All of them and more are part of the same group.'

Ekins and Grove looked at me with expressions of shock, even disbelief. Ekins spoke first.

'Yet Nat Whetham does not defend against these traitors?'

I assured them that I was working on bringing the group down.

'I must know who Sam Goodly really be. Also this Jim Roding. He study me aplenty when we eat at the Sun inn.'

I suddenly thought of one more item. 'And Jeanne, or Joan the Whore, she be controlled by this Sam Goodly.' Ekins' mouth dropped open. He was speechless. After several seconds of silence.

'I knew Jeanne when she were a child. I cannot believe that she

215

would be a traitor.'

I had my reply ready.

'So methought. Yet she do.' For Grove's benefit, 'Captain, Jeanne or Joan the Whore came to my room in dead of night, when I were sleeping, and coupled with me. I could not stop her. Now she would have me give her information. Information about troops going.... north.'

'Robert, what of your wife? Surely ye would push Jeanne away, put her off?'

'Captain, ye do not know her. She be a woman possessed. She takes a potion to make her....ravenous for men. When she came to my room, she... she... aroused me too much in my sleep. 'Twas too late to stop her. I did not think she could do so.'

I explained her modus operandi. Ekins and Grove looked at each other; in this puritanical age, a woman doing what Jeanne had done was, well, unthinkable.

'Amelia must not know, she would be heartbroken. But ye really do not know Jeanne. Nor do her sister, I think.'

I felt deeply ashamed, but could not think what more I could say. Ekins answered at last.

'Robert, 'tis not the pressing matter yet. We must help ye get to the bottom of the matters of which ye ask us.'

So far, I had not mentioned Maud. Why was she involved, and how? I did not know. I hoped that Whetham had released her by the time of my return to Northampton. I thought that it was time to tell of her.

'Gentlemen, there be more. I found Lady Sorrell's maid, and took her to Whetham. He has arrested her, since she would not say a word. His men must have her now.'

Grove asked how I knew of her.

'I talked with her at the market. She were buying fresh food for

Lady Sorrell's supper.'

Ekins demurred.

'Her maid? A maid would not do her shopping, Robert.' Now I was unsure what to say.

'So she told me,' I said, plaintively. 'We thought to capture her, and plant another. I saw her in the house for passing messages, with Sam Goodly. She be too educated for a maid, mayhap.'

"Tis a veritable spider's web,' said John Grove, 'I never heard such a tale.'

I was loth to say more, my guilt at the trail of bodies that I had left behind was gnawing at my conscience as the conversation unfolded – not to mention my guilt at betraying my wife with her sister. Master Ekins chipped in.

'If she be educated, she be no kitchen wench, Robert. Nor even handmaid. Perchance she be a companion.'

Grove concurred with this. I spoke first.

'Why would a companion be buying food. And why would she be carrying messages – dangerous messages?'

The conversation ground to a halt, as none of us could think of more to say that would enlighten us. We agreed to leave the matter and sleep on it for now, whilst I went to Amelia and Johnny, and tried to find rest from the rigours of the task that I faced.

When I returned to the hall, Amelia was playing with Johnny there. She looked up as I walked across to her.

'Husband, has ye got what ye wanted from Master Ekins and captain Grove?' I felt hurt by this comment.

'Amelia, 'twas just a question. I would share my time back here with ye and Johnny. If ye knew what I must do in Northampton, ye would know how pleased I be to see ye both.'

She looked at me without any emotion. I could not but help to contrast her with her beautiful sister. 'Aye, if ye say so,' she said.

'God's blood, can ye not be pleased too? Or would ye rather I go back now?' I was angered by her manner.

My father crossed the hall on hearing this, and chided Amelia.

'Daughter, I know how hard it be for Robert at this time. If ye please, do not push him away from ye.'

She managed a wan smile, and returned to playing with Johnny. I, exasperated, turned away from her, picked up my snapsack from the floor where I had left it, and returned upstairs to our room. My father meanwhile put a hand on Amelia's shoulder, and pulled her round to speak to her.

'Child, ye would lose your husband? Robert be a good man, and 'twould rend his soul if ye spurned him. He loves ye dearly. 'T rends my soul to see ye thus. The war has been hard for all, but for soldiers such as Robert, even more so. He has seen much death and hurt, and I would not have ye add to 't.' She sighed.

'He would stay in Northam'ton rather than with his son and I, methinks.'

'I know 'tis not so, child. He may not tell ye of his work, nor even I. I beg ye, ask master John, if ye'll not hear me.'

A few moments later, I returned to the hall, ignoring Amelia and my father, crossed to the outer door, and went outside. Ten minutes later, I was in the tavern, drinking its strongest ale. I could not handle her attitude towards me, as well as all my growing regiment of demons.

I returned to the hall two hours later, drunk, bleary eyed, and demanded food of the kitchen wench. Captain Grove and Master Ekins were horrified to see me enter in such a state, and even worse, my wife burst into tears, fled upstairs, leaving our son with my father. Father called to me to come and sit at his table. I could barely stand, and when I tried to do as he asked, fell giggling insanely in a heap on the floor. Captain Grove summoned one of the garrison soldiers; they picked me up and half marched, half dragged me upstairs to our room, where they dumped me on the bed to sleep it off. Both returned to the hall, where Grove asked my father to join them, and the three of them sat together talking quietly, while Johnny played nearby. Master Ekins spoke first, to my father.

'Your son is truly in a bad way, now that Amelia pushes him away, master John. I would know what we may do to help. Perchance talk to Amelia? She has such a destructive streak, has she not?'

'Aye. She feels hurt that he be not here with her, but Robert has his orders. She refuses to accept that.'

'Indeed, and he works for a very hard master in Nat Whetham. I know him not, but by reputation. Robert needs must tell her all, yet he may not.'

'Mayhap he takes her to Northampton with him?'

'Nay, 'tis not possible. Whetham would not have it. No more would Robert. Amelia would be in mortal danger, Johnny too. We have heard....stories.' This from Master Ekins.

'Stories? What stories?'

'There have been murders, master John. Robert must not have Amelia threatened so as to distract him, and disrupt his work.'

Their quiet discussion continued for another hour or so, but they came to no firm conclusion; all three of them realised that I and Amelia must be brought together again somehow. A thorny problem.

Late in the day, after the small garrison had eaten supper, I dragged myself downstairs, my head pounding, and eyes red, face white. I truly looked a mess again. Master Ekins and Grove sat talking, and seeing me appear in the hall, called me to go to them. Captain Grove spoke angrily to me.

'Captain, ye are a disgrace to your rank. If ye please, go to the scullery, and wash yourself. Then we may order ye supper.'

I nodded groggily, and wobbled over to the scullery door. One of the workmaids opened the door wide, and called me in. She pointed to a large pail of cold water.

'Watter may fix yer 'ead, captain. Dryin' cloth uvver there.'

When I reappeared a few minutes later, I felt a little better, though still unkempt and bleary eyed. I tottered to where Master Ekins and captain Grove were sitting, and without asking, took a seat. Master Ekins opened the conversation, 'Robert, ye needs must speak with your wife. She were sore hurt by your state this afternoon.' He put a hand up as I started to answer.

'Hold hard. I know she be lonely, be unhappy with ye away. 'Tis only natural, man. We must talk about your work, try to find a way to help ye.'

I felt my guilt well up yet again.

'I have done things of which I am truly ashamed, Master John. Colonel Whetham cares not that I be away from Amelia, that he offends my conscience. He would take Jeanne soon, give her to his men to wring information from her. How can I face Amelia, when I knows what they would do to her?'

'Ye must face her, talk to her,' was Ekins' reply.

'Yet I may not tell her of my work. How would she understand, if I do not?' I sighed.

Grove's answer was more constructive.

'Do not reproach her, Robert. She needs ye. Tell her that ye would take her to Northampton with ye, but may not. Tell her that your work troubles ye greatly, but ye may not yet tell her of it. Above all, tell her that ye love her. 'Tis not so hard, methinks.'

'Aye, ye're right. I will try.'

Ekins added, 'Go to her room, man. Not in this hall, in so public a place.'

I nodded, and got to my feet. 'I thank ye both.' But I felt very unsure of myself, to add to the burden of my massive guilt.

I climbed the staircase slowly, and then walked along the corridor to Amelia's room, knocked – my nerves jangled – and entered. She was sitting in a chair, looking downcast, and was absentmindedly sewing one of Johnny's small pairs of breeches. As I approached her, I saw her stiffen, and look up at me.

'Lia, I know that ye're hurt that I cannot be with ye. I... my work...it be under military orders. If I were to leave it without Whetham allows it, I could be hanged for a deserter. Mayhap ye would wish to come to Northampton with me? 'Tis too dangerous, my love. People...lasses, lads...have died for helping me. It trouble me so much, so very much.'

She looked at me as I sensed her growing sense of fear.

'Died, Robbie? How so?'

'I.... needs must.... discover traitors. They kill to avoid discovery.'

Amelia was at a loss to know how to answer.

'They tried to kill me too, but I fought them off. Forget not that I must yet be a soldier, think, act like a soldier. I truly wish 'twere not so.'

The question that I dreaded most slipped from her lips.

'What of my sister, Robbie? Has ye seen her?'

I took a deep breath, thinking hard how to answer.

'Jeanne be for sure with them.'

Her hand flew to her mouth.

'Jeanne....with traitors?'

'I would not tell ye, though I must. Colonel Whetham may yet take her.'

She looked at me aghast, and realising what that meant, burst into tears. I pulled her to me, and held her, while she sobbed, and at last, pulled away from me.

"Tis your duty to, to, hand her over to him?'

I nodded sadly, as I felt my guilt well up even more.

'Aye. Yet I seek not to. Whetham allows me but three days away. I fear that he may take her whilst I be here.'

She shook her head in disbelief, then looking around her, 'Robbie, have ye eaten? Ale do not sate your hunger.'

I shook my head. Taking my hand, she stood, wiped away her tears, smoothed down her skirts, and pulled me to go with her, down to the hall. I did not resist.

I realised that I had not seen Johnny, and asked where he was, as we reached the stairs.

'Worry not,' she said, 'I asked master Ekins's maid to look after him. Let us have time without him.'

As we entered the hall, both Ekins and Grove, who were still seated smoking pipes and talking, looked at us, and their relief was palpable.

"Tis better to see ye together,' from Grove, with a cautious smile.

I smiled back, if a little weakly. Nonetheless, I was relieved that Amelia seemed to have come round a little, at least for now.

'Lia, would ye like to sit with our friends, or just ye and me?'

She wanted to sit away from Grove and Ekins, so we found two empty seats, and sat together. Master Ekins called for his kitchen maid to come and see to our needs.

'Have ye any food, mistress? We have not eaten.'

The maid answered 'Aye', and returned to the kitchen, from whence she came out again two or three minutes later with bread, cheese, and meat, plus a jug of small ale and two pots. I and Amelia were more than ready for some food, and tucked in at once. The food certainly improved our mood. After eating, Amelia brought up the subject of Johnny.

'Johnny is of an age when he should be schooled, Robbie. Master Ekins's maid and I try to teach him his letters, but we be not teachers.

222

How thinks ye we may school Johnny?'

I hadn't really expected that, but realised that, at the age of seven, he should be in grammar school if he were to receive a decent education.

"Tis a little thorny, I think. I were sent to Wellingborough grammar school, and stayed with a cousin of my father's. Wellingborough be no place for a child, with the troubles there. Northampton, no, not safe. Have ye cousins that could help, mayhap?'

Lia thought carefully.

'Only my uncle Tom. Could your father help?'

I felt that my father had enough to worry about.

'He may know of someone, but I fear he be much troubled with business. Let us ask Master Ekins? His brother? Cousin? He lives at Chester House. 'Tis close to Wellingborough. If he has childer, mayhap he has a teacher in his house?'

She thought that a good idea, and we settled on talking it over with John Ekins on the morrow. After that, we indulged in small talk, during which Amelia asked me about Northampton. She had never been there.

"Tis prosperous, for sure. Many army men, some with wives, and the hostelries do good business. But, 'tis dangerous because of my work. The city sells many boots and other leather goods to the army. 'Tis a large market with many stalls, much good food. When 'tis safe to go, I will take ye, ye would love the market,' I said, hoping that it would help to make us feel more as one. I remembered the locket that I had bought, which was still in my secret pocket, pulled it out, and gave it to her.

'I did not have time to find a chain,' I said. She seemed much pleased with it, and I hoped it would continue to improve our fraught relationship. She had not seen a market for several years, when the war had made it too risky for stallholders to travel to Rushden, and, indeed, Rushden's inhabitants to travel further afield for a bigger market in such as Wellingborough or Kettering. I remembered that there was still the issue of Ned Mawle's stealing some of my father's stock, about which so far I had still not said anything. I decided to confide in Amelia.

'When father spoke with Ned Mawle, Lia, he also discovered that the stock did not match his bookkeeping. I fear that Ned may be stealing from my father, but I did not tell my father that I knew of't, since I had to go away. I worried that father would challenge Ned about the shortfall, and I not here to help.'

She was a little surprised, to say the least, but privately, she was pleased that I had taken her into my confidence. She was quite an independent woman – she had to be, during my long absence in the army – which was unusual in our time; men usually took all the decisions.

"Twould sorely hurt your father. He has treated Ned so well,' she replied; 'Perchance ye should speak with Ned on your own.'

'I already did, my dear, but I did not see the matter resolved.'

I had put the fear of God into Ned Mawle that day; perhaps Ned would have learned his lesson, though I doubted it. It made a change from my problems in Northampton! Then I considered it a little further, and realised that Ned of course had been put up to it by none other than the officer who was so interested in me in the Sun inn, Jim Roding/Watterson. I subconsciously spoke aloud, 'is there nowhere I can leave it behind?'

Amelia looked startled.

'Robbie, what say ye?'

'Oh, I am sorry, I were thinking about Ned. And that....Will Watterson. He be... in Northampton now.'

'What?'

'Aye. Ned were put up to 't by Will. Will Watterson calls himself Roding now.'

I realised that I should not have told her, but could not see the harm in it - yet.

'So this, this Roding. He be trying to harm ye?'

'Damn fool' I thought. 'I must tell her now.'

'He harms not myself, but those who have helped me. Wears an officer's uniform now.'

She recoiled in shock.

'God in heaven! He could, he could... harm Johnny and ... myself? And he knows us all.'

Now, I had to tell her.

'Aye, I fear 'tis so. 'Tis why ye are safer here. Whetham will have him, I think. Mayhap not yet.'

I sought to reassure her.

'Worry yourself not. But I would ask ye, if ye please, take care, for ye both.'

At least, I mused, Amelia was beginning to understand what I had to do, and its risks. I would rather she did not know too much, she would be terribly upset; would I lose her if I told her of my time in the war and working since? I did not know.

That night, we slept together, and for the first time since the sixth day of last month, February, and happily for both, we made love. I felt an awful guilt afterward for succumbing to Jeanne's dubious charms. However, once I fell asleep, I did not wake again until the seven o'clock bell, followed by the knocker-upper, and fortuitously, my demons had more or less left me alone that night.

Monday 19th March 1649

The day proved to be ordinary at first. After breakfast, my father headed off to his chamber to work , while I went to pay Ned Mawle a visit at the old house. As before, I found Ned sitting at the desk, writing in the ledger.

'Good morrow, Master Ned.' Ned looked up, and immediately

looked fearful. And shifty.

'Good morrow yerself, maister Robert. What… brings 'ee to me this day?'

'I would check the stock against your ledger, Ned.' He looked thunderstruck.

"Tis… in order, maister.'

'I would be the judge of that, Ned. Show me the stock, if ye please.'

Ned rose, and took me into the other rooms of the house, pointing out the sheets of leather, then the completed boots. I mentally noted the quantities of each. Returning to the ledger in the front room, I demanded to see the relevant entries in the ledger. Ned showed me, then stood there shaking, as I compared the quantities I had seen with the entries in the book. Again, there was a discrepancy of five sheets of leather and ten pairs of boots.

'The figures do not tally, Ned. If ye please, explain.'

Ned became a gibbering wreck, remembering his cut ear, and his hand involuntarily shot up to it. He tried to explain that his accounting was wrong.

'Then let us go to my father's chamber, and check against his main ledger.'

At this, Ned sank to his knees.

'I beg ye, please forgive me.'

I wanted to know why the discrepancy, but Ned did everything in his power to avoid answering.

'Did I not say to ye, last time we spake, that ye needs must be honest with me?'

Ned nodded, but said nothing.

'Ned, I could force ye to tell, but I would avoid hurting ye. Come, we will talk with my father.'

Ned hung his head.

"Twere that Will Watterson, maister. 'E threaten me wife and childer if'n I gi'e 'em not to 'im.'

I had my evidence.

'Very well. Tell me all.'

Ned's initial shaking reduced as the story flooded out. Watterson appeared every few days, demanding more leather and boots. When Ned tried not to give in, he cut off Ned's smallest child's ear. His wife was terrified, and begged Ned to give him the stock.

'I can't save 'er 'n' me childer frum that man. 'E be marv'lous cruel.'

I answered this.

'Ned, he be in Northampton. I know him, I watch him. Governor Whetham will soon have him – and if he do not, I would slit his damned throat.'

Ned gulped, and put his hands together.

"Ow do 'ee plan to save me Liza 'n the childer, captain?"

I was only too aware that I could not keep them safe, but said, 'Ned, ye must be patient. Whetham would have Will and his… his… friends soon.'

I bade Ned good day, with a warning not to help Will if at all possible.

By the time I returned to the hall, I was hungry, so looked for Amelia and Johnny, and suggested an early lunch, after which we could have some time out in the hall's park. The weather, fortunately, had so far been kind to us, and it would be a good opportunity to relax and enjoy the spring sunshine for a while.

Lunch, as always at Rushden hall, was a simple affair, usually consisting of bread, perhaps some butter, and cheese or a slice or two of meat. The food had never been lavish, certainly not since I was quartered there, and I missed the good food at the Sun in

Northampton.

'We would not be fat at Rushden hall!' I said to Amelia, 'But I fear I eat too well at my billet in the Sun inn, in Northampton. 'Tis very good food, and much of it.'

She laughed, and patted my belly.

'Aye, I noticed your paunch, husband.'

It almost felt like the time before I went to war, at least for a while.

After our repast, we enjoyed strolling around the expansive park of the hall, hand in hand, and watching Johnny run around, picking some of the flowers that were beginning to show in the spring sunshine. Northampton, Whetham, Watterson, and all the mayhem of the intelligencing ring could be on the moon for a while. My father came out of the hall after a while, obviously heading for his old house. I called to him, and quickly told him that I had talked to Ned Mawle about Watterson.

'I fear he still robs ye, father. But I have put the fear of God into him again. But he may yet dread Will Watterson more than myself or ye.'

He expressed his gratitude. I watched him walk off towards his old house with a renewed spring in his step.

I and Amelia savoured the afternoon, playing with Johnny on and off, even lying in the grass together for a while. I dreaded going back to Northampton, but for now said nothing to Amelia about it. It would come all too soon.

Supper was a much more congenial affair than of late. There was a little better repast than usual, which I learnt had been put on mainly out of my father's pocket; he was grateful to me, and the three of us, as well as Johnny, tucked into it with more than usual pleasure. I knew that the next day would be a further holiday for us, but after an early lunch the day after, Wednesday 21st March, 1649, I must hurry back to Whetham's domain. It was a date that I would remember for the rest of my days.

Tuesday 20th March 1649.

The following morning, breakfast passed off much as usual, after which I suggested that Amelia and I might find a boatman to take us for a trip on the river Nene. The Nene is a shallow river, and though Amelia could not swim – her heavy clothes would inhibit swimming anyway - there was little risk for me. Master Ekins' maid could look after Johnny for a couple of hours while we enjoyed our free time together. Johnny of course clamoured to go; but we were adamant. It would not be safe and he would probably drown if he should fall in, whereas I and Amelia were likely to survive. The maid was expert at persuading the small child to do as he was told, and then I and Amelia walked hand in hand out of the village towards the bridge to Irthlingborough. The river was narrow by the bridge, so it was popular for fishermen who plied the river fishing, usually by nets, and working in pairs of boats. The fish sold well in the little market at Irthlingborough in this time of straitened circumstances for the people of the area. A fisherman would also welcome the chance to earn a few silver pennies rowing I and Amelia up river a way, then back again.

We easily found a fisherman who would take us, and his shallop looked watertight enough, so we clambered aboard, and off we went. It proved to be a lovely relaxed morning, and all went well for us, arriving back at the little wooden jetty by Irthlingborough bridge around twelve o'clock. As earlier, holding hands, we walked happily back to the hall, and the prospect of a simple lunch. Johnny of course was overjoyed to see us, and threw his arms around his mother's neck the moment she leant down to pick him up. After a relaxed lunch, I and Amelia decided to walk to the local church and back. It was such a beautiful spring day, both of us felt relatively happy and relaxed in the sunshine. At supper, we chatted with Master Ekins and captain Grove, and the sergeant of the now depleted garrison. By the end of the evening, a tired me and Amelia and Johnny retired to our room ready for a good night's sleep.

Wednesday 21st March 1649.

The next morning, though we had not made love again, we looked almost like newlyweds at breakfast. Until I mentioned that I must return to Northampton after lunch, and I could not go churching with her – which was not really possible anyway, with no preacher. I told Amelia that I wished I could stay just as we were for good, but dare not do so. I dare not risk Whetham's wrath. It somewhat dampened our mood, but with the weather deteriorating, and rain showers occurring from time to time, we stayed indoors and talked of our future. Amelia brought up the subject of her sister, which rather shook up my easy mood, and my feelings of profound guilt welled up in me again.

'What to do about Jeanne, Robbie? Could ye perchance free her from the bad people's clutches?'

I was at a loss to know what to say.

'I know not, truly. She seem fixed in her evil ways. I fear Whetham may take her afore I may do anything for her.'

Amelia had to ask.

'Wouldst he….. hang her?' I sighed as I tried to form an answer that would not upset her too much.

'Much worse, I fear. His men.. are.. much skilled with hot irons, burning oil. She would beg to die long 'fore they had finished with her. She has little to tell, I think. Yet they would try to get more.'

Amelia's expression darkened.

'I would have not told ye, but 'tis the truth. I would think on 't, if I may help her.'

Grove heard the conversation, and interjected.

'Robert, torture be illegal, I think.'

230

'Aye, but ye know as I do, when intelligencers be involved, 'tis done anyway.'

'Mayhap 'twill not come to that.'

"Tis to be hoped not. I... have not heard of Whetham having it done, but he do threaten.'

My father heard some of the conversation as he came to join us, and immediately tried to change the topic.

'I hope ye would be soon back in Rushden, Robert. Amelia must not get down again, I think.'

I replied that I hoped I would be able to return quickly.

'But 'tis in Whetham's hands,' I added, with a sense of impending gloom.

Lunch came all too quickly, and I packed my snapsack and arms, then went to the stable and readied my horse, after which I came back into the hall to say my goodbyes to Amelia and my father, then my small son. I held Amelia in my arms, and kissed her gently.

'I would come back as soon as I may, my love. Do not be downhearted, I beg ye.'

She returned my kiss, and then picked up Johnny, asking him to kiss his father. Johnny kicked up a fuss but I kissed him anyway, then briefly holding Amelia's arm, walked out of their lives again for my next trip back to the city, with a heavy heart. I preferred not to look back. I would rather not see Amelia's tears again, I felt too depressed and anxious already.

Chapter 15: Maud and Margery

Unlike my ride back to Rushden, I took the slower route for my return to Northampton, crossing the river at the London Road into St Thomas's Gate and the city. I was surprised to overtake two men wheeling a large handcart, on which was obviously a body under an old sheet. I slowed, and asked who was the body. One of the men answered me.

'Dunno cap'n, it be a young woman. Fished 'er out o' the river but 'alf an 'our ago. Takin' 'er t'the Guild'all fer th' constable.'

I do not know what prompted me to do so, but I wanted to see the body.

'If ye please, may I see her?' I said to the carter.

'Aye. Mayhap ye'll know 'er. But she ain't a pretty sight. Jack?'

They pulled the sheet away, and the body that they revealed came as a profound shock. It was the naked body of Maud Smith. She had clearly been beaten and burned, her fingernails were missing, and I realised, her feet had been burned almost to the bone and blackened half way up her calves. One of her eyes was missing, leaving a mangled mess. I had seen much during the war, but this so shocked me that I turned away and vomited. I could barely stop myself bursting into tears.

'I know the woman. She be Maud Smith. She were alive four days ago when I last saw her. Do ye know what befell her?'

The men both shook their head.

'She were found at dawn this morrow, maister. In th' river, by the bridge yonder. 'Tis all we know.'

'If ye please, treat her poor body with care. A silver penny each for your trouble.'

They eagerly took the silver, and doffed their rough caps to me, before I rode on. I was overcome by a very black mood indeed, so when I stabled my horse at the Sun inn, settled her, and dropped off my snapsack, I then sought food myself, before walking to the Guildhall and Whetham's office.

As soon as I entered the Sun's taproom I called for a best ale, and sat in my usual corner seat to drink it, hoping that it would steady my shredded senses, before steeling myself to go to Whetham's office. The state of Maud's wrecked body affected me greatly, and my nerves felt as though tied in knots. I could not confront Whetham in this state; I was too close to tears. I kept imagining Joan the Whore in the same state and what it would do to Amelia and my marriage. Two other officers came over to me, and asked to sit. I pointed to the other two chairs.

'Aye, if ye please, do so. But I be not good company. I have seen the body of the young woman found in the river. 'Twas an awful sight.'

One of the officers replied, 'Word has it that she were done great ill by the Governor's men.'

"Tis so, I fear. I needs must visit our good colonel in his office, but I have need of strong ale afore I go.'

The other officer noticed my irony when I said 'good colonel'.

'Ye might quiet your tongue, captain. Whetham does not welcome such words if they get back.'

I shrugged, and studied my ale, then drank more. The second officer, also a captain, prompted, 'Ye seem most troubled, captain. Did ye know the woman?'

I spoke quietly, trying to steady my shaky voice.

"Twas me that arrested her.'

The other two looked at each other, then the first replied.

'Aye, 'tis hard when ye know the prisoner. Best not, methinks.'

I realised when the Guildhall clock struck five that I was overdue at Whetham's office. I took my leave quickly, and walked to the Guildhall, where I was speedily admitted to Whetham's presence. 'Come in, captain. Ye are late. What kept ye?'

'I chanced on men bringing Maud Smith's body from the river. She was cruelly used by your men, Governor, most cruelly. I am deeply troubled by 't.'

Whetham looked at me, but said nothing, and sat tugging at his beard. There was suddenly a loud commotion outside in the hall, and a woman's voice demanded imperiously, 'Out of my way, cur! I will see Whetham!'

The next second, the office boor burst open, and a small woman stalked into the office. I judged her about forty-five, dressed all in black, but in beautiful velvet clothes of the highest quality, relieved by an exquisitely patterned lace collar, and wearing an expensive hat that was now out of fashion over beautifully coiffured black hair. She walked with a slight limp, and used a polished black cane, which she pointed at Whetham.

'Are ye the one that used my poor daughter so monstrously, dog?'

Whetham was not used to being addressed like this, and rising to his feet, snapped at her.

'Who be ye, to speak to me thus, madam?'

'Milady to ye, cur! I am Lady Margery Sorrell. I take it ye are Whetham?'

Her black eyes flashed with a cold fury as she said it. Whetham was taken aback by the scorn in her voice.

'I am your Governor, milady. Nathaniel Whetham, lieutenant colonel.'

I tried to introduce myself, since I realised now who Maud was, and felt horribly responsible. She turned a little towards me.

'Quiet, worm! I speak to this dog!' and prodded Whetham's ample stomach hard with her cane, forcing him to take a step back. It slowly dawned on Whetham too: 'Your daughter... were... Maud? That I arrested four days ago?'

I tried again to interject. 'Milady, she..'

234

I was cut short as Lady Sorrell's cane stabbed me viciously in the midriff, causing me to sit down heavily on the chair behind me, 'I told ye, be quiet, worm!'

Whetham now thought to go on the offensive.

'Lady Sorrell, Maud were exposed as a traitor. We have evidence of her wrongdoing. My captain here brought her to me for questioning, but she would not talk. My men would.. persuade... her.'

Lady Sorrell's black eyes blazed even more furiously – if that were possible.

'She were but a child, Governor' - she spat the word out - 'But seventeen years. Ye, dog, did not have to torture her so. Torture, dog! A child! What are ye?'

She whacked Whetham across the face with her cane as she said the last words. His shock at being attacked so, by this small, furious woman, left him speechless. He had never in his life been treated like this by a mere woman. 'I tell ye what ye are!'

Recovering, he said, 'A man-'

'Man? Man? Ye are snivelling cruel cur! Tom Fairfax shall hear of your cruelty. He is a close friend. Torture is illegal. He will have your plums for a necklace!'

She now turned those flashing black eyes on me. 'And who are ye, worm?'

I stood up, doffed my hat.

'Captain Robert Barker, milady. I observed your daughter at a house where intelligencers pass messages. 'Twas I brought her to colonel Whetham. She told us she were Maud Smith, your maid.'

I got no further.

'Ye did not think to bring her to me, worm?'

I now received a painful whack of her cane.

''Tis servant's place to speak for her mistress, thinks ye?'

'We thought to place our maid in her stead...'

'To spy on me? Ye dares to spy on me, worm?'

I groaned inwardly. Now she turned back to Whetham, and continued to berate him. Whetham's temper was boiling now.

'Madam – milady – 'tis part of my job to catch traitors. Your daughter played with traitors, and were burned for it. If ye continues to attack me, 'twill be your turn next in my prison. Mayhap 'twill cool your accursed temper!'

It was a red rag to a very angry bull....or, perhaps more accurately, cow. Lady Sorrell picked up a large crockery inkpot and threw it at Whetham with so much force that the stopper flew out, and he was covered in sticky black ink. It splashed across his face and neck, and ran down onto his white collar then inside his doublet and onto his shirt.

'Guards – arrest this curséd woman – NOW!'

Two guards came into the office with their half pikes held out, and would have grabbed Lady Sorrell's arms, but she held up her hand in an imperious gesture.

'Ye has no power to arrest me. I am your Governor's superior. Step away!'

They looked at each other, and did as they were ordered. She turned back to Whetham.

'Colonel, see that my poor daughter's corpse is carefully wrapped with fresh white linen and brought to my house this eve. Your guards here can do it – give them something useful to do, instead of seeking to assault their betters.'

Turning back to me, she said, 'Ye, worm, what has ye to say for yourself?'

I sought to placate her.

'Milady, I may only offer my sincere condolence. What is done is done, and may not be undone. I be deeply sorry for 't.'

She looked me up and down. 'H'mm. At least one of ye has a soul.'

She turned on her heel, and saying 'I bid ye good day,' over her shoulder, walked out through the ranks of the guards, who were keeping a straight face with great difficulty, as she left the building, summoning her coachman. From inside, we heard her carriage wheels and horses clop-clopping over the cobbled roadway, as the carriage moved off.

After she had gone, Whetham tried to recover some of his shattered dignity. He slammed the office door, having told his guards to return to their posts, and sat down at his office desk.

'God's teeth! What a marvellous temper on that woman! I never have seen the like.'

I answered in a way that I would not usually dare to do.

'Aye, colonel, 'tis true. Yet how would ye feel if 'twere your daughter? Much the same, I think.'

Whetham looked at me with an astonished expression.

'Captain, did ye not know her name? She spoke well, did she not?'

'Aye, sir, she spake uncommon well for a maid. But...her clothes were a maid's. She said her name were Maud Smith. Yet, sir, 'twas not I that tortured her. Killed her.'

Whetham was angered by my obvious insubordination.

'Captain, Lady Margery be my superior and may speak so, but if ye please, remember your place.'

I, too, was angry, and didn't feel contrite.

'Aye, sir, I know my place, yet I but speak the truth. I fear ye would do the same to my sister-in-law, be her so lowly a toy of the traitors. She knows little, and I will get ye what she knows. But I beg ye, do not do as ye did to Maud Sorrell.'

As Whetham steepled his hands in front of his face, and looked at me over his fingers, I continued my insubordination. I had ceased to care.

237

'And I must tell ye, sir, if ye take Joan, I would no more work for ye. Even if my life be forfeit.'

Whetham was clearly shocked at this.

'I give ye my word, captain, if ye can make Joan talk, I would not harm her.'

'Sir, I saw Maud myself this day, 'twas an awful sight. My mind be much disturbed by 't. I did bad things, saw bad things in the war, but never so bad as this. I may not face more of 't.'

As a tear ran down my cheek, Whetham realised how disturbed was my state of mind.

'Captain, think ye I am immune? I would see this business over. Truly, I would. Ye may trust my word. Now, I would that ye return to the Sun inn, and leave this behind ye. For this day. If ye please, attend me on the morrow, we shall talk more on 't.'

I stood, saluted, and left Whetham's office, walking out, past the guards, who were looking at me questioningly. I did not, could not bear to, return their gaze. Once outside, I felt so weighed down by my guilt, that I at first could not return to face my fellow officers at the Sun and headed instead to the now almost empty marketplace. Lady Margery's insults had stung me greatly, coming after the awful shock, the horror, of discovering that Maud was her daughter – and only seventeen! - she looked so much older. Then there was her mangled body. I could not get the image out of my mind. I walked slowly to the market cross, and sat on its base, head in hands. The thought of Joan the Whore, my sister in law Jeanne, suffering the same fate made my stomach revolt again, and I could not help retching and then vomiting, until one of the market traders who was preparing a new stall for the market on the morrow came over to me to ask if I was all right. I smiled weakly at him.

'I thank ye, Master, I be a little sick at my stomach. I will be all right, methinks, when I have eaten.' The trader asked if I was sure, then walked back to his stall, which he was fitting up from materials on a handcart. Seeing the handcart triggered the image of Maud on the handcart earlier, and more tears flowed, which I strove to hide behind my hands. I had never felt so low, so utterly miserable and distraught. I thought that my best recourse was to walk back to the inn, and order a best ale. Drowning my sorrows in a good strong ale would at least deaden my overwhelming guilt for a while – but I worried about the night to come, when my demons would surely return to torment my soul even more. I wondered if some good wine would keep those demons away for a while more effectively than the ale.

As I walked slowly back towards Guildhall Street, I felt a hand on my left shoulder, and spun round, instinctively pulling my pistol out and cocking it in one swift movement. When I faced the owner of the hand, I realised it was just the market trader who had asked if I were all right earlier. The man jumped back and raised his hands. I uncocked my pistol and put it back in my pocket, and apologised to the man.

'I be much troubled this evening,' I said, 'Ye startled me.'

The trader put his hands down, then raised one, palm out.

'I would not take a pistol ball, captain. I would just ask if ye now feel better.'

I made myself smile.

'I go for some food. Mayhap I feel better soon. I thank ye for your concern, and bid ye good evening.'

The man looked much relieved, and stood while I walked slowly, shakily, towards the Sun inn. He did not think it wise to turn his back on such a touchy soldier with a pistol in his pocket until I was well away from him.

I, for my part, felt embarrassed that I had reacted so precipitantly towards a man who only thought to help me, and I feared that I might snap and attack one of my fellow officers, since I was feeling in a very volatile state of mind. It would not be wise to leave my pistol in my room, even in the snapsack, but I decided to return first to my room,

239

and leave my cloak and tuck there. Then I would order the ale and food. Vomiting had left me feeling hungry, and that too made my temper even more edgy than it would otherwise have been. Rather than go in through the front door, and have to walk through the taproom full of soldiers, I went to the stable, checked that my horse was properly stabled, and then in via the back door, quickly slipping onto the stairs, and out of sight of the taproom. I unlocked my room door, entered, took off my cloak, hat, and tuck, and threw them onto the bed. I splashed water over my face from the fresh pail of water, and dried it off, afterwards left my room, making sure to lock the door, and made my way down to the taproom. It was not as full as I expected, though it was a Wednesday evening, and fortunately no-one had taken my usual seat in the corner. Seeing the kitchen wench, I asked for the strongest ale, and food, then sat, and for once removed my hat. I did not have to wait many minutes before she returned with a wooden tray containing a jug of ale and a pot, plus a plate of meat pie, a chunk of fresh bread, butter and cheese, and a bowl with some root vegetables, mashed into an unidentifiable mix. It was steaming, and I sniffed it; it smelt very good. The meat pie proved to be game in a tangy sauce with apple, herbs, and other things that I could not identify. I did not care, it smelt delicious, so I tucked in at once, burning my mouth with the hot meat. Sam Goodly appeared, and asked to sit with me, so I flapped a hand and nodded, then fanned my open mouth. Goodly laughed.

"'Twas a tad hot, Robert? Have ye not learned to be careful when eating Meg's hot pies?"

A swig of the ale cooled my burnt mouth, and three more swigs of the strong ale slowly improved my mood a little. The meat pie was delicious – if only the cooks at Rushden hall were as good – and as I downed more of it, my mood lifted further. After I had finished the meat pie, I asked the kitchen wench for a dessert; she brought stuffed quinces with almonds and other nuts. I was in my element at last. My mood became merry under the influence of the alcohol, and I happily played several games of Noddy with Sam Goodly. I lost each one, costing me a few pence each time, but I did not care. I intended to drown my guilt in alcohol and high jinks while I might. As the evening wore on, I and Goodly ordered sack, which we quaffed in ever greater quantity, both of us becoming more and more convinced we could sing like skylarks – much to the annoyance of the other officers present. Off-key raucous singing punctuated by bouts of insane giggling is not enjoyable to those who have to endure it! The only time our caterwauling stopped was when one or other had to go to the privy to relieve himself; even that did not endure well, as both of us became too inebriated to find the privy and pissed anywhere we could find in the yard. The landlord was far from amused, but his rebukes fell on totally deaf ears, as we tried to get him to join in our attempts at songs. Finally, the landlord threatened to throw both of us out onto the street, and demanded we retire to our rooms. By this time, we were so drunk that we had to be almost carried to our rooms. Not wishing for our respective beds to be soiled by our failing to wake and wetting ourselves, we were dumped on the floor of our respective rooms by the inn staff who helped us.

For Sam Goodly, it was merely a drunken stupor for much of the night. For me, however, it became a night of abject terror as my nightmares came back to me with a vengeance. I woke the occupants of nearby rooms several times during the night with my screams and howls as my demons came to torment me in my dreams. The too real jabs of their wicked knives, imagined oil poured over my body and ignited, and wailing, twisted images of Maud, the dead lads, and the other corpses that my efforts to discover the spies had left in my wake came to torment my subconscious. I repeatedly woke with sweat pouring from me, shaking, and once even biting my tongue; twice I tried to find my piss-pot and failed, wetting myself in the process. By five o'clock in the morning I was a total wreck. Worse, a total almost sober wreck, as a mood of utter gloom descended on me, and I broke

241

down in tears of frustration and despair, hammering the floor with my fists – much to the anger of the occupants of neighbouring rooms woken by the noise.

Thursday 22nd March 1649.

When the Guildhall clock struck seven I was wide awake, fully sober, with a pounding headache, face haggard and pale, and eyes like ripe tomatoes. I was as unpretty a sight as anyone could imagine. And to top it all, I was to go to Whetham's office as soon as he arrived for work.

Somehow, I managed to wash myself, find clean clothes, and stagger downstairs to break my fast. Before I could sit at my usual table, my bowels and stomach erupted in anger at the abuse of their equanimity, and I had to rush to the privy to vomit and explode in diarrhoea – the biggest problem being which to deal with first. Somehow I managed to cope, and came back into the taproom looking even worse than before. Several of my fellow officers looked at me, and averted their eyes to the ceiling or tut-tutted pretentiously at my appearance. I struggled to get some food down, and asked for a pot of milk instead of my usual small ale. Eventually I managed to eat enough to feel a little better, as my inevitable dehydration reduced with drinking more of the milk, and I went shakily back to my room to dress for going to Whetham's office.

I was admitted to Whetham's office to find him in a grim mood. Other officers had already complained to Whetham about my appalling behaviour the evening before and during the night. The colonel was far from amused, and I found myself on the receiving end of the dressing down of my life. I sat there, looking downcast, then burst into tears and sobbed uncontrollably as Whetham lashed me with his tongue for about fifteen minutes, and threatened demotion or worse should it happen again. He expected his officers to behave with a modicum of decorum, no matter what they felt like.

Eventually, he said to me, 'God's blood, what ails ye, man? I know ye were much disturbed by the death of the young woman yesterday,

242

but your behaviour last evening were disgraceful. Could ye not go to the church and seek solace of the preacher?'

I confessed that I had not even thought of it.

'Or even take yourself a whore for the night?'

That touched a nerve, and Whetham was shocked and surprised to see me start sobbing again. He had still not properly realised the depth of my worrying about Jeanne, let alone my ever-burgeoning guilt at the things that I had done, seen, or caused, and could not atone for.

'Would ye have more time with your family, mayhap?'

I nodded. A plan was forming in my mind that I dare not whisper to anyone, least of all to Nathaniel Whetham. But I said, 'I would first attend Maud's burial. I feel so sorry for the girl. 'Tis the least I could do.'

Whetham was not unhappy that I should do so, but his motives were not so much to alleviate my grief as to salve his own conscience.

'I will grant ye that. Lady Margery may not welcome ye, but pray do not anger her more. I would not have her attack me again. 'Tis not good for my temper.'

Remembering her fury the day before, I smiled weakly through my tears.

'After the burial, ye may have a few days at your home. We may not afford to let these traitors think we be weak, captain. We must plan to take them all down as soon as we may.'

I had no choice but to say, 'Aye, sir. The priority must be to discover who owns the house where messages be passed. Also who 'tis that passes them from inside the house. They must be the key.' Whetham reminded me that Joan the Whore had not yet returned the false letter that I had given her to pass to the intelligencing ring.

'Aye, sir. She would visit me again, I think. When least I expect.'

Then, thinking to deflect too much interest in Jeanne from Whetham, I went on.

243

'I would visit mistress Joan soon. I would make her talk.'

Whetham's reply made my heart sink.

'Ye must make sure she do talk, captain, else I will do't.'

After a further hour of discussions, I was given leave to go, proceed to find out about the funeral for Maud, and attend her burial. It would give me little comfort, but at least I could show my contrition to Lady Margery. My involvement in Maud's horrible death, if she found out, would horrify Amelia, and probably undo much of the bridge building that I had tried to bring about during my short stay with her. After leaving the Guildhall, I walked up Drapery and Sheep Street to the church of the Holy Sepulchre, went into the church, and asked the preacher about the burial. The latter told me that she would be buried the following morning.

'But are ye invited, captain? Lady Margery has given tickets to those whom she would have attend.' This was news to me, though tickets for funerals of rich people was the norm.

'I did not know, preacher. Mayhap I would knock at Lady Margery's door and ask if I may attend.'

The preacher opined that I might try.

'Captain, Lady Margery be a very private person. She may not welcome ye. If ye please, why would ye attend?' I answered honestly.

''Twas I who took her to colonel Whetham. I trusted him to treat her fairly. I regret it greatly, and w-' The preacher cut in.

'She were grievously hurt by Whetham's men, I hear. I suggest ye sit far back in the church. If ye please, do not disturb Lady Margery. Ye would do well to avoid rousing her wrath.'

I thanked the preacher for his advice, and slowly walked back towards the marketplace. As I walked, I pondered the thorny problem of how to find out who owned the message house. 'Mayhap neighbours would know,' I mused, 'Or a local preacher. I may try neighbours.'

I resolved to walk there that morning, and look around the vicinity. I could also watch the comings and goings from the alley nearby. It might give a clue.

Chapter 16: Plan and Perfidy

Crossing the marketplace, I found some of 'Arry's pals wandering around, begging what scraps of food or money that they could; it is illegal, and they would be for a whipping if they were caught. I decided to ask their help again. With care, no-one will get hurt. An older boy approached me.

"Ave a ha'penny to spare, cap'n?'

I responded with, 'If ye would like to earn a penny or two, I have a task for ye.'

The lad was plainly nervous of helping me.

"Twas 'ee 'at caused 'Arry 'n' Joe to be killed. Oi dun't wanna lose me loife, maister.'

'Aye, nor would I want ye to. If ye are careful, 'twould not happen.'

'What d'ee want, then?'

I ushered him away from the marketplace to the shadow of All Hallows church.

'Does ye beg from houses, er…?'

'Jez, maister. Aye, sometoime, Oi does.'

'Would ye knock on a door, see who answers, tell me after? 'Twould be worth a silver penny.'

Jez nodded. 'If'n that be all, maister.'

I suggested a way to be less conspicuous. 'Ye could knock on more doors. 'Twould look better.'

Jez agreed to do it – but wanted to know where.

'House with a broken pane, off Guildhall Street.'

That was different. 'Nay, maister. That 'ouse be trouble.'

So I tried a different tack.

'Do ye know who lives there, Jez?'

"Tis a woman, maister. But 'er dun't live there. 'As a way to 'ouse in next street.'

Progress at last!

'How do ye know?'

Jez had even more information.

'Oi see'd 'er. 'Er comes out 'f 'ouse in next je'y. 'Ouse wi' sign o'fleece uvver 't door.'

The fleece? I probed a little more.

'How do ye know 'tis the woman from the house with the broken windows?'

Jez was quick to answer.

'Oi see'd 'er come to winder, maister. 'Er teks and gives packets ter men what comes.'

I was delighted.

'Jez, ye needs not go to the house. Two silver pennies for your information.'

I left a delighted Jez in my wake too. Now it was time to reconnoitre. Then something struck me, and I came up sharp. Edwin's house too had the sign of the fleece over the door. 'God's blood,' I thought, 'be there no end to this web?"

I made my way to Guildhall Street via Derngate Street, Swan Street, and the back alley that I used before, edging along a narrow jetty that opens onto Guildhall Street fifty yards down the road from the narrow lane where the house with broken windows stands. Almost opposite is another lane, narrower still, and I could just see the house with the sign of the fleece over the door. I decided to stay hidden and watch it carefully. After waiting an hour or so, the door opened, and a middle aged woman stepped out into the lane. She looked strangely familiar; as she turned and I caught sight of her face, I realised that I knew that face. Jen, Edwin's maid-of-all-work. I was in deep shadow, and wearing my dark clothing, so she didn't appear to notice me as she walked to the end of the lane, then turned right towards the marketplace. I decided to follow her at a distance.

As my rising excitement took its effect, I felt much better, and was rather relishing finding out more about this nest of vipers. I turned around, walked quickly back along the short jetty, turned right, and almost ran along the back alley to another narrow jetty about a hundred and fifty yards up the street. From there, I could observe her walking past. After about ten minutes, when she had not appeared, I moved carefully to the end of the jetty and looked towards where she had come from. There was no sign of her. So there must be another house involved? Or was she visiting a friend or relative? Yet another mystery to solve. Should I stay put, or should I return to my previous place for watching the house of the fleece? Staying put seemed like a better option, so I stood in the dark shadow and waited. And waited. And waited. Jen did not reappear. I concluded that my next option was to pass the information to Whetham. Whilst the latter might not be keen to see me again so soon, this information would be valuable – just in case someone spotted me, and stuck a dagger in my ribs. Having mulled over my options, I decided instead to go back to my previous watching place and wait there. Jen did not appear there either. Now I was in a quandary. Where could she possibly have gone? I reckoned that my best option was to return to the Sun and a decent lunch, after which I could find Jez, and quiz him about possible places she could have gone. But I must be very careful indeed; I did not wish to be responsible for another needless death of a child.

I did not feel very much like eating a hearty lunch, so settled for a pot of small ale, and a penny-pipe of tobacco. It helped calm my nerves, and also to think. I decided to see if Jez was in the marketplace, but not talk to him there. The church was more secluded, and harder for someone to eavesdrop – provided there was not a service in progress. There was no sign of Sam Goodly, and other officers were few this day; so after a leisurely lunch and smoke, I headed to the marketplace and sat on the base of the market cross. It was not long before Jez appeared at my side.

'Got any other tasks, maister?'

'Aye. I were looking for ye.'

I looked around, and there was no-one anywhere near us, but nonetheless I spoke quietly.

'I did see the woman, Jez. She came out, as ye said, and walked towards the Guildhall. But she disappeared, and I would know where she went. Could ye tell me of the back alleys and jetties near the house?'

Jez suggested that he could show me, but I was afraid of putting him at risk.

'Jez, I would not place ye in danger. Could ye tell me where the lane by the house of the broken window goes? Mayhap a back alley?'

Jez was sure that there was a back alley. He reckoned that he could go and have a look.

"Twould be a risk, Jez. If ye were seen, ye could end like Harry. These people be very dangerous.' Jez, however, was not to be deterred.

'I could go p'chance just ar'er dawn?'

'Perchance, with great care. Perchance just before dark.'

Jez was keen.

"Tis Friday on th' morrer. They may be at church, maister. Oi would see ye on th'morrer late.'

He scuttled off, and spoke to other people who were strolling in the marketplace, begging for some money. He certainly seemed more street-wise, more aware of how to appear as just a beggar than poor 'Arry had.

I suddenly had an idea. If it were Jen, as I believed, she would need a horse to go back and forth to Wellingborough; it would have to be stabled somewhere. I decided to go and explore the back alleys near Jen's house, so walked back there, using as before the back alley on the opposite side of the road, heading towards Swan Street. I walked along the back alley to the same jetty as before, and came out almost opposite the lane where Jen lives; I decided to take a chance, and walk along that lane, and see where it came out. There was no sign of life in Jen's house, and I carried on, until the lane ended at another wider street, which, when I turned left, I realised, was Swan Street. Further up Swan Street was what I expected, a livery stable. As I passed it, I could see through its open gates that there were several horses lodged there. Some were jennets, small amiable horses that were popular with women. So that was almost certainly where Jen went. Almost opposite the stable was another narrow lane, which I turned into, and walked briskly along, until I came out back on what was actually Guildhall Street. I was serving no useful purpose by standing watching Jen's house, or the house with the broken window, and decided that I would go to All Hallows church and listen to the afternoon service. It would be a welcome break from my duties.

I found the quiet and serenity in the church soothing to my tangled nerves, and sat quietly meditating after the service ended, when the small congregation of townspeople mostly departed. A few did much as I did myself, and sat quietly praying or whatever else they may have been doing with bowed head and calm demeanour. One woman saw me, and came to sit by me.

"Tis good ter sit a-quiet in th' church, sir. Ye be soldier, I think?'

I indicated a 'yes' with a quick nod, and she went on, 'Aye, soldiers be good fer trade, methinks. Ye bain't from Nor'am'ton?'

'Rushden, mistress. Mayhap ye knows a stable nearby to rent a jennet?'

She looked surprised.

'Jennet be too small fer 'ee, maister. They be good stabble on Swan Street. Out of 'ere, do ye know Saint Goiles Street? Ye c'n go darn Saint Goiles, turn roight opp'site Guild'all, darn Guild'all Street, then fust roight up je'y to th'end, 'n' it's opp'site, on Swan Street. Or roight darn Swan Street heself, stabble 'll be on left soide. 'T 'as the soign o' the swan ridin' on 'oss outsoide.'

I thanked her kindly, and realised that I had wrongly assumed that Jeanne/Joan lived off Derngate Street, when in fact she lived off Swan Street. In a generally unfamiliar city with few street name boards – the majority of people could not read and write - and a maze of streets and narrow lanes, it was easy to make such mistakes, unless one bought the services of a local guide.

When I left the church I noticed that the second-hand stall was still there in the market, and walked over to take a look. I spotted a silver chain that would suit the locket that I had bought for Amelia, and bought it. Again, it cost me a pretty penny – nine silver pence. It was a good chain, though, and I knew that Amelia would be pleased with it. She had little jewellery, and a discrete silver chain and locket would not look ostentatious in these puritanical times. I paid and secreted the chain in my inner pocket.

As I continued to wander around the few stalls left, my mind wandered too – onto the thorny subject of Jeanne/Joan. I was increasingly concerned that colonel Whetham could just take her and have her tortured just as he did Maud. The question was what to do to prevent it. Firstly, I needed as much information as Jeanne would or could give me about her activities, to pass on to Whetham, and so far that was not materialising. The additional factor that I had to consider was that Jeanne was in reality just a sideshow, but was distracting me – and Whetham for that matter – from the much more important players in this game of cat and mouse. I thought first that I would visit Jeanne, and see what I could get out of her by simple persuasion.

I resolved to do it this morning. So I walked back to Swan Street, going via the junction with Derngate Street; this enabled me to have a good look at the stable if Jeanne was not in. I made no attempt to avoid being seen, and it took less than ten minutes to be standing before Jeanne's rather shabby front door in the unnamed lane. I knocked, and waited for an answer. No-one appeared, so I knocked much more loudly. This time, I heard shuffling footsteps, and the door opened cautiously. Inside was a tired looking Jeanne, her hair unkempt, and in her smock.

'Oh, 'tis ye, Robbie. Ye'd best come in,' then stood aside for me to enter.

Her speech was a bit slurred, and there was the faint smell of her potion hanging around the parlour. She must have been hooking another of her targets, I surmised. She pointed to a chair, which I sat in, whilst she took the other. I started the conversation.

'Jeanne, ye have not handed back the letter that I loaned ye.'

She looked a little blankly at me, then her befuddled brain slowly registered what I was talking about.

'I would bring it ye this night, if ye wish,' she slurred. 'Ye must be needful of my services, indeed, Robbie.'

I shook my head, though mused that I would find it hard to say no.

'Whetham be on your trail, woman. Ye would not want his, er, attention, I think. I have seen what his men do to a woman'- I shuddered involuntarily - 'and 'tis not a pretty sight. I would have the letter, but I would also have information, if ye please. Who be your controller?'

She looked at me with an angry expression. 'Ye knows I cannot tell ye.'

I reckoned that it was time to stir her pot. 'I know who 'tis, but not his real name, woman. He be Sam Goodly.'

She just stared blankly at me, then, 'Nay, 'tis not.'

'He comes to your house, Jeanne.'

Still she looked blank, then shook her head. I was becoming irritated.

'I have seen the man. He says he be major Sam Goodly, though we know 'tis not his real name.'

She looked bewildered. I carried on.

'He speaks as a gentleman, do he not? He wears the uniform of

252

Fairfax's Life Guards. I have seen him go into your house, tell ye off. Do ye not deny 't.'

She just shook her head, said nothing.

'He takes letters ye give him, passes them to another. I have seen him do't. And he brings ye letters. He tells ye what he would have of ye. Like who to, to, snare, with your woman's wiles.'

She paled but still refused to say anything.

'Very well,' I said, 'I would have my letter, if ye please.'

She went to the writing box, which I realised was unlocked, and extracted the letter. The letter had either been unopened, or more likely had been opened and expertly resealed. Once opened anew, it would betray which. I snatched it from her hand.

'Ye will tell all, Jeanne. Or suffer Whetham's red-hot irons, other horrible cruelties. Ye will talk, or die in agony. And be found in the Nene, like Maud.'

Her mouth fell open. Mayhap she knew Maud, I surmised.

'I would not have to tell your sister of such a death for ye, Jeanne. Not at the hands of Whetham's men. But 'twill come to pass, if ye do not tell.'

She still said nothing, so I bade her good day, and let myself out.

I returned to the Sun, partly in order to eat a lunch, partly to write a report for Whetham. I wrote the report, sanded it, folded it, and put it in my secret pocket with the letter, after which I donned my coif and went downstairs to order lunch. I was still not feeling so well that I could face the Sun's usual large meals, and ordered just a plate of bread, butter, cheese, plus a jug of small ale and a pot. I reasoned that I could order some more food, if I felt the need later on. In the event, that was the case, so I asked for cold meats and more bread, and had they some more of the nice pickle from the other day? The wench said, yes, they had, so I was able to eat a quite hearty lunch anyway. It would not go amiss, before having to face Whetham again, methought.

I was finding the prospect of talking to the Governor daunting, to say the least. After eating my fill, it was still early, so a penny-pipe of tobacco would fill my time and calm my nerves. There were no other officers who would come and sit with me after last evening's débacle, and not even Sam Goodly turned up. I decided on reflection to risk Lady Sorrell's wrath, and visit her house as my next task.

I walked to the start of Drapery, turned up the hill, then almost the full length of Sheep Street to Church Lane and along it to the front entrance of Lady Margery's house. I walked tentatively to the door and knocked. A servant opened it, and asked what I wanted.

'Captain Robert Barker. I would speak briefly with Lady Margery, if ye please. If she would be so kind as to see me.'

'Wait, if ye please. Lady Margery be in mourning for her daughter. She would not be disturbed.' After a short while, Lady Margery appeared at the door.

"Tis ye, captain Barker. What do ye want of me, pray?' I put on my expression and tone of deepest respect.

'I would ask ye, if ye please, if I may attend your daughter's burial. 'Twould mean much to me, I be sore afflicted by your loss.'

She looked me up and down and sighed ostentatiously.

'I would permit it, but if ye please, not in your uniform. As a private person only.'

She turned and called her servant.

'Give captain Barker an invitation card to Maud's burial, if ye please. As Master Robert Barker.'

She turned back to me.

'Master Barker, I cannot say ye are welcome, but I respect your wish to show contrition for Maud's untimely, awful death. If ye please, stay away from myself and my family henceforth.'

The servant handed her the card, which she passed to me.

'That is all, I bid ye good day,' she said, and closed the door behind

254

her, before I had time to answer. I folded the printed card, and consigned it to my secret pocket, then turned around, and walked away from the house. It took around fifteen minutes to walk back to Drapery, and turn the corner to the Guildhall. I looked at the old building, sighed loudly, and went up the flight of stairs to the door. The guards admitted me, with, 'Oh, 'tis 'ee again, captain. Ye're near living in the Guildhall lately.'

I ignored the comment, and merely said, 'I needs report to the Governor, I have papers for him.' Whetham's door was open, and he appeared at it, and signalled to me to come in.

I quickly recounted what I discovered that morning regarding Jen, the stable, and how I had obtained permission from Lady Margery to attend her daughter's burial on the morrow. I purposefully left out my visit to Jeanne/Joan. Whetham was increasingly surprised and angered at the size and complexity of the net of spies in the city, and was more determined than ever to obtain the real identity of major Sam Goodly.

'He may be a gentleman, as ye says; yet no person seems to know him. Surely some person must know such a man!' And banged his desk with his fist, making his heavy crockery inkwell jump.

I could do no more than agree; yet no-one would admit to knowing anything about him. Privately, I realised that I had no option but to get the truth out of Jeanne, whatever it took – and rather myself than Whetham's men, surely. Whetham asked how I was expecting to uncover the real identity of Sam Goodly.

"Tis a thorny problem, if no-one knows the man. We know who he is not, yet not who he is,' I said, in a statement of the obvious.

'My men might discover it, yet we must take all at once. If we do not, others would hide, and we may not catch them. I would not wring it out of the man at this time.'

'If he be as tough as Maud, he would likely say nought. I must watch more, use urchins more, 'tis all I may do. He may yet betray himself. He is not as clever as he thinks, I suspect.'

Whetham said nought, just dismissed me with a flap of his hand, and returned to whatever he was reading before he admitted me to his presence. I reckoned that the burial on the morrow might expose more information, if I observe the mourners carefully, but said no more, and started to make my way back to the Sun inn.

Soon after I returned to the Sun and my room, where I washed the dust out of my hair and beard, and generally tidied myself up, I went downstairs to the taproom, and sat in my usual corner. Before I even had a chance to order food and drink, Sam Goodly arrived, and asked if he might join me. I, though, not feeling very sociable, and looking forward to returning to my Amelia for a longer period of time, decided to take the opportunity to try to tease some more morsels of information from the man.

We both ordered a slice of meat pie with its side order of baked apples, and some decent red wine to accompany it. I said casually to Goodly, 'What regiment did ye fight in at Naseby, Sam?'

The other looked somewhat nonplussed, and stammered.

'Oh...er....I was in the first line, in...in...L-L-Langdale's regiment of horse. Aye, that was it...Langdale's regiment of horse. 'Twas an unexpected question, Robert, and a while ago now.'

I, however, knew enough about Naseby's battle order to realise that Goodly had now betrayed something important: Sir Marmaduke Langdale's regiment of horse was both a northern regiment, and came under Prince Rupert. A Royalist! I would play dumb for now.

'Langdale's regiment of horse? I must confess, I know not of it. Who was its divisional commander, pray?' Goodly suddenly realised that he had made a serious mistake.

'Oh, er.....'twas on the left wing, first line. I....I...may not recall the commander's name.'

I replied that I knew my own divisional commander – lieutenant general Oliver Cromwell – that I was on the right wing, part of colonel Robert Pye's cavalry, and my commanding officer was colonel

Thomas Sheffield.

'I thought ye said that your regiment was Whalley's, Robert?'

'Aye, it were. At Naseby, Whalley's regiment were split in two, and half went to Bob Pye.'

I knew my regiments – whereas Sam Goodly was floundering; now I dropped the mortar bomb that will really put Goodly on the spot.

'Bob Pye's regiment was facing Langdale's regiment of horse, Sam.'

Goodly coloured immediately, and tried to get out of the hole that he had dug for himself.

'Aye, aye…..'tis true, forsooth, I fought for king Charles. When his recruiting officers came, my father forced me to join. My father is dead these three year, Robert. I volunteered later to fight for general Cromwell.'

'Did ye, indeed? I wonder if 'tis why Whetham does not trust ye, Sam, and interrogated ye? He does not like those that change their coat, I think.'

I smiled disarmingly at Goodly, who gave a half-hearted, embarrassed smile in return.

'Aye, could be so, could be so. A man must go with his heart, Robert. In these troubled times, we must do what we must, methinks.'

'Who were your father, Sam?' Goodly had no choice but to answer – he must know his father.

'He was Sir Amyas Goodly, Robert. Has – had – land in north Essex, good land. He had fifty tenants, or thereabouts, farming sheep.'

'Methought that your speech were educated for a soldier, Sam. Ye must have gone to a good school.'

"Aye, 'tis true, I was educated at the College of Eton.'

I repeated my disarming smile.

"Twould have been good for ye. I had my schooling at Wellingborough grammar school. My father has a fine business, but 'twould not run to Eton! My own son must start schooling this year, Sam. I would that I could send him to Eton.'

Goodly, too, could manage a disarming smile.

'I am sure he would do well there, Robert. Mayhap ye could find the money somehow. 'Tis not so much, I think.'

I thought it time to change the subject now, as the wench from the kitchen came with our food and drink.

'Ah, food,' I said, 'my belly do think my throat were cut! I be truly ready for this. I thank ye, my dear.'

The kitchen wench smiled at me, and gave a small curtsey before returning to the kitchen. Goodly, however, did not receive his yet.

'Robert, that smells good indeed! My belly thinks likewise.' He sniffed appreciatively and beamed at me; but I was too busy now tasting the pie to respond. I took a draught of the wine, 'God's blood, that tastes like nectar, Sam. Yours'll be on its way.'

The kitchen wench brought Goodly's food and wine, and he too tucked in – only to burn his mouth with the pie, as I did the day before. It was my turn to mock him gently.

'More haste, less pain, Sam! The wine would soothe it, methinks,' and winked at Goodly, who just looked back at me with a pained expression. Neither of us said much as we demolished our respective meals, and I made a silent resolution not to get drunk. I did not want to be suffering a hangover at the burial tomorrow, and even less to be on the receiving end of another tongue-lashing from Whetham. Once was surely enough.

After I finished eating, I said, 'I swear the food here gets better each day, Sam. 'Twas a handsome meal, methinks. I never had such food, nor yet at Hampton Court palace.'

Goodly's ears pricked up.

'Ye were at Hampton Court, Robert? How come?'

"Twas simple, some of my regiment were sent with Rossiter's men to take king Charles there from Holdenby in '47. I were at Newmarket, and went from there, when Rossiter's men stayed briefly.'

'Indeed? So ye were in London, some… two year?'

'Aye. Under canvas through two winters. 'Tis why I could not go home to Amelia and my son.'

That somewhat dampened the conversation, and I was pleased when Goodly changed the topic to the many rumours circulating. We discussed the currently hot topic of Ireland. Stories kept surfacing of yet more atrocities against Irish civilians, and Goodly was clearly well versed in them. It did nothing to encourage my equanimity this evening; I carried enough of my own guilt, without it being stoked with such stories from over the Irish Sea.

'I would not hear of such, Sam. 'Twas bad enough fighting five year and more, I saw and did too many bad things. I wish 't could be righted. My demons yet come to haunt me in the dark hours, Sam.'

We had talked long enough, and after the Guildhall clock struck nine, I announced that I must retire to my bed. In truth, I wanted free of this dispiriting subject. I could use the time to write my next report for Whetham, and a copy for Master Ekins, for when I arrived back at Rushden. There was still wine in the jug, so I took the jug and my pot with me to my room.

Back in my room, I tried to settle to write my report, and found that I could not. My mind kept wandering to the funeral service for, and burial of, poor Maud Sorrell on the morrow. More wine helped little; I fell asleep in the chair, and when I awoke needing my piss-pot, I felt even more unsettled and groggy from the wine. I undressed, had a quick wash, and having put my smock on, got into bed. I lay awake, and was still awake when the clock struck one o'clock. The pie hung heavily on my stomach, and my head had begun to throb. I blew the candles out, but nothing helped. I just wished that I were going

259

straight to Rushden instead of the church of the Holy Sepulchre, come the morning.

I fell into a fitful sleep, and woke again just before the Guildhall clock struck four. This time, I could not only not get back to sleep, but I was wide awake, and my mind was working feverishly. I lit the candles and sat in the chair, then picked up the quill and started writing my reports. The cold air of the room refreshed me somewhat, and though I shivered from time to time, I continued my writing. After finishing the report for Whetham and duplicating it for Master Ekins' eyes, I sat awake and thought…..and thought…..and thought some more. My mind was fixated on the subject of Jeanne Rately, aka Joan the Whore. I gradually firmed up a plan in my mind. And went over it many times, thinking through each 'what-if?' as it occurred to me.

Friday 23rd March 1649.

As the funeral service was to be at nine o'clock in the church of the Holy Sepulchre, I needed to rise earlier than usual, break my fast earlier too, and be walking to the church in my best civilian clothes by a half past eight, if not a little earlier. Although wide awake much earlier than usual, I was far from my best due to the effects of the previous evening's over-indulgence in meat pie and trimmings, as well as most of a jug of wine to myself. However much I tried to make myself presentable, I could not hide my pallid face and reddened eyes. I decided to keep my sash of rank with me in a pocket, but wore my usual high-crown hat, complete with its blue ribbon denoting my regiment and rank. Hats are worn in church by everyone except the preacher, and I hoped that the blue ribbon would not anger Lady Margery. So long as I kept well back away from her family and friends, I expected that she would not notice me at all.

After a quick breakfast, and avoiding other officers, I was out and walking up Drapery in the direction of the church of the Holy Sepulchre just before half past eight. I was thankful that it was a pleasant cool spring morning; burials on a rainy day are most depressing, and I did not need any more to weigh me down. I arrived at the church early, and was ushered in by a sidesman who scanned my invitation card, and handed it back, passing me a black scarf to wind around my hat – fortuitously hiding my ribbon of regiment and rank. I chose a spot close to a pillar in the round body of the church where I would be hard to spot from the nave where the family and other invitees would be sitting or standing. If needs be, I could move to another spot when the other people arrived.

Firstly, Lady Sorrell and some of her relatives arrived, and took up their positions in the nave, followed by others at intervals. I had a shock when I noticed none other than Sam Goodly stride into the nave, and take a position in the pew occupied by Lady Sorrell and her family. It was even more important now not to be noticed, and I rose, quietly moving into the south chancel, in a corner well away from the others, and as far as I could arrange it, hidden from them by another pillar. It was clear from greetings exchanged between family members of Lady Sorrell that Goodly was either a family member or a close friend.

The mourning bell of the church tolled twenty times. Thrice for her being buried as a child, the remainder for each year of her age. The preacher gave a fairly standard sermon – Presbyterian, not Anglican – followed by her biography and a list of all that was good about Maud, then Lady Sorrell stood up, went to the lectern, and gave a short speech, further describing the girl's marvellous good nature, and denouncing the grotesque way in which she died, and the man responsible – the Governor, lieutenant colonel and cruel dog Nathaniel Whetham. Afterwards, the congregation walked out of the church to the graveside, where the lead coffin awaited, ready to be lowered into the open grave, and there was a final prayer offered up by the preacher. I had watched the last part from behind another grave with a high gravestone well away, just close enough to hear. As soon as the prayer finished, I slipped away, and made my way back to the Sun.

Chapter 17: Rubicon and Rushden

I had become too heavily weighed down by my guilt to care any more. Whetham could have me executed for my next step, and it mattered not to me. I would put my plan into action regarding Joan the Whore. I went up to my room, and exchanged my high-crown hat for a black coif, then made sure that my pistol was primed and at half cock, my dagger in its sheath and my tuck securely hanging from my belt. I folded two sheets of paper and fitted them into my inner pocket. I made sure that a shortened quill and ink bottle – securely stoppered – was in my snapsack, along with the sand shaker. Then I put the snapsack over my shoulder, and walked out of the Sun and in the direction of Swan Street and Joan's house. It was about half an hour after ten o'clock when I knocked on her door. At the second attempt, she appeared, as before in her night attire; I pushed her inside, followed her, then closed and locked the door behind me.
'What is this?' she asked me.

I said nothing, but grabbed her wrist, twisted it behind her back, and forced her to go further into her parlour, where I made her sit on an open-backed chair, taking the other wrist, and pulling it, too, over the back of the chair and with some thick cord that I had brought, tied her wrists together and to the back of the chair. She was almost too shocked to speak, but managed to gasp out, 'What do ye want, Robbie? Why do ye tie me so?'

'Ye will – WILL - answer my questions about your intelligencing, Jeanne. Who is't ye do it for?'

'I m-may not tell ye.'

I sighed loudly for effect.

'I would not hurt ye, Jeanne, but will if I must. Ye must talk, or Whetham's men will make ye.'

She simply shook her pretty head.

'So be it,' I said.

I tore open her smock, took one of her breasts in my hand and squeezed it – hard. I felt her wince, saw her grit her teeth, but still she said nothing, just shook her head again.

'Jeanne – or is it Joan here and now? Ye're a bigger fool than I thought. Whetham's men would make ye talk with hot irons and burning oil. Would ye suffer that, instead?'

She still shook her head, though a tear formed in her eyes. I took her breast in both hands, and squeezed so hard that a small amount of blood oozed from the nipple. She wet herself, and a moment after, gasped, 'Stop! Stop, I beg ye. I will talk.'

'Very well, talk. Who gives ye your orders?'

She gasped as I let go of her breast, then blurted it out.

'Simon Sorrell. Simon Sorrell, Esquire.'

'Ah! This makes sense.' I thought. I extracted the paper, ink and quill, and wrote a sentence.

'Now, why do ye have a writing box, seals of dangerous, nay treasonous, sign? Ye do not write nor read, I think.'

'I do read and write a little, Robbie. But Simon uses them. He comes to my house to write. Writes ciphers.'

I wrote some more.

'For whom?'

She did not really know.

'He takes them to a house. He collects and gives them to another.'

'The house with a broken window in a jetty 'tween Guildhall Street and Swan Street? Jen's house?'

'Aye, 'Tis the one.'

'Who was it brought ye to intelligencing?'

The answer left me near speechless.

264

'A lady. Simon Sorrell's sister-in-law, Margery Sorrell.'
'I do know the lady,' I said, 'Why did ye do't?'
Her answer left me almost speechless again.
'I came to Northampton with nought. I were taken in by another,
took me to Lady Sorrell's house. I cannot...tell ye all... They
beat me till I said I would do't.'
I quickly regained my composure, and wrote this down.
'What more do ye know, Jeanne?''
She shook her head.
"Tis all I durst tell.'
Writing some more, I continued.
'I would save ye from Whetham's men. I would save your life.
Be your maid here?'
She nodded.
'Ring the bell, if ye please, and she will come.'
I complied, and the maid's footsteps creaked down the stairs.
When she came in, she looked at Jeanne and then me, wide-
eyed.
'What passes here, child? Why be ye tied?'
I answered.
'Mistress, I needed to make her talk. Now I would save her life.
Has she man's apparel here?'
The maid, Peg, nodded.
'Dress her in't. Has she a nag?'
Again, Peg nodded.
'Man's saddle?'
'Men's and lady's. What have ye done to her? Her pap, 'tis going
black and blue! Untie her, I beg ye.'
I realised that she was still tied, in what must have been an
uncomfortable position, so I did as she bade me. When Jeanne's
hands were free, her first instinct was to try to slap my face, but I

caught her wrist.

'Nay, Jeanne. I told ye, I would save your life. I did not want to hurt ye, truly I did not.'

I turned my attention to Peg.

'Dress her, hide her hair under coif or cap. Ready her nag. Be ready in one hour. I will return then, and she must away with me. Out of the city. I will copy my scribbles. If ye please, when we are gone, take them and the writing box to Governor Whetham at the Guildhall, with my letter.'

"Twill be done, captain. I will be sure to do as ye says.'

'I hope 'twill be enough to satisfy Whetham. I must face his wrath later.'

I turned to Jeanne.

'If I fail, Whetham will give ye to his men. Afore they were done with ye, ye would beg to die. I cannot let it be so, even if I am arrested for't.'

I had a thought: what would Peg do now?

'Peg, how will ye fare without Jeanne?'

'Fear not, captain. I were a dressmaker afore Joan. I made her whore's dresses. I can make dresses again.'

I took my temporary leave of the two women.

'I must away now to attend to my affairs. I will return in one hour – ONE HOUR. Jeanne must be ready to ride. I bid ye farewell till my return.'

I unlocked the door, and walked out, then back to the Sun inn.

'How will I tell Whetham,' I mused to myself, as I walked, 'he will be much angered with me.'

It was too late to change my mind. Jeanne must be taken to relative safety, away from Whetham's brutes. Back at the Sun, first I found the landlord, and told him that I would be away for about a week, and would need my room on my return. Next, I repaired to my room, and wrote a simple letter to Whetham, outlining what had transpired, with the new intelligence I had obtained, and then made a copy of it to take with me back to Rushden. I packed the papers into one thick package and sealed it, then secreted it in my doublet's inner pocket. When all this was completed, I packed my clothes into my snapsack, donned my sash of rank, and took all of it to the stable, where I saddled my mare. I left the Sun by the backyard entrance, and turned left thence along Derngate Street, rather than my usual route in the opposite direction, which was Drapery, and St Giles Street. I reasoned that my best route was not via Wellingborough, where Jeanne would be too well known. It is further but safer to go via the Dern gate and take the Bedford road, then via Cogenhoe and Grendon. The main risk would be the narrow lane round the park of Castle Ashby, where I might be challenged. The hour was soon nearly up, and I rode out onto Derngate Street, then turned down Angel Lane and Swan Street, arriving at Jeanne's house soon after. Peg had been as good as her word, and Jeanne's nag, a small placid jennet, was ready with a small man's saddle. Jeanne herself was ready with her golden curls hidden by a black coif, and shapely figure approximately concealed by a dark brown doublet and breeches, brown stockings, and nondescript shoes. She would do. Peg wished us both luck. 'God go with ye, both. Fear not for me, I shall fare well enough.' Jeanne with some difficulty and my help mounted the jennet, and we rode away, continuing east along the narrow lane on which her house stood, via the next narrow lane to a bigger street that connects with Derngate Street, after which we headed to the Dern gate.

There was a large amount of cart traffic at Dern gate, along with groups of mounted soldiers and footsoldiery. As I had surmised, the guards saw my sash of rank, merely saluted, and signalled me and Jeanne through. I returned the salute, and walked on with Jeanne following closely behind like a servant. The guards should have checked Jeanne especially, but were too busy with the other traffic. I and my companion headed out of the city on the Bedford road, crossing the Nene and its tributary on the way past Great Houghton, then took the road to Little Houghton and Cogenhoe. The small village of Cogenhoe was very quiet, farmers and traders from the village no doubt having gone to Northampton's busy market, and I and my charge continued on to Grendon. We had to make the detour around the large park of Castle Ashby, once a Royalist stronghold, now garrisoned by Parliamentary troops; I hoped that we would not be challenged by any who might be patrolling the narrow lane. Luckily we only meet two footsoldiers, both looking bored, who saw my sash of rank, and as at Derngate, merely saluted and stood aside. They exchanged greetings with me.

'Captain, 'tis a good spring day! God be with ye.'

I replied easily.

'Aye, 'tis good weather. I wish ye a good day, trooper,' as I returned the salute, and then, 'Come, lad, look sharp." They looked a little quizzically at my "lad", but did not feel it wise to challenge an officer of my rank. There was now a long uncomfortable ride through Grendon village to Wollaston, which meant crossing the main highway from Wellingborough to Olney on which mounted patrols were a frequent sight, before entering the large village of Wollaston itself. Part way, Jeanne required a privy, of which naturally there was none, so I had to help her dismount, and unhooked the breeches from the doublet she was wearing, so that she could have a pee by the roadside – common enough, but usually women found it easier when, on the rare occasions they travelled, they wore just their skirts and, as normal, nothing under them. At least the skirts preserved some dignity. Jeanne had no such opportunity, though I sought to look away, before helping her back on with the men's clothing, and then onto the horse. She was obviously in pain, wincing as I helped her mount the horse, and her sore breast chafed against the rough cloth and tight doublet. My feelings of guilt surfaced briefly, but I suppressed them, reasoning that I was saving her from a terrible end at the hands of Whetham's men, and she would soon be in Rushden.

Approaching the main highway, I sat and watched as two mounted columns trotted past, heading north. Seeing no more coming, I urged Jeanne to keep up with me as we crossed the highway as quickly as possible, and continued on towards Wollaston. She lagged behind a little – her horse was much smaller than mine – but she more or less kept up, and in ten minutes or so, we were heading into Wollaston's busy marketplace. My horse easily pushed her way through the people congregating around the few market stalls, and cleared a way for Jeanne on the small jennet. Soon, we were heading out of the village towards Irchester and a short distance further on, Rushden. It had taken over two and a half hours to reach Wollaston, now about another hour would see us at Rushden hall.

We entered the stable yard at Rushden hall around mid-afternoon, neither having eaten nor drunk anything since Northampton. Jeanne looked fit to drop, her face pale and haggard, and I had almost to lift her off the jennet. I gave the stable lad two pennies to take the horses and settle them in the stables, whilst I helped Jeanne up the steps into the entrance to the scullery corridor, and into the large room used as the garrison dining room. As we entered, I spotted Amelia sitting talking with my father and a woman whom I did not know, and Johnny playing nearby. Jeanne walked shakily in front as she entered the hall, and her sister looked up and then looked Jeanne up and down. Recognition suddenly dawned.

'Jeanne...? Is't ye, Jeanne?'

She got up, rushed forward, and threw her arms around Jeanne in an embrace, at which Jeanne yelped, and pulled away. Amelia looked stunned.

'What is't..?'

Jeanne undid the doublet, pulled the shirt up, and exposed her breast, now heavily bruised, and with some congealed blood still on the nipple. Amelia looked at it aghast, as Jeanne said, with bitter irony, 'Your husband truly knows how to woo a girl, sister.'

Amelia looked from her sister to me.

'Wha... Did ye..really do this, Robbie?'

'I would not hurt her, but needed make her tell me of her...work. Whetham would take her for treason, and give her to his men .... I brought her to Rushden to save her life, Lia.'

Jeanne was near to fainting, but I caught her, and eased her gently into a chair, as Amelia looked on horrified, white faced. She was as if transfixed, looking at Jeanne's miserable state.

'Lia, would ye take her to your room, get these rough clothes off her, and find some woman's dress, if ye please.'

She tried to pull Jeanne up with an arm, causing her to cry out again, so I intervened, pulling Jeanne forward, then lifted her up with an arm around her waist, and walked her gently towards the staircase. Amelia gathered her senses, caught up, and did the same on Jeanne's other side. Between us, we managed to get her up the dark stairs, and along the corridor as far as our room, where I pushed the door open with my foot, and we deposited her into a chair. I left her with Amelia, and came back down the stairs.

My father spoke first.

'Robert, the more I see of ye lately, the less I know ye. To hurt a woman so. How could ye do 't?'

'Father, ye have not seen what Whetham's men would do to her. I have seen much in the war, yet never such as they do. I made Jeanne tell what she knows, sent it with other reports to Whetham afore I brought her away. I hope 'twill be enough to keep him from taking her. I must return a week hence, face his wrath.'

The woman whom my father had been talking to spoke.

'So this is Robert, your son? Will ye not introduce me?'

'I beg your pardon, lady. Captain Robert Barker, my son. This be mistress Elizabeth Watson, Master Ekins's affianced.'

I stood, and did a little bow, doffing my hat at the same time.

'I knew not that Master John were affianced, mistress Elizabeth. I wish ye both a long and happy life together. God be with ye both.'

Putting my hat back on, I sat down on a bench next to my father.

'Mistress Elizabeth, I would ye did not see the war that I must fight. 'Tis not a pretty sight, yet I have seen far worse. Done far worse. 'Tis the nature of England's fate at this moment. Truly, I would 'twere not so.'

She smiled sweetly at me.

'Fear not, captain Robert. I am not a tender blossom. My husband to be, Master John, has told me something of your

271

work. Soldiers must needs do their duty.'

Amelia came back down the stairs, and called to me.
'Husband, what is wrong with my sister? She has fainted,
methinks.'
I stood at once.
'If ye please, I would be excused. I know what 'twill be,
methinks. She takes a potion to help her whore and snare the
intelligencers' targets.'
I accompanied Amelia up the stairs, and entering our room,
found Jeanne insensible in the chair. Taking a pot, I filled it with
cold water from the pail, and splashed it into Jeanne's face. She
stirred and mumbled, but did not come round. I filled the pot and
tried again. This time, she opened her eyes, and slurred her
words.
'Robb...Robbie...'tis... ye. F-f-fuck me, Robbie....' and then
passed out again.
Amelia stood for a moment with her hand flying to her mouth,
then, 'Robbie..?'
I held my hand up, "Tis the potion, Lia.'
I filled the pot again, this time poured it over her head, then
lifted her forward by her shoulders, and shook her, after which
she revived somewhat.
'Oh, Robbie.... My head! My head!'
Amelia picked up a towel, and wet it with the cold water, then
handed it to me. I rolled it, and held it over her brow. Slowly,
Jeanne came round some more, with her face a deathly white,
then taking the towel herself, held it across her brow and
temples.
'God's blood, my head throbs.'
She was still in most of the men's clothes, but had removed the

coif, and now her golden curls were limp and dripping with the water, her eyes bloodshot and the pupils dilated.

I said to Amelia, 'I know not what 'tis that she takes, but 'tis to make her .... ravenous for men. 'Tis how she do the whoring for the ring of traitors.'

Amelia looked closely at Jeanne.

'I smell...something... on her, Robert. 'Twill make her ill so as to die, methinks?'

I nodded, then answered.

'Aye, 'tis marvellous strong stuff. She ...she...came to my room one night while I slept. Forced herself on me.'

Amelia looked at me with a mixture of shock and horror.

'She...fucked....ye, Robert? She...made ye do't? Ye did not...did not...stop her?'

I nodded slowly.

'Ye has no notion of her with the potion, my love. She were...unstoppable.'

'My sister, husband? Mine own sister?'

'Aye, 'Twas her job. She be skilled at it, marvellous skilled. I be sore ashamed, so sorry, Lia. Whetham would have me do it with her again and again. I would not. 'Tis mayhap why he would arrest her, let his men...torture her.'

A tear ran down my cheek.

Amelia stood there looking askance at me, almost as white as Jeanne at that moment. She slapped my face, and I made no attempt to stop her.

'Ye could not make me feel worse, Lia. Jeanne forced herself on many of Whetham's officers.'

Jeanne was now coming round rather more, but still looked ghastly, her face ashen, eyes red and unfocused.

'I fear I know my sister less even than my husband,' from

Amelia, 'I, I, hath much to hear of, I think. She were a lovely girl once.'

I could only nod, then took the towel back, wet it, wrung it out again and handed it to Jeanne, who sat there a little more upright, and groaning now. I turned to Amelia.

'I will leave ye to see to your sister. She should recover now.'

I returned downstairs.

My father and Elizabeth had heard the exchange, and both looked at me as though I had two heads, as I entered the hall, and sat by my father.

'My son, how could ye…. With your sister-in-law?'

I hung my head.

'Father, ye have not seen Jeanne when she ... be…. aroused by the potion. I fear the man who made her take it has done her much harm.'

Elizabeth asked me, 'And who is't who gave it her, captain?'

I was unsure how to answer this sensitive question.

'He, er, calls himself Sam Goodly. Dresses as a staff major. But 'tis neither his name nor rank. His brother were Sir James Sorrell. He were killed at Naseby in '45. I may not tell ye more.'

Master John Ekins appeared at the foot of the staircase, and called me to come with him. I, as before, excused myself, and went with Ekins, who led me to his office, and, after motioning me to sit, closed and locked the door. I initially greeted him.

'I would wish ye and your affianced a long a happy life together, Master John. Happier, than mine, I think.'

Ekins nodded and thanked me.

'Aye, Elizabeth would be a fine wife, I think.'

John Ekins was about thirty-seven, old for a first marriage, and Elizabeth nearer Amelia's age, which all the more surprised me, but I chose politeness, and did not make any comment.

'We marry next Saturday, 30th March. You are most welcome, Robert, and your Amelia. And Jeanne Rately, if she so wish.'

'I thank ye warmly, Master John. We would surely come.' Now we got down to business.

I opened my doublet, and took out the copied packet of letters for Whetham, and handed them to Ekins. 'Ye will find these most illuminating, Master John. I would that captain Grove reads them too.'

I sat and watched as Ekins rapidly read my rather poor writing – my hand was still shaky after the bad night before – and asked me what several words were. After he had finished reading, he looked concerned.

'H'mm. 'Tis a pretty story indeed, captain. Ye has more to tell, methinks.'

I told him about Edwin – Edward Marston's – maid-of-all-work, Jen, being the intermediary for the letters, the fate of Maud Sorrell, the deception of Sam Goodly.

'Ye have told all to Governor Whetham?'

'Most all, Master John. He do not know yet of Jen's part in all this.'

'He should be a'ready to arrest this nest of vipers, methinks. Yet, are there more, do ye know?'

I could not hide my doubt.

'Mayhap there are, Master John. I do not yet know Will Watterson's part in 't. Or if there be more that we know not of."

Ekins also had his doubts.

"If mayhap there are more, captain, 'twould be folly to arrest any at this time. Too quick, and others would disappear. Ye needs must take all or none.'

I thought it wise and a matter of courtesy to ask if Jeanne might stay at the hall for a while, until we can decide what is best for her.

'Your Amelia may be a companion for my Elizabeth. Mayhap Jeanne can earn her keep as a maid for her, or mayhap as a nanny for your Johnny. If she so wish.'

I thought the latter might suffice; after all, Jeanne had learnt her letters, even if she claimed to be less than good at reading and writing. That would remain to be seen.

'If my father would return to his own house soon, mayhap Jeanne could be his maid. Or mayhap Amelia and I may take a house. 'Twould help her, methinks.'

The issue of Jeanne was shelved for now. I crossed my fingers and hoped that Whetham would now forget about her, and concentrate on the remainder of the group. For now, Amelia might perhaps coax more information from her.

I realised that I must not stay too long before returning to Northampton, and face Governor Whetham, a prospect that I did not relish one iota. I considered the Wednesday following Ekins' marriage, which would be the 28th March. Today was the 23rd; so I reasoned that Thursday 29th would be better. For myself, anyway; and if Whetham wanted to arrest Jeanne, he would have to come to Rushden, which would of itself create a delay. 29th it would be. In the meantime, I thought that Master Ekins might write to Whetham, explaining the situation vis-á-vis Jeanne, and prepare the ground at very least. I would ask Ekins the following day. Also, I needed to placate Amelia somehow, now that I had confessed my, well, adultery – even though I felt that it was not really my fault.

There was some noise from the hall now, as the few remaining troopers came in for their supper. I excused myself from Ekins, and returned to the hall, where Amelia, Elizabeth, and my father were still there, and I went over and joined them. I asked if anyone had checked on Jeanne, but they had not.

'She would feel better for some food to counteract the potion, I think. I would bring her down to eat with us. If ye all permit.'

No-one demurred, so I took that as a 'yes', and went back upstairs to my and Amelia's room, where Jeanne was sitting in the chair still, though dressed in some clothes that her sister had loaned her. She looked rather more presentable now, albeit still pale and with reddened eyes.

'If ye please, come down to the hall, and partake of some food, Jeanne,' I said.

Jeanne rose unsteadily to her feet, swayed somewhat, then asked for my arm, and walked shakily with me out of the room, and along the corridor. I held her arm tightly as we both descended the stairs, and all eyes were on Jeanne as we entered the hall. I steered her to a bench, and she sat down rather heavily next to her sister, to whom she turned and smiled weakly.

Amelia asked, 'Are ye feeling better, sister? Ye were very sick an hour past.' Jeanne smiled back.

'Aye, Lia, 'tis not so bad now. My pap hurts as much as my head now, I think,' darting a look at me, 'but 'twill mend, methinks. I would fain have some food if ye pleases. The potion, 'tis very strong.' Elizabeth looked at her.

'Why do ye take this...potion, mistress Jeanne?'
She answered warily.

'I were forced to. Could not go a-whoring without. And I must go a-whoring for … these …. people, or be beaten. Whipped.'

'Ye are here safe, now. Robert and your sister would keep ye safe, methinks.'

'I hope 'twill be so, mistress, er, Elizabeth..?'

Elizabeth nodded.

'Aye, I am Elizabeth Watson of Bletsoe, Master John's affianced. We marry Sunday after Easter, here in Rushden's church.'

'I truly wish ye both well, mistress Elizabeth. And God bless your union.'

John Ekins came and joined us, and called for food to be served. Two kitchen wenches came with the supper, of the usual potage, a tasty pork concoction with root vegetables, herbs, and some dried fruits, with bread and butter, cheese, and various sweetmeats. Next came jugs of small ale, best ale, and red wine. It made a pleasant meal, which, with pleasant conversation, was altogether a relaxed and congenial affair such as even I had become unused to these last few weeks. Jeanne started to recover some colour in her cheeks, though the less welcome colour in her eyes remained for now. After the meal, the menfolk – Ekins himself, I, and my father, John – all repaired to a room that I had not even suspected to exist, Ekins' own closet, where all partook of a decent wine and smoked a pipe of tobacco or two, whilst we played cards. The womenfolk remained where they were and chatted, as they got to know one another better. Amelia asked the inevitable question.

'Sister, mayhap ye would tell us of your life after our parents died? 'T cannot have been easy for ye.'

Jeanne instantly clammed up, and sat there looking downcast and a little pale again. Elizabeth chided Amelia.

'Tush, Amelia, 'tis clearly a thorny matter for your sister. She will tell ye in her own time, I think.'

Amelia blushed. 'Sister, I did not think the memories so painful for ye. I would not press ye, if 'tis too hard for ye,' and put an arm round Jeanne's shoulders. The latter burst into tears, at

278

which Amelia, rather shaken at her sister's reaction, pulled Jeanne to her, and did her best to comfort her sister.

Elizabeth said, 'Amelia, ye must be gentle with your sister. She has suffered much, I think.'

She poured a goblet of the wine, and passed it to Jeanne, who gladly took it, and sipped at it cautiously. Elizabeth now changed the subject, and asked Jeanne if she liked sewing.

'I fear I have ten thumbs, mistress Elizabeth. Never have I been able to sew well.'

Amelia chipped in.

"Twas I that sewed, mistress Elizabeth. Jeanne, methinks, had other talents. Like her beautiful hair. I always envied Jeanne's locks.'

The conversation meandered on, with Jeanne obviously becoming very tired, until Elizabeth suggested that her sister take her up to have an early night. Elizabeth turned to Jeanne.

'Mistress Jeanne, would ye share a bed mayhap with your sister, or prefer a room to yourself, perchance?'

Jeanne indicated that she did not want to be alone in this strange house, so Amelia agreed to share with her on this, her first night at the hall. She helped her sister, who had stood, and was teetering somewhat, steering her to and up the stairs to her own and Johnny's room in Ekins' own part of the house. I would have to take Johnny into my and Amelia's erstwhile shared room, and sleep there.

Having shown Jeanne to her own room, Amelia collected Johnny, and settled him in the truckle bed in her and my former room, then returned to the hall to ask Elizabeth where her husband and his father were.

'Worry not, Missus Amelia, I will go and send your Robert to his son.'

279

I was not particularly pleased to have to be sleeping alone apart from Johnny, but in the event, it was not such a worrying matter that it might otherwise have been, when I had a bad nightmare yet again, and woke my worried father and Johnny with my wails and yells.

Chapter 18: Potion and Plan

This night proved to be far from quiet regarding Jeanne, and Amelia too. Amelia was woken during the night with the unexpected sensation of a naked woman's body against her back, and a hand fondling between her legs. As she became suddenly awake, she near leapt out of bed, and fumbling at first, managed to strike a flint on some tinder, blow it, light a slow match, and then apply it to candle. A naked Jeanne was lying on the bed facing her, smiling broadly.

'Come back to bed, sister, ye surely wants me.'

Amelia's reaction was to slap her sister hard across her face, then storm out of the room, and come and pound on my door. She managed to wake half the house, and worried faces appeared in the corridor. Elizabeth came out to her, asking what the problem was.

'Amelia, dear, what is't? What ails ye?'

I opened my door sleepily – I had only shortly before managed to get back to sleep after a nightmare – Johnny woke up, and I repeated Elizabeth's question.

'Amelia, wife, what is't? Ye've woken half the house.'

Amelia was white-faced, and could barely get her words out.

'Robert, Robbie, my sister..... she....she tried to .... she touched me. Touched me! Where she should not!'

I looked at Elizabeth, and both could not resist laughing.

'She touched ye, wife? Is't all?'

Amelia however, thought it no laughing matter.

'She be evil, Robbie! Come!'

She took my hand, and pulled me along the corridor back to her room, where, as I and the two women came in, Jeanne was giggling almost insanely, white face and red eyes, as earlier.

'Have ye all come to play with me?'

She lay there still naked, and indeed, playing with herself. Amelia

281

stepped forward, and slapped her across the face again. More giggling came from Jeanne, and her giggling did not abate, though both hands went to her face. I turned to the other two.

'God's blood, she has brought the potion with her! But how? Check her clothes.'

Elizabeth stepped forward and checked the pockets of her man's clothes, pulled Jeanne's own clothes out of the small bag she brought.

'Nothing in her clothing, Robert.'

Jeanne tried to sit up, but I pushed her back down.

'Where be the potion, Jeanne?'

She just giggled even more, began to look decidedly groggy, and was starting to slur her words.

'Search, and….. ye shall find...' she slurred, through her giggles.

Amelia interjected.

'We have searched her clothes, there be nought else, surely?'

Elizabeth was far less naive, and said quietly to Amelia, 'Pull her legs apart, Missus Amelia.'

Each took a leg, and pulled them apart. There was a cord, ending in a red tassel. Elizabeth looked meaningfully at Amelia, pulled the cord, and out came a dark red glass bottle, sealed tightly with a stopper. Jeanne giggled even more, whilst Amelia looked astounded. Elizabeth dried the bottle, with a little difficulty removed the stopper, then sniffed the liquid inside.

'It smells queer, like Jeanne's breath smells now. 'T must be the potion.'

'Indeed,' I said, 'She must have great need of 't. We must lock it away.'

Elizabeth was even more thoughtful.

'Aye, indeed, captain. We should seek a physician on the morrow, who may know what 't is.'

282

While we conversed Jeanne had passed out, so I looked around, found a pot, filled it from the pail, and splashed it hard into her face. She woke slightly, managed to get out, 'Fuck me…. Lia….. c'mon….' before she passed out again.

Amelia, turning to me, 'She was .. thus.. with ye, Robbie?'

I nodded.

'Aye, indeed. Th'potion makes her…. ravenous for men….now it seems, women, too, I think.'

Amelia could hardly believe what she had witnessed.

'My sister has….has...come to this?'

Elizabeth was much more worldly-wise.

'Not all the world be so puritan as yourself, Amelia.'

I could not resist saying, 'Mistress Elizabeth, I have not even seen my wife without her clothes. Not even on our wedding night. Yet I have seen all that her sister has to offer a man.'

Amelia was quite angry at this.

'Robert! In front of Master Ekins's intended! Ye should be ashamed.'

Elizabeth smiled and turned to her.

'Amelia, ye do not offer yourself to the world when your husband sees ye unclothed. Were not Adam and Eve in the Garden of Eden without clothes?'

Amelia reddened, but said nothing.

We had not noticed my father come in whilst we were talking. He surveyed the scene.

'What passes here?' before spotting the naked, unconscious form of Jeanne on the bed.

'What is't with Jeanne? Surely her nakedness should be covered?'

None of us had thought anything of it, but Elizabeth again took control, stepped forward, and pulled a sheet over Jeanne.

'She did't herself, Master John, she had brought a phial of the potion, and taken some of it. She, er, made advances to her sister, while Amelia slept.'

His mouth fell open, rather like a fish out of water, I heard him gulp, and then he managed to get out, 'How...so?'

'Master John, 'tis better ye do not know.'

A moment later, Ekins entered the room, similarly surveyed the scene.

'God's blood, what is't that passes here?'

Elizabeth again took charge.

'My dearest, Jeanne smuggled a phial of the potion into the house. She took some, and woke Amelia by touching her where she should not. The potion has caused her to faint again. We must seek a physician on the morrow, ask what it is, how may we seek to help Jeanne.'

Ekins asked how Jeanne had managed to bring the potion in, and Elizabeth bent to his ear, and whispered to him. He looked thunderstruck. 'Is there nought she would not do?'

Now I spoke, ''Tis the potion's power, Master John. She cannot resist its power.'

Ekins shook his head in disbelief, and signalled to me to come outside. I complied.

Outside the room, he asked me to come to his private office, so that we could talk in private, and not be disturbed. 'If ye please, tell me where she came by this potion.'

I knew only too well part of the answer.

'She were forced to take it by those that use her in their treason, Master John. We must keep her from it at all cost.'

We talked of the intelligence that I had gathered for a while.

The hall clock struck four. 'Let us repair to our beds, captain, and we must decide what to do on the morrow.'

I readily agreed, since I was very tired by now, and went back to the bedroom, where Amelia was sitting in the chair, and Elizabeth on the bed, both gazing distractedly at Jeanne's unconscious form. I spoke first.

'My ladies, I feel that we serve no purpose here. Lia, would ye stay with Jeanne, or mayhap we do't in shifts? She may be very sick when she awakes.' Amelia cautiously agreed to do it.

'Mistress Elizabeth, I would thank ye for your great help this night. Methinks ye wish go back to your room now?'

Yes, she would, and bade us both good night. I took Elizabeth's place sitting on the bed. I had great difficulty deciding what to say.

'My love, I would ye had not seen this, but methinks ye sees why I could not leave Jeanne to Whetham's men. 'Tis not her fault. When she be recovered, mayhap she will tell ye how it came to this.'

Amelia looked at me with a sad expression on her face, said a cautious, 'Aye', and suggested that I go and get some sleep.

'Husband, we must talk on the morrow, and see what is to be done. Elizabeth has been such a great help this night. I had not thought any of this possible.'

I stood, bent over and kissed her, then held her hand for a second or two, before retreating to my and Johnny's room, where the latter was crying and kicking up an awful fuss. I managed to calm him down, but it was clear by the time all who went to the hall's dining room the following morning that not one of us had managed to sleep any more that night. The only one missing was Jeanne.

Friday 23rd March 1649.

Amelia was the first to report on the night's concluding events after we had all returned to our rooms shortly after four o'clock. Jeanne had been unconscious for quite some time, not returning to some semblance of consciousness until after five o'clock. She woke with a raging thirst, and badgered Amelia for a drink; Amelia lit a candle, and went to the kitchen, from where she brought a jug of small ale back to the room. Jeanne was wider awake when Amelia entered the room, and started complaining loudly of a bad headache. There was nothing Amelia could do, except wet a towel and put it on Jeanne's forehead. It seemed to do little good. Jeanne, however, vociferously demanded more of her potion, and tried to hit Amelia when she refused. After a short time of putting up with Jeanne's tantrum, Amelia locked her in the room, and sought Elizabeth's help. It took the two of them to stop Jeanne's violence, and then only by tying her to the bed with a sheet. Eventually, Jeanne calmed down somewhat, lying there with a thunderous look on her face; but at the time when her sister was ready to break her fast, and asked Jeanne if she would eat, the tantrum started again, so Amelia simply left the room, and locked her in. It was abundantly clear that Jeanne was going to be very difficult to cope with.

With John Ekins, my father, John Grove, I, Amelia, and Elizabeth, a plan of action was soon arrived at. The first thing we needed to do was to get the potion to a physician, the one that Elizabeth indicated in Wellingborough. I volunteered to go, and took charge of the bottle. We also agreed that we needed a strong maid to sit with Jeanne, to help her with her toilet needs, and to make sure that she drank regularly, even if she would not eat. I, of course, had seen her like this before, though not as violently as this day; I suggested that we try to get Jeanne to eat as soon as possible, since the potion's effects would probably last longer if she did not. Elizabeth volunteered to show a maid how to manage Jeanne, and I offered money for the usual maid to look after Johnny, so that my own work was not adversely affected. Although I felt a little better now, I looked even more gaunt and haggard than the days since Maud's death, after last night's drama and loss of sleep.

Shortly after the discussion, the kitchen maids brought us some breakfast, and I, having brought Johnny down with me, sat my son at the table between myself and Amelia, so that we could eat and drink with minimum fuss. I especially had a bigger than usual breakfast, since I had to prepare my horse, and then face a two hour ride to Wellingborough, the consultation with the physician – if that one was able to help - then a two hour ride back again, after which I would have to pay the stable lad well to look after my horse, or else settle her in the stable myself. I left the table as soon as I had eaten, and returned to my room, readied my snapsack, checked my pistol – I would not ride anywhere without it now – and laid out my outer clothes for the journey.

I made my horse ready within about half an hour, after which I returned to my room, and clad myself for the journey with my high-crown hat, sash, tuck and belt, and my thickest cloak. I set off from the hall at half an hour after nine o'clock, and headed out for Irchester and Wellingborough by the usual back lane. I was fortunate that the day proved dry, overcast, a cold wind, but the going was good, and I made good time. I rode into the marketplace at Wellingborough as the church clock struck midday, and decided to go straight to the physician's house in Church Street, at the sign of Asclepius. It took but a few minutes to find the physician's house, and I was quickly admitted. The physician was not pleased to be disturbed on Good Friday – even though Parliament had banned the public celebration of holy days in '47, so he was working as a normal day,when, in fact should have been on his knees in church, as I too should have been. The physician was curious why I wanted to know what the potion is composed of, but on being told that it was a military matter, he asked no more. He opened the bottle and sniffed it cautiously, then declared himself baffled by the smell.

"Tis an oriental medicine, methinks,' he said, 'but ye should seek the apothecary two houses up the street, over the road.' I thanked him, and did not offer money, since no real help was forthcoming. The next apothecary was both equally unhappy to be disturbed on Good Friday, and was little more help. He thought that it might contain something like a tincture of nightshade, or an opiate from Turkey or the East.

I said, 'It has a great power to make those that take it sleep, and develop great thirst.'

The apothecary thought it best to avoid taking it, or else take a very tiny drop indeed, and drink plenty with it. He could offer no antidote.

I was about to leave, then thought, and asked, 'Be there others who might sell such a potion?'

The apothecary of course did not want to aid his competitors, but having demurred, he felt somewhat needful of talking when I produced and fingered my knife. He suggested I try an apothecary in the next street. He demanded a shilling for his information.

I gave him two pennies, saying, "Tis all that your information be worth, master 'pothecary.'

I rode to the next street, and rapidly identified the apothecary's shop, a very small house which was easy to miss. This apothecary was less displeased at being disturbed on this very holy day; he was clearly olive-skinned, probably of an Eastern origin, and was dressed in a silk gown and small silk turban, completing his Eastern appearance, so I guessed was probably not a Christian.

He also sniffed it, and said, 'Aye, 'tis a potion that I have sold betimes. 'Tis very powerful strong. There be no antidote for't.'

'What is't, master 'pothecary?'

He would not tell me, but confirmed that it came from Turkey or thereabouts. 'Sultan needs it for his seraglio, captain.' So I tried another approach.

'How long before it cease to make a person sick, master 'pothecary, after a person stops taking it?'

The apothecary did not know, but thought two, maybe three weeks.

'Drink much vatter," he said. I then asked him who bought it here in Wellingborough.

'Master Marston's maid,' came the answer. 'Mistress Jen?' I asked.

He confirmed that it was indeed Jen.

I gave him a shilling, then settled on going to the Star of Bethlehem tavern, and taking lunch there. Unlike the last time I ate at the Star, I was wearing my sash and ribbon of rank. When I walked in, the buzz of conversation fell silent, and I felt as if all eyes were on me. I looked around, saw that the chair in the corner was empty, so took it. The barmaid Mary came across to me, and realised that she knew my face, then realised who I was.

'God's blood, maister...captain! Ye gave me a start. 'Tis 'Ob, innit?' I smiled.

'I would have some food and a good ale, Missus Mary. Your husband keeps a good kitchen here.' She curtseyed, and returned to the bar, then shouted through to the kitchen. A few minutes later, she brought to me a tray with a wooden bowl of steaming potage of mutton, beans, and carrots, flavoured with herbs, plus a jug of ale, and a wooden pot.

'Did ye foind yer Joan, maister?'

'Aye. As ye said, she be, er, dangerous to know. But my wife were pleased to hear of her.'

'Ye on army business, maister?'

'Aye, but of little import.'

'Ter do wi' they Diggers?' Mary was nothing if not inquisitive.

'Mayhap. And other matters.'

She looked at me inquiringly, but deciding that retreat might be better than valour, curtseyed again, and returned to the kitchen. I noticed that I was still of more than casual interest to some of the drinkers, but chose to finish my food and enjoy it, rather than provoke anything. When I had finished eating, Mary came over and offered a pipe and tobacco, as well as wine or more beer. I politely declined.

'Nay Missus Mary, I must be on my way. But I thank ye.' I finished my pot of ale, went to pay my tally, and after donning my cloak – I did not remove my hat, this time – I left the tavern, with some twenty pairs of eyes watching me closely.

Armed with the information that I had gleaned from the apothecary, though it was of little value in treating Jeanne, it raised certain questions regarding the intelligencing ring. Why would Jen be the one to buy it? I had much to ponder, and thought that the key answers would be likely to come from Jeanne – if we can release her from the clutches of the potion. Learning more of the potion would probably need the services of either a physician or apothecary in Northampton, or possibly even one in London – which I could not effect.

As I passed the Golden Lion tavern I heard the church clock strike two o'clock, and then was out of the town; a little over half a mile further on, and I crossed the broad expanse of the river Nene, and headed through the little hamlet of Chester-on-the-Water, then about another half mile, and I was in Gipsy Lane, heading for Irchester. I would be back at the hall around four or half past.

As I arrived at the stableyard, I heard the hall's clock strike the half hour, so it must be half past four; the small detachment of militiamen was practising arms drill in the hall park. I heard their muskets fire a ragged volley whilst I was settling my mare in the stables. I had removed the saddle with its accoutrements, and was removing the reins when the stable boy came in and offered to take over. I was happy to delegate the task, and gave the lad a silver penny for his trouble. 'See that ye do it well,' I said, 'or I would have my penny back!' The lad grinned at me, and started to brush down the mare. I picked up my snapsack and went into the scullery passage and the dining hall. It was empty, so I went straight upstairs, and knocked on the door of Ekins' private office. 'Enter,' came Ekins' voice, then as he saw it was I, 'Come and take a chair, Robert. Your Jeanne is marvellous poorly, she screams and kicks, and demands the potion. It takes Amelia and Elizabeth both to manage her.'

I sat opposite him, and recounted what I had learned in Wellingborough.

'This mistress Jen, captain, what thinks ye? How does Jeanne get the potion from her?'

''Tis a goodly question, Master John. By my reckoning, mistress Jen and Simon Sorrell esquire are in 't together. The matter we must discover is how Jeanne met mistress Jen. Afore she were at Northampton. We would not know unless Jeanne be recovered.'

Ekins threw in another possible way.

'Mayhap Governor Whetham's men could … persuade her, think ye?'

I flinched, 'More like, she would die rather than tell. Just as Maud.'

We sat looking at each other, deep in thought, for a few seconds, before Ekins spoke again. 'Captain, ye must return to Northampton soon as may be, methinks. The answer will not be found in Rushden.'

It was not something that I relished, as I would first have to explain to Whetham why I spirited Jeanne away out of the city. Whetham had not forbidden it, but it was nonetheless a provocative action, since I knew that Whetham considered Jeanne merely a traitor to be wrung for information, then hanged or pressed, if she survived that long. She had talked with little resistance to my inflicting some pain, so she might talk rather more readily, even if only shown the torture instruments, but the likelihood was that someone would get to her and kill her before she could tell what she knew. I did not believe that Whetham's gaolers were all honest; a bribe to the right one, and Jeanne would be found dead. My best argument would be that Amelia was more likely to coax better information from her.

I voiced my thoughts to Ekins, who agreed with my reasoning, but urged caution.

'Much depends on how soon Jeanne is well enough to talk, and respond to her sister. We should talk with Amelia.'

I suggested bringing her into the office immediately, so Ekins despatched his maid to bring her. When they returned, I spoke first.

'My dear, we have discussed Jeanne. We must keep her from Whetham's men. Their cruelty be too much to stomach. Think ye that ye could persuade her to talk, tell us more of how she were brought to intelligencing?'

Amelia looked rather at a loss to know what to answer. 'She.. she … be too sick, husband.'

Then when the initial surprise had worn off a little, 'I would rather not be involved in your work, Robbie.'

'I would fain ye were not. But 'tis the best chance to save her life, my dear. Aye, she be too sick presently, but she will mend. Then she may tell ye more.'

Ekins now ventured his thoughts.

'We would not have ye at risk, Missus Amelia. Methinks ye would want to hear of how she came to this pass? Is't not so?'

She had to admit that it certainly was so.

'Master John, I would not break my sister's confidence.'

'Even to save her life, my dearest? Whetham would be hard to convince that she should live. She be guilty of treason in his eyes.'

Amelia sighed, and fiddled with the ribbons of her bodice.

'Aye, I suppose 'tis true. We must agree what he may be told.' Ekins again interjected.

'We must hear what she tells ye, then agree what may be told to Governor Whetham. We may not have much time, my dear, for such niceties.'

We agreed that this must be the basis of our actions now, and we must hope that Whetham does not take precipitate action vis-à-vis Jeanne. And, indeed, place blame on any of ourselves. Aiding the commission of treason is a capital offence.

I thought that I could stretch my time away from Northampton until the following Thursday, 29th, or maybe the Monday, 2nd April, due to attending Ekins' marriage. We must make the most of the time remaining that we can be together as a family again, and enjoy the spring weather. If need be, I could use the excuse that I could not leave until the end of Easter Week, due to the daily church services celebrating the Resurrection and Ascension and beyond. In the meantime, I would help Amelia and Elizabeth to make Jeanne drink plenty, since it was difficult with just the two women. I told myself that it would be in Jeanne's best interest.

Sunday 25th March, 1649: New Year's Day

By the third day, Jeanne had calmed down considerably, and appeared to have sunk into a deep depression, though Amelia and Elizabeth managed to persuade her to eat a little, and to drink plenty. Elizabeth spoke to Amelia.

'I will look after Jeanne, so that ye may spend time with Robert, and the maid can look after young Johnny.'

I and Amelia enjoyed the morning walking to the church to listen to the new preacher, and after the sermon sat on the low wall surrounding the churchyard talking and listening to the birdsong, all the noises and sights of spring. Meanwhile, Jeanne had opened up to Elizabeth.

'After the troopers burned our house, we moved in with Uncle Tom in Wellingborough. I were fifteen. Uncle Tom came to me every night, did wi' me as he wished. Papa found out, and he were goin' to hurt Uncle Tom, so when the soldiers came looking for Diggers' leaders, Tom told 'em Papa were one of 'em. They took him away, and we never saw him again. I found I was with child. I told Uncle Tom to try to stop him, but 'e beat an' kicked me till I lost the child. I were never able to 'ave another. Mama lost heart. She got the ague later in '47, an' just gave up 'n' died.'

When Amelia and I returned to the hall, we went up to our room, where Elizabeth and Jeanne were sitting talking, as our son played with a toy. Elizabeth asked Amelia, 'Please come outside, Robert can look after Jeanne.'

Amelia's earlier much improved mood was shattered by Elizabeth's telling her Jeanne's revelations. Amelia was utterly mortified and collapsed into Elizabeth's arms, sobbing so much that Elizabeth had difficulty helping her to a chair further along the corridor. When the sobbing subsided enough, Elizabeth left Amelia, and came to me.

'Please, Robert, go to Amelia. I will stay with Jeanne.' Ekins heard the voices and Amelia's sobbing. He came out of his office and around the corner of the corridor, saw me trying to comfort Amelia, and took us both to his private office, where he sat us down, gave us a goblet of sack each. After Amelia recovered her composure enough, I persuaded her to tell us what Elizabeth had said that upset her so. When I heard what she told me, I went white with fury.

'I'll away to Wellin'borough and kill the dog!'

'There will be time enough, Robert, to deal with Tom Rately,' said Ekins. 'Mayhap Justice Pentelow will arrest him, if ye make a formal complaint. Ye would have my backing.'

Elizabeth had much empathy with Jeanne, getting her to eat and drink, to talk about her past, and was pleased to help, for which I and Amelia were extremely grateful. I commented to Amelia, 'I would have plenty to pass to Whetham on my return. I hope 'twould both help arrest the intelligencing ring, and save Jeanne's life too.' She certainly should be saved from Whetham's men, from what I had heard so far.

After what had transpired, Amelia ate hardly anything at

lunchtime.

'I would pray go to Jeanne and sit with her. She may say more.' Elizabeth replied.

'I think 'twould be unwise. Jeanne still must recover from the potion. She's in a fragile state, and may go silent instead. Amelia, why not you and Robert make the best use of your time together trying to relax and enjoy some normality before Robert has to return to his duties?'

I tentatively agreed, and suggested going to the old neglected formal garden. We decided to go and find a seat in the cool spring sunshine, listen to the birds, and simply chat about what we might do once this worrisome time was over.

'My dearest, is it worth chatting some more about Johnny's schooling? Mayhap we could afford to do what Sam Goodly suggested, find out the cost to send him to Eton College?'

Always assuming, of course, that the college was open during this febrile time. Having earlier talked to John Ekins about the matter, he proposed to me two other schools, Oakham and Uppingham, both of which took boarding pupils, at least, in more settled times.

'Neither is too far away, so it would be possible to visit Johnny at intervals. Another might be Huntingdon Grammar School. 'Twas attended by no less than Oliver Cromwell himself.'

I was not sure that it would take boarders, but all three schools were within about twenty miles of Rushden, so were good possibilities to be considered.

Amelia and I spent the whole afternoon chatting easily about our future life, neither confronting the two issues that would also have to be addressed: Jeanne's future, and where we would live, once we had left Rushden hall. Neither of us felt like facing the realities of our life even a year from now. Not least was that the war was only temporarily over; the Irish civil war had not been resolved, nor the likely return of Charles the son, and the possibility of his leading a

Scottish army again into England to try to take the throne.

There was another unspoken issue: intelligencing. There were more spies around than ever, and the presence of Royalist clubs starting up, like the Swordsmen, implied that mischief making would not go away whilst Charles the son was still alive. Rich noblemen like the earl of Northampton were prepared to fund them in order to further their own ambitions based on overthrowing Parliament and putting Charles the son on the throne, but in their thrall. I thought to myself, 'While 'tis like this, I could be forced to return to active duty anytime,' but I would not tell Amelia, and spoil her better mood.

At suppertime, we expected Elizabeth to have more revelations, but she had not drawn anything more out of Jeanne. A maid had been asked to take some food and drink to Jeanne; she came back to report, 'She eats but little, drinks some, sits looking like she be very low.'

Elizabeth, John Ekins, I, and Amelia sat in a group at the top table. The few garrison troopers sat the other end of the room well away from our group, so we were able to chat and take our meal in relative peace, even though from time to time bawdy humour drifted across from the other end of the room. John Ekins asked, 'Might Jeanne be well enough to eat with us all yet?' Elizabeth answered this question.

'My dear, she should be well enough on the morrow, I think. Two of us might accompany her, since she mayhap could faint or try to run away.'

I asked, 'Mistress Elizabeth, might Jeanne be better now with her sister?'

Elizabeth agreed. 'Mayhap 'twill calm Jeanne more to be with her sister.'

This resulted in a more relaxed atmosphere, and we all finished the day in a better frame of mind. Amelia suggested, 'Would Jeanne be better if Robbie and I sit with her just now?' All concurred – so long as we did not try to press her for more information about her past, especially her whoring past, for now.

Jeanne appeared less than pleased to have me enter the room along with her sister, but she did not demur. There were only two chairs, so I sat as best I could on the bed. Amelia asked, 'Sister, would ye care to take a turn in the park on the morrow, with Elizabeth and myself? If 'tis not too cold or raining.'

Jeanne looked at her a little blankly, then nodded.

'Aye sister, 'twould be good to be out of the house, methinks.'

We tried to talk with her about some innocuous subjects, such as what food she would like on the morrow, but her answers were as if she were half absent. After an hour, I suggested leaving the room, and seeing if Elizabeth would take over; Jeanne merely shrugged.

'Jeanne, we are not gaolers. We want ye well again. Amelia would like her sister back, I think,' I said. Amelia nodded, and smiled at her sister.

'Aye, sister, 'tis so. I have missed ye since .....' Jeanne looked up at her.

'Since our mother died? 'Tis what ye would say?' Amelia nodded sadly.

'Aye, I wish we had those days again, I wish there were no war, I wish Robbie had not gone to war.'

I reached out and held her hand as a tear welled up in her eyes. Jeanne just looked down impassively and said nothing. I turned to Jeanne.

'Jeanne, sister, we cannot change what has passed. Only the future.... For us all.'

Jeanne still sat looking down and said nothing. I stood.

'My dear, I will away to the dining hall. Mayhap Elizabeth be still there. I will ask her to attend ye both.'

I smiled at Amelia, and with a quick squeeze of her hand, turned and left the room. My footsteps echoed along the corridor and down the staircase. Amelia told me what happened next.

297

After I had gone, Jeanne started to cry, and tears started to run down Amelia's cheeks too.

'Robbie wants 't to be better for ye, too,' she said.

They heard Elizabeth's lighter footsteps coming up the stairs, then along the corridor, and she entered the room to find them clinging to each other. She quietly closed the door, and returned to the hall.

When Joan stopped crying, she started to talk.

'Sister, 'twas awful for me. I could not stand Uncle Tom fucking me near every night. I sneaked out one night, and slept on the street. This woman picked me up, took me home. Mistress Jen, her name was. Took me to a house in Angel Lane. Master Marston's house. He made me work, but didn't touch me. Then mistress Jen were goin' to Northampton and made me go with 'er. Took me to a large 'ouse, owned by a lady, it were. Aye....Lady Sorrell. That lady - ' she spat the word, '-made me lie with 'er brother-in-law. Master Simon. If'n I wouldn't, they both beat me. Black an' blue, I were, till I did as they said.'

She resumed crying, and her sister took her in her arms again.

'Shhh, Jeanne. Let it out.' After Jeanne's crying subsided, she started talking again.

'Nex' time mistress Jen come, she brought the potion. They made me tek it. When I took it, couldn't stop meself. Desperate to fuck. Man or woman. Felt so sick after. And desperate for more of the potion. Master Simon took me away to the 'ouse in the lane off Swan Street. Got mistress Meg to live in wi' me – 'ad to, I were real sick after each time I took the potion. Needed 'er to look after me. Then they told me I must go after army officers, make 'em crave for me, to get information. If I wouldn't, they'd kill me, they said. If I told any'un, they'd kill me, too, they said. So for last year, tha's what I've done. Gave me lots of gold for doin' it, though.'

Amelia realised the significance of all this.

'Jeanne, I must tell Robert. He will make a report to Governor

298

Whetham, hope Whetham doesn't charge ye with treason.'

Jeanne shook her head.

'Does 'e have to?'

'Aye, that he does. If you wouldn't be charged and hanged. Probably worse, if what Robert says be true.'

Jeanne resumed her crying, with Amelia again doing her best to comfort her sister.

'It was not your fault, Jeanne, sister. There be no shame in it for ye. The shame be all those who took ye so.'

Her sister's crying gradually subsided. She said, 'They all knew me. Called me Joan the Whore. I hated it. Hated it. But I had to put up with it or be beaten.' Amelia tried to comfort her again.

'Jeanne, let us call Robert and Master Ekins, so ye can tell them what ye told me. They will do their best to protect ye.'

Jeanne nodded uncertainly, eventually turning her tear streaked face to look directly at her sister.

'Lia, I know 'tis for best. Let us call them, while I feel I may do 't.'

Amelia let go of her sister, and went far enough down the stairs that she could call me and Master Ekins.

'Robbie, Master Ekins, if ye please, come.'

We ascended the stairs, and she ushered us into her and my room, to where Jeanne was looking down at her lap. As we entered, she looked up, then away. Amelia addressed us both.

'Robbie, Master Ekins, Jeanne would tell ye what she told me.' Then to Jeanne, 'If ye please, Jeanne, tell them. For me.'

As the story came out from Jeanne, in fits and starts, neither I nor Ekins were surprised, but we both felt desperately sorry for Jeanne, and, indeed, her sister. I waited till Jeanne had stopped talking.

'I must write down what ye have told us, Jeanne. I will report it to Whetham. I do truly hope he will forgive ye. He and I will go after those that treated ye so, so, monstrously. They will pay an awful price for their treason.'

'Must ye tell the Governor, Robbie?'

'If I do not, Whetham will have ye put to the torture, Jeanne. I could not live with my conscience, were I not to tell him. He would not want your story known, ye may have no fear of that.'

I asked Master Ekins if we might speak privately, now that I had what I needed for Whetham, so we decamped to his office. I began what I wanted to say.

'Master John, I will pen my report shortly, and mayhap ye too will write a report. May I ask that our reports go to Governor Whetham, with additional letters, from me, and yourself, explaining what has happened. I would also write a date when I expect to be back with the Governor. 'Twould be good if we could send them by fast army post rider? He would surely receive them within the day.'

'Aye, Robert, 'tis a sensible action. I will pen my report on the morrow. We should catch the post-rider if we are ready by ten of the clock.'

And so, we had a plan, and parted, already thinking about how to write our respective reports. I now felt dreadfully oppressed by my guilt, and my apprehension at the prospect of both telling Whetham, and of going back to face him. I must sleep alone save for Johnny, while Amelia slept in the same room as Jeanne. Neither I nor Amelia relished yet another night apart.

I took Johnny to my and Amelia's room, and put him to bed, then settled down to write for a while, since it was early still, and there was nothing better to do with the time. I wrote until I heard the hall's clock strike nine, then decided to go to bed myself, since it was hard to write legibly with only one candle; more light and Johnny would not sleep. I left the single candle burning for now.

I had been in a restless sleep for some three hours when my demons came to haunt me; and they haunted me with renewed vengeance. Not just Jeanne, but Maud, 'Arry and his pal, Emma, and even Ned Adkin and one other of whom I may not speak visited my disturbed sleep to taunt me with their bloodied bodies and fearsome expressions. I tossed and writhed more and more, until suddenly I screamed and fell out of the bed, waking in a heap on the floor. My father, in his room next door was awakened by the noise, and came into my room, soon followed by Amelia, and then the garrison sergeant. Amelia turned to the sergeant, as he came in.

'I am most sorry, sergeant, my husband has these awful nightmares. 'Twas the war, d'ye see? If ye please, leave us.'

The sergeant looked angry, then doubtful, but grunted, and went back whence he came. She found me as before, white faced and sweating profusely, as well as shaking like a leaf.

'Oh, Robbie, what shall we do with ye? How shall we stop your nightmares, husband?'

Very shakily, I lied to her. "Tis worrying about going back to Whetham, my love. It unquiets me much. I must be back as soon as I may, the longer I be here, the more I fret on 't.'

'My son, ye must use this time with your wife well. Forget Whetham for now. What will be, will be, ye cannot change it by fretting.' My father did not wish to admit his own fretting about it.

'Master Ekins and I are to send our reports to Whetham by fast army post rider, on the morrow, father. Let us all hope that pleases him. I am so sorry to have woken ye. I would ye go back to bed, and try to sleep more.'

Meanwhile, Johnny was wide awake and snivelling. Amelia tried to quieten him, but he was having none of it. I intervened.

'I will see to him, Lia. If ye please, go back to bed.'

I kissed her, and waited until everyone had left me alone with Johnny, who I now persuaded to lie down, then blew out the candle and returned to bed. My demons, however, had other ideas, and I now repeatedly woke feeling terror and sweating, shaking, and an awful sense of foreboding.

Monday, 26th March, 1649.

Eventually, morning arrived, as the knocker-upper called everyone to wake at seven o'clock. I looked as if I had had no sleep, but I must get up, do the necessary, then likewise for Johnny, before breaking my fast, after which starting to write again. It was a rather gloomy group of us that assembled in the hall for breaking our fast. I was not the only one that looked pale and red-eyed; my father, Master Ekins, Amelia, and now Jeanne, who was with us, all looked somewhat the worse for wear after the previous night's drama. Johnny was his usual rosy-cheeked self, except that he was unusually cantankerous, to be expected after the lost sleep. We ate in near silence.

As soon as we were done with the breakfast, I and John Ekins left the others, and headed upstairs. We returned to our respective rooms, and each did the same: out with quill and paper, and wrote our reports and letters. The reports took not much over an hour to complete, and seal, then I repaired to Master Ekins' office, where we combined all the reports and letters into one sealed packet, ready for the fast post-rider, who would, as usual, stop at the hall around ten o'clock.

Just after ten, there was a clatter of hooves, then a loud knock at the front door of the hall. It was the fast post-rider, pretty much on time, which was a relief, especially for me. I took the packet out and bade the rider farewell, with a request to take a good care that Whetham received it at the Guildhall quickly, and to be sure that it had gone into his hands. The rider looked at me with a frown, but said that he could be relied upon. I gave him two silver pennies as a bribe.

I revealed to Amelia that I expected to go back to Northampton later in the week, on the following Sunday, the 1st April, or certainly no later than the next day. She was not happy to hear that news, but knew that go back I must. We would have a week together, and it would end with John Ekins' and Elizabeth's marriage. That would be a happy day, especially for this couple of the gentlemanly class.

As Jeanne slowly recovered during the next few days, we enjoyed more time together, and the two sisters were much happier in each other's company, as well, I thought, in mine too. My nightmares became less fearsome and less frequent, so that I was able to sleep more. Captain Grove, who had been away on military business – we were not allowed to be privy to where, or why – returned, and he too responded to the rather better atmosphere in the hall.

Even more heartening for me, though sad, was that Jeanne played wonderfully with Johnny. She clearly had a way with children, and was starting to teach Johnny his letters. If only her uncle had not damaged her so!

The days went by quickly, until the post-rider brought a letter from Whetham to me, thanking me for my service, and telling me not to return. A copy was delivered to Master Ekins. The letter to Ekins also said that the intelligencers would be arrested in a few days.

Wednesday, 4ᵗʰ April 1649.

Master Ekins and Elizabeth had a fine wedding last Sunday, raising everyone's spirits. Now, today, Wednesday, the day started normally. Even I, though my nightmares still troubled me even if to a lesser extent, felt brighter. It was almost midday, when there was a clatter of hooves and wheels at the front of the hall. A banging on the front door, and a sergeant and two troopers, all in armour, were shown into the dining hall, where I, Amelia, Jeanne, my father, Master Ekins and his Elizabeth, and captain John Grove, were sitting talking.

The sergeant surveyed the room, pulled out a document, then said, 'I have a warrant for the arrest of mistress Jeanne Rately, also called Joan the Whore, for the crime of treason. If ye please, where is she?'

A paling Jeanne stood.

'I be Jeanne Rately, sergeant.'

The two troopers stepped over to her, and took hold of her arms.

'Ye will be taken to Northampton, to the Guildhall for interrogation and trial.'

I stood, shouting.

'No! No! She must not be taken!' The sergeant was unmoved.

'Take her to the cart, lads.' The troopers steered her towards the door.

I tried my best to stop them, as did Ekins and captain Grove, but they dragged Jeanne out to a waiting cart and threw her into the back of it. The sergeant remained, but Master John Ekins stood too, and shouted at him, 'Get ye out of my house!'

I, meanwhile, slipped to my knees, then keeled over forwards, and pounding the floor with my fists, 'They must not have her! They must not have her!' over and over again, tears pouring down my face.

My guilt had finally taken over my mind, spirit, and soul, and I lost all of my sense of reason.

Chapter 19: Confessed and Confounded

I was told that I raved and screamed myself hoarse for three or four days, without sleep or food, as my demons terrified me every waking moment, and I tore out clumps of hair, bit my arms, and generally behaved like a madman. Amelia and Elizabeth took turns to persuade me to drink, but after I finally quietened down enough and became manageable again, both were so exhausted that a maid had to take over caring for me.

Eventually, I started to eat a little, andAmelia sat with me for a longer while each day, coaxing out of me the story of my time in the army, and what had caused my demons to become so bad. As more of my story escaped my lips, she first became more and more shocked, and then more and more immune to the horrors that I had both witnessed and done, or latterly caused, myself. One horror remained, and I would not reveal it, much to her chagrin – my most important secret, my great service for which I was thanked personally by general Cromwell in London.

Three months after the trials, there was the clatter of hooves at the front of the hall, then a banging at the door. In walked none other than Nathaniel Whetham, Governor of Northampton, with two of his guards. He asked for me. He was shown into the dining hall, where I and Amelia were sitting quietly.

'Good morrow, captain Barker, Missus Barker. I hope that captain Barker is much restored?'

'He heals but slowly, Governor.' I gazed at Whetham with a profound disinterest.

'I must give my grateful thanks to captain Barker for his great service to Parliament, and General Cromwell, Missus. Thanks to his good work, the malefactors in my city are taken and have gone to the gallows.'

I did not care, since Jeanne, so far as we knew, had received a similar, perhaps worse, fate. Amelia felt her temper rising.

'Why, pray, should he be troubled with that, Governor?'

'I have brought Robert's gold for his service to General Cromwell, two hundred pounds, and pay for his work for me in Northampton, a further fifty pounds. All in gold.'

He dumped a heavy leather bag on the table.

'Governor, ye could keep every penny of 't if I could but have my sister back! That my husband and my sister should suffer such, such cruel usage for gold, 't breaks my heart. Ye be a cruel, heartless man to treat them so. D'ye have a wife? Sister? What would they feel, Governor, to be treated so?'

His answer astounded us both.

"Your sister, Missus Barker, is outside. My men will return her to ye. As for Robert, such are the times we live in, Missus Barker. We all must do our duty, hard though it may be.'

'Duty?' snapped Amelia. 'Duty? The price of duty be too great, Governor! Gold can never be enough for your precious "duty"! I hope my sister did not suffer at the hands of your men. My sister and my husband? 'Tis too much, too much, d'ye hear?"

He stood, bowed slightly, saluted, turned and walked out, followed by his two guards. We were never to see him again. A minute or two later, Jeanne walked unsteadily into the hall. She looked thin and careworn, her hair tangled and unwashed, her dress torn and dirty. We both welcomed her warmly, and Amelia rushed to her sister and embraced her. We would hear her story that evening.

Jeanne was not tried for treason, nor given to Whetham's men, thank God. After my and Master Ekins' reports, and her own story, she became an important witness with her evidence hastening the various members of the intelligencing ring's passage to the gallows. All were convicted except for two: Lady Margery Sorrell and Will Watterson. Lady Sorrell was simply too high in the echelons of powerful people, with a panoply of friends in high places, for Whetham to risk putting her on trial. Will Watterson could not be found, so he, too, escaped the others' fate.

Amelia returned to pressing me hard to tell her what my great service to Cromwell, my unspoken secret, was. I could not bear any more of her nagging me, and eventually gave in and told her. I started by describing my service at the Old Artillery Yard, in London, and ended with the terms offered to gain a volunteer for the task, part of which was that the volunteer's name would never be disclosed. I described how I had been outfitted with mask, wig, and gown, to hide my identity.

Amelia thought all the theatricals hilarious, and joked about my having become a player in a pantomime. I replied, 'Lia, 'twas necessary, or someone could have discovered who I was, and I could have been hunted down and murdered. The task was done in the utmost secrecy.'

She jabbed me in the ribs, and laughing, said, 'Husband, why such secrecy? Anyone would think that ye'd killed King Charles himself!'

'That, my dear, is exactly what I volunteered to do. If what I did were discovered, all our lives would be forfeit if Charles the son was to succeed in ousting Cromwell, and taking back his father's throne.'

'But....but....? Ye....truly didn't..... kill the king, did ye?' She was not laughing now.

'My dear, 'twas I swung the axe that took off the king's head.'

Chapter 20: Epilogue

Whetham was sent to become governor of Portsmouth in September 1649, and his place taken in Northampton by his deputy, major Thomas Lydcott, who was raised to lieutenant colonel.

In the late spring of 1651, Robert and Amelia are living in Northampton, with their son now a pupil at the grammar school there. As Prince Charles's Scottish army evades confrontation with Cromwell north of the Tay, and is rumoured to be marching south at speed, war again rapidly approaches. The new governor, Thomas Lydcott, sends a message to Robert ordering him to become an active counterspy again, and his wife now demands to work alongside him. Robert's father appears to be near death, and Ned Mawle effectively runs the part of his leather business in Rushden. Rumours abound, spies proliferate. Arms are removed from local mansions, as support for Charles grows among Presbyterian communities, and one of Cromwell's commanders, Edward Massey, goes over to Charles. Militias are mobilised. Unlike his father, Prince Charles is a competent tactician, and a serious threat to the fledgling Commonwealth.

Amidst this febrile situation, a new cell is working feverishly in the Midlands to undermine Cromwell, and it is Robert's task to uncover them. It is thought that the great battle will be near Coventry. If Charles takes that fortified city, he will be near impregnable, so it is crucial that Robert succeeds.

If you have enjoyed this novel, please consider posting an honest review to Amazon. Thank you.

Printed in Great Britain
by Amazon

70473860R00180